FORGE BOOKS BY RENEE PATRICK

Design for Dying
Dangerous to Know

DANGEROUS TO KNOW

DANGEROUS TO KNOW

✳ A Lillian Frost and Edith Head Novel ✳

RENEE PATRICK

A TOM DOHERTY ASSOCIATES BOOK · NEW YORK

DANGEROUS TO KNOW

Copyright © 2017 by Renee Patrick

A Forge Book
Published by Tom Doherty Associates
175 Fifth Avenue
New York, NY 10010

www.tor-forge.com

Forge® is a registered trademark of Macmillan Publishing Group, LLC.

The Library of Congress Cataloging-in–Publication Data is available upon request.

ISBN 978-0-7653-8186-6 (hardcover)
ISBN 978-1-4668-8459-5 (e-book)

Our books may be purchased in bulk for promotional, educational, or business use. Please contact your local bookseller or the Macmillan Corporate and Premium Sales Department at 1-800-221-7945, extension 5442, or by e-mail at MacmillanSpecialMarkets@macmillan.com.

First Edition: April 2017

Printed in the United States of America

0 9 8 7 6 5 4 3 2 1

To Ann and Vincent Keenan

✳ Acknowledgments ✳

A good cast is worth repeating. So began the closing credits of numerous films of the 1930s made by Universal Pictures, coincidentally the studio where Edith Head ended her career. It's appropriate to cite that maxim here, given that so many people who were indispensable in launching the first Lillian and Edith book proved so again with this one.

Our agent Lisa Gallagher has been in our corner every step of the way, at all hours of the day and night. Our editor Kristin Sevick challenged us to be better in the sunniest manner possible. Thanks to everyone at Tor/Forge, especially Tom Doherty, Bess Cozby, Alexis Saarela, Patty Garcia, and Justine Gardner. Gerad Taylor crafted another glorious cover for us. Mary Beth Mueller and Noelle Noble proofed every sentence in this book except this one.

We will be forever grateful to the Malice Domestic community and particularly its grants committee. Eddie Muller continues to provide invaluable guidance and support.

We turned time and again to the books by Edith Head's trio of biographers: Paddy Calistro, David Chierichetti, and Jay Jorgensen. (Other works we consulted are listed later, in the author's note, so as not to spoil the plot.) Our ongoing gratitude to the staff at the Academy of Motion Picture Arts and Sciences's Margaret Herrick Library, and to the archivists at Paramount Pictures.

Vince thanks Bob Sobhani and the whole crew at Magnet Management. Rosemarie thanks her colleagues at Fred Hutchinson Cancer Research Center. We both thank every bookseller and every reader who shares our love for a bygone Hollywood.

On with the show.

There's a foreign legion of women, too. But we have no uniforms, no flags, and no medals when we are brave.

—Marlene Dietrich, *Morocco*, 1930

DANGEROUS TO KNOW

LORNA WHITCOMB'S
EYES ON HOLLYWOOD

Ah, December in Los Angeles, the season when our starlets simmer with jealousy contemplating their East Coast cousins. What sets them off? The furriers' shop windows full of mink and silver fox. Pity the poor sweltering sirens whose sole chill is the cold shoulder from producers; the only snowflakes they see are made of soap, strewn on soundstages to turn Culver City into Chamonix . . . Overheard on the Warners lot from a fluttery female watching George Brent walk by: "Now I know what started those forest fires!" . . . Does Gotham's high-society smuggling case have tentacles reaching all the way to the movie colony? Albert Chaperau, self-styled producer and diplomat, stands accused of helping Park Avenue plutocrats evade Customs duties on gowns and jewels freighted in from Europe. Comes word local luminaries may also have benefitted from his extra-legal largesse. We hear the brouhaha began at a diamond-encrusted Manhattan dinner party in October, but whoever has the skinny on that swanky soiree isn't talking.

1

※

"THE FOOD WAS too rich, for one thing. So were the guests. The dinner party was a dud long before the Nazis got involved."

I looked over at Edith Head, a blur of motion behind her sketch pad. "But you've heard my Chaperau saga before. More than once."

"True, dear, but your account is so entertaining."

"You can't buffalo me. This is about Lorna Whitcomb's column this morning. Are Paramount stars involved?"

"One hears rumors, so one seeks facts. You were there, eyewitness to history. Humor me. Don't mind my sketching. I can draw and listen at the same time. It's the essence of the job."

A trace of paint fumes perfumed Edith's office in the Wardrobe department at Paramount Pictures, olfactory proof she had finally arrived. The suite had formerly been home to Edith's mentor, Travis Banton. She had assumed Banton's responsibilities in March when the studio opted not to renew the brilliant but bibulous costume designer's contract. Paramount hadn't been in a hurry to bestow his title or office on Edith, though, the formal announcement coming after she'd been doing his job for months. Her first official act as Paramount's lead designer had been to have her new domain repainted, the walls now a soft gray. "Like a French salon," she'd said. "A muted palette places the focus on the actress, where it should be. Besides, if I don't change something in here no one will take me seriously."

Edith's personal transformation was more dramatic. She'd

abandoned her bobbed hairstyle in favor of bangs with a chignon
at the back. The new coiffure was a touch severe when paired
with Edith's owlish spectacles, but it suited her businesslike demeanor perfectly. I'd complimented her on it when I'd entered
the office that morning. She'd waved me off. "Copied from Anna
May Wong. A new look for the new position. With my unfortu-
nate forehead, I'm afraid the options are rather limited. Then I
remembered how striking Miss Wong's hair looked when she returned to the studio to make *Dangerous to Know*. I haven't decided if I'm going to keep it."

I owed my presence at the infamous dinner party, along with
a bounty of other opportunities, to my friendship with Edith. If
she wanted to hear the story again, then she'd get the full road-
show rendition. My goal: uncork a spellbinder to make her set
aside her sketch pad.

"The entire trip happened at the last minute. That's how it
is with Addison." Meaning Addison Rice, the retired industrialist
who had inexplicably seen fit to give me a job. "His wife, Maude,
was about to sail for Europe with a companion, but the grim news
from the Continent was giving her second thoughts. Addison
decided to see her off in New York, and asked me to come along."

"Because it's your hometown," Edith said.

"I think it was more he wanted company on the trip back. It
was a whirlwind jaunt. We waved our handkerchiefs at the *Queen
Mary*, leaving me enough time to race out to Flushing and visit
my uncle Danny and aunt Joyce."

"How are they?"

"Dying to meet you. I gave you some buildup. While we were
in Gasparino's Luncheonette, Addison ran into a familiar face on
Fifth Avenue."

"Albert Chaperau. The producer."

"Who'd been haunting Addison's parties, looking to meet
people. So thrilled was he to see his bosom pal that he finagled

us invites to a Park Avenue dinner. Instead of going to a picture at Radio City Music Hall, Addison and I turned up like foundlings at the home of a state supreme court justice."

I described our hosts. Judge Edgar Lauer, a bluff man in his late sixties, wore the authoritative air of someone who handed down verdicts even when he wasn't on the bench. His fiftyish wife, Elma, made a more vivid impression, thanks to the wardrobe she'd chosen for the occasion. "That gown," I whispered, still thunderstruck lo these six weeks later.

Edith looked up from her sketch pad, but her pencil kept moving. I hadn't won her over yet.

"Picture a floor-length sheath of white silk jersey," I said. "With a gargantuan royal-blue bow covering most of the bodice. The points of which unfortunately emphasized Mrs. Lauer's sagging jawline."

"It sounds quite audacious."

"That's one word for it. It wasn't designed for a matron entertaining at home. It was meant to be worn in some Parisian boîte by a woman half her age."

"Someone like you?" Edith said with one of her patented closed-lipped smiles. "I don't believe you ever told me what you wore that evening."

"I made do."

"With what, exactly?"

"You've seen the dress. Ice-blue satin with a square neckline and short matching jacket."

"For a formal dinner?" Edith raised an eyebrow. Now I prayed she'd continue sketching, not wanting to earn her undivided attention this way.

"Didn't I say it was a whirlwind jaunt? That was the best outfit I brought."

"You are the social secretary for one of the most prominent men in Los Angeles, and you weren't prepared for the possibility of a formal dinner? A floor-length dress, evening shoes, and a wrap would have taken the same amount of space."

"Not the way I pack." It didn't seem the time to point out how far I'd come in the year since I'd been a failed actress turned shopgirl without a pair of evening shoes to my name. "It's not as if Addison had a tuxedo. He wore blue serge!"

Edith closed her eyes with tremendous forbearance. "Go on."

"The Lauers throw more sedate affairs than Addison's. Their guests hail from politics, industry, and the *Social Register*. Albert Chaperau was completely out of place. You've seen his picture in the newspapers? Heavyset fellow, head like a salt block? All these staid sorts and there's Chaperau, filling the air with ideas like so many soap bubbles, not caring that virtually all of them were destined to pop and leave only slickness behind."

"A taste of Los Angeles," Edith said.

"Truth be told, I enjoyed having him there for that very reason. He was just back from Europe and had a whole slate of projects he'd discussed abroad, including an American version of his film *Mayerling*."

"I know it was a huge success, considering it's in French," Edith said. "But how does he propose to get that ending out of the Breen Office alive?"

"That was my first question. Actually, my first question was, 'Can Charles Boyer star in it again?' Chaperau said the murder-suicide of Crown Prince Rudolf and his young love was a matter of Austrian history, and any American retelling would be true to the record."

Edith clucked dubiously, just as I had.

"Dinner was served," I went on, "the first course a deathly white cream of mushroom soup. I was seated next to Serge Rubinstein, a financier who'd cornered the market in coarseness. Addison mentioned he'd just sent his wife off on a tour of the Continent. Chaperau asked where she was visiting. 'I wouldn't

put faith in maps much longer,' he says. 'Those poor souls in the
Sudetenland didn't think they were in Germany.' Everyone at the
table had recently been in Europe and had a dire report to con-
tribute. Judge Lauer believed the Austrian Anschluss and the Su-
deten crisis had only whetted Hitler's aggression. Mrs. Lauer
said their summer shopping had been spoiled by the mood of
despair. All the while Addison is turning paler than his soup."

"The poor man," Edith said. "He must have thought he'd dispatched his wife into near-certain doom."

"For his sake I wanted the war talk to stop, so I went to my
can't-miss subject. Who should play Scarlett O'Hara in *Gone with
the Wind*?"

"Still stumping for Joan Bennett?"

"She's only the perfect choice. Admit it. But sadly, no one took
the bait, because Chaperau insisted on polishing his credentials.
He announced he was recently named attaché for the government of Nicaragua. Which came as a surprise, because I thought
he was French. Rubinstein asked what a banana republic needed
with a picture maker, and Chaperau held forth on films as a universal export, shaping ideas around the globe. He claimed Hitler himself knew this, and it was why the exodus of talent from
the UFA studios in Berlin distressed him. Then Judge Lauer
weighed in. 'Hitler's a madman who must be stopped. We're fool-
ing ourselves if we think otherwise.'"

Edith made a quiet sound of satisfaction. Whether at the
judge's politics or her own still-in-progress sketch, I couldn't tell.
Time for bold methods. Time for me to *act*.

I stood and began staggering around the room. "Throughout
the conversation, Rosa the maid had been refilling glasses. Now
she stops and slams her tray onto the sideboard." I performed the
scene, reeling into Edith's desk. My Rosa had a clubfoot, my
hammy instincts getting the better of me. "Mrs. Lauer asked if
she was all right. But Rosa, her face bright red, was not." I gave

my next words a Teutonic twist. "'I am happy to work in your home, Mrs. Lauer. But first and foremost, I am a true German. I love Adolf Hitler. And I will not abide anyone speaking this way about the Führer. If these insults do not cease at once, I will stop serving. The choice is yours.'"

Edith finally put down her pencil and gaped at me. I had her captivated at last. Game, set, and match, Frost.

"It was so quiet after Rosa's outburst, I was certain everyone in the dining room could hear my heart racing. Then Rubinstein asks, 'Is Park Avenue part of the Sudetenland, too?' Judge Lauer, an old hand at pronouncing sentences, stands up. 'Then you may go at once, Rosa.' The maid storms out one door, Mrs. Lauer scurries out another in tears. I went after her. She was still apologizing to me when Rosa appeared, wearing a coat as black as a nun's habit. She looked at Mrs. Lauer and said, 'Madam. There remains the matter of references.'"

Edith hooted with laughter. "Rosa certainly has her nerve. Marvelous accent, by the way. You sound like Marlene Dietrich."

"Addison's is even better. We've been telling this story a lot. Rosa's request hit Mrs. Lauer like a bracer. She drew herself up and asked Rosa if her sister still worked as a retainer for the former Grand Duchess Marie of Russia. 'Not only will I *not* provide you with a reference,' she proclaimed, 'but perhaps I will telephone the grand duchess and let her know what kind of blood runs in your family.' To which Rosa replied, 'Only good German blood, madam, something the grand duchess already knows. Much as you know there are telephone calls I, too, can make.' With that, Rosa moved past us and out into the night. Mrs. Lauer and I linked arms and returned to our soup."

"Remarkable," Edith said. "But of course it wasn't over."

"Oh, no. Throwing Manhattan's most awkward dinner party since the Gilded Age wasn't enough. The next day, Addison and I belatedly made it to Radio City to see *The Mad Miss Manton*."

"Ah, Stanwyck." Edith sighed, with me happily taking a second chorus. Barbara Stanwyck was one of our favorite people.

"While the picture played, the Lauers' world collapsed. Rosa Weber, freshly unemployed, marched into the U.S. Customs offices and spilled every bean in her possession. The Lauers, she told the authorities, were guilty of smuggling, along with Albert Chaperau. It seems Mrs. Lauer cleaned out various ateliers on her summer excursion to Paris. Chaperau then transported her purchases in his luggage, which bypassed Customs inspection owing to his dubious diplomatic status as a representative of Nicaragua. Consequently, Mrs. Lauer avoided paying import duties on the clothes. A few days later, Albert Chaperau—right name Shapiro—was taken into custody at his suite at the Pierre. He was in white tie and tails at the time, having been at the Stork Club until four in the morning. I say if you have to be arrested, that's the way to do it."

Edith nodded in agreement.

"Customs men also raided the Lauers' apartment, hauling cases of couture away. By then Addison and I were back in Los Angeles. A Customs agent, gruff man name of Higgins, drove out to ask us about the dinner party. He said last year the Lauers hadn't declared a load of fancy clothes and jewelry, costing them more than ten thousand dollars in duties and fines. Agent Higgins made it clear the Customs Service was not in the second-chance business. He also said Mrs. Lauer had hied herself to a sanitarium. I felt for her. She didn't strike me as particularly black-hearted or criminal. Just another rich woman insulated from the real world. Plus she agreed Joan Bennett would make a splendid Scarlett O'Hara."

"I almost sympathize with Mrs. Lauer for going along with Mr. Chaperau's proposal," Edith said. "I had no idea I was supposed to pay import duties on the gowns I purchased when the studio sent me to Paris this summer. There I am on the dock, suddenly owing a fortune! A man from the New York office had to come down and set matters right. Mrs. Lauer's outré dinner party gown had been smuggled in by Mr. Chaperau, I take it."

"It's now being held as evidence. Your turn to spin a yarn, Edith. What have you heard about Chaperau's West Coast operations?"

"Only that he appears to have made his services available to at least one figure at Paramount. The place is in an uproar. An encore of your account of the dinner seemed in order."

Typical Edith, gathering intelligence on behalf of the studio where she spent every waking moment. I pressed her for the suspect star's name knowing she'd keep mum. Such was her loyalty. Were Paramount under siege, tiny Edith would hoist a pike and defend the Bronson Gate.

Bested, I asked, "What were you sketching away madly on?"

"Dorothy Lamour's costumes for the new Jack Benny picture."

"Speaking of Jack—"

Edith huffed out a sigh. "I haven't forgotten my promise to get you into an early screening of *Artists and Models Abroad*." In addition to starring my favorite comedian, Jack Benny, and my personal Scarlett O'Hara, Joan Bennett, *Artists and Models Abroad* boasted a fashion show sequence already being touted in fan magazines: a parade of gowns from the finest designers in Paris. Schiaparelli and Lanvin, Maggy Rouff and Alix. I was champing at the bit for an advance look, and my eagerness undoubtedly chafed Edith given her costumes were being upstaged by the haute couture.

Edith's receptionist knocked on the door. "Pardon me, Miss Head, your next appointment is here."

Marlene Dietrich coasted into the office, crooked smile first. She wore a pale green daytime suit with a subtle checkered pattern and slightly flared skirt. The matching emerald veil on her low-crowned hat did extraordinary favors for eyes that required no help.

Edith and Dietrich embraced, the actress bending to kiss the diminutive designer on both cheeks. Edith introduced me, my knees knocking at the prospect that Dietrich had somehow heard my cut-rate imitation of her. "But Lillian and I have already met," Dietrich said, her accent an ermine wrap around every syllable. I sounded nothing like her. "At a party hosted by your lovely employer Mr. Rice. Perhaps you remember?"

"How could I forget? You played the musical saw." The image of Dietrich flicking her dress to one side, tucking the handle of the blade between those impossible legs, remained a high point of my Hollywood sojourn.

Dietrich crossed those legs now as she sat down and took immediate possession of the room. I rose, preparing to leave the ladies alone.

"Thank you for arranging this opportunity to consult with your esteemed guest," Dietrich said.

I cocked an expectant eye toward the door only to discover that Dietrich gaze again aimed squarely at me. Apparently, *I* was the esteemed guest.

What had Edith walked me into?

2

⁛

I'D BE IN the dark a while longer; Dietrich was dictating the pace of the conversation. "Edith, what's wrong? I can tell you do not feel at your peak."

"Actually, I'm as fit as a fiddle."

Those eyes narrowed. "Do not lie to me. I have a sixth sense when it comes to discomfort. Where does it hurt?"

"Honestly, I feel fine. A headache after working late—"

"Your liver. That's the problem. All headaches are caused by harassment of the liver. You need artichokes. Have a few for lunch and dinner and you'll see an improvement. Now. Have you spoken with Travis?"

"I have, and he's intrigued."

"Of course he is! It is a magnificent opportunity. Only Travis could do justice to these clothes." Dietrich's eyes shifted to me. "My director, Frank Capra, is preparing a film about George Sand. Have you read her writing?"

The hazards of a Catholic education. The nuns who'd taught me weren't about to let any libertines near the syllabus. At least I'd known Sand was a woman. "Who hasn't?" I hedged.

"A pioneer of fashion, in whose footsteps I humbly tread. She will wear men's clothes at first, as was her wont. But as she falls in love with Frédéric Chopin, she becomes the essence of femininity."

"Who will be your Chopin?"

"Spencer Tracy."

I tried to picture a bust of Tracy's massive head atop the upright piano at my old boardinghouse. One of our most unpre-
tentious actors playing a tortured composer? At a loss, I turned
to Edith, who naturally knew what to say. "A fine choice. Making Chopin's ethereal genius earthy and accessible."

"Exactly! Which is why Travis must design my wardrobe. We
shall work together, Edith, to convince him."

Edith nodded, forever inscrutable. "Consider me your ally."

"You always have been. Enough about that. To the subject at
hand."

Edith turned to me. "Marlene has a personal matter where I
believe you can lend some assistance," she said.

"I'm happy to try."

"It's very simple," the actress said. "I'm looking for a young man."

Aren't we all, I bit my tongue to prevent myself from saying. I
glanced at Edith. The thick round lenses of her eyeglasses prevented any meaningful contact, and I wondered again if that's
why she chose to wear them. "I don't understand. You want me
to find him?"

"At the very least I'd like to know where the boy is, that he's
all right. His name is Jens Lohse."

Her pronunciation made his surname sound almost like
"louche." I requested Dietrich repeat the name and spell it as well.
She did so.

"May I ask why you wanted me to do that?"

"Something I read in a self-improvement book. Helps me do
my job. Visualizing names makes them easier to remember."

"My mother did the very same. 'Memory training,' she called
it. To build self-reliance." She looked at Edith. "You were right.
She's definitely the one."

Floating several inches above my chair, I said, "Tell me about
Jens."

"A gifted composer and pianist. From Austria originally, but

I met him in Berlin. He was a whelp then, sneaking into cafés and nightclubs, learning at the feet of Kurt Weill, of Friedrich Hollaender. Soon he was writing songs of his own. 'The Trouble with Sin' was his great triumph there. Are you familiar with it? Very saucy, very knowing." She cast her eyes modestly toward the floor, an effortless and automatically seductive gesture. "I have taken a stab at it once or twice myself."

"I'm guessing Jens made his way to America."

"Yes, like so many of us he fled Germany after the Nazis rose to power. Because of his Jewish background and his writing of 'decadent music.'" She packed an impressive amount of contempt into two words. "I reconnected with him in Los Angeles. Still brilliant, but without a foothold in his new land. And at an added disadvantage because at first he didn't speak the language. But his is a buoyant spirit, and such people always find a way to survive, to flourish. He would play the piano anywhere they would pay him. Beer halls, society parties, places beneath his talents." Dietrich laughed. "Quite a picture, my dear Jens. He would arrive at the home of some studio executive in that wretched jalopy of his, a car you could smell a mile away and hear two miles off. But he would set the party ablaze with his gift . . . and his enormous book of music. He always kept it close at hand. He'd hear a new song and immediately scribble enough of the notes so he could fumble his way through it. It's how he learned English. You can never stump that boy. He will play anything at the drop of a hat. Provided you toss a little silver into that hat, of course."

"You see him regularly, then."

"Yes." Another bashful look. "I am toying with the idea of a nightclub act. To amuse myself between films. Jens was the only accompanist I considered. We would rehearse every week."

"He missed an appointment, I take it."

"Last Thursday. He didn't telephone, so I telephoned him,

very upset, only to learn he no longer lived at that address. Never mind, I thought, he is to entertain at a party I am attending the next night. I will deliver my tongue-lashing then. I arrive at the party and ask the bandleader to speak to Jens, and he tells me Jens has been replaced because he missed several of their engagements. At this point I know something is terribly wrong, because Jens is a complete professional."

In my experience, musicians demonstrated a pronounced tendency toward flightiness, but I kept that opinion to myself. "Then you should contact the police."

Dietrich tutted at me, and I felt all of eight inches of my five feet eight inches of height. "But I've done this! I spoke at length with a detective named Wingert." She hurled the name like a blade, the W rendered as a V, the T as hard as a diamond. She then spelled it for me without prompting.

"What did Detective Wingert tell you?"

"Little of consequence. He said Jens had moved out of his home, which I already knew. Jens had run out of money and was adrift in the city, staying with friends. But Jens was a proud boy and had arranged for his landlady to receive messages for him. He also kept his car at his old address. That's where this Wingert found it. Which, you see, tells me everything."

I blinked twice. The second time didn't clarify matters. "I'm afraid I don't see. Where does Detective Wingert think Jens is?"

"Mexico!" Dietrich barked the word as if it were explanation enough. "Jens's visitor's permit was due to expire, so for weeks he had spoken of going to Mexico and applying for a visa there. That's what this Wingert believes happened."

"And you disagree."

"I don't disagree. I simply recognized in this Wingert a, a . . ." She snapped her fingers trying to conjure the right word, Edith and I both instinctively leaning forward to aid the effort. "A functionary's mind-set. Mexico is the convenient solution, therefore

Mexico it must be. He will not consider other possibilities. Darker possibilities."

"Such as?"

Dietrich sat back, a scatter of creases decorating her flawless brow. "Jens was in turmoil the last few times he played for me. As I've said, I can sense these things. Finally, I confronted him. 'What is wrong? You must tell someone. Tell me!' But he said he couldn't. He was too frightened of . . . them."

"Did he say who 'they' were?"

"He didn't need to. I knew, and Jens knew I knew. That's why he confided in me as much as he did." Genuine loathing stoked the fire in her eyes. "The Nazis did something to Jens. They're the only people he feared. The only ones I fear."

"Miss Dietrich," I said after gathering my thoughts, "I'm not entirely sure what I can do for you. Detective Wingert's theory sounds plausible. And if the Germans did do something—"

"Not Germans!" Dietrich interrupted. "Nazis. Already all my countrymen are being tarred by the brush of National Socialism."

"Forgive me. But if this darker possibility is true, I'm the last person in the world who can help."

"Do not be modest. Edith tells me you're a clever young woman. I know of your adventure with her last year. Unraveling a murder on this very lot, and doing so with the utmost of discretion."

If we'd been that discreet, I thought, *you'd never have heard about it.*

"A special circumstance," I said.

"Nonsense," Dietrich declared. "You travel in the circles where Jens entertains. I can hardly ask questions without attracting undue attention. But you can learn where Jens is without raising, as they say, a fuss. Surely this is possible?"

It wasn't, as far as I could see. I was struggling to articulate this view diplomatically when Edith spoke up.

"Of course it is. Isn't that right, Lillian?"

In the year I'd known Edith I'd learned an incontrovertible truth: she did everything for a reason. I trusted she had one now. I smiled with a good measure more confidence than I felt. "Any suggestions on where I should start?"

"At the capital of the German colony here in Los Angeles." Dietrich smiled enigmatically. "The home of Salka Viertel. The writer. The earth mother of all refugees from the fatherland. Jens is a staple of her Sunday salons. Salka has a ready piano and a ready ear for him. Regrettably, I avoid these gatherings. Too much history with some of the participants. But I will give you her address and inform her you are coming."

I had but a moment to appraise Dietrich's elegant script—*165 Mabery Road, Santa Monica*—before the actress closed her hand around mine.

"Tell me," she commanded. "What is your birth sign?"

"I—My birthday's June sixth, so—"

"Gemini. You possess vitality, speed. You are definitely the person to help me. All my women friends are Geminis."

"I'm not," Edith said.

"But you, Edith, are a unique case. Lillian, I will have your horoscope cast by my personal astrologer on the Santa Monica pier. She has one tooth and the wisdom of the ages. I had Edith's horoscope done years ago. Do you remember, Edith, what it said? 'Better times are coming.'" Dietrich beamed. "And look at you now!"

3

"I WON'T ASK why you sandbagged me," I told Edith as we walked toward the Paramount commissary. "I'll use my storied detective skills. You want to design Marlene's George Sand costumes."

"That picture isn't being made."

"It's not?"

"Mr. Capra has already moved on. He's started shooting footage in Washington, D.C., for his next picture, with that young actor James Stewart."

We passed a brunette in a plaid skirt, who offered Edith a tentative smile. "No gum, Stella," Edith said in reply, leaving the poor girl stricken as she rooted in her purse for a wrapper.

"But Marlene thinks the George Sand movie *is* being made."

"An actress must always retain her optimism. The sad truth is Marlene herself was the sticking point. I understand Mr. Cohn at Columbia refused to make the picture with her despite Mr. Capra's insistence."

"Because she's supposedly box office poison?" That was the phrase bannered across ads taken out by the Independent Theatre Owners back in May, urging studio heads to steer clear of performers who'd top-lined too many flops. Dietrich, Katharine Hepburn, Bette Davis, Joan Crawford, all of them had to swallow news of the imminent demise of their careers along with their soft-boiled eggs that morning.

"Yes, and what utter foolishness. Mostly women on that list, you'll note. And every one of them will be on top again soon enough, mark my words." Edith turned to me. "You're not far wrong about my motives, of course. It's early days for me in this job. If Paramount can land a bigger name they'll cast me aside. Thus I'm doing everything in my power to make myself of value to the studio. That includes asking you about Mr. Chaperau and currying favor with every star I can get. And no matter what the Independent Theatre Owners say, Marlene Dietrich is a star."

"You don't have to convince me. What I'd like to know is how I'm supposed to find her missing composer."

"But you don't have to, dear. Given Mr. Lohse's immigration status it's likely he did go to Mexico to secure a visa. But you can make Marlene feel better. This Detective Wingert may not have taken her seriously. You can call your friend Detective Morrow for a more thorough report, make inquiries with Mr. Rice and his circle of friends. I doubt it's necessary for you to visit Salka Viertel, although I hear she's a fascinating woman. If you can reassure Marlene her friend has gone to Mexico, you'll be doing me a great service."

Edith made it sound simple, but I harbored a healthy skepticism about the entire enterprise. Not wanting to voice my doubts, I said, "I wish I understood this Mexican visa business."

"I'm taking you to someone who can explain it."

Naturally. "I have to ask. Do you really think Spencer Tracy as Frédéric Chopin is good casting?"

"Heavens, no. A dreadful idea. It almost makes me happy the picture fell apart."

THE COMMISSARY WAS a sea of meline turbans, the lightweight fabric wrapped tightly around the head of each ravenous actress so her hairstyle would look exactly the same after lunch. Edith dispensed greetings as she strode toward the loudest table.

Crowded with food and scraps of paper, it was ringed by half a dozen voluble men. The adjacent tables, I couldn't help noticing, were vacant, a buffer against the raucous conversation. Not seeing any waitresses willing to brave the din, I snagged a piece of piping hot cornbread from a basket on the table.

"Good afternoon, gentlemen," Edith announced. "Mind if we join you a moment?"

Boisterous hellos and mock grumbling followed, then the men went back to the business at hand. One of them would call out a letter, which they each scribbled on cards ruled into five-by-five grids. "Frank, did you say 'A' or 'K'?" one of the men bellowed. He got two As and three Ks in response.

Edith and I took seats next to two men. One had the sober style of a New England banker, wearing a double-breasted gray suit and navy tie. Only his tousled hair hinted at an independent streak. Alongside him was a smaller man in a tattered argyle pullover, shirtsleeves rolled up, ready to arm wrestle. He had the impish face of a cherub hidden in the corner of a painting as an artist's joke, engaged in some secret act of deviltry. The man said in a Germanic accent, "And I have the last letter, and I say to L with the lot of you. *Bon chance*, gentlemen."

The men bowed over their cards as if they were hymnals and set pens to scratching. After a moment I understood they were constructing words out of the letters written on their grids. They tackled the task with rapt concentration: clearly money was at stake.

Edith indicated the man with the accent. "Lillian Frost, may I present Billy Wilder. His writing partner Charles Brackett. They wrote *Bluebeard's Eighth Wife*."

"I loved that movie!" I said.

"You loved the beginning, maybe." Wilder remained focused on his card. "The couple meets in the department store and buys a pair of pajamas together. Him the top, her the bottom."

"Guess whose idea that was." Brackett pointed at Wilder. "You should see our next picture, *Midnight*. Lord knows we wrote enough on it."

"Multiple drafts of dazzling sameness." Wilder raised his eyes to Edith. "I understand Claudette Colbert gave you a time."

Edith shifted uncomfortably. "She has her own opinions, to which she's more than entitled."

"Pish. She's stubborn. And thinks she's French. Is she truly buying her *Midnight* wardrobe in a department store rather than have you do it? What is the studio coming to?"

"I believe she said since her dialogue was off-the-rack, her dresses might as well be, too."

The table erupted in hoots and laughter. Wilder gave Edith a gallant seated bow. Touché.

"We stopped by, Billy," Edith said, "because I wondered if you could tell Lillian that story about your stay in Mexico."

"Ready your handkerchiefs, men," Brackett called, receiving a chorus of "aye, ayes."

Wilder muttered a few words in a foreign tongue. "It's not a sad story. It's a simple one. I had a visitor's visa. In 1934, it expired. I went to Mexico for a new one."

"Why Mexico?" I asked. "You don't sound Mexican."

"We have a trained ear at the table." Wilder smiled while still laboring over his card. Brackett, I noticed, had written down many more words than him. "There is a system of quotas in place, so many immigration visas for each country. European nations go through their allotments quickly, with legions of people fleeing the fascists. But in Mexico, the visas go begging. So I packed a grip and crossed the border." He set his pen down but continued to stare at the letters gathered on the page. "It was a risk, because I did not have the proper paperwork. It was in Berlin, and I was not about to go back for it. I am Jewish, and if I presented myself looking for documentation, a very stern gentleman would say, 'It is here, on this train. Come this way.' I sat before the American consul and explained my situation. He walks around the desk as I talk, nodding, yes, yes. Finally, he asks, 'If I allow you to return to the United States, what will you do? How will you make money?' I tell him I am a writer, I write scripts. Little do I know he is a fan of the movies. 'Write some good ones!' he says. He gives me the stamp"—Wilder pantomimed the gesture—"and sends me on my way. He did not have to do so. In another life, I am still there, waiting for my chance to enter this country."

"Cue the violins," Brackett said. "I still say there's a hell of a picture in that situation."

"Too depressing. You'd need the right angle. Why do you ask about Mexico?"

"There's a composer who may have gone there for the same reason," Edith said.

"Always it is good to know composers. Friedrich Hollaender—he's Frederick Hollander now—introduced me to Lubitsch and saved my life. Who is the composer?"

"Jens Lohse," I said. "He wrote a song called 'The Trouble with Sin.'"

Wilder hummed a snippet of an unfamiliar melody. "I know this song. 'The sable under the table.' It's clever. It's not Hollander, but it's clever."

"Do you happen to know Salka Viertel?"

"A little." Wilder shrugged. "She is a writer, too. Mainly for Miss Garbo. But as Miss Garbo seldom acts nowadays, Miss Salka seldom writes."

"She seldom acts?" Brackett raised an eyebrow. "Then who the devil have we been writing for?"

"You seek your composer at Salka's?" Wilder peered at me cryptically.

"Possibly. Any advice?"

"Salka's friends are my people but not my crowd. They look

to yesterday while I prefer to think about tomorrow. They wait to go home while I am waiting to get paid."

"Hear, hear!" another man cried.

"To put it yet another way," Wilder continued, "they were compelled to leave Europe. I *choose* to be in Los Angeles, because I want to make pictures."

"He promised the little man in Mexico," Brackett said.

Two men at the opposite end of the table began arguing whether "grith" was a word. Brackett's benediction didn't end the dispute. They were still going at it hammer and tongs when a waitress finally ventured over. "You writers don't knock off this racket, you're gonna get moved into your own room."

"We would welcome the solitude," Wilder said.

"Your game would probably improve." Brackett pointed at his partner's card. "Look at the dross you've come up with."

The waitress turned to Edith and me. "Can I get you anything?"

"I was told to have artichokes for lunch," Edith said.

"Artichokes? Good Christ, is Marlene here?" Wilder sat up straight and rolled down his sleeves, the specter of Marlene putting him on his best behavior.

4

ADDISON'S GLOSSY BLACK Cadillac Fleetwood waited by Paramount's Bronson Gate where I'd left it. I marched over to Rogers, the liveried chauffeur.

"Finished! We can head back to the house."

Rogers grunted and continued squatting on the car's running board. He took a drag on his cigarette. Then another. At long last he rose, crushed the butt under his boot, and slid behind the wheel, leaving me to open the rear door myself.

The universe didn't want me to get a big head. It had given me access to a car, courtesy of Addison Rice. It also provided an operator for said vehicle who didn't care for me one iota. Rogers had been in Addison's service for years, his face and hands nut brown from front-seat exposure to the California sun. Our relationship had gotten off to a perfectly civil start, until Addison suggested Rogers teach me how to drive. My first and only lesson led to a white streak in Rogers's hair, a certain skittishness whenever he passed a Bentley, and a regular deduction from my paycheck to cover the damages.

From that day forward, Rogers proved singularly immune to my charms. That chill didn't stop me from chattering to him incessantly out of a misplaced confidence I could win him back.

"There may be more driving," I warned him.

Rogers sucked on his teeth and tossed his chauffeur cap onto the seat next to him.

· · ·

AT ADDISON'S MAMMOTH manse, purchased with the proceeds from the many radio parts he'd patented, I stopped by my desk to ensure there was no pressing business then set off in search of my employer. I found him in the solarium, slumped opposite a stocky man. Donald Hume was not only Addison's attorney, he handled the legal affairs for any number of Los Angeles luminaries. He certainly looked the part, brown hair graying with distinction, his procession of immaculate black suits giving the impression he was always off to a funeral worth attending. Addison greeted his counsel's counsel with a castor-oil face.

My boss mustered a smile as I approached but couldn't mask his agitation. "Lillian! How was your lunch with Edith?"

"Lovely, but I'm afraid it's what we expected given Lorna Whitcomb's column this morning. Albert Chaperau snared at least one person at Paramount in his scheme."

Addison winced. "That name now provokes an immediate need for bicarbonate of soda."

I'd gone into my meeting with Edith anticipating she'd inquire about Chaperau. Two weeks earlier, Agent Higgins from Customs had returned to the house with more questions about the felonious filmmaker. Addison had been in constant contact with his attorney ever since.

Donald lit a cigar, turning it in the flame with a safecracker's grace. "I don't suppose Edith mentioned who's under suspicion."

"She didn't breathe a word."

Addison wiped his brow. "To think I invited that common criminal into my home."

"Be fair," I said. "If anything Chaperau's an uncommon criminal. Not every bounder gets himself accredited as a Nicaraguan commercial attaché."

"Higgins says he wants to know about my previous dealings with Chaperau. I don't like the sound of that word. I didn't have 'dealings' with the man, I asked him to some parties." Addison heaved a mighty sigh. "I could use a party now to take my mind off this lunacy."

"We talked about this, Addy," Donald said. "No one loves your parties more than me. But they're why Customs is interested in you. Chaperau might have exploited your hospitality to further his smuggling racket. Use Maude's absence as a reason to lower your profile until this matter's sorted. Nothing more elaborate than a quiet evening of bridge, like tonight."

Addison wasn't the only one who longed for one of his signature blowouts, complete with elaborate theme. It fell to me as social secretary to organize the bashes, a charge for which I often felt woefully ill-equipped. Thanks to Uncle Sam's scrutiny we had but a single charity breakfast on the horizon, leaving me with little to do. If we didn't schedule a shindig soonest, I feared I'd be looking for another job.

Donald paced the solarium floor. "It's beyond me why Customs is pursuing this case, especially when it hinges on the testimony of a Nazi maid. With the press they've been getting?"

Coverage of the Reich had changed markedly in the last month, since the two nights of mayhem when dozens of Jewish citizens in Germany and Austria were killed and countless synagogues and Jewish businesses vandalized, the streets littered with broken glass. The ferocity and apparent coordination of the attacks, along with the subsequent arrest of tens of thousands of Jews by the Nazi regime ostensibly for their own protection, had transformed the conversation about German aggression. Regarding Adolf Hitler as a menace only to his own people and their neighbors could no longer be done. I knew, because like most Americans I'd tried.

Addison's face clouded; he'd been reading the newspapers closely too. "Damn it, I wish Maude would come home. But she insists on maintaining her schedule."

"She knows she's safe in England," Donald said. "Might as well be in Pomona for all the risk she's facing."

"But how long will that hold?"

"For the foreseeable future, Addy. Hitler's a bastard and an anti-Semite, no question. But he's Europe's problem. They'll deal with him before he becomes a true threat. Lindbergh's right on the money: The real danger is Russia. Europe will wake up to that soon enough. Don't let the news wear you down. Remember, it's not just what you're hearing. It's who's saying it. You know my rule. Life's like playing poker. Once the hand is dealt, first you check your cards then you—"

"Check your dealer," I finished along with him, prompting a chuckle from Addison.

Donald feigned indignation. "Some wisdom is worth repeating. Back to this Chaperau business. We now know Paramount will be doing their own legwork, and lots of it. It would benefit us enormously to be privy to that information. Any chance you could keep your ear to the ground there, Lillian?"

"Edith *did* ask me for a favor."

"Do it," Donald directed. "Whatever it is."

I side-eyed Addison. "It would mean helping Marlene Dietrich."

Addison sat up straight. Funny how Marlene's name instantly improved the male posture. "You agreed, I hope."

"It could be tricky, what with you being more partial to Garbo."

"Nonsense. They're both wonderful. Marlene played the musical saw for me!"

"Now *that* was a party," Donald said rapturously. "Customs better wrap this Chaperau investigation up fast, Addy. We need you entertaining again posthaste. It's like keeping an artist from his canvas."

·   ·   ·

ADDISON HAD A new wave of patents to discuss with Donald.
Back at my desk, I resumed my march through the Rices' Christmas card list.

"Is this where I buy in to the crooked bridge tournament?"

I was happy to have my steady diet of good cheer interrupted,
especially by Charlotte Hume. Donald's wife was his sole con-
cession to a Hollywood lifestyle. The up-and-coming starlet, her
dark hair and gimlet eyes a fan magazine fixture, had broken out
last year in *The Defense Rests*, thanks to a big scene where she collapsed on the witness stand being cross-examined by Robert Taylor.
Donald had coached his spouse on her technique, earning a fair
bit of press for himself in the process. The Humes hadn't batted
an eye when Addison hired me as his untested social secretary,
Charlotte serving as benevolent Beatrice, my guide through
Paradise in *The Divine Comedy* that had become my life. She looked
immaculate in a dark gray suit with a Persian lamb collar, her
sandalwood perfume complementing the scent of leather she
always carried from horseback riding.

We exchanged kisses. "Donald tells me you're toiling for Marlene Dietrich now." Charlotte's sleepy voice contained too much
Virginia molasses for studio vocal coaches to eliminate. "You
know, I was up for a part in a Capra picture with her."

"The Chopin film with Spencer Tracy?"

"Lord, wasn't that a terrible idea? I'm talking to Mr. Capra
about a part in his new picture, a senator's daughter who tempts
poor Jimmy Stewart. Utterly thankless, but it's Capra." She
sighed. "I'm still holding out hope. For Scarlett."

Charlotte, owing to her recent fame and southern upbring-
ing, had not only been floated as a possible Scarlett O'Hara in
Gone with the Wind but had tested for the role—twice. Jimmie
Fidler even pegged her as a frontrunner in March, but she'd since
fallen back to the pack.

"Oh, I know it'll be Paulette Goddard in the end. But Mr. Selznick keeps bringing in unknowns, saying he wants a new face. He's testing another one this week, the latest antebellum belle fresh from amateur theatricals. Thanks ever so, Mr. Selznick." She fanned herself with her hand. "I told David O. I was born to play the part, that *Gone with the Wind* was like reading about my own life. Do you know what he told me? He said every actress fed him that line. Including Katharine Hepburn, and she hasn't been further south than Pennsylvania Station."

I couldn't help laughing. Recalling what Edith had said about actresses and their reliance on undying optimism, I decided to buck Charlotte up. "You're still in the running. Soon it'll be Selznick on line one, Capra on line two."

"From your lips to the good Lord's ears. Will you be playing bridge with us tonight?"

"I should get started on that favor for Dietrich instead."

"You sound a touch dubious, sweetie."

"It's not the kind of thing I usually do. But I'll be helping Addison if I stumble through it."

"Then stumble away, I say. Horse-trading's a way of life out here. And I'm a horsewoman from way back. Hollywood's a big business and a small town. Favors are coin of the realm." She paused. "As are rumors. Speaking of, let's review who else is in the running for Scarlett."

I ABANDONED GLAD-TIDINGS duties in favor of the latest *Photoplay*. I'd barely started the article averring that even his best friends didn't know the real Tyrone Power when Addison crept into view. "Donald and Charlotte are brushing up on their hand signals for bridge. You have to tell me what you're doing for Marlene."

I explained what Dietrich wanted. "I wasn't sure about pitching in. But if it will help you—"

Addison dismissed my reservations with a flick of his hand. "Anything for Marlene and Edith. My car's at your disposal. Besides, you've already met Jens Lohse. Or at least heard him."

"I have? Where?" As soon as I posed the question, I knew the answer.

"Here. He's played several of my parties."

"Since I've been working for you? So I hired him. I hired him and didn't know it."

"Come now, Lillian, it's not like you booked the Jens Lohse Orchestra. He sits in with a few bands. The two of us happened to fall into conversation one night he was here."

Classic Addison, the most democratic person I'd ever met. He'd invite a bevy of stellar names to his soirees and would be as likely to wind up deep in conversation with a waiter as Clark Gable. What's more, he'd be able to recall the person's name and face without relying on mental gimmicks like I did.

"March, it was. Our Spring Has Sprung affair. We'll have photographs on file. Jens will be the sad lad at the piano. Go see what your quarry looks like."

IT DIDN'T TAKE long to dig out the pictures, which brought back the vivid aroma of cherry blossoms on a warm March night. Chilled punch on every table, hot music by Tim Turner and His Troubadours.

Attacking the ivories in one photograph was a thirtyish man blissfully unaware of the camera. His too-large houndstooth jacket made his shoulders appear gigantic. A curtain of fashionably long dark hair hid his eyes but left a slight smile for the world to see. He looked vaguely dissipated, like he was meant to die of consumption in the last reel and spare the heroine a difficult choice.

At the edge of the frame, only a few feet from Jens, was yours truly. I did not appear to be enjoying myself. I seemed overwhelmed, biting my lower lip and staring at the floor, agonizing over whether I'd ordered too much food or not enough. Oblivious to whatever music Jens was playing.

The booking agency put me in touch with Tim Turner—right name Lou Mandelbaum—who told me Jens was his third-string eighty-eighter, he had no contact information for him, and the Troubadours were available to play for Addison again anytime.

I studied the photo of Jens. He'd plied his trade in this very house.

Now I felt obligated to look for him.

5

⬚

THE GOOD NEWS was I already had plans to play bridge with Gene Morrow, giving me a ready-made opportunity to ask about the LAPD's efforts to find Jens Lohse. After that, the bad news came in spades—likely the only correct reference to cards I'd make all evening.

Drawback number one: the get-together was at Gene's house, a two-story Victorian wedged on a Bunker Hill incline. Gene rented the upstairs to the Lindbloms, a Swedish couple with an impossibly well-behaved brood of five children. He treated his tenants better than himself, tending to their needs while neglecting his own accommodations. Age and the neighborhood's decline were taking their toll; the house was creaky and drafty, and every room on the west side picked up the scent of the Shell gas station on the corner. Hardly environs conducive to romantic sentiments. And on that subject . . .

Drawback number two: we were playing bridge because Abigail Lomax enjoyed the game, meaning Abigail would be in attendance, and her presence was also not conducive to romantic sentiments. Gene and I didn't see each other as much as either of us would have liked. His cases demanded odd hours, while Addison's frenetic social schedule kept me jumping. When we could steal away together, chances were good Abigail would be our third wheel. Gene felt an understandable obligation toward the childhood friend turned widow of his longtime partner. Many's the time I'd arrive to meet Gene at a restaurant or movie theater only to discover Abigail—sweet, always-a-kind-word Abigail—holding our table or our tickets, Gene later whispering an apology, saying she'd otherwise be cooped up home alone. As far as I could tell Abigail had no designs on Gene whatsoever. She was forever telling him he didn't need to invite her everywhere, but I couldn't help noticing she seldom said no. More troubling, Gene continued to ask.

Which brought us to drawback number three: bridge required a foursome, and recruiting the quartet's final member was my responsibility. The caliber of his play was irrelevant, so long as he was an available male who could, in theory, be paired off with Abigail both for the evening and the happily ever after.

For the assignment I'd selected Warren Fisk, one of Addison's accountants and a devotee of the game. He was also such an unassuming milquetoast I had difficulty recalling his name. Fortunately, I had Hiram Beecher's hints at hand. Beecher was the former lard salesman turned authority on business communication whose book *How to Be at Home in the World* had become a national sensation and my personal bible. *Why do people remember jokes? Because silliness sticks in the memory!* he'd advised. A warren is where rabbits live, so I'd picture a rabbit the same sandy shade as Warren's hair wearing his horn-rimmed glasses, leaping in a perfect parabola. Damned if it didn't work like a charm.

Warren sprang from his car outside Gene's house the instant he saw me. "I would have picked you up," he said.

"No need for that"—*leaping rabbit*—"Warren." As we climbed the rickety steps to Gene's door he took my arm, and it dawned on me he might have the wrong idea about why I'd asked him along.

"DON'T TELL ME you and Edith are at it again," Gene said.

"We're not *at* anything. She wants to do a favor for a friend and I'm in a position to help."

Once inside I'd buttonholed Gene, busy propping up a leg of his wobbly card table with a *Saturday Evening Post*. Gene sighed and squinted up at me. I took in his dark brown hair and realized two things: he needed a trip to the barber, and I'd missed him and his easy self-confidence. I was glad I'd freshened my face powder and lipstick before coming over.

Gene pushed himself to his feet. The table still wobbled. "No surprise Miss Dietrich didn't get the white-glove treatment she's accustomed to. Don't get me wrong. Carl Wingert's thorough. But he doesn't go for social niceties. Still, I'll call him." He held my gaze for a moment. "Oh. You want me to do it now."

"It wouldn't be a bad time. The game hasn't started yet."

"Yeah. We wouldn't want to interrupt the game." Gene was no fan of bridge, either. He glanced at Abigail. "Let me see what I can do."

As he stepped out of the living room I walked over to Abigail. She sat by herself dealing cards while—*leaping rabbit*—Warren built drinks at Gene's modest bar.

"Some solitaire to pass the time?" I asked.

Abigail giggled. "Just making sure Gene has all fifty-two cards." Her fingers moved dexterously, laying out four suits in record time, then executing a fleet shuffle.

"Better keep the stakes low," I told her. "Matchsticks only. Remember, what little I know about bridge I learned from *Grand Slam* with Loretta Young." My relationship with Abigail would have been so much simpler if I could have disliked her. But it was impossible to harbor ill feelings toward this slip of a woman with her huge Kewpie doll eyes and halo of tight brown curls. The hint of helium in her voice filled her every utterance with wonder, perfect for her job as a schoolteacher. Abigail had already endured so much pain—her husband, Teddy, gunned down in the line of duty—that I felt petty for questioning her motives or her sincerity. Like everyone Abigail encountered, I wanted to do something for her. And I had something in mind.

I leaned in and nudged her. "What do you think of our fourth?"

"He seems very nice. He certainly knows his bridge."

"That's why I brought him over."

"And I can tell he's quite taken with you."

"What?" I recoiled so fast my head swam. My best-laid scheme ganging aft agley before card one had been dealt. "Forget me. I wanted to put you two together."

"As partners? That doesn't make sense."

"No, I insist. Bunny should play with you."

"Bunny? Who's Bunny?"

"Have I got a nickname already?" Bunny—*No! Leaping rabbit!*— Warren hopped over with a tray of weak-looking whiskey high-balls, believing he had a tiger by the tail.

"No, um, Warren, sorry. I meant someone else."

"Lillian seems to think we should be partners tonight," Abigail said.

"I don't agree. Only way to keep the game interesting is to team the novices with the old hands. You are a novice, aren't you, Lillian? I'd be happy to show you what I know."

How was this evening unraveling so fast? "Or . . . or," I found myself shouting, "the ladies could take on the fellas!"

"Maybe next time," Abigail said in the soothing voice she undoubtedly used on surly children. "Tonight you and Warren should be together."

She'd already committed his name to memory, too. "Fine. As long as I'm the dummy. Being the dummy works for me."

"You might want to be the declarer for once," Abigail said. "It wouldn't hurt to try something new."

Same to you, I longed to holler in her face.

Bridge, a game of clues and evidence, should have been right

up my alley. But it had never captured my fancy. I played solely
for the snacks, preferring the five-card stud poker my uncle
Danny had taught me around the kitchen table in Flushing. Abigail and Warren did their best to convey some of bridge's stra-
tegic intricacies, but having two people hold forth on a subject
you didn't care for didn't mean you learned twice as much. It
meant you listened half as long.

When Gene finally returned, I pounced on him with relief
and dragged him into the kitchen. Where, to my dismay, I saw
neither hide nor hair of any snacks.

"Where's the food?" I asked, keeping a lid on my alarm.

"Are we doing food? We really expect to play for that long? I
have pretzels somewhere. And sandwich fixings."

"Grub courtesy of Loaves and Fishes Catering. Did you reach
Detective Wingert?"

"Yes, and he's not exactly thrilled Miss Dietrich is second-
guessing him. I wouldn't be either, given what he told me. There's
nothing to work with. It's tough to consider Jens Lohse missing
when he has no place to be missing *from*. He hasn't had a fixed
residence since he got bounced from his last place for not paying rent. Lohse convinced the landlady, a Mrs. Fuchs, to take
messages so he could still get work as a piano player, and she let
him leave his car there. Wingert gave it and his place the once-
over and found nothing out of the ordinary. He's pretty sure
Lohse went to Mexico to get his visa."

"Who gave him that idea?"

Gene blinked at me. "Your pal Marlene did."

"Wingert didn't talk to anyone else?"

"Who else is there? Nobody knows where Lohse lives."

"If Jens went to Mexico, why is his car still here?"

"Because it's a heap. Wingert says the shape it's in, it wouldn't
make it to Long Beach."

"Then how did Jens get to Mexico?"

"By bus. Or thumb. There are ways, Frost."

Ravenous, I scavenged sandwich supplies. The drawer containing the cutlery was stuck. Gene pounded the countertop to work it loose. "It doesn't sound like this Wingert investigated at all."

"He did exactly what I would have done." Gene's words were chillier than anything in his icebox. "Miss Dietrich may not be satisfied, but the LAPD did its job."

So much for using my vaunted connections to unearth more information on Jens. Gene and I prepared a platter of substandard sandwiches in silence, presenting them to our partners as if they'd been hand-delivered from Chasen's. I was paired with what's-his-name. Within an hour the four of us were playing gin rummy, and I was home in bed by ten thirty. Another giddy night in Hollywood's social whirl.

6

ADDISON'S ANNUAL SANTA Breakfast for Hollywood Helping Hands—or the Brentwood Boys Brigade, as I thought of them—wasn't about to organize itself, so Saturday meant a hard half-day at my desk. The breakfast was Addison's favorite charity event, because he could don the suit of the world's most famous fat man and ho-ho-ho to his heart's content. Our youthful charges received a hearty breakfast with gallons of cocoa, plus photographs with Santa and toys handed out by the biggest stars of the silver screen. Charlotte Hume had graciously agreed to fill in for Mrs. Rice as hostess, leaving every other aspect of the following Friday's festivities, from answering the first doorbell chime to peeling the last peppermint stick off the damask curtains, my responsibility.

I was scratching my head at some paperwork I'd obviously filled out myself when the telephone rang. My gratitude for the break proved short-lived.

"How's tricks, princess?" came a chipper voice.

"Hello, Kay." Kay Dambach and I had once lived in the same boardinghouse and been nigh on inseparable. Then the aspiring newshound had landed a gossip column earlier in the year, a direct result of her indirect involvement with the murder case that brought Edith and me together. *Katherine Dambach's Slivers of the Silver Screen* had limped out of the gate, picked up by a handful of newspapers and hampered by a lack of scoops. I had taken to cutting short if not outright ducking her telephone calls; her re-

lentlessness since climbing onto the lowest rung of success's ladder, forever badgering me for dirt on Addison's parties, had put
a strain on our friendship.

She started in again. "The ol' blank page blues have me down.
You don't have any tidbits for Mother, do you?"

If she only knew. "I'm afraid not. It's been pretty quiet around here."

"About that. Addison's name is usually stamped all over the
Hollywood social calendar, yet he hasn't hosted a bash in weeks.
What gives?"

I cursed myself for blithely wandering into Kay's trap. "Mrs.
Rice is traveling, that's all. Say, she might have a few observations
for your readers when she returns."

"Oh, goody. A matron back from abroad telling me the French
have a word for it. That always plays." She sighed. "Are you sure
this has nothing to do with Addison being at that New York dinner where the smuggling racket was cracked? Scuttlebutt is
some Paramount people may be implicated."

Clever Kay, ferreting out the facts. "No, Addison's simply being a good boy. I should run. I'm rather busy."

"Doing what, if Addy's not throwing any parties?"

"You're forgetting the Santa Breakfast. It's the highlight of the
holidays!" I proceeded to talk Kay's ear off, telling her who had been
invited and how many rashers of bacon stocked, until she threw
in the towel. She was, I had to acknowledge, a fair little reporter.

I hung up the receiver. After a moment, the unannounced
woman cleared her throat again. The first cough had been so soft
I'd assumed it was a dewy leaf brushing against a windowpane.

"Forgive me," she said, "but I seem to be turned around."

"Striking" scarcely did her justice, but one had to start somewhere. She resembled a precocious child's drawing of a beautiful woman: vivid slashes of brow above wide eyes, ebony hair
parted dramatically down the middle. And as in a child's drawing, her features were strangely flat and lifeless.

I leaped to my feet nonetheless, slamming my knee resound-
ingly against my desk. I recognized the woman. Hedy Lamarr
had appeared in exactly one American film—*Algiers*, with Charles
Boyer—but she was already being promoted as the world's most
beguiling creature, the latest in a line of luscious European exot-
ics like Greta Garbo and my new best friend Marlene Dietrich.
In person Lamarr more than lived up to the billing, even when
dressed in a belted camel trench coat and clutching a borrowed
man's fedora. I hadn't been told to expect the actress, but famous
faces turned up at Addison's on a regular basis.

"Happy to help, Miss Lamarr," I said, massaging my kneecap.
"Where are you to meet Mr. Rice? The dining room? The con-
servatory?"

"His laboratory." She gave the word a foreign spin, pronouncing it like Boris Karloff. "He promised to show me his inventions
this morning. You're lucky to work for such a brilliant man. I
should have paid closer attention to the directions I received at
the door." She pointed back down the hall with surprisingly thick,
utilitarian fingers. She had a mechanic's hands.

I was setting her back on course when Addison ambled by,
carrying what looked like a shoebox with a telephone dial on it.
"Hedy! There you are! Did Lillian waylay you?"

"Hardly. Is that what I think it is?" Animation stole into the
actress's eyes for the first time.

"Yes, my Magic Tuner. Allows you to change the station on
your radio from another room using static frequencies. The
Philco people have a similar product in the works, but I've made
a few refinements of my own."

"You must explain this fascinating device to me after I powder my nose." After a second round of directions Lamarr excused
herself, leaving Addison and me with nothing but his Magic
Tuner and a protracted silence for company.

"Hedy's very interested in engineering," he said.

"So I've heard."

"Asked more intelligent questions about radio equipment than the people who used to work for me."

"It's grand to meet people with common interests."

"Thought I'd show her what I've been tinkering with. Given the global situation I've been spending more time in the workshop. And Hedy tells me she's quite bored with the roles they're giving her."

I was perhaps the only person in the world who'd accept Addison entertaining a goddess while his wife was abroad at face value, taking them as partners in scientific inquiry. "I can imagine," I said. "I've only seen her in *Algiers*."

"Which I screened again recently. I forgot Charles Boyer was in it. He's a fine Pepe Le Moko, but seeing him reminded me of *Mayerling*, which only made me think of Albert Chaperau. Now Donald tells me Chaperau may not even have produced *Mayerling*, can you imagine? Everything the man told me could be a lie! And I introduced him to people! My friends!"

Addison may have been fabled for his frequent, grandiose parties, but he took sociability seriously. He genuinely loved people, from walks of life high and low. That enthusiasm was the reason I enjoyed working for him. Now here he was, reduced to showing a crateful of wires to Hedy Lamarr instead of entertaining the town, the notion he'd betrayed some communal trust eating him alive. As he wandered off to wait for his ardent admirer, I vowed to do what I could to aid his cause.

JENS LOHSE HAD formerly resided in a shabby bungalow court off Vine Street in Hollywood. Beige paint flaked off cottages huddled around a balding courtyard, the stooped palm tree at its center like an abashed stand-in.

Mrs. Fuchs, the owner-manager, had propped her bungalow's

door open so she could survey her empire from the shade. Her hair was the same vague blue as her cardigan. She nodded at the photograph of Jens I'd dug out of Addison's files.

"That's him, only he don't live here no more," she said, her voice hoarse from hollering at tenants through doors. "Police even came by asking about him. What'd he do to you?"

"He entertained at my boss's home. We're thinking of hiring him again." Neither statement technically a lie. I was unduly proud of myself.

"Leave a telephone number and I'll tell him you were here."

"You've been taking his messages for some time, then."

"Six weeks or so, since he came clean about not having rent money. I don't abide freeloaders. But it's not Christian to keep a young man from earning his livelihood. He needs to look stable, like he has a permanent address, or he can't get work." She settled herself in her chair, drawing the sweater around her shoulders. "I know a thing or two about show people."

"I'm sure you do. Is Jens a stable young man?"

"For a piano player." She cackled. "He never gave me no trouble, 'cept when I had to tell him to knock off his music when it got late. Always noodling on that keyboard."

"Would it be possible to have a look at his bungalow?"

Mrs. Fuchs's eyes flicked to a door across the courtyard. "No. New tenant already moved in, soon as my son and I repainted. There's nothing of his in there, anyway. We hauled it all out, including that ancient piano of his. Gave it to my church with Jens's blessing. Everything else is at the junkyard, 'cept a box of odds and ends he asked me to hold on to for him." She leaned forward, stopping just short of the sunlight. "Why do you need a look at his place to hire him for a party?"

An excellent question, Mrs. Fuchs. "He borrowed some music the last time he played for us. I'll get it from him later. Did I see Jens's car out back?"

"The convertible? He's got to leave it somewhere, although if you ask me it couldn't move with a stick of dynamite under it. Gonna hang a 'for sale' sign on it soon."

I went out to an alley behind the bungalow court. A trickle of water ran down its center from an unseen source toward some unknown estuary. I hadn't set foot back here before speaking with Mrs. Fuchs and had no idea what Jens's car looked like, but there was only one convertible. The boxy LaSalle sagged on knock-kneed axles, its accordion roof in tatters, bright yellow finish faded to the color of advanced jaundice. The passenger door shrieked as I opened it. Twigs were strewn across the seat and floorboards, the wilderness laying claim to the car. I forced the door shut and inspected the trunk. It was locked.

Taking a circuitous route back, I passed what Mrs. Fuchs indicated had been Jens's bungalow. A voice came through the patched window screen, that of a young woman singing scales.

There was no trace of Jens Lohse here anymore. I didn't know why I'd bothered to come.

I returned to Mrs. Fuchs's cottage. "Would it be possible to see the box Jens left behind?"

"Must be some special music he borrowed from you. Is Bing Crosby after it?" Still, she padded to a closet and retrieved a box, placing it on a table where I couldn't readily abscond with it. No treasure trove lay within, merely a broken watch, some blank postcards from Vienna and Berlin, and a stack of books.

The topmost one I recognized. Jens had read Hiram Beecher's *How to Be at Home in the World* as thoroughly as I had, the pages of his copy dog-eared. Had I introduced myself to Jens at Addison's party, we would have had a subject to discuss. Flipping through it I didn't turn up any marginalia or scraps of paper. Next was a book by an author named Karl May. A western, judging by the cover illustration, and in German, no less.

The final book came as a mild surprise: a second copy of

Beecher, this one so new its cover creaked. A gift not yet presented to its recipient, the inscription inside written in purple ink
with impudent flair.

> Felix,
>   It worked for me.
>   Jens

As I repacked the box's contents, some of Hiram Beecher's
wisdom came back to me. *The sound of a person's own name rings like
a bell in their ears, the purest note they'll ever hear.*

"Mrs. Fuchs, you've been a tremendous help."

"No bother," she said crisply.

"Thank you for offering to put me in touch with Jens. He's a
talented man, and he wouldn't be able to succeed without people
like you."

A tremor of pride ran through her body. "It's nothing, really."

"Don't sell yourself short, Mrs. Fuchs. All artists need patrons,
and not all patrons provide money. Some simply leave a door
open." I paused. "I heard Jens may have gone to Mexico for a new
visa. Do you think that's possible?"

"He never mentioned it to me. I suppose it is."

I nodded as if she'd said something profound, then wrote
down my home telephone number and took two dollars from my
purse. "When you hear from Jens, Mrs. Fuchs, could you do me
the great favor of letting me know at once?"

"Certainly." She glanced at the paper I'd handed her. "Right
away, Miss Frost. Lillian."

Ol' Hiram was right. It did sound good.

7

⠿

THE KEY TO one's wardrobe for a Sunday salon by the shore, Edith would advise, was the hat. A maroon sailor, say, boasting enough brim to spare my face the ravages of the sun, topping a gray jersey dress with a wide maroon belt.

Rogers, naturally, didn't compliment my choices when he picked me up in Addison's car. Well, I'd show him.

"Our hostess is Salka Viertel," I babbled to the back of his neck. "She used to be an actress, but now she writes scripts. Exclusively for Greta Garbo. She wrote *Queen Christina*, can you imagine? They say if you want Garbo in your picture, you've got to go through Salka. She holds these get-togethers every Sunday for artists coming from Europe. Composers, novelists, intellectuals, all discussing the state of the world. A bit highbrow for me. I'll be in over my head unless this week's *Your Hit Parade* comes up. It'd be swell if someone I've heard of is there. Garbo's too much to ask, but fingers crossed for Charlie Chaplin. He sometimes stops by."

I was so busy arguing that Fredric March, who'd played Vronsky to Garbo's Anna Karenina, would make a superior Chopin to Spencer Tracy that I didn't realize the Cadillac had slowed to a stop outside a white English-style house. Honeysuckle ran riot on the surrounding fence, and two lofty pine trees sheltered the front door. I couldn't see the ocean from where I sat but I could smell it, sense it on my skin, feel it soothing my blood. Even from the car the house seemed a sanctuary, the sort of home you would strive to be worthy of, a reward for a life well and fully lived.

"You're out of luck." Rogers addressed the windshield. "I seen Chaplin's car before. It ain't here."

"WE HEARD SUCH foolishness about living in Santa Monica. 'You will become rheumatic, suffer bronchitis and gout. Seal up your windows to spare yourself disease.' But who would deny themselves this?" Salka Viertel raised her hands to take in the totality of her abode. The living room with its fire crackling in the hearth, the view of the hills rising from Santa Monica Canyon, and everywhere the enticing scent of paprika. Simply agreeing with her was scarcely sufficient. I wanted to collapse into her arms and never leave.

A handsome, solidly built woman of about fifty, she had reddish hair and perceptive gray eyes. Knowing the value of plumage, she'd accessorized a simple brown dress with a vivid blue scarf guaranteed to draw attention as she darted about tending to her guests. It felt like a privilege to have her to myself for a few moments. I gushed compliments about the house then thanked her for welcoming me on Marlene's behalf. At the mention of the actress's name, Salka pulled me closer, her eyes sweeping the room.

"Careful when invoking dear Dushka." Her accent endowed every word with intrigue. "Greta may appear at any moment, and she and our mutual friend have only the most fragile détente. Out of necessity, my loyalty is to Greta."

"I understand." Organizing Addison's parties had taught me Hollywood relationships were like icebergs: only fractions of them were visible, the most treacherous parts lying beneath the surface.

"Dushka and I are, of course, close. I knew her first, in fact.

We acted together in Max Reinhardt's company a lifetime ago. Even then, she had her . . . dramatic temperament. It is on full display, I fear, in her concern over young Mr. Lohse."

"Do you know him well?"

"Not as well as I should, because he requires no special care from me. Jens comes in, helps himself to some food, takes a seat at the piano if no one is already there, then plays and chats with whoever happens along. He's very . . ." She glanced at the ceiling while she groped for a word. She unconsciously patted my forearm as she did so, the maternal gesture warming my heart. "Jens is self-reliant, which is why he will fare well in this new country. So many of my guests still struggle with the language, the lack of career opportunities. One of Vienna's finest surgeons— he's here, I'll introduce you—now supports himself as a masseur. And every week brings more newcomers. I never need worry about Jens. He's always at the piano, making someone laugh." She paused. "A strange boy, though."

"In what way?"

"I don't want to speak ill of him. He has such talent. He can always conjure up a tune to make a recent arrival feel at home. He knows every folk song in Europe. And the way he teaches himself to master new pieces, scurrying around with that enormous book of his. Like an encyclopedia. He'll play anywhere he can reach in that wretched roadster. It's his worst feature, that car." She cocked her head, again noticing an unflattering pigment in the portrait she'd painted. "That, and he can be aggressive about getting work. He's a pushy sort, forever pinning you down about your plans, exploiting every person he meets."

"Sounds very American."

"It does, doesn't it? I wish he were here, so I could speak with him."

"Where do you think he went?"

"I don't think he went anywhere. I've gone longer than this

without seeing him. Dushka is the one who insists the poor boy
has vanished." Salka's smile showed near-infinite reserves of com-
passion. "I understand how Dushka views life. She is a star. When
someone is drawn into her orbit, she believes only a cataclysm
can tear them loose. My attitude is different. The cataclysm is
happening now, as we sit by this lovely fire. People are constantly
being cast adrift. The best you can do is offer safe harbor. Jens
floats in, and he floats out."

I pictured Jens, bobbing like a cork on the open sea, clinging
to his book of music. "Is it possible he went to Mexico to secure
a visa?"

"Absolutely, if his visitor's permit had expired. *Mein Gott*, I don't
envy him the trip. We did it ourselves, my husband, Berthold,
and our boys. We stayed at an ostentatious hotel Jack Dempsey
built in Ensenada, with a casino attached. America's answer to
Monte Carlo. The Depression ended that dream. We were the
only guests! After three days we had claustrophobia. We were
grateful to cross the border again."

"And as for the theory the Nazis played a role in Jens's alleged
disappearance—"

"Preposterous. Make no mistake: people are disappearing all
over Europe because of them. They are ruthless. Jens knows it,
as do all people with their eyes open. Jens is keenly aware of what
is happening and speaks out against the Nazis. But the idea the
Reich even knows who he is?" The noise of dismissal she made
left no room for argument. "My fervent hope is you have wasted
a trip, and Jens comes through that door with a tale to tell. But
you are welcome to stay. Ask the others about Jens."

Recalling the inscribed book Jens left behind, I said, "I will.
Is Felix here?"

"Which Felix? I know several. You must mean Felix Auerbach,
the composer. I haven't seen him or his wife, Marthe, today, but

it's early yet. Help yourself to food. Dinner will be later, but for now there is *apfelstrudel* and *gugelhupf* in the kitchen."

"That first one sounds like apple strudel," I said. "And if the second is anything like that, you'll find it hard to get rid of me."

MUSIC FLOWED FROM every room, spilling into the yard where it accompanied the racket from a pitched Ping-Pong match. Talk was abundant but polyglot, the exchanges in English delivered in accents so strong as to be borderline indecipherable. I received my share of curious, welcoming smiles, but my forays into conversation died aborning. I was too much an obvious interloper. After a second pass through the house for another slice of *gugelhupf*, which turned out to be a heavenly ring-shaped coffee cake, I retreated to Salka's garden to reassess.

A defunct incinerator hid behind a lilac bush that had bloomed its last. I contemplated it while gorging on *gugelhupf*, so I didn't hear the man as he approached.

"This bush. It knows the fire is near, so it surrenders. Everywhere there is death."

Oh, brother. All the rays of sunshine came to me. The man's appearance bolstered my initial impression. He wore rough corduroy trousers and a black turtleneck despite the sun, and I pegged his weight at 90 percent eyebrow hair. His hunched posture channeled a lifetime of disappointment directly to his face.

"There's always hope," I said. "Maybe it'll come roaring back."

"This is what Salka thinks. You are American, *ja?*"

"Yes. Lillian Frost. Glad to know you."

"Gustav Ruehl." He stated his name as if expecting me to recognize it.

"How do you know Salka?"

"The way everyone does. Exile."

"What is it you do?"

"I am a writer."

"Anything I might have read?"

"I do not recite my curriculum vitae on Sundays. Others here should be known to you. Mostly composers today." He reeled off a roster of all-stars in a sport I didn't follow, stabbing a finger at each man as if casting them out. "Arnold Schoenberg. Bronislau Kaper. Ernst Toch." The rest he dismissed with a wave.

What modern music needs, I thought, is a series of baseball-like cards. Picture on the front, vital statistics on the back. *Wrote nine symphonies. Conducts with his left hand.* "There is a composer I was hoping to meet. Jens Lohse."

"He is not a composer. He writes musical doggerel." Ruehl peered at me. "Who are you, exactly?"

"A friend of Salka's. Not an exile, but—"

"Not a truth-teller, either. Why are you here?"

I fumbled for a reply. Ruehl pounced on my weakness. "Why are you looking for this Lohse? Perhaps you work with the men who wait outside watching the house."

"Men outside? I don't understand."

"And now you play the innocent!" Heads turned as Ruehl's belligerence grew. "Why are you asking questions? Does Salka know you do this? She abides this intrusion?"

I sputtered, desperate to silence him. My unlikely savior was a sturdy brunette who looked all-American but shushed Ruehl in fluent German. Ruehl started to protest, then tossed up his hands and turned to cast blame at the dormant lilac bush. The brunette, dressed for the office in a brown-and-maize suit, led me away from him and toward Salka's house. "Sorry about that. We don't usually let Gustav talk to people until their third or fourth visit."

"I think he's upset I haven't read his book."

"Nobody here has. They all own it, though." She introduced

herself as Gretchen Corday. "Gustav is one of the worst *bei-unskis*. They mainly speak German to other Germans about Germany. What matters to them is that you're *bei uns*. With us."

"You don't sound like a *bei-unski*."

"I'm something even rarer. California born and bred. My mother's from Stuttgart, though, so I have an in with Salka and her friends. It also helps I work in pictures. I'm a secretary over at Lodestar. Did I hear you asking about Jens Lohse?"

"I'm looking for him about a job. I gather he's not here."

"No, he isn't." Gretchen's voice sounded like it came from the bottom of a well.

"Have you seen him lately?"

"Not in about two weeks. And our paths cross pretty frequently." Her manner gave me the distinct idea Gretchen made sure of that; she was clearly carrying a torch for the tunesmith, and was at Salka's hoping to encounter him.

"Someone said he went to Mexico to clear up immigration trouble."

"That's not true. If he was taking that trip, he'd have gotten advice here first. Salka and half her guests went to Mexico for the same reason. They could have told him what to expect. Jens never makes a move without getting the lay of the land."

"Do you know where he's currently living?"

"Anywhere he can rest his head, I'm afraid. Funds are tight so he's been staying with friends, sleeping on sofas." The shadow as we entered the house cloaked Gretchen's face as she said, "I put him up a time or two myself."

"I've seen him. Lucky you." I hated to pry, but couldn't think of another way to keep her talking. "Does he have a girlfriend? He was drawing interest when he played for my boss."

"Oh?" A pause, then, "Was she blond?"

"She could have been. Do you know her?"

"Not really. But the last time Jens stayed with me, I found a few blond hairs on his coat. He was out of sorts, so I asked if he'd quarreled with his little blonde. It must have struck a nerve, because he was gone first thing the next morning."

But he'd still slept on her sofa, I noted. Dietrich's conviction that Jens was missing had received its first validation. Time to test Dushka's other theory. "Is Jens a *bei-unski*? How does he feel about what's happening in Austria?"

"How do you think he feels? His country's been taken away. Every spare minute he and I volunteer at the Hollywood Anti-Nazi League. Pitching in around the office, doing whatever we can. Jens is very passionate about it." Aware of how she'd described her would-be beloved, Gretchen backtracked. "But not as passionate as he is about music. He wants to score pictures at the studios and plans on studying composition. He's written such wonderful songs. Do you know 'The Trouble with Sin'?"

"I don't, sadly. I'd love to hear it."

After some internal debate, Gretchen took my arm again. She directed me to a room with a baby grand piano and no visitors. Once she closed the door firmly, she took her place at the ivories. "I won't do it justice. I have absolutely no training. But I love to play this one." She closed her eyes as if in prayer, hands suspended over the keys. She brought them down to peck out the melody, talk-singing the verses before belting out in a choir-loft alto.

In Paradise, the story goes
Two strangers met without their clothes
A circumstance they didn't mind at all

But gratis of a certain snake
They came to realize their mistake
And fled when the Almighty paid a call

And there we have the sinner's plight
When you give in and take a bite
Forbidden fruit will lead you to a fall

The press of lips, the gift of sable
The gin that lands you 'neath the table
Feel so nice, but there's a price
That's the trouble with sin

The fare is steep for each transgression
That's how you know you've learned your lesson
Which you dismiss with the next kiss
That's the trouble with sin

She wasn't blushing but strangely I was, her little-girl-lost performance adding spice to the saucy lyrics. "There's more," Gretchen said, "but Jens—"

The door burst open, a seething Gustav Ruehl beyond. "I knew it!" he cried. "Why you do play this Weimar nonsense for an outsider?"

Gretchen's German wouldn't allay his wrath this time. Ruehl crooked a crooked finger at me. "I demand to know why you are here! You were sent to put us under scrutiny, *ja*? You are with those men in hats outside who watch us day and night. Land of the brave, home of the free, yet government eyes always on us. It is Germany all over again! The smiling faces do not fool me! I insist—"

Salka Viertel's voice, calming but firm, preceded her into the room. She scolded Ruehl, who muttered in response after a final poisonous glance my way. Salka beckoned to Gretchen, who reluctantly led Ruehl from the room. Salka turned to me, pity in her eyes. "Poor Gustav hasn't eaten. You've caused something of an uproar, I fear."

"I didn't intend to. Perhaps I should go."

Her nod confirmed that was the wisest course of action. From one of the bookshelves she plucked a leather-bound volume called *The Prophet's Holiday*. "Gustav's masterwork," she said, pressing it into my hands. "I want you to have a better sense of him. Bring it back on your next visit."

ROGERS SLOUCHED BEHIND the wheel, acknowledging my return to Addy's Caddy with the merest movement of his head. "Have you noticed anyone watching the house?" I asked. "Possibly men with hats?"

He didn't want to answer, but I'd piqued his interest. "Guy in the blue Ford up the street there has been eyeing the place."

"He's wearing a hat, too. He might be a government man. Let's see what he does when we leave."

What he did was pull out after us. Rogers drove to the road running parallel to the shoreline, the Ford remaining a short distance behind. When there was a break in traffic, Rogers swung around in a sudden, provocative U-turn. The man in the Ford, caught off-guard, glanced down at his dashboard as we roared past. He made no attempt to pursue us.

"That'll teach him," Rogers said. "After all, we're Americans." I had the feeling it was the only positive thing he could think to say about me.

0

⁘

"LILLIAN!" MRS. QUIGLEY called up the stairs. "The show's about to start!"

No one needed to tell me when *The Jell-O Program Starring Jack Benny* began. Listening to my favorite comedian was a Sunday night ritual for me and most of America. I stepped into my pink carpet slippers and headed down to join my landlady. Miss Sarah Bernhardt sprawled on the lobby floor, wholly unimpressed by my choice of footwear. Served me right for trying to win over a dusky Burmese.

Gathering up Miss Sarah, I went into Mrs. Q's apartment. The aging ex-chorine stood her post in the kitchen, stirring her bottomless pot of stew. She wore a housecoat of many colors, and one side of her permanent had gone flat where she'd fallen asleep on it. "Help yourself if you're hungry."

The *gugelhupf* had been hours ago, so I dished out some dinner. I'd been one of Mrs. Quigley's tenants for almost two years. Thanks to the generous salary Addison paid me, I could have afforded bigger digs. But no place I'd scouted was as homey as the first place I'd ever lived on my own, complete with its prowling feline empress. I'd started paying additional rent and had a handyman pry open the painted-over connecting door to the smaller adjacent apartment so I could colonize its closets, the arrangement a triumph for all concerned.

The three of us settled in for the broadcast. Announcer Don Wilson declared that this week's show was emanating from

Radio City in New York. "I saw a movie there on my last trip," I said.

"Shush," Mrs. Quigley sensibly replied.

The standard silliness—Jack's wife, Mary Livingstone, razzing his stinginess, crackpot crooner Kenny Baker missing the point of, well, everything—was underway when the lobby telephone rang. Mrs. Q, bent close to the radio so as not to miss a wise-crack, didn't hear it, so I ran to take a message.

The voice rattling down the line asked for me in hushed tones. "It's Mrs. Fuchs. From yesterday. I thought you'd want to know there's a man here looking for Jens Lohse."

"Right now? Is he from the police?"

"He said he was Jens's friend, so I invited him in for tea." The sound on her end was briefly muffled, and I pictured Mrs. Fuchs cupping the receiver to throw a nervous glance over her shoul-der. "If you move fast, you can talk to him yourself."

Mrs. Fuchs clearly hoped to pick up a few additional dollars from me. Going to the bungalow court seemed a less reckless option than letting her brave a stranger solo on my behalf. I dashed upstairs for my shoes and coat. On my way out I poked my head into Mrs. Quigley's. "Where did you go?" she said over Kenny Baker's singing. "Jack's going to do a detective skit called 'Murder at the Movies'!"

Of course he was. And I was going to miss it.

ON ENTERING MRS. Fuchs's bungalow I spied Jens's box of meager possessions, a homely centerpiece between two cooling cups of tea. I also observed she was alone.

"What kept you?" she asked, clutching her cardigan. "Did you see him?"

"I had trouble finding a taxi. He left?"

"I kept him here as long as I could." She sounded hurt. "He

got restless, so I mentioned Jens's car. He went to have a look and hasn't come back."

I scampered to the alley, which, naturally, was pitch dark. The only illumination came from a flashlight wielded by a man conducting an inspection of Jens's jalopy. I cleared my throat.

The man's blond head snapped up like a dog hearing a whistle. At the same instant, he doused the light. I blinked into the blackness and felt for the bungalow behind me.

The light snapped on again, much closer than I expected. The man had moved with stealth. I glimpsed blue eyes and cheekbones fashioned by God's top sculptor. "May I help you?"

"I was hoping we could help each other. I understand you're looking for Jens Lohse."

A faint clucking sound emerged from the man's throat as he pieced together Mrs. Fuchs's stalling tactics. "Then you would be seeking him, too, Miss . . ."

"Frost. Lillian Frost. And you are?"

"Peter." He spoke with a precise and curiously airless quality, as if calibrating each syllable in advance. A tense smile settled on his thin lips. "I assume this is about money. Is that what you want?"

Mrs. Fuchs probably does, I thought. "No, it's not."

"Are you sure? It's my experience most things are about money. Jens is a friend, then."

"Not exactly. I'd like to offer him a job."

"You see? It *is* about money." His shoes scuffed concrete. "You must have a favorite of his songs. Which is it?"

A test. Luckily I had an answer. "'The Trouble with Sin.'"

"A bit earthy for me. Always popular with the ladies for some reason."

Turnabout, I had learned from Sister Luke in grammar school, was fair play. "Which Jens Lohse composition tops your hit parade?"

"He's written so many. I'd have to say 'Pick a Star.' Lovely melody, simple sentiment. 'Choose the right celestial fire / And you may find your heart's desire.'"

He could have invented a title for all my knowledge of the Lohse songbook, but quoting the lyrics convinced me. "So we are both after our musical genius," Peter said. "When did you last see him?"

"It's been well over a month," I hedged. "And you?"

"Too long." As my eyes adjusted to the darkness I saw Peter's fingers graze the trunk of Jens's car, the gesture almost intimate. "I came by hoping to surprise him, only to learn he hasn't lived here for weeks."

"Same thing happened to me. No one knew."

"He's good at keeping secrets, our Jens." A last lingering brush of the car's faded finish, then Peter's hand withdrew. "Do we know where he is?"

"I'm trying to find that out. What he left behind isn't very helpful, at least not to me. I gather Mrs. Fuchs showed the items to you. There's not much. A book I read, a western, some postcards—"

"The Karl May. *Winnetou and Old Shatterhand.*" Enthusiasm crept into Peter's voice. "I enjoyed those books as a child. Far from an accurate depiction of the West, but then May never set foot past Buffalo. Motion pictures take similar liberties. Did you see *The Plainsman*? A silly enterprise that ran roughshod over history."

Normally I bristled whenever someone criticized a Paramount picture, out of loyalty to Edith. But Edith hadn't touched a stitch of the costumes on *The Plainsman*; it was a Cecil B. DeMille production, and DeMille maintained his own costume unit. That was a sore spot with Edith, and consequently with me. Plus I hadn't cared for the movie. Perhaps our mutual disdain for DeMille's sagebrush saga could provide common ground.

"Oh, I agree." I nodded vigorously. "Why don't we go back inside? We can look over Jens's things and pool our resources."

"If you don't mind, Miss Frost, I think I'll take my leave. It's been a pleasure meeting you."

"Wait! What about finding Jens?"

"I'm sure he's fine, wherever he is. I'll see him again soon enough. We share many friends." He touched a finger to his hairline and again switched off the flashlight. He retreated down the alley, blond hair ghostly in the shadows.

I scurried to Mrs. Fuchs's bungalow. She waited in the doorway, her best scowl in place. "Did Mr. Ames tell you anything?"

"Was that the name he gave you, Peter Ames?" It sounded a bell in my head, as if I'd heard it before. "No. He went out of his way not to tell me anything."

"That's what I thought. Shifty fella. Didn't care for him."

"Had he visited Jens before?"

"Never set eyes on him in my life." She sighed. "Then the whole thing was a waste of time."

"I do appreciate it, though." I fished a few more dollars out of my purse in gratitude.

"Please, I'm happy to help." She still tucked the money into her cardigan. No martyr, our Mrs. Fuchs. "I'm only sorry I missed the Benny program."

"I was listening before I came over. It's from Radio City tonight." A second bell tolled. *Radio City.* On my New York trip with Addison, we'd gone to Radio City Music Hall to see a movie. *The Mad Miss Manton,* with Barbara Stanwyck as a daffy crime-solving heiress. Henry Fonda played opposite her as the stuffy newspaperman turned love interest.

Named Peter Ames.

A common enough handle that it could be a coincidence, I supposed. But if you were caught off-guard and needed an alias, why not select one from the silver screen?

Pondering the possibility, I wandered over to the box of Jens's possessions. I absently examined the western by Karl May, the author "Peter" had so enjoyed as a child.

During our conversation in the alley, I had completely forgotten the book was in German.

9

▦

I DECIDED THE next morning to invoke Rita of Cascia in making my case to Edith. Rita was the patron saint of lost causes—one of several, lost causes abundant enough for the Vatican to have saints working in shifts. If Marlene wanted to find Jens, I'd say, she'd do better with Saint Rita pounding the pavement. I was fresh out of miracles.

But Edith had access to higher powers of her own. "It's uncanny that you're calling," she said. "Can you come to the studio at once? Mr. Chaperau's scandal has claimed a victim. Some representatives of the government were on the lot this morning interrogating George Burns."

"George Burns?" I barked the comedian's name loudly enough to bring a quizzical Mrs. Quigley from her apartment. I waved her back inside. "Was he involved?"

"It looks that way. As you might imagine, it's a matter of some import. Mr. Groff wants to speak with you."

Barney Groff? Paramount's stern security chief? A man who, legend had it, once made Chico Marx burst into tears with a single glance? A man with all the charm of a rusty stiletto, who cared for me neither a jot nor a tittle, requested my presence?

I told Edith I'd be there, then dialed Addison. He sounded subdued even before I explained the situation.

"Donald informs me Albert Chaperau was indicted in New York this morning on charges of smuggling and conspiracy, along with Mrs. Lauer. Agent Higgins then requested I report to Customs tomorrow for further questioning." Addison chuckled out of habit. "I won't require Rogers today. You help Edith and learn what you can."

ONE WANTED TO look sharp when calling on Paramount's powers that be. I broke out a navy blue sheath with a boxy jacket I'd saved for just such an occasion, accessorized with a necklace of chunky coral beads. Edith handily outclassed me in a reddish-brown dress with a gathered yoke boasting three rows of black dome buttons. She was always fashionable but never flashy, and sometimes I wondered why I bothered. She still sported the chignon, the hairstyle apparently agreeing with her.

"Thank you for coming," Edith said. "I hope it's not an inconvenience."

"It might be for the federal agent who followed me here."

Edith stared at me. "What?"

"I picked him up yesterday outside Salka's house. He was at it again this morning. Trailed me right to the gate. Rogers is down there now making with the *malocchio*. But it's not my car, and I hate involving Addison in this."

"Not as much as I regret putting you and Mr. Rice in this position."

"Couldn't be helped. We'll discuss Jens after my audience with Mr. Groff." I nodded at the sketch pad in her hand. "More work on Jack Benny's next picture?"

"Yes. Did you hear his show last night? The last skit—a detective burlesque, very funny—ended with a joke priming the audience for *Artists and Models Abroad*."

"I missed it," I said huffily, peeking at Edith's pad. The sketch showed a woman in a gold halter top held around the neck by a thick chain. Golden links draped in loops over, and did precious little to conceal, an exposed midriff. A brief matching skirt, saved from criminal trespass by sheer harem pants, completed the en-semble. "Jack's latest has exotic slave girls?"

"Several of them. Too risqué?"

"Maybe a touch."

"Nonsense. The young ladies who'll wear these costumes will be bright, smiling chorus girls above reproach. Any immorality will be in the eye of the beholder."

"Tell that to the Breen Office."

"I have, on multiple occasions."

Edith's secretary announced her next visitor. "So this is where the congregation is meeting," George Burns said in his signa-ture rasp. "Good. Always happy to stop here, Edie. It's peaceful. Like a betting parlor after the last race is called." The comedian looked dapper in a pin-striped navy suit and two-tone shoes. His eyes practically disappeared into a face that seemed old be-yond its years yet emanated a playful spark. His fingers twiddled an unlit cigar.

Edith introduced me, and I told him I'd had the pleasure of meeting his wife, Gracie Allen, the year before. I could have added that Edith and I had lent a hand in apprehending a murderer on the set of his film *College Swing*, but that seemed a lot for a man to absorb at once.

"If you've met my better half, I'm going to prove a real dis-appointment." Burns shifted the cigar to his other hand. "I'm told you also know Albert Chaperau. The man who's going to end my career."

"I'm sure it's not as bad as all that," Edith said.

"Let's revisit the subject in six months and see who's right."

"How did you meet Chaperau?" I asked.

"Through friends. He was taken by the fact we're both Na-thans. His right name's Nathan Shapiro, mine's Nathan Birnbaum. Chaperau couldn't get over it. Me, I wasn't so impressed. Where I come from, I know plenty of Nathans. I see one every time I

look in the mirror. Frankly, I'm not too enamored of him lately."
Burns smiled thinly, craving a laugh he knew he didn't deserve.
"A few years ago, 1936 it was, we're all in New York at the same
time. Me and Gracie, Chaperau and his wife, Paula. We have dinner at the '21' Club. And I notice the bracelet Paula is wearing.
A lovely thing. The bracelet, not the wife. Normally I don't make
a practice of noticing bracelets, but this one is wide."

"Wide?" I was lost.

"Tell me something, Lillian. That is your name, isn't it, Lillian?
I know it's not Nathan. You've met my Gracie, seen her in pictures. Notice anything particular about her clothes?"

He would have to pose the question in front of Edith. After
a moment, I shook my empty, empty head.

Burns moved the cigar back to his other hand, and Edith took
this as her cue. "Sleeves," she said solemnly.

"That's right. She always has full- or three-quarter-length
sleeves. Do you know why? Because she was scalded on one arm
as a girl and hates for anyone to see the scars. So I stay on the
lookout for jewelry she can wear."

"Like a wide bracelet," I said.

"Exactly. That night I took Chaperau aside. Gracie would love
that piece, I said, where can I buy one like it? Chaperau says you
don't have to buy one like it, I'll sell you that one. I said I don't
think Paula will take too kindly to that. He told me not to worry.
That's when I should have started worrying. Who sells jewelry
right off his wife's arm? I wouldn't try it. I don't know another man
who would. But I'd gotten it into my head I wanted it. Because
it was perfect."

"Wide," I said.

"Wide. Chaperau says it's mine for two thousand dollars. I get
the money, I buy the bracelet. I had no idea he'd smuggled it
into the country. I send him a note later saying Gracie loved the
bracelet—she did, by the way—and I sign it 'From Nathan to

Nathan,' knowing he'll get a kick out of it. He asks me for a photograph, I sign it the same way. And that's how I landed in the soup.
He travels with the picture and the G-men found it. Fans like
him I don't need."

He lapsed into silence. "Surely the government wouldn't ha-
rass you over that," Edith said.

"I'm pacing myself. I'm not proud of what happened next."
Burns contemplated the cigar. "Earlier this year, Chaperau showed
me papers he'd gotten. Credentials from some country."

"Nicaragua," I prompted.

"That's the one. And he explains how he can bring in goods
under diplomatic cover and save us a few hundred dollars. Not
that I'm looking to save the money. But Chaperau tells me everyone does it. Politicians, society people in New York. I knew it
was wrong, but didn't want to say it was wrong. You get in a situation like that, you don't want to be the rube."

I understood. I'd met enough show people to know even those
at the top of the profession viewed their position in society as
tenuous at best. Years of living in run-down theatrical boarding-
houses and being treated as second-class citizens made them extremely conscious of status. For Burns to be included in a dodge
reserved for the upper crust was a greater windfall than any money
he might save.

"So I went along. When I bought Gracie gifts in Europe, I let
Chaperau take them back into the country. I did it in May, then
again in October. I was in New York when he came back from
that trip, so I stopped at his hotel, picked up the jewelry, brought
it to California." More seemed forthcoming, but Burns abruptly
stopped talking and fussed with his cigar. The stogie, I realized,
was more than a prop he'd use to time his jokes, or a baton to
conduct conversation. It was an essential part of his character, a
meditative object.

Edith not only sensed his distress but intuited its cause. "What

else did you bring to California, George? Items Mr. Chaperau
had smuggled for a friend, perhaps?"

The question compelled Burns to set the cigar alight at last.
"Gracie always says you're a smart cookie, Edie. The government
men asked me the same thing. They were more forceful about
it." He took a contented puff, the fragrance indicating Burns didn't
skimp on quality. "It's funny, I've sat under those pepper trees I
don't know how many times and never thought I'd be grilled
by federal agents there. *My* agent, maybe, but not Uncle Sam's.
It's where we first met, Edie, remember? Back when we were making *College Holiday.*"

"I do indeed," Edith said with a wistful half smile. "As for this
friend—"

"Do the feds know who it is, and does he work for us?" Among
studio grandee Barney Groff's many dark gifts was the apparent
ability to materialize at will. He glided into Edith's office as if
mounted on casters in a suit the color of midnight, and placed a
hand on Burns's shoulder. "Tell me now, George, if we're still in
the woods on this business."

"If I were you, Barney, I'd start building a campfire."

"Goddamnit. Give me a light, George. Do the government
boys know who it is?"

Burns sparked Groff's cigarette. "No names, but they hinted
pretty hard they know something. Maybe Chaperau told them.
Maybe he travels with signed photographs of everyone he roped
into this scheme. The *putz.*" Burns glanced over at Edith, then me.
"Forgive me, ladies. I'm not myself today."

"Think nothing of it, George," Edith said.

"I've met Chaperau," I added. "*Putz* is the word."

If nothing else, I made George Burns laugh.

Groff ended our exchange. "So you stay mute, give them
nothing. We make them prove—"

"Hold on, Barney. As soon as I heard Chaperau was arrested

I told myself and more importantly I told Gracie I'd be honest with the government right down the line. I'll own up to what I did. Pay restitution, suffer the consequences, answer every question truthfully. If they ask if I transported jewelry for someone else . . . I have to say yes."

Burns's sincerity moved me. But Groff, bless his black heart, was already hatching plots. "Suppose they don't ask about this individual *by name*. There's no reason you'd have to mention him, right?"

Burns drew on the cigar. "I hadn't given it that much thought."

"That's the boy. All I need's a little room to maneuver. Who's your lawyer?"

"Good man, Bill Donovan in New York. He knows the president."

"Let's hope we don't have to call on Roosevelt just yet. You've got the right attitude, George. Face the music squarely and it'll all come out in the wash. Paramount will back you to the hilt, and your reputation won't suffer a bit. Don't you agree, Miss Head?"

Edith nodded without wholly endorsing Groff's view. "What matters is you'll be able to face Nathan in the mirror again. And Gracie, too. How is she these days?"

I wanted to hear Burns's answer but Groff pulled me aside. In the past he'd barely acknowledged my existence. I was the one who'd brought Gene and the LAPD into his Paramount fiefdom last year, and while ignominy was averted my presence didn't evoke pleasant memories. Now he was galled at having to include me in top-secret powwows. "Christ, why'd they have to ambush the poor bastard? We could've put them together in an office somewhere, had his lawyer present. A goddamn train wreck, this is. Miss Head informs me you attended the dinner where this whole smuggling enterprise came tumbling down. Tell me about that night and this *putz* Chaperau. Spare nothing. I need an angle to work and fast." I did as Groff asked while Edith kept George Burns occupied. She got the better end of the deal, serving as Burns's willing audience, her hand permanently pressed over her mouth as she laughed.

"I don't get it," Groff said after he'd wrung me dry. "Why is the government pursuing a penny-ante noncommercial smuggling case?"

"Well," I said, "the law was broken."

Groff's disparaging look contained a soupçon of pity for my naïveté. "I said *noncommercial*. We're not talking about enemy agents bringing in radium, for Christ's sake. It's people ducking a few measly bucks in taxes. What's more American than that?"

"Maybe that's the point. The government wants to set an example with the war looming."

"So they build their case on the say-so of a Nazi maid? None of this makes a lick of sense. They've got Chaperau and that judge's wife dead to rights. What's the point of coming out here and putting Paramount in the crosshairs? Why go after George Burns when you can hang a judge?"

"He's better known than the judge," I said helpfully.

"Since when is Uncle Sam in the publicity business? What, they need a tumble in Winchell's column? The longer this thing's in print, the more it reminds people the government's in bed with some Kraut dishwasher. This stinks to high heaven. Something else is afoot here." Groff spun dismal designs in his mind, subconsciously baring his teeth as he did so. "If you hear any whisper about the government's case from Mr. Rice or his attorney, I trust you'll share it with your friends." He didn't phrase it like a request.

His demeanor suddenly sunny, Groff wheeled toward Burns. "George, let's you and I parley in my office. We'll figure out our options and get you clear of this imbroglio."

A slump-shouldered Burns said his good-byes. "You know what gets me, Edie? Here I am fighting for my livelihood over a bauble when I should have come to you. You'd have found something for Gracie to wear. Maybe not gold and diamonds. But it would have looked good on her. That's all a woman wants."

I ASSUMED EDITH and I would dissect the conversation, sharing breathless can-you-believe moments as the scent of Burns's tobacco lingered. But upon closing the door behind her visitors, all thought of pending scandal was banished. "Now," she said briskly, "tell me about your weekend."

I gave a précis of my peregrinations. "There's not much more I can do," I concluded. "Wherever Jens is, he'll eventually come back and contact Mrs. Fuchs. When he does, she'll tip me."

"I can't thank you enough. You've gone beyond the call."

"Yet I can tell from your voice," I said, "there's further still I can go."

"Possibly. Would you excuse me a moment?" She picked up her telephone and had one of those distinctly Hollywood conversations, all cryptic remarks and half-finished questions. She set down the receiver with a flourish of accomplishment. "I thought I knew the name Felix Auerbach. That was Boris Morros, the head of our music department. An émigré himself. He said Mr. Auerbach is a highly regarded composer under contract to Lodestar Pictures."

"And you want me to talk to him."

"Only if you have time. Boris can arrange a meeting with his counterpart at Lodestar to pave the way."

I only hesitated a moment. After all, Addison *had* encouraged me to help Edith. "If I go to Lodestar, I could speak to Gretchen about this Peter Ames character. He reads German and took pains to hammer any trace of an accent out of his voice. I'm thinking he's another émigré, maybe a regular at Salka's. Gretchen might know him."

"An excellent notion." Edith had undoubtedly drawn the same conclusion, but let me lay claim to the idea myself. "Then this trip will mark the end of your efforts on Marlene's behalf. Don't let me delay you."

I could forgive Edith for chivying me along. She had a busy day ahead, slave girls to half dress.

10

THE G-MAN DILIGENTLY dogging me likely needed a rest. He and Rogers could remain at Paramount while I visited Lodestar. But the necessary deception required an accomplice.

After a few rondelets of ring-a-levio with the Lodestar switchboard ladies, I tracked down Gretchen Corday, taking messages for a B-picture producer named Huritz. She divined the reason for my call. "Have you heard something about Jens?"

"Several things. I've got an appointment at Lodestar's music department about him."

"I tried to help Jens land a job there!"

"The thing is," I said, "I've got car trouble. Do you know the best streetcar route?"

"Forget that. You're getting a lift courtesy of Mr. Huritz. Where should we pick you up?"

ANDREZJ CYBULSKI WAS a slender, ascetic man with a mane of silvery hair meant for center stage at a concert hall. His office at Lodestar Pictures had been styled in his chilly image down to his faithful factotum. She presented Cybulski with a sheaf of papers, removing each one as he signed it with a sound like a whip crack.

"Yes, Jens Lohse approached me about a job. A second-rate Frederick Hollander, since you asked, a pushy lad who exaggerated his notices. I turned him down. Imagine my surprise when I encountered him on the lot some time later. He'd started studying composition with one of our employees. Not that instruction would have helped."

Crack.

"Yes, as a matter of fact it was Felix Auerbach. Every studio has a brilliant German writing difficult music on their payroll. Felix is ours."

Crack.

"No, he's not here. Our brilliant Mr. Auerbach can't be bothered to work on the lot because he claims the constant noise is a distraction. Do you hear any noise, Miss Frost?"

Crack.

"If you wish to speak to him, Miss Rascoe can provide his address. He also owns a cabin in the hills—an aerie, he's actually called it—where he presumably composes his more groundbreaking and therefore unpleasant work and no one is inconvenienced, save the coyotes."

Crack.

"Should you happen to find Felix, please be so good as to ask him to report to work. We need a new song for Laurence Minot's picture *Murphy's Murphy Bed*. Will there be anything else, Miss Frost?"

Crack.

GRETCHEN AWAITED A report, her black skirt billowing as she paced the forecourt outside the music building.

"Did you know Jens is studying here with Felix Auerbach?"

"He is?" Her voice shrank, which only magnified the pain it contained. "He hasn't mentioned it to me."

I wondered how one-sided their relationship was. Jens may have slept on Gretchen's sofa, but could he pick her out of a lineup? Then again, no one seemed aware Jens was under Felix's tutelage. Wouldn't he sing such news from the rooftops if he was seeking employment?

"Do you know Felix?" I asked.

"Not well. He comes to Salka's every once in a while. He's one of the *bei-unskis* I told you about, doesn't mix very much. I don't think his wife, Marthe, even speaks English." She paused. "Marthe's beautiful, though. A lot younger than him, too."

"Ever listen to Felix's music?"

Gretchen's eyes circuited their sockets. "Salka played a recording one afternoon, made the whole room fidgety. Except for another of her regulars, Arnold Schoenberg. He was flattered, I guess, because Felix had written the piece using Schoenberg's technique. Twelve-tone composition, I think it's called? I'm no expert on it."

Neither was I. From what I knew, Schoenberg's work was to music what Elsa Schiaparelli's avant-garde designs were to fashion, acclaimed as the epitome by those in the know while leaving the hoi polloi flummoxed. All I knew was I couldn't dance to one and couldn't wear the other.

Gretchen squinted as I described the man calling himself Peter Ames. "I can't picture him," she said, "but I haven't met everyone who frequents Salka's. I guarantee he and Jens aren't friends. In the past month Jens knocked on the door of anyone who was even a passing acquaintance looking for a place to sleep."

We studied the red brick beneath our feet for a moment. "What now?" Gretchen asked.

"I could pay a visit to Felix Auerbach and find out when he last saw Jens. The music department gave me his address."

"Then you're on studio business. Wait here. I'll arrange a car for you."

Who was I to argue with such diligence?

• • •

A DIFFERENT LODESTAR driver picked me up, this one a lanky fellow who moved with a languid ease verging on disinterest. I told him our destination and he grunted. "You're going to see Mr. Auerbach. I've driven him home before."

Home was the El Royale Apartments on North Rossmore in Hancock Park, one address that could tempt me to abandon Mrs. Quigley's. The magnificent Spanish-style building was an underhand stone's throw from Paramount, the electric-green script of its rooftop sign beckoning to me whenever I passed it.

The car pulled up to the entrance like it belonged there, which it did. "Shall I wait?" the driver asked. "The Auerbachs are in 402, if that helps."

The information sped me past the doorman. I flew through the splendid arches of the El Royale's lobby without stopping to admire the gorgeous inlaid oak floor and ceiling. On the fourth floor, I rapped softly on the Auerbachs' door, then hammered as loud as I dared. I pressed an ear to the wood and heard dust settling.

The white-haired elevator operator told me he'd last seen the Auerbachs "maybe a week ago," each carrying a suitcase. The doorman had no idea where the Auerbachs' hilltop aerie was, which posed a problem considering the address wasn't on file at Lodestar, either. A promising avenue of inquiry had hit a dead end, my modest bag of tricks emptied.

Sorry, Marlene. I'd done all I could.

"Nobody home?" The Lodestar driver, smoking cross-legged against the sedan's grille, smiled pleasantly. I considered him and reconsidered my options. He was older than I would have expected, in the vicinity of forty, hair already graying. He stood well over six feet tall, as lean as if he'd been whittled out of pemmican. His suit was as trim as he was, his brown-and-white Oxfords a subtle hint of flash. Perhaps the sign of a man willing to bend the rules.

"What was your name again?" I asked, knowing he'd never offered it.

"Simon."

"You said you've driven Felix before. Ever take him to his place in the hills?"

Simon took a contemplative drag on his cigarette. "Up in Pacific Palisades? Yeah, now and again."

"Any chance you remember where it is? It looks like he and his wife went there."

"It's rather remote. I relied on Mr. Auerbach's directions." He turned toward the hills. At his left temple, the side I couldn't see from the backseat, the skin was bone white save where it was mottled with decades-old scars that remained a furious red. "But I'm willing to try. This is studio business, right?"

"Absolutely."

A few blocks down Rossmore, I became convinced a car—not the one from that morning, but a different one—was shadowing us. Riding with Rogers of late had transformed me into a paranoiac, I told myself, but the gray car was still with us a few turns later. Desperate for distraction, I quizzed Simon. "I haven't met Felix Auerbach. What's he like?"

"Very serious. Doesn't say much. Composer, isn't he? Never heard his music. What kind of stuff is it?"

I pondered what I knew of Felix's oeuvre. "Difficult," I said. "Have you driven his wife, Marthe?"

"On occasion."

"I hear she's lovely."

"I wouldn't know about that."

The gray car continued drifting along behind us like it didn't have a care in the world.

"I don't suppose you've seen this man with Felix." I handed Simon the photograph of Jens from Addison's collection.

Once we were on a straight length of road, Simon glanced at

it. "Seen him? I've driven him in this very car. He's a student of Mr. Auerbach's, isn't he? Hans something or other?"

Never would I use the phrase "stab in the dark" cavalierly again. "Jens Lohse. When did you drive him?"

"Several times over the last few months, either from the studio to the Rossmore apartment or back."

"Is that customary, providing taxi service to Felix's students?"

We reached a red light. Simon pivoted toward me, the slash of scarred skin exposed in the rearview mirror. I willed myself not to look at it. "No," he said. "But Mr. Auerbach requested it. I figured Jens was taking advantage of the studio's generosity toward Mr. Auerbach until I got a load of his car. Lord, what a heap. Felix sent me to pick him up once after it broke down on Western. Bald tires, steam spewing out of it like in a silent picture." He laughed a bit too avidly at the memory. "Poor bastard needed a lot of rides."

"Sounds like you don't have a high opinion of Jens."

Simon faced front again. His eyes met mine in the mirror and stayed there. "I didn't like him, Miss Frost. He was a touch too slick and acted above me because I work this job. But he's the one scrounging rides." The corners of his eyes crinkled, so I assumed he'd smiled. "Besides, if my passenger doesn't work for the studio, I don't have to like him."

"And if he does?"

"Then he—or she—is the most talented person it has ever been my privilege to transport."

THE GRAY CAR no longer drafted in our wake as we climbed into Pacific Palisades north of Santa Monica. A short distance into the hills the earth was singed black, burnt trees clawing air faintly smelling of smoke. The presence of great swaths of green nearby only made the landscape more alien.

"Big fire up here last month," Simon said. "Hope the Auerbach place survived." I slid across the rear seat behind Simon as if he could shield me from the hell that had swept through not long ago.

We proceeded slowly, Simon navigating in silence and occasionally reversing course. He then nodded in satisfaction. "There's the horse trail I've been looking for. Okay, now I've got this licked."

The road, more a rutted track hacked through trees mercifully spared in the blaze, scaled a promontory. The rustic flagstone house at its summit had a balcony that projected over the canyon below. Simon stopped the car and the wind became our sole accompaniment, emphasizing how isolated the Auerbachs' cabin was.

"I don't see a car," Simon said. "You sure they're here?"

"That's what I was told," I lied. "Let me check."

"I'm coming with you. You get coyotes and mountain lions up this way."

Forest fires, coyotes, and mountain lions. Three things I never worried about growing up in Flushing. California had made me a different person.

No one answered my knock. Simon hollered hello through cupped hands a few times, the only response the breeze. He tried the front door. It opened.

"That's a good sign. Maybe they're out for a walk." Simon didn't sound convinced. He hadn't sold me, either.

We ventured inside. The cabin felt small, most of the space given over to a fireplace and an upright piano. The sink in the simple kitchen held a few days' worth of dirty dishes.

"Looks like someone left in a hurry," I said.

Simon mounted a narrow ladder. "Must be the bedroom up here. I'll go."

I moved back into the living room. On an end table was a

photograph of a couple I presumed to be the Auerbachs. Felix, of stocky build, balding pate, and imperious gaze, loomed protectively over his blond wife. Marthe was as stunning as advertised, the forthright smile on her face the only decoration the room required.

"The bed's not made," Simon called from the second floor. "I don't know. Place feels deserted to me."

I told him I agreed and stepped onto the balcony. A single chair faced the house, an empty glass on the floor next to it. The view of the canyon, now a patchwork of lush greens and scorched blacks, took my breath away. It truly was an aerie, I thought, running my hands along the wooden railing.

I felt the scrape first, then leaned over to inspect the small, fresh gouge in the wood. Gripping the rail tightly, I peered over the edge. About a hundred feet down, an object was visible amid the still-verdant brush. My eyes scanned the terrain around it. The strangled cry from my own throat told me that was indeed a shoe far below, the leg it had flown off of extending from the undergrowth.

Simon insisted on making the descent alone. I watched from on high as he cantered down the slope, wincing with every footfall that brought forth a cascade of rocks and soil. I knew what he would find long before he nodded up at me with grim finality. Jens Lohse had died far from home and nowhere near a piano. The sporadic call of birds would have to be music enough for him.

11

❖

"YOU'VE CHOSEN YOUR property well," Gene announced from the Auerbachs' balcony, "when you can still admire the view after hell's paid a visit."

Simon had taken me down the hillside to a hamburger stand, where I'd telephoned Gene from a booth beribboned with flyspecked menus. A second call to Paramount sent Rogers homeward. I'd be a while.

Squad cars arrived at the Auerbachs' cabin first, several officers trekking down to stand watch over Jens Lohse's body. Gene and his partner Roy Hansen drove out from downtown. Hansen never entered the house, marching straight to where Jens had fallen. He skirted me without a glance, Hansen not exactly a dues-paying member of the Lillian Frost Fan Club. Gene had greeted me with a curt "Miss Frost" then spoke with Simon, last name Fischer. ("With a 'C,'" he'd stressed.) After consulting with the uniformed men, Gene escorted me onto the balcony. I hugged the wall of the house. I'd had my fill of panoramic vistas for the time being.

Gene, having no such compunction, gauged his men's progress. "It's going to take time to move the body. He's been down there a while. You want to tell me what this is about?"

"I told you the other day. Edith asked me for a favor."

"This constitutes a favor? Running all over town, deceiving that driver?" Gene nudged his hat back on his forehead. I'd not only ignored his advice, I'd found the body of a man an LAPD colleague had insisted was in Mexico. Gene's frustration would not be easily dispelled.

He glanced into the house at Simon, who stood at sleepy attention. "What's his story? Fischer?"

"He drove me here. The end."

"Has he taken good care of you?"

I was happy he wasn't looking at me when he asked. It meant he didn't see my eyes moisten at his concern. "Yes. He's been very considerate."

Gene nodded, then signaled Simon to join us. Simon strolled out as if expecting to be dispatched to Bullock's for a parcel. "It's early yet," Gene said, "but suicide's the best bet. Lohse came to a place he'd been to before and threw himself to his death. Miss Frost, hadn't you heard Lohse had been behaving oddly of late?"

"Yes." His assessment jibed with what Dietrich had said.

"Only question is how did Lohse get up here? It's unlikely he walked. There's no car outside." Gene inched closer to Simon, crowding him. Simon stared placidly back and didn't retreat a step. "Somebody drove him. You're a driver. Was it you?"

"No. I never drove Lohse here."

"Right. Only to and from the Auerbach apartment, you said. How often did you do that?"

"Five, six times."

"What did you make of him?"

"I never formed an opinion."

"You sat in the car together and had no thoughts on the man?"

Simon shifted his shoulders, not quite shrugging. "I had to keep my eyes on the road."

That wasn't what Simon had expressed to me—*I didn't like him, he was a touch too slick*—but I wasn't about to point that out to Gene now.

"You drove Felix Auerbach here," Gene said. "How often?"

"Once, maybe twice."

"When was the last time?"

"I'm not sure. End of summer, maybe? That's when he was spending time here."

"And four months later you remembered a route you'd only taken twice? With half the hillside charred?"

Simon scratched the scarred flesh at his temple. "Yeah. How about that?"

"I can see why Lodestar hired you. Did you just drive Felix or was his wife there, too? Marthe?"

"I've driven both Mr. and Mrs. Auerbach to their apartment in town. It was only Mr. Auerbach on the trips to the cabin."

"Was Mrs. Auerbach already here?"

"I wouldn't know."

"How about this? Was there a car here?"

Simon thought briefly, then nodded.

"There we go. That's something." Gene grinned. "Tell me about the Auerbachs. They a happy couple?"

Now Simon flashed some teeth. "They never argued in the car."

"Must've made the drive easier. Any idea where they might be?"

"Not a one."

Down below, Hansen uttered an oath. Maybe a coyote or a mountain lion, I hoped.

Gene flipped pages in his notebook. "It's my understanding Felix and Marthe Auerbach are not American citizens."

I couldn't help myself. "What difference does that make?"

"I'm wondering if they found Lohse's body and panicked, given their legal status. It's obvious someone was here. Food was eaten, bed slept in."

"Goldilocks," Simon suggested.

"That could have been Jens," I said. "He didn't have a fixed residence. He might have known the cabin would be empty."

"It's possible. Your thoughts, Mr. Fischer? The Auerbachs seem the flighty type to you?"

"I don't speculate. Lodestar hires writers to do that." Simon spread his arms wide in a show of helplessness. "I just drive."

"It's good for a man to know his place, I always say." Gene held Simon's gaze a long moment, then opened the balcony door. "Miss Frost, would you excuse us? Mr. Fischer and I have to cover this ground again."

Inside, I watched Gene and Simon continue sparring, two men competing to see who could give the least away. I was happy to be excluded from the balcony and the temptation to look over the railing at Jens's body. *Forbidden fruit will lead you to a fall,* Jens had written in "The Trouble with Sin," the lyric no longer the least bit amusing. My thoughts took a morbid turn, wondering if when he'd penned those clever words he'd had a premonition he'd plunge to his death on the other side of the world.

My eyes fell again on the photograph of the Auerbachs, Marthe's face, at once youthful and cultured, framed by blond locks. I recalled Gretchen's story of finding blond hairs on Jens's coat. A doomed romance with the wife of one's mentor seemed a potent motive for suicide—particularly given the location from which Jens had taken his final leap.

If he'd actually taken the leap.

Gene had to supervise the removal of Jens's body, so Simon ferried me home. The canyon walls cast shadows making the road more treacherous. Simon drove at a measured, even stately pace, inquiring if it was too fast. He took a silver flask from the glove compartment—"Four Roses bourbon, a nip for those nippy nights"—and offered it to me. I declined, his solicitousness more than I could bear. Here he was being courteous when I was the reason he was involved in this mess, subject to Gene's badgering. If my first Lodestar driver had stayed with me for the day, odds were I'd never have made my way to Felix Auerbach's hilltop haven and Jens Lohse would still be lying alone at the bottom of the canyon, his body prey for scavengers.

"On second thought," I said, "pass me that flask."

The bracer prepared me for the difficult task ahead. "You've probably realized by now this wasn't strictly speaking Lodestar business."

"It was going to be whenever that body was discovered. A dead man at the home of a studio employee is studio business."

"True, but it's my fault you're part of this and I'm sorry."

"Better use of an afternoon than driving some producer's wife to the beauty parlor." His eyes—a chilly, antiseptic gray—again found mine in the rearview mirror. "I imagine you're wondering why I didn't tell your friend what I thought about Jens."

Your friend. He'd picked up on our relationship even though Gene and I had been publicly cool to one another. Not much escaped Simon's attention. Another reason to be impressed with him. "I was curious about that, yes."

"Never tell the mucky-mucks a goddamn thing. Learned that in the army and it's served me in good stead. About the only thing I learned in the Great War, in fact." He took a pull on the whiskey himself before returning the flask to its nest.

We reached the main road and motored toward the heart of Los Angeles. The shadows lengthened and I grew drowsy. Blame the bourbon, blame the steady tattoo of tire against road, blame—

"Miss Frost? Does the car behind us look familiar?"

I felt like I'd downed several cups of coffee as I spun around. Sure enough, the gray car from earlier was back.

Simon didn't require a vocal response. My body language told him enough. "I noticed you noticing it this afternoon."

"When it didn't follow us up the hill to Felix's cabin, I forgot about it."

"It's tricky trailing somebody up those roads, so they waited for us to come back down. I thought I spotted them when you telephoned the police. They'd already followed us to Mr. Auerbach's apartment. They probably knew where we were going." His eyes were once more on mine in the mirror. "Makes you wonder if they knew what we were going to find."

BODY FOUND IN CANYON

LOS ANGELES, DEC. 5 (AP)—The body of Jens
Lohse, 28, was found today in a secluded canyon in
the Pacific Palisades. A Los Angeles Police Department spokesman said the body of Mr. Lohse, a musician, was discovered in a heavily wooded area directly
beneath a Pacific Palisades residence by Lodestar Pictures employee Lillian Frost. An autopsy will be conducted by the Los Angeles County Coroner's Office
to determine the time and cause of death.

12

✦

"PREPOSTEROUS. JENS WOULD never take his own life. Never, do you hear?" Marlene Dietrich paraded the length of Edith's office, every pivot in her black suit showcasing her long legs, the matching shako on her head only adding to the martial air of her movements.

"We don't have all the facts yet," Edith said in her cold-cloth-on-the-forehead voice. "But you did indicate Mr. Lohse had been upset of late. At the very least we must acknowledge the possibility—"

"No. This is not the Jens I know. If he killed himself, where is the note?" Dietrich spun toward me, her eyebrows thin as rapiers. "There was no note, was there?"

"Not that I saw."

"You see? And it was Lillian who found him!" Dietrich triumphantly waved a hand as high as the feather on her hat.

"Not everyone leaves a note in these circumstances," Edith said.

"Jens would have. He always expressed himself."

Jumping from the balcony of Felix Auerbach's cabin would make a pretty strong statement, particularly if he'd been carrying on with Marthe. But I didn't voice the thought, because the absence of a note troubled me, too.

Dietrich was back on maneuvers, talking more to herself than us. "No, my poor Jens was murdered. And the Nazis killed him. They denounce me every chance they get. Jens was always mocking them and their attitudes in his songs. We are—this saying I like—peas in a pod, Jens and I. We antagonized people with long memories and apparently long arms, reaching from Berlin nightclubs to sunny balconies in California. Jens and I spoke of this often. He was writing a song about it for me, the guilt of being miles from home amidst such turmoil. The Nazis are to blame for his death."

"It seems unlikely," Edith said, no doubt as prelude to soothing Dietrich's nerves.

But now Edith faced the glare of Dietrich's wide, knowing eyes. "Years ago I hired bodyguards when hooligans threatened to kidnap my Maria. Should I do so again? Will every German who is not a friend of the Reich require bodyguards? Few Americans understand what a menace Hitler is. I'd kill him if I had the chance. I know how I would do it. He fancies me, you know, this . . . Führer."

I couldn't be sure, but I thought Dietrich spat on the floor of Edith's office as she said Hitler's title.

"He wants me to return to Germany," Dietrich continued. "Work at UFA again, be the Fatherland's great star. Goebbels has made overtures."

"You wouldn't do it," I said in a near whisper.

"If it placed me in the same room as that monster, I would." Dietrich tilted her head upward, absorbed in the action flickering on some inner movie screen. "I would present myself to Hitler as a fawn helpless before the might of his charisma. He would accept this as truth, I think, and that vanity would prove his undoing. I would offer myself to him. I would be naked, of course. Except for a single . . . poisoned . . . hairpin. An idea from a mystery novel. A technician from the studios can make one for me. Edith, perhaps you know someone. Armed only with that weapon, I would finish him. With great pleasure."

Edith swallowed. "That would be quite a sacrifice."

"Yes. Although perhaps I could escape. I dress myself as his body cools. I ease the door to his bedchamber shut. I tell his lackeys I have exhausted the great leader with my lovemaking and need the night air to settle my nerves. Who would deny me that? I might make it to safety before the dogs were set on me. And if not . . . it would be a better death than any written for me in a picture, don't you agree?"

She smiled at that phantom screen in her mind. Edith and I exchanged a look, struck dumb by the potency of this fantasy.

Dietrich clapped her gloved hands together, story time over. "No one comprehends the nature of the world we are entering. We need strength from our leaders and instead receive only capitulation and appeasement. What hope is there for civilization when an English monarch abdicates his throne for a flat-chested American? I should have seduced that poor man when I had the opportunity."

I wondered what kind of hairpin might have accompanied Dietrich on her assignation with King Edward VIII. Edith wisely steered the discourse back to terra firma. "It's a curious world indeed, but we're doing all we can to make sense of it. You did right by Mr. Lohse. His death is now being investigated by the authorities. What you need is a distraction. You should think about your costumes for the role of George Sand in Mr. Capra's production, how you'd like the transition from masculine to feminine to be played out, if you want elements from one in the design of the other. I'm always available to discuss ideas." Edith tried to throw her last line away, but put too much English on it and came off sounding a touch needy.

"If God and Mr. Capra are willing." Dietrich planted herself in front of me. "I thank you, Lillian, for all you have done for me and for Jens. I cannot hope to repay you, but you must permit me to try." She pulled me to her, holding me several seconds longer than was necessary, resting her head on my shoulder like a weary child being carried home. I was enjoying the experience until it occurred to me she might have a hairpin under her hat, and then I started to fear for my life.

With an embrace of Edith, she was gone, pulling the air out of the room with her. It was as if a tempest had blown through, the pressure slow to normalize in its aftermath.

I exhaled and sank into a chair. "Does talking to Marlene cause the bends?"

Edith polished her glasses and smiled without displaying a single tooth. "One gets used to it."

"I'm relieved this Jens business is over. I finally get my name in the newspaper and it's because of this. Thank God they got my job wrong and didn't mention Addison. I hope Lodestar goes easy on Simon, that poor driver."

"I hope I haven't caused any problems for you. But are you sure it's over?"

"Don't start." I paused. "All right, you can start, but let's finish quickly. Gene still wants to know how Jens got to the Auerbachs' cabin. And Marlene raised a valid question about the lack of a suicide note."

"Does Detective Morrow have any notions on the subject?"

"He thinks Jens didn't write one. He also suggested the Auerbachs may have found the body and fled in a panic, taking the note with them."

"Quite possible," Edith said, her skeptical tone at odds with her words. "Of greater interest is the absence of something else."

"What?"

"Mr. Lohse's music book. In which he wrote down every song he encountered in an effort to improve his English, his musicianship, and his employability. By all accounts, Mr. Lohse took it everywhere. But it wasn't at the cabin, was it?"

I shut my eyes and pictured the Auerbachs' living room, specifically the piano. On which there wasn't a scrap of sheet music to be found.

"No," I said. "But it didn't occur to me look for it."

"Undoubtedly Detective Morrow will inventory what's in the cabin. I ask only because the book wasn't discovered at Mr. Lohse's former residence or his car. It seems unlikely he would go to the home of his music teacher without it. Even if he went there with the intention of killing himself. If something were removed from the Auerbach cabin, it would be that book as opposed to a suicide note."

The headache that started directly behind my left eye told me Edith was onto something.

"I'm sure all will be explained once the Auerbachs are located." Edith made her voice three-strip Technicolor bright. "Now! How about lunch with my gratitude?"

"I'd love to, but unfortunately I have to return to work. Today's my chance to get ahead on Addison's Christmas shopping while Customs interviews him about Albert Chaperau. Any developments on that front?"

"None I'm privy to, although Mr. Groff has burned copious quantities of midnight oil." Edith's voice turned grave. "I'm sure he'd want me to say any information you can relay from Mr. Rice's meeting would be held in the strictest confidence and much appreciated."

"First Marlene, now all of Paramount. At this rate, the whole town will owe me favors."

13

✳

SHOD AGAIN IN carpet slippers I decamped to Mrs. Quigley's, her radio blaring as her favorite gossip columnist took to the air.

"This is Jimmie Fidler in Hollywood, where the latest looks are always in the bag . . . sometimes the diplomatic bag."

I knew a veiled Albert Chaperau reference when I heard one. So much for packing up all my cares and woe after an afternoon at Addison's.

A knock at the front door interrupted my nightly nuzzle with Miss Sarah. I set the cat down and went to answer it, hoping Jimmie didn't dish any Chaperau dirt in my absence.

Two men waited outside. One lingered in the shadows, hat brim down as he cleaned his fingernails with a matchstick, doing everything in his power to avoid being seen. His cohort, in contrast, provided almost too much to look at. Beneath a crown of red hair his left eye protruded slightly, as if his head had been pulled out of a vise at the last possible moment. Worse, he possessed a truly engaging, even roguish smile.

"Good evening, miss." The redhead spoke in a whispery singsong suited to addressing a spooked horse. "We're looking for Lillian Frost."

"That's her there," Mrs. Quigley volunteered, wandering out into the lobby.

The ginger gent channeled extra wattage into his grin, and I almost ran for the stairs. "My name's Mr. Knoll." He spelled it for me, in case at some future point I wanted to enter it into the record. "That's Mr. Garrett. We're your escorts for the evening."

"And where are you gentlemen supposed to be escorting me?" I asked in a level voice.

Knoll snapped his fingers and Garrett handed over several familiar cards. Urchins pressed them on strangers on the streets of downtown Los Angeles. The outline of a ship's prow on the left, four aces on the right, THE S.S. *LUMEN* emblazoned across the top. THREE MILES FROM SANTA MONICA—BUT A WORLD AWAY!

"The gambling ship!" Mrs. Quigley said. "I see the advertisements in the newspapers all the time!"

Knoll dropped a few of the cards into her palm. "You keep those, dear. Each one good for a free turkey dinner onboard. Cuisine by Jean-Claude of Lyon. Bring your friends."

Things were getting entirely too chummy. "And if I don't want to go?"

"Why wouldn't you want to? Hospitality is our business," Knoll said. "Oh, I feature it. You're concerned no one knows your plans. Mrs. Quigley here is informed. Call Detective Morrow and share your whereabouts, if that appeals."

His knowing about Gene sounded like a fait accompli. I took Knoll up on his offer, marching to the telephone and dialing Gene's desk. Another detective answered and I left a detailed message, silently thanking Knoll for spelling his surname.

"I'll tell you all about the boat when I get back," I said to Mrs. Quigley. I glanced down at Miss Sarah. Her face indicated that if I never returned, there was a slight chance she'd remember me.

MY THIRD TRIP to the shore in as many days. Soon I'd be suffering from the gout Salka Viertel had mentioned. Once we were underway in a black sedan I didn't recognize as one that had followed me, Garrett couldn't stop talking. He served up succinct critiques of every restaurant and diner we passed, a veritable Baedeker of beaneries. This place had lethal coffee, that one a blue plate special worth driving out of your way for. He nodded at the Hi-Hat Café and said they offered decent toast.

"How do you rate toast?" Knoll wheezed.

"They don't burn it much," Garrett said reasonably.

Never had I missed the taciturn Rogers so deeply. The lights of Santa Monica Pier couldn't appear fast enough.

Garrett parked the car and we walked underneath Christmas lights and wreaths. Passersby undoubtedly assumed we were a foursome out for an evening of waterfront fun, temporarily one woman short. Knoll and Garrett, veterans of escort duty, had their technique down to a science. I glanced around for Marlene Dietrich's single-toothed soothsayer. Maybe she could tell me if I'd survive the night.

Knoll indicated a neon arrow at the end of the pier. "This way. You ever been on the *Lumen* before?"

I shook my head. I hadn't set foot on a boat since Mikey DeFarlo's cheap-date cruise on the Staten Island Ferry.

A sign beneath the arrow boasted of continuous water taxi service. We crossed an arched bridge to a float, where a boat waited. The *Maybelle* was a narrow launch enclosed by glass for most of its length, canvas awnings supplying additional protection from the elements. Garrett clambered aboard, extending a hand to help me. Knoll jumped on and nodded at someone on the float, the *Maybelle*'s engine instantly roaring in response.

The launch lurched away from the pier, swerving around the costly cutters berthed nearby as it made for the mouth of the harbor. The other passengers huddled at the front of the taxi, studying the fine print on the cards inviting them to the *Lumen*. Aside from a young couple lost in each other's eyes and lips, we had the stern of the *Maybelle* to ourselves. Knoll leaned out into

the spray, letting it cool his face. Garrett approached me as soon
as the launch cleared the breakwater. I decided this wasn't a coincidence and gripped the railing for dear life.

"The free turkey dinner's not bad," Garrett said. "For a free
dinner, that is. You're better off paying for the prime rib. Unless
you prefer veal scallopini."

I nodded and almost heaved over the side, not wanting to con-
template veal scallopini at the moment. On a dinghy this size, I
couldn't even countenance soda crackers.

True to its name, the *Lumen* bristled with lights, Christmas
coming to the high seas early. From the look of her, she had once
been a proud oceangoing vessel, the kind of four-masted ship on
which Charles Laughton would have tried in vain to break Clark
Gable's spirit. (Repeated viewings of *Mutiny on the Bounty* consti-
tuted the bulk of my maritime service.) But the *Lumen* had been
extensively, almost cruelly overhauled, everything past the bow
gutted so a squat structure could be erected behind it. The light-
show, with multiple beams probing the early winter darkness
like octopus tentacles, couldn't glamorize what was essentially a
warehouse on the briny deep.

Several such ships were tethered along the Southern California coast just past the three-mile limit—and theoretically beyond the state's jurisdiction, so prohibitions against gambling did
not apply. Whether this legal strategy held water was still being
debated in the courts. One could read coverage of the latest developments in the local newspapers across from advertisements
for twelve-minute water taxi rides to the *Tango* or the *Rex* or the
largest of them all, the *Lumen*. Those aggressive enticements were
partly why I was willing to accompany Knoll and Garrett on this
brief voyage; any business spending that much money to promote itself had to have a fighting chance of being legitimate.

The launch motored up to the *Lumen*'s landing stage, illumi-
nated like a theater box office with a battery of ushers in red jack-

ets at the ready. Not that I required their assistance. The *Lumen* was perfectly stationary as I stepped aboard, three massive hawsers holding it in place.

Knoll and Garrett steered me through the casino. I glimpsed a bank of forlorn slot machines and some sparsely attended roulette tables. At the far end of the hall, a dance band desultorily tuned up. From below drifted the scent of freshly grilled beef. From everywhere else I smelled fish.

I was whisked through a STAFF ONLY hatch, down a flight of metal stairs, and along a series of drab corridors. Knoll rapped on an unmarked door. As he opened it, Garrett whispered, "I'm gonna hit the galley. Get some shrimp."

The door barely cleared the desk beyond, a mammoth piece of furniture apparently hewn from what had been the rest of the *Lumen*. The balding man seated behind it was every bit as solidly constructed. He'd shucked his jacket and rolled up the sleeves of his crisp white shirt, ruby tie in a flawless Windsor knot. He possessed both a large stomach and hungry eyes, never a good combination. His placid face had stared out at me from the pages of many a newspaper.

"Miss Frost," he said. "Malcolm Drewe."

The owner of the *Lumen* had made his reputation during Prohibition, running liquor from Canada in a fleet of speedboats. Once the law of the land had been set to rights again, Drewe parlayed his profits into a host of ventures: pool halls, automobile dealerships, real estate speculation. But testing the limits of seafaring law was his grand obsession. Rumor had it several of Drewe's former bootlegging cronies were silent partners in the *Lumen*. But it was Drewe publicly waging the battle in the courts, promising to equal the splendors of the French Riviera while paying track odds daily.

And he had hustled me out to a ship where the normal rules didn't apply, in order to make conversation.

"Have you been well looked after?" His question may have been directed at me, but those voracious eyes sought out Knoll.

"Treated her like your special guest," Knoll answered. "Haven't given her the grand tour yet."

"Make sure you bring her by the dining room. Let her sample some of our fine fare."

The counterfeit congeniality only ratcheted up my unease. "I'd rather you just tell me why I'm here." I wanted to sound calm. My words simply came out hushed.

Drewe smiled. "Straightforward. I appreciate that. You're here because you found Jens Lohse. To be precise, you're here because you were looking for Jens Lohse. Never thought anybody would turn over rocks searching for that sheeny except me. I'm interested in your interest in him."

So you get to drag me away from my home on a whim? I didn't yell, knowing to keep my anger in check. "I was doing a favor for a friend."

"Then we're in the same business. Who's the friend? Maybe I know him, too."

The circumstances seemed to preclude prevarication. "Marlene Dietrich."

Knoll snorted. Drewe sighed. "I hoped we could avoid this kind of silliness. Did your employer Addison Rice tell you to hunt up Lohse?"

"Addison had nothing to do with this, so please don't say his name again. You've obviously done your research, Mr. Drewe. Did you hear a story from about a year ago involving me, Paramount Pictures, and the police?"

"Some rumblings, maybe."

"My interest stems from that. Jens played piano for Miss Dietrich. She was worried about him. I said I'd look around. I found him. And now I'm out of it." I paused. "Honest."

Drewe leaned forward, bare forearms on the blotter, eyes boring into mine. "I'd love to have Miss Dietrich out to the *Lumen*," he said finally. "Could you mention it to her?"

"Absolutely. Can I ask if you're having me followed?"

"When you spot a tail, Miss Frost, it means the person wants you to know they're there. Either that, or you're dealing with incompetents. I don't qualify on either score." He reclined again. "Lohse could tickle those ivories. He played on this ship, you know. He was briefly a member of our band, the Lumenarias. You probably heard them as you came aboard. As for my interest in him, it's not altruistic like Miss Dietrich's. Jens had something that belongs to me. I paid for it. So I'd like it now."

I opened my mouth. Closed it again. Started over. "I don't understand. Why are you telling me this?"

"Because once I pay for something, it's mine. So here's the deal. You come across anything Jens left behind, do me the courtesy of letting me know." He scribbled on another of those ubiquitous free turkey dinner cards. "Call this number day or night should you stumble on any objects of interest."

"But I'm not looking for objects of interest. I'm not looking for anything. Jens is dead. I really am out of it."

"You're hardly the person I would have expected to find Jens's body. You strike me as capable of more surprises."

"Have I already met one of your people looking for this whatever-it-is?"

The slight frown on Drewe's face unleashed an icy feeling in my heart. Even Knoll took a step back. "You met someone else on the prowl for Jens? Where?"

I swallowed hard, and told Drewe about my encounter with Peter Ames. Drewe listened intently, writing Ames's name on a pad of paper. "Helps me remember names, seeing them in my own handwriting," he said. "Little trick from a book I read."

"*How to Be at Home in the World*, by Hiram Beecher?"

"You read it, too?" Drewe beamed like I'd just signed my house over to him. "I'm an extravagant admirer of Mr. Beecher's. Gave copies to all the boys."

"It's why I spelled my name for you before," Knoll chimed in. "Saves time."

"This Ames fellow is unknown to me," Drewe said. "But now I'm interested in *his* interest. The fact that you encountered him proves you and I should remain in touch. Your path crosses his again, you dial that number I gave you."

There was no point in protesting that our paths wouldn't cross. Drewe wasn't listening to me. "Could you at least tell me what it is you're looking for?"

"I don't want to limit your initiative. I'd rather make it easy on you. Call if you find anything at all."

I'd had it with people making it easy on me, and with Hollywood's favor economy. Edith had sworn looking for Jens wouldn't inconvenience me, yet here I was shanghaied and missing Jimmie Fidler. I was through helping people. From here on out, I'd be Lillian Frost, bad Samaritan. "That's a lot of work for a turkey dinner that's already free," I said.

"Don't crack wise with me, Miss Frost. You're not pretty enough to get away with it. Marlene Dietrich's not pretty enough." Drewe stepped out from behind his desk, and I turned green for reasons that had nothing to do with the swells nudging the ship.

With his dress shirt and tie, Drewe wore thick-soled boots and dark brown work trousers. Both were freshly stained with mud, the pants bearing arcs of what I prayed was not blood, as if Drewe had stood too close while bringing a mallet down.

He didn't look at me as he crossed to the office's porthole, comfortable in the knowledge his attire was having the desired effect. "Don't mind the clothes. I've got a hog farm out by Fullerton. First place I made any real money. Still go there on occasion to take care of business. Bring in the pork we serve on this very ship." He turned to Knoll. "Another reason to take Miss Frost to the dining room."

"Will do, sir." Knoll grinned.

"There's two ways of judging a man. How willing is he to get dirty, and how well does he clean up." Drewe nodded at his own profundity and gazed out at the sea. "Usually we close the *Lumen* for the winter. Weather's too unpredictable. But people want a break from their families during the holidays—Christ knows I do—and we'll be here to take their money. We were open Thanksgiving weekend and made a killing. I'm not a gambling man myself, but I have to make a bet. What if we lose this lawsuit and I'm forced to scuttle the *Lumen?* Better bank as much as I can now. I'm also willing to bet if anyone can find my property, it's you. There'll be a nice finder's fee should you come across." He peered out into the night for a moment, not liking what stared back. "That'll be all," he said softly.

Knoll touched my arm. I refrained from screaming and slipped free of his grip. I was prepared to swim back to Santa Monica and walk to Mrs. Quigley's from there.

14

GOOD OLD PREDICTABLE Gene. Knowing what he considered the earliest acceptable time to call, I positioned myself by Mrs. Quigley's telephone. Came the first ring, I pounced.

"You're alive," he said. "You can tell me about your misadventure at sea while I drive you to work."

"You know me. Always willing to accept a ride."

I set about the task of dressing deliberately. If Gene was coming all this way, I wanted to make an impression—and force him to partake of the house coffee. Mrs. Quigley, her taste buds ravaged by an excess of champagne and oysters during her Ziegfeld Follies days, brewed java strong enough to bring Pony Express riders to their knees. You couldn't pour it down the drain behind her back, because it would eat away the pipes. You could only quaff the stuff, contact a clergyman, and hope for the best.

I was still assessing my accessories when Mrs. Quigley greeted Gene at the front door. After a suitable interval, I staged my dramatic entrance to Mrs. Quigley's apartment in a black collarless suit with red fabric buttons and a red and pink scarf shot through with gold thread, black toque angled over one eye as if I had something to hide.

Not that Gene noticed. He sat at the kitchen table, warily regarding a coffee cup at arm's length. It was still full.

"Good morning, Lillian!" Mrs. Quigley said. "Let me fix you some coffee."

"No need, Mrs. Q. I had a cup after I answered the phone."

Gene held up the cards Knoll had left promising the night of
a lifetime about the *Lumen*. "Souvenirs?"

"Lillian's friend left those," Mrs. Quigley said. "We should
all go!"

"Remember, the free turkey dinner is strictly from hunger.
You're better off paying for the prime rib."

Mrs. Quigley's crest fell. "I should have known you don't get
something for nothing. Your coffee's growing cold, Detective."

"TWO CUPS, FROST. She topped me off like we were at a diner.
Be ready to take the wheel if I black out. Tell me about Mr.
K-N-O-L-L."

I regaled Gene with my nautical narrative. "You shouldn't
have gone with them," he said when I finished.

"They wouldn't have taken no for an answer. Besides, they
knew about us. I mean, they knew I knew you." I felt myself blush
and studiously ignored it. "They made no bones about where
they were taking me, they suggested I call you, and the boat's a
public place. I assumed I'd be safe."

"They could have lied about where you were going. And don't
assume you're safe on the *Lumen*. Malcolm Drewe was a tough
customer in his rum-running days. Men died because of him."

"He's not running rum now, though."

"No, he's taking on the city, county, state, and federal gov-
ernments at once. The days of the gambling ships are numbered
and Drewe knows it. Mayor Bowron got elected beating the
reform drum, and Earl Warren, the attorney general, plans to
ride gambling clear to the governor's mansion. He'll scuttle
those ships himself if he has to. Drewe sees the writing on the
wall. He's a bastard but he's no fool."

"And he only hears what he wants to hear. He didn't believe
me when I said my part in this was over."

"He'll believe me. I'm going to have words with Mr. Drewe."
His fingers flexed against the steering wheel, and I felt safe for
the first time since returning to dry land. Gene, my rough-hewn
guardian angel. "Did it sound like Jens stole something from him?
Or did Jens sell Drewe something, then not deliver?"

"If Jens stole from him, I think Drewe would come right out
and say it."

"So do I." Gene paused. "Do you think Drewe could have
killed Jens?"

"I— Why? Was Jens killed?"

Gene nodded. "Autopsy results came back. Coroner fixed
Jens's death at some time Thursday, the day before you started
looking for him. Jens took what looks like two direct blows to
the back of the head that aren't consistent with the injuries sus-
tained in the fall. Condition of Jens's body meant the doc couldn't
conclusively say those blows caused his death, so I went back to
the Auerbachs' cabin. Still empty, by the way. No Felix, no Marthe. Based on the shape of the cranial injuries I examined the
fireplace poker. Somebody cleaned all the fingerprints off the
handle, like it had never been touched. Scrubbed the rest of it
pretty good, too, but they missed where the hook curves in. That
spot still had . . . residue on it."

I appreciated Gene's tact, but found myself picturing the scene
nonetheless. Two swings of a fire iron, and Jens's music had been
silenced.

My voice trembled. "So someone struck Jens, then threw his
body off the balcony to make it look like he'd jumped?"

"That's the thinking. The body might not have been found
for weeks if it wasn't for you. We're searching for Felix Auerbach.
Lodestar claims to have no idea where he is, insisting he's on va-
cation. We're bringing in your driver again, Fischer, and some of
Felix's studio colleagues."

"What about Marthe Auerbach? Couldn't she have killed Jens?"

"And then heaved him into the canyon by herself?"

"I would have thought swinging the poker was the hard part."

Gene shrugged, taking my point.

"I have nothing to base this on," I continued, "but it's possible Jens and Marthe were having an affair. Maybe it went sour."

"Or Felix tumbled to it, and that's his motive. Naturally, we want to talk to both halves of the happy couple, wherever they are. And now there's Malcolm Drewe, beefing about what sounds like a busted business deal. Jens sells him a bill of goods and fails to come across, Drewe's boys brace him and get carried away, and now Drewe expects you to lead him to the dingus. Any thoughts on what it might be?"

"Not really."

Gene glanced over at me. "I speak fluent Frost, you know. I can tell when 'not really' means 'well, kinda.'"

I told Gene about Jens's music book. Ever-present in life, wholly scarce in death. "Interesting notion," Gene said. "Yours?"

Take the credit. Just take it. "Edith's, actually. It occurred to me the book could be in the trunk of Jens's car, which was locked."

"We can certainly open it now. The owner won't complain."

"Could you do something else for me?"

I practically heard Gene's guard going up, like steel shutters closing. "Depends what it is."

"I want to talk to the detective who dealt with Marlene Dietrich."

"Wingert? Forget it. He hates you."

"Why? What did I ever do to him?"

"Landed him in hot water. Thanks to you, the brass thinks he gave Dietrich the brush."

"But he didn't! Even you said he did everything he was supposed to."

"Sure, but when a civilian then finds a body by asking a few questions it reflects poorly on the department as a whole. What do you want with him?"

"I just want to be sure he didn't overlook anything."

"Like this music book? If it turns up, what then? Call Drewe for more dinner and dancing past the three-mile limit?"

"No. I'd call you. After seeing if Jens finished a song he was writing for Marlene. It would help bring this to a close for her."

Gene looked dubious, but I was used to that by now. "I can sound Wingert out about talking to you. Keep your expectations low. Any dinner plans?"

"Not at the moment," I said brightly, glad I was dressed for an evening out.

"Good. Abigail said something about a new place she wants to try in the neighborhood."

Abigail. Strange how you could like a person yet loathe the sound of her name. "Keep me posted," I said.

ONE ADJUSTMENT I had yet to make to Los Angeles life was planning for Christmas with the mercury high enough to keep Saint Nick in seersucker. At least my chosen musical accompaniment produced a wintry chill, even if it was ill suited to yuletide chores: a brooding orchestral piece, jagged notes conjuring an atmosphere of dread without coalescing into a melody. When Addison entered aghast, I lifted the phonograph needle.

"What on earth was that racket?" he asked.

"Something I had the record store send over, by a composer named Felix Auerbach. I won't play it again until you're out. Or ever. What happened with Customs yesterday?"

His voice brimmed with relief. "Twenty minutes! I wait all day, then I'm in and out in twenty minutes! A handful of questions about how Chaperau broached the subject of his diplomatic papers, that's all. Donald's due with the latest. I pray this is over and done with before Maude comes home. I'd love to spare her this burden. Speaking of which—"

"I sent a wire reminding her about the Customs duties. I've also arranged for a representative from your New York law firm to be on hand when her ship docks to assist with any problems."

"Splendid. I can't afford even a hint of impropriety."

"As for your Christmas plans, we're all set for the boys' breakfast on Friday. I've laid on extra helpings of gruel. And I believe this single item should dispense with the bulk of your holiday shopping." I spun a catalog toward him. "Behold the tantalus. From Greek mythology. Twin crystal decanters in a frame, the sweet nectar therein inaccessible without a key."

"Hence tantalizing."

"Give that man a cigar. The frames come in a range of finishes. Chrome for business associates, silver plated for well-wishers, et cetera. But you have to set aside time to make some decisions."

Addison huffed. "Maude usually handles that sort of thing."

"I arranged a tie-up with our friends at Coronet Liquor Store. Each set of decanters will be full of the hooch of your choice. A tasting, naturally, is required. Mr. Coronet himself will be here with a selection of his finest potables at seven sharp."

Addison rubbed his palms together. "Now *that* is a capital idea. You'll stay and assist?"

I remembered Gene's indistinct dinner invitation. "This should be a solo mission, sir."

"We'll be happy to pitch in. We can toast my legal legerdemain." Donald Hume approached my desk, followed by Charlotte. She had selected her demure day dress—blue silk with a pleated skirt and narrow white stripes—to complement Donald's club tie, yet on her it managed to say cocktails more than brunch. In her hand, a bouquet of daisies bound with violet ribbon.

"There's the free man now." She bussed Addison on the cheek, then me. "All praise to his high-priced mouthpiece."

Donald bowed modestly. "Spoke with a friend of a friend in Customs this morning, Addy."

"Why? Things had gone so well."

"Too well, I feared. Never hurts to know exactly what they're after. The hand had been dealt. You'd checked your cards and your emotions. I simply wanted to—"

"Check your dealer," the three of us finished.

"Mock my sound advice at your peril. I gleaned the odd tidbit. We should discuss briefly."

Addison led his legal counsel away. Charlotte curtsied and offered the bundle of flowers.

"For me?" I said with surprise.

"From my very own garden. I thought you could use them, after reading you'd found a dead body. What in heaven's name was that about?"

"Blame Marlene Dietrich." I gave her the short version.

"*She* got you into this?" Charlotte perched on my desk with easy elegance, flaunting the bold chin that had already made her a caricaturist's dream. "You are nothing if not thorough. For your next trick, why not get cracking on who's going to beat me out for Scarlett O'Hara? David O. better make up his mind soon. They're burning Atlanta in a few days."

"I heard that! How's that supposed to work without a leading lady?"

"Slap a wig on a stuntman and hope the flames are high enough. I think it's a brilliant idea." She tapped a lacquered fingernail on the image of the tantalus in the catalog. "As is this. So clever. Donald and I need an elf like you helping us make merry. How do you do it?"

"Two steps. First, write down every last thing you have to do. Second, grow up Catholic. Guilt makes a mighty motivator."

"Whatever your secret, sugar, it's working. You've taken to this like a duck to bourbon."

"You're sweet to say so. I'm just making it up as I go. I still feel like I'm on probation."

"We all feel that way. And probation doesn't end until we reach the glory land. A tip from someone who grew up Baptist."

"I could use a few parties to plan, even if all the work makes me break out in hives. I'm going a little stir-crazy."

"There's the Santa breakfast, which is the other reason I stopped by. You have to walk me through my role."

We were well into reviewing Charlotte's hostess duties when Donald returned. "Addison wants us to attend tonight's tasting," he said. "The man needs Maude back posthaste."

"I can't. There's an Anti-Nazi League meeting."

"I'm sure they can foil the Führer without you."

"But they're planning the next radio show! I may get to do a bit on it."

"You sure Selznick will be happy about that? I've said before I don't see the percentage in someone in your line getting overly political."

"Be serious, dear. Jack Warner is on the League's board of directors. Fredric March, Bette Davis—"

"So it's a kaffeeklatsch." Donald winked at me. "You're not going to topple fascism. You want to show off your clothes."

"Of course. Why does anybody do anything?"

"Jens volunteered for the League," I blurted out, taken aback by how the late musician continued to occupy my thoughts.

"Who? That poor boy you found?" Charlotte patted my arm. "I wonder if I ever saw him there. I'll mention him tonight. Maybe we'll acknowledge him on the air."

"That would be lovely," I said, "I have a question for Mr. Rice's legal counsel. What do you know of Malcolm Drewe?"

"I know not to gamble anyplace you can't readily walk away

with your money. I haven't met the man. I can only pass along some sage wisdom dating back to the birth of the great state of California." Donald flashed a grin. "Never trust a man who owns a pig farm."

I told him I would bear that in mind.

15

✦

THE LITTLE HAND reached the five without word from Gene
about the evening's events. I was surprisingly jake with that. After
barge-toting and bale-lifting for Addison, the notion of sampling
the cuisine at some newly minted hash house alongside Abigail
held little appeal.

Not that going home would set the night on fire. I bailed out
of the streetcar several stops early in search of the standard balm
for my soul: a movie.

I'd already seen *Thanks for the Memory*—I never missed a chance
to admire Edith's handiwork—but revisiting the clothes and Bob
Hope warbling "Two Sleepy People" with Shirley Ross was easily worth fifteen cents at the neighborhood discount theater.

Alas, the newsreels focused almost maniacally on the upheaval
in Europe, the repeated shots of Adolf Hitler exhorting crowds
poisoning my mood. I hadn't seen the first two episodes of the
jungle serial, and my fellow filmgoers, more interested in win-
ning a set of dishes in the bingo game between features, chat-
tered over Hope's amiably corny jokes, their cigarette smoke
filling the auditorium. I wandered out before the picture ended.

Not having much of an appetite, I opted to cull dinner from
my icebox. A lanky figure sprawled across Mrs. Quigley's front
steps. I thought his shoes looked familiar. Then he took a sur-
reptitious sip from a flask.

"Hello, Simon. Nice to see you again." And I meant it. My former driver reminded me of some of my uncle Danny's vagabond

pals. Sailors and salesmen, older gents with colorful stickers on their suitcases and unfamiliar scents on their clothes. You couldn't help feeling a thrill when they appeared on the doorstep unannounced. The wider world had come to call.

Simon rose to his feet. "Good evening, Lillian. Apologies for turning up like this."

"I already said it was nice to see you again."

"That's right. You did." He moistened his lips as if craving another jolt of whiskey, but instead pocketed his flask. "Spent the day being interrogated by your friend Detective Morrow. Made me wonder how you were faring."

"He mentioned he'd be seeing you when I talked to him this morning."

"Bet he was more abrasive with me." Simon chuckled and glanced down the block, baring the patch of scarred flesh at his temple in the streetlamp's glow. "So you're okay then?"

"Yes, thanks." Again I felt a pang of guilt at entangling him in my affairs. The next words tumbled out of my mouth without any input from my brain. Once uttered, though, my brain raised no objections. "I was about to get dinner. Would you care to join me?"

Simon leaned back, the better to cock an eyebrow. "It would be my honor," he said with a quaint formality.

NO ONE HAD ever written home about the grub at Cavanaugh's, but the fare served our purposes. I'd recommend the joint to Malcolm Drewe's man Garrett if I had the bad luck of seeing him again.

Lost for an opening move in the conversation, I yammered about the movie I'd seen. "Don't go to pictures much," Simon said.

"Check, please."

"Occupational hazard. You hear people in the back of your car describing them all day, you lose interest."

"But you enjoy being a driver."

"Maybe it doesn't show much ambition on my part, but I can't take being trapped in an office all day."

"Who's the most famous person you've ever driven?"

"All the big Lodestar names. Bruce Fleming, Madge Granger. Drove Clark Gable once. Quiet fella."

"He's going to play Rhett Butler."

Simon smiled from what seemed a long distance away. "Is that good?"

"Wow, you really don't follow pictures."

"I don't deal with stars much. Stars want to drive themselves. They need to go fast and all of them think they're wizards behind the wheel. Mostly I deal with the moneymen. And people with money aren't automatically interesting. They just have money. Hear those executives talk and they sound like the pants-pressers they used to be."

I scraped gravy from my Salisbury steak, but upon seeing what lurked beneath hastily put it back. "Was Felix Auerbach interesting?"

"I've been talking about him all day."

"Talk about him some more."

Simon weighed coleslaw on his fork as if the fate of our dialogue hinged on it. "He genuinely is interesting. Probably his European background. Or maybe it's that he bothered to learn my name. He asked me about the war. He sees me as a person. While I *don't* see him as a genius. That's a tough racket, being the guy who has to think things up. I'd rather be the one in the front of the car. You get to read the signs that way."

Simon, I suspected, seldom required signs to determine which way to go. "How about Marthe?"

"How about her?"

"Did she know Jens?"

"Jens played piano in her house while her husband yelled 'fortissimo' or some such at him. I'd wager she knew him."

"That's not what I meant. Is it possible they were . . ." I faltered, thrown by a vision of Sister Frederick wagging a judgmental finger at me. "Were they a couple?"

"Sometimes I'd drive Felix home for a lesson with Jens and find Jens's car already there. Once about three months ago, I drove Jens to Felix's apartment. Then, two hours later, drove Felix there from the studio. Jens led me to believe he was going to Felix's for a lesson, but Felix was still at work."

"And Marthe was home?"

"Somebody let him into the building."

"It sounds like they were lovers." This time I said the word like I tossed it around regularly. *Hand me my robe, lover. It's over there, behind my lovers.* "Did you tell Felix?"

"It's not my place to tell Felix."

"More importantly, did you tell Gene?"

"You know my policy. Don't volunteer information. Keeps conversation to a minimum."

"But you told me."

"That's different." He picked up a piece of fried chicken. "I want to keep talking to you."

SIMON OFFERED TO doctor my postprandial coffee with bourbon, pay the check, and walk me home. I said yes to all three. I told myself it was the lack of a third wheel that felt so liberating, but I was truly enjoying his company.

As we strolled to Mrs. Quigley's, he asked about my job. "I know Addison Rice from the papers," he said.

"I suppose you think he's a crackpot."

"On the contrary. He made a fortune building things and now he's enjoying the fruits of his labors. I admire the man. While I'm extending compliments, I'll also say I admire you."

"Me? What did I do other than cadge a lift from you?"

"You're not like most people I've met here. You didn't fall for the Hollywood dream."

"It's more like the Hollywood dream didn't fall for me. My uncle Danny painted sets at Paramount's New York studio, so I know every second of movie magic comes from hours of toil."

We rounded the corner onto my street. I glanced up at my abode and came to a dead stop.

"What's wrong?" Simon asked.

"I thought I saw light in my window. Maybe a car—"

There was no mistaking it this time. The stab of a flashlight's beam against my curtains, visible for only an instant. Simon pressed me against the closest building, a clapboard slat digging into the small of my back. He stood as close as he could without touching me, his eyes not moving from my window. I could smell the coffee and bourbon on his breath, found myself staring at the scarred patch of his skin as if it contained a code I had yet to decipher.

"Front-facing unit on the second floor, right?" he said quietly. "Give me your keys."

I did so without hesitation. Simon darted up the block and eased open the door to Mrs. Quigley's. I edged toward the street, the seconds elongating. Nothing moved in my window. Some perverse alchemy transpired in my stomach; base Salisbury steak had been turned into lead.

I'd stepped toward the police call box on the corner when the clatter erupted behind my building. Headlights swept up the alley toward me. I leaped clear of the onrushing car and turned back in time to glimpse the man in the passenger seat. A black watch cap concealed his hair, which I already knew to be blond. Only his eyes registered, alive with canine ferocity and a spark of recognition. I trusted there was one in mine as well.

Peter Ames.

As the taillights shrank I sprinted toward Mrs. Quigley's. I heard my landlady shriek and pounded on the front door. It opened an instant later. Miss Sarah tried to escape. I grabbed her out of instinct.

Simon sat halfway up the stairs, blood pouring into his face from a gash on his scalp. "Yep, it was a flashlight," he said. "Solidly made, too."

"Mrs. Quigley, can you call the police?" As she bustled away I hurtled upstairs, pausing to give Simon a handkerchief.

Chaos reigned in my apartment. The armchair overturned, the bedsheets scattered. Books had been pulled from shelves, drawers emptied. I picked my way to the connecting door and found the adjacent unit untouched. Peter Ames didn't know I paid for two flats. Not that he would have found whatever he thought I possessed.

Just to be safe, I searched my closet and confirmed my mother's brooch was where I'd left it. I'd lost the only keepsake I had from her once, and I couldn't bear the thought of it happening again. Stepping back into the violated room I could hear Mrs. Quigley consoling the man who, to her, was a stranger.

"The police will be here any moment. Can I get you anything, you poor man?"

"Some coffee would be lovely," Simon replied.

Mrs. Q scampered off for a cup of her witches' brew. The poor man, indeed.

16

✵

THE BEAT COP Officer Macklin knew Mrs. Quigley well, both of them tracing their people back to County Roscommon. Once I ascertained nothing had been stolen from my apartment, they settled in for a gab session. Other tenants prairie dogged out of their doors to investigate the rumpus. By the time Gene arrived, the proceedings had taken on the air of a parish mixer. When he clapped eyes on Simon, though, the party was over.

"Can I ask what you're doing here, Mr. Fischer?"

I'd bandaged Simon's wound myself, my old department store gift-wrapping skills paying unexpected dividends. "After our conversation today, I wanted to see how Lillian was getting on."

"How she's getting on isn't any of your business." Gene's words carried a force that didn't derive from his badge.

"You're going to begrudge a man an act of human kindness?" Simon drew on his cigarette. "What a world."

Gene gestured up the stairs. I led the way to my flat. He surveyed the scratches on the door's lock, then the damage that lay beyond. "This is about Jens Lohse," I told him.

"Because you saw Peter Ames fleeing the scene?"

"Yes, although I doubt that's his name. I think he got it from a Barbara Stanwyck movie."

Gene blinked at me. "You realize how nuts that sounds."

"I'm aware, yes. But the fact remains Peter or whatever his name is thinks I have something that belonged to Jens."

"Which isn't far removed from what Malcolm Drewe thinks."

After more terse fact-finding questions, Gene asked, "What happened to our having dinner tonight?"

"You didn't call by the time I left."

"I telephoned Addison's just after five, then tried here."

"I went to the pictures."

Gene nudged a book with his wingtip. "You made plans with Simon?"

"Not at all. When I got back, he was waiting. We went for a bite. He walked me home, and we walked into this."

"And you don't find that suspicious? Him whisking you to dinner right when someone is tossing your apartment?"

I invited him, I thought, but questions about the night's convenient timing had indeed been fluttering around my head. Still, my capacity for denial exceeded even my gift-wrapping prowess. "He was attacked! Peter hit him on the head!"

"Right where the wound makes a mess but does little harm. If I was going to clout a guy for show, that's where I'd do it." He shook his head, at either the wreckage of my flat or my credulity. "I don't like this, Frost. You shouldn't, either."

He was right. But I could try denying that, too.

"We checked Jens's car, trunk and all," Gene continued. "No music book. And I heard back from Wingert."

"Let me guess. He won't talk to me."

"His wording was more indelicate, but that was the gist of it."

"You've got to try again. Please."

"I knew you'd ask, and I was going to say no. But given tonight's festivities, I'll swing by and ask in person. He was a sorehead before this, though. Remember that when I disappoint you."

"You never disappoint me, Gene."

For a moment, he seemed ready to reply in an equally complimentary vein. Then he waved his hat toward the door. As we went downstairs, I decided a gesture on my part was called for.

I beckoned Simon over. "I think you should tell Detective Morrow what you told me about Jens and Marthe."

Cigarette smoke clouded his grimace, then Simon did as I requested. "You didn't see fit to share that this morning?" Gene asked.

"It's gossip. I don't spread gossip. But as Lillian thinks it's important, I'll make an exception."

Putting his hat on, Gene turned to me. "I don't want you staying here tonight."

"I wasn't planning on it."

"Where would you like to go?" Simon asked. "I'll drive you."

"That won't be necessary." Gene's words slipped past clenched teeth. What a night. My apartment ransacked and now two would-be Lancelots jousting in the lobby. I spoke before Simon had a chance to parry.

"I'd welcome a police escort. Addison's is too obvious a choice. Let me telephone the one other person I trust."

EDITH LIVED, AS I expected, in a darling house. The yellow cottage possessed an Italianate feel befitting its location overlooking the Silver Lake Reservoir. Under the moonlight, with the song of mockingbirds echoing over the water, it was possible to believe you were on the shores of Lake Como. Or at least the movies' version of it; I'd never visited the Continent.

A path wended its way through a small garden to the front door, which opened before I could knock. The woman who greeted me shared Edith's petite size, but at first I doubted it was her. Dressed in a vibrant yellow blouse with puffed sleeves and a billowing violet skirt, she indulged in a broader palette than I'd ever seen her display at Paramount. Even her hair was different, the chignon abandoned for thick ponytails held by red ribbons.

She looked for all the world like a child wandering out to wish a beloved pet good night.

She pulled me to her at once. "I'm ashamed it took this ordeal to have you over at last. An ordeal of my making. Of course you'll stay the night."

I wasn't about to say no. I wasn't about to say anything until I got something off my chest. "You look so different!"

She glanced down at herself, then peered up at me with the faintest smile. "I'm on my own time, for once. You can't show all your colors at work. You'd lose your capacity to surprise."

Crossing the threshold made me feel a passport was necessary. We were suddenly south of the border, the house's interior chockablock with Mexican pottery and other artifacts in a style at once haphazard and meticulously organized. I couldn't comprehend how someone who slaved at the studio for twelve hours a day could also possess a home that felt so comfortable. I decided I was entitled to hate Edith a little for managing to achieve such an enviable balance.

"The kitchen's where all meaningful conversation takes place. Bill, our other guest is here."

Bill Ihnen bounded over to me. Edith's longtime friend and colleague, an accomplished art director, was at the tail end of an evening out, clad in a tuxedo with his tie unknotted. His red rose boutonnière drooped fetchingly, only a splash of champagne required to revive it. A hint of contented belly peeked over his cummerbund. He kissed my cheek and inquired after my safety.

"I'm fine," I said, "but I have the feeling I'm interrupting a war council."

"Some late-night shop talk is all." Edith set a bottle on the table. "Fernet-Branca. An Italian liqueur. I was recently introduced to it by Madeleine Carroll."

"From *The 39 Steps*? I saw it thirty-nine times and still don't understand why she was upset about being handcuffed to Robert Donat."

"I couldn't agree more. Madeleine's doing her first American film at Paramount. *Café Society* with Fred MacMurray. She's a joy to work with, a true member of the international set. Plus as the title indicates, it's a dress picture. Lots of fun to be had."

"And her ladyship got you hooked on this?" I lifted the bottle of brown liquid.

"It's guaranteed to save you on the day you want to kill yourself."

"But I don't want to kill myself."

"Then think how much more you'll enjoy it!" Bill poured three generous drams into cordial glasses. "Be advised to sip this."

"When did I develop a history of guzzling?" Taking heed, I treated the liqueur like sacramental wine. The distinctly medicinal odor would have slowed me down in any case. Its bitter taste, containing notes of menthol, eucalyptus, and regret, prompted gagging, which I kept at a genteel level. "That's an interesting flavor."

"Mostly saffron, I'm told. With a host of other spices including myrrh."

"You mean what the Wise Men gave the baby Jesus? They couldn't have been that wise." I nudged my glass away, not wanting to hurt Edith's feelings. I told them about my evening, Edith and Bill taking turns making the appropriate sounds. At some point, the glass miraculously returned to my hand.

"Now that I have a place to rest my weary head," I said, "you two can get back to your important discussion."

"Honestly, it's nothing," Edith said. "I'm picking Bill's brain about running an entire department."

"Which she's doing marvelously." Bill winked at her. "And of course rehashing this Chaperau business."

I reached for the bottle and topped off my nightcap. Lord help us, the Fernet's insolent taste had grown on me. "Addison said Customs is wrapping up their investigation."

"I've heard otherwise," Edith said.

"G-men storming the Bronson Gate any minute." Bill held his own glass out for a refill.

"Paramount *is* making a film from J. Edgar Hoover's book *Persons in Hiding*. Perhaps the Bureau wants to weigh in on the costumes."

"You know Hoover's already read the script," Bill said. "Without anyone at Paramount giving it to him."

"If federal agents do crash the place," I interjected, "nothing says you have to talk to them. You don't have to volunteer information to people simply because they're in charge."

Edith turned to me so quickly her ponytails flew. "That doesn't sound at all like you, Lillian."

"You're right. It doesn't. I'm not myself. The Fernet's going to my head."

"Time to let the slumber party begin." Bill pecked Edith on the head, tugging her left ponytail as if signaling the streetcar to stop. "Alert me if Hoover busts down the doors, Edo."

I cleared the kitchen table as Edith showed Bill out. In the wastebasket I spied a wad of crumpled tissues bearing telltale signs of eye makeup. Had Edith been crying on Bill's shoulder? Was the strain of her new position taking a toll?

Or could it be something else? I wondered where Edith's salesman husband was and how he'd take to his wife entertaining a tuxedoed man in the wee hours, workaday woes or not.

Edith returned and tidied up my tidying up. "Again, Lillian, I feel dreadful. When I asked for your assistance with Marlene, I thought it would be a few phone calls, perhaps a nice drive. Not intruders in your home."

"Don't blame yourself. I had an ulterior motive." The Fernet

had loosened my tongue. "I wasn't just helping you. I was helping Addison by hanging around Paramount's Chaperau investigation and telling him what I learned. I've been feeling guilty
about it."

"Lillian, please. Firstly, I expected you to share this information with Mr. Rice. Secondly, you always feel guilty. Lastly, I ab-
solve you. Strategy and a healthy self-interest are a benefit to a
woman." She appraised the kitchen. "There. Did I forget anything?"

"Possibly. Where's Charles? Is he on the road?"

"He . . . we . . . no." It was a night of firsts, seeing Edith so casual, then finding her flummoxed. "Charles and I are no longer
together. We got a divorce." She said the words cautiously, testing them out like a new roadster.

Now I got to be at a loss. "I— When?"

"Shortly after my promotion. One major change, I felt, deserved another. As did Charles. We parted amicably."

My interactions with Charles had been limited to a handful
of chance meetings at Paramount. He was a genial if distant man,
drifting from job to job, transacting the bulk of his business with
John Barleycorn. What I remembered most about him were his
immaculate suits with their flawless accoutrements. I'd long suspected that Edith dressed him, too. I didn't know why I was surprised to learn their union had been put asunder. Edith scarcely
spoke of Charles when they were married. Why should she mention him once they'd divorced?

She only invoked him now to pivot away from the subject.
"You'll stay in Charles's old room tonight. Although I did want
to ask about Detective Morrow's theory regarding this . . . other
gentleman you were seeing."

"Simon? I wasn't seeing him."

"My mistake. You were merely dining together." She adjusted

her glasses, although her vision seemed plenty sharp to me. "Detective Morrow suggested Simon might have been party to the break-in."

"Yes. But that's ridiculous."

"On the contrary. You must admit the timing is remarkably coincidental."

"So it's coincidental. So what!" My vehemence startled me.

And also Edith, who leaned back. "I only mean the theory bears consideration."

"No, it doesn't. Why would Simon be in league with Peter Ames?"

"That we don't know. It's worth remembering Simon professed to be friendly with the still-missing Felix Auerbach. It could be Felix pulling everyone's strings."

A cogent argument, but one I had no interest in hearing as it presupposed a man would only spend time with me to facilitate a burglary. I was confounded by my feelings. Worse, I was snapping at Edith, who had taken me in after a long day. I tried to find a polite way to end the conversation only to draw a complete blank.

Edith mercifully sensed my frustration. "It's far too late to discuss these matters now. Several hours' sleep will put you right. Let's make up your room."

I almost asked if she had a hair shirt I could wear as a nightgown. I doubted rest would alter anything, anticipating a night of self-recrimination amidst twisted bedsheets. But my ticket was punched for the Land of Nod the instant my head met the pillow, the only thought I could articulate: *Edith always knew what to do. Why didn't I?*

LORNA WHITCOMB'S
EYES ON HOLLYWOOD

. . . Word from under the pepper trees that federal agents investigating the Albert Chaperau smuggling case have unleashed their bloodhounds on the Paramount lot. We hear a couple of funny men may soon be playing serious roles before a New York judge . . . Will David O. Selznick keep fiddling while Atlanta burns? The ersatz Atlanta that is, constructed amidst the detritus of the Selznick International backlot. The set will fall to the match on Saturday with cameras rolling but still no Scarlett in sight . . . Douglas "Wrong Way" Corrigan received an airplane hangar full of cash for his life story from RKO, but the flyboy's not spending his windfall on fancy autos. The aviator has been seen taking the streetcar to the studio. Either he's tight with a penny or he doesn't want to end up in Pasadena by mistake . . .

17

❖

EDITH'S SKILLS EXTENDED to set decoration. The gauzy salmon drapes in her guest room transformed the act of waking into a delight. They permitted the dawn to suffuse the room incrementally, making me feel I was steeping in the morning's promise. I stretched every muscle, inventorying half-remembered images from the night's dreams, discovering uncharted cool patches of the pillow like some drowsy da Gama.

I rolled over, reluctantly opened my eyes, and stared into a monkey's grinning face. I then screamed like a banshee that had been fleeced at a clip joint.

By the time I realized the monkey was a primitive yet gruesomely handsome figurine, Edith had hustled into the room. "Good, you're awake," she said. "And you've met my friend. Bill found him in Mexico. Isn't he striking?"

"And rather alarming to see first thing in the morning."

"That's why he's not in my room. My housekeeper is fixing breakfast. We have a busy day ahead."

I threw back the covers, relieved the previous night's tension had dissipated. "What's up?"

"I've been on the telephone. Salka Viertel is hosting an impromptu wake for Mr. Lohse today. If you care to attend, I'll gladly take you. But first, if you could accompany me to the studio. Another person ensnared in Albert Chaperau's web would like to talk to you." As she left, Edith turned the simian rictus away from me.

• • •

I'D HAD THE presence of mind to grab a change of clothes before leaving my apartment, a navy skirt with a matching knitted jacket that was thankfully conservative enough for mourning. I called Addison and explained my pending absence. Once he extracted a solemn vow I'd be present bright and early for the next day's Santa breakfast, he gave his blessing. I enjoyed a hearty meal, which I manfully kept down as Edith pell-melled us to Paramount in her car.

We checked in at Wardrobe first, Edith dispensing with half a dozen urgent matters in the time it typically took me to pour my morning coffee. Next, we hustled to the studio of John Engstead, Paramount's portrait photographer and Edith's close friend. We picked our way through a jumble of furniture and bizarre props—an enormous pair of scissors, a firecracker taller than me—toward Engstead, an eternally sunny man who embodied the unforced grace he captured with his lens. After kisses all around, Engstead said, "One of your stars is here, the other en route. I'll leave you to it."

Several lighting stands rubbernecked around a table laid out with a full English tea service. The backdrop behind it somewhat confusingly depicted Paris. A mannequin sat propped in one of the two chairs, clothed in pink chiffon.

"Where'd star number one go?" I asked.

"She hasn't budged." Edith gestured at the mannequin. "Meet Cynthia."

"Really?" My own excitement baffled me. Cynthia was the plaster of paris brainchild of artist Lester Gaba. Acclaimed for his soap carvings, Gaba had been asked to bring the same level of realism to department store mannequins. Cynthia was the result, a figure so lifelike she boasted freckles and two different-sized feet. Her verisimilitude made her an unlikely luminary, invited to parties at the Stork Club and El Morocco, sporting hats custom-made by Lilly Daché, her comings and goings chronicled in gossip columns. I knelt humbly before her. "She was in the display window at Saks Fifth Avenue when I was in New York. People lined up to see her."

"Mr. Gaba treats her like a living person, so we do, too. I'd catch myself talking to her and he'd apologize and say she had laryngitis. Most peculiar."

"Someone should follow me around saying that. It'd spare me a world of trouble. Why is she here?"

"John is taking publicity photographs. She appears in *Artists and Models Abroad*."

I leaped up. "Are the gowns from the fashion show here?"

Edith pursed her lips. "No. I'm afraid you'll have to make do with the clothes I designed."

Oh, for a little laryngitis. Before I could apologize for my blunder, the other star of *Artists and Models Abroad* arrived. A smiling Jack Benny walked toward us with his distinctive show-pony stride. "Well, we're all here. Edith, how are you? You must be Miss Frost, a pleasure. Hello again, Cynthia. You look a little peaked." He patted the mannequin on the shoulder and chuckled.

Hearing that voice emerge from a genial midwestern face instead of every radio I'd ever owned produced a shiver of glee. To my mind Jack Benny was more than the funniest man in America. He was a genius who had turned his radio show costars into a family and created a world I was eager to visit every Sunday night.

Then the figurative penny dropped. Had it been a literal one, Benny would have stooped to pick it up. The man who famously played a tightwad was involved in Albert Chaperau's smuggling scheme. He segued to the subject at once.

"Now about this Chaperau business, Lillian. You've met the man. You know what he's like. I wanted a chance to talk to you, set the record straight."

"You don't owe me an explanation, Mr. Benny." Saying his name made me sound like Kenny Baker, the boy tenor on his radio program. Like that, I'd become a character on his show. I'd met enough performers to grasp what was happening. I'd heard George Burns's story, now I had to listen to Jack Benny's. It was a matter of equal billing.

"Please, Lillian, it's Jack." He fanned his hand at me. "You should know I didn't want anything to do with Chaperau. The whole thing was Mary's idea." Mary being Mary Livingstone, his wife and costar. Already he sounded like he was reading a radio script, with the usual quota of gags about him being miserly with money. "Mary and I, we decided to spend our summer in France, you see. We did Paris, we did the Côte d'Azur, all of it. And while we were in Cannes, we, we ran into this fella . . . Chaperau. Now, we'd met him here in Los Angeles socially and wanted to be civil, so of course we had lunch with him. It was a lovely meal, you know, right there on the beach, with the striped umbrellas. And I mention some jewelry I bought for Mary in Paris, a diamond bracelet and a pair of lovely clips to match. And Albert, uh, Chaperau, he tells me how he's now some kind of diplomat. Who can bring Mary's jewelry into the country under a sort of, of diplomatic flag, and this is a courtesy diplomats—not just him but *all* diplomats—extend to friends and business associates. And Mary, being a practical woman, says yes." He took a step back, like a magician who'd completed a trick. "Now I ask you. If the people who work in our government, who make and enforce our laws, don't feel there's anything wrong with taking advantage of what I took to be a friendly gesture, why should I? Why am I being, you know, being unfairly punished? Not even punished, persecuted is what I'm being."

He was rehearsing his legal defense on Edith and me. I didn't know what to tell him, in part because I didn't know how I'd react under similar circumstances. If Chaperau had offered me the chance to save hundreds or even thousands of dollars in import duties, would I have played along? More importantly, would my moral compass point true north when things went south, as George Burns's had?

Who was I kidding? I'd been educated by the strictest nuns in Queens. What Jack Benny had done was wrong, and he should have known better.

Edith cleared her throat. "It's a thorny subject to be sure, Jack. Am I right in thinking the jewelry you'd bought was delivered to you in Los Angeles by George Burns?"

"Unfortunately, yes. It's my fault for putting George in that position. You know, he and I have been friends for years. Since Flo Ziegfeld gave God his big break." He paused for a moment, and I realized he was waiting for his laugh. "If I'd picked up the jewelry myself or let Chaperau bring it to me, George wouldn't have to say a word, not a word. It's another friendly gesture gone awry, is what it is."

"George indicated that if charged, he planned on pleading guilty." Edith spoke with deliberation. "He also said if he's asked if he brought jewelry to you, he would have to say yes."

"I won't blame a friend for telling the truth to the authorities," Benny said, his equanimity instant and apparently bona fide. "I've spoken to George and everything between us is fine, just fine."

"Then would you plead guilty, too?" I asked.

"No, I won't. I won't. This whole thing was presented to me as aboveboard, perfectly legitimate, and I'll tell every judge in the country that. Bill—George and I have the same lawyer, Bill Donovan, wonderful fellow, very connected, used to be in the Coolidge administration, you see—anyway, Bill convinced George to plead guilty and wants me to do likewise. Says it's the fastest way to make this blow over. NBC, who carries my radio program, is already in a tizzy over this, and the General Foods people are up in arms about how it might affect Jell-O sales.

George confided in me that he and Gracie are about to lose their sponsor. But I refuse to plead guilty when I didn't do anything wrong, when there's a, a big misunderstanding. And anyway, Mary doesn't want me to do it."

I was beginning to understand who wore the pants in the Benny household.

"Contesting the charges might keep you away from the studio," Edith said. "Won't they have to postpone filming *Man About Town?*"

"It's a small price to pay. No, I'm sticking to my guns." Benny sidled closer to me, arms folded across his chest. "Now, Lillian, you know Albert Chaperau."

"I wouldn't go that far, Mr. Benny."

"But you've made his acquaintance is my point. He's offered to transport goods for other people, hasn't he?"

"I don't know. I can only say he never made the offer to me. But then I haven't been to Europe." For once, that statement didn't leave me feeling impoverished.

"Still, he's the sort of fellow who has several schemes going at once, isn't he? Did he, did he mention any other ploys? To you, or Addison, or anyone else you know? Maybe at one of Addy's wonderful parties?"

He smiled at me, all guileless innocence. I resisted the urge to ask Edith to borrow some hip waders from wardrobe, because Jack Benny was clearly on a fishing expedition. If he planned on pleading not guilty to the smuggling rap, he'd have to mount a case. And in clumsy, disingenuous fashion he was asking me to help build him one—which I felt conflicted about doing no matter how much he made me laugh, because I knew he was guilty. I'd submit to a grilling by an attorney or a Customs official, but a comedian was an entirely different kettle of fish.

My eyes broadcast my distress to Edith, who smoothed the situation over like the nap on a suede jacket. "Excellent questions,

Jack. But Mr. Groff already asked them when he interviewed Lillian the other day. Part of the studio's plan to wage this battle in the courts if necessary. Every habit and mannerism of this Albert Chaperau recorded for posterity. You put your Mr. Donovan in touch with Paramount's legal representatives and you'll soon have all this unpleasantness behind you."

John Engstead glided back into view. With velvet glove finality, Edith said, "Lillian and I should let you get to work. You don't want these emotions registering in your photographs."

"Quite right, Edith. We're promoting light entertainment here. I can't thank you two enough."

We left Benny in Engstead's capable hands. As we walked away, Edith muttered, "If he insists on pleading not guilty, Paramount won't back him up. I hope his attorney convinces him to change his tune."

"This investigation doesn't sound over by a long shot."

"Mr. Groff used the term 'witch hunt.'"

At the door, I glanced back. Jack Benny sat opposite Cynthia, comically dainty teacup in hand. He smiled and sent a final wave in my direction. My favorite entertainer in the entire world, acknowledging me and me alone. I so wanted the moment to feel better than it did.

18

❖

"YOU DON'T HAVE to drive me to Salka's," I told Edith.

"I owe you. Besides, it might do some good if I got away from the studio. Give the girls free rein for a spell." She sounded like she was parroting advice from a trusted source she didn't quite believe. "You really should acquire your own license. Driving's an easy skill to learn."

"Ask Rogers if that's true. Provided he doesn't light out for the hills when you raise the subject."

What I'd wanted to say to Edith was *Please don't drive me to Salka's.* She handled her car as if she were constantly trying to make up ground at Le Mans. I was never more conscious of how thick her eyeglass lenses were than when she was behind the wheel. But I felt obliged to attend the wake. I'd found Jens's body, so in a sense I was responsible for the proceedings. I wanted to see how Gretchen was bearing up. And Salka, I reasoned, might know where Jens's music book was. Not that I was searching for it. But the sooner it was located, the sooner I'd be left alone.

The *Lumen* bobbed in the distance, a toy abandoned in a gargantuan bathtub by an enormous child. A multitude of cars lined Salka's street. I inhaled sharply as I spotted a familiar vehicle. "There's the man who followed me," I said.

"In the blue Ford?" Edith peered at the driver, studying that morning's paper, his hat visible over the headline blaring that Father Charles Coughlin, the controversial radio commentator, had sued a Detroit newspaper for libel.

She pulled alongside his car. "Good morning, sir. Will you be long?"

The man fumbled with his paper. "Pardon?"

"If you were leaving, we could have your space. Parking's at a premium, what with the sad news."

The man touched his fingers to the brim of his hat and started the car. Edith drove several feet forward while I gaped at her.

"What? If he's here to watch people, he'll want to watch us. We might as well have a spot to leave the car." She swung into the newly vacated space.

SALKA CLUTCHED ME to her bosom the instant I breached her doorway, as if mere contact with her could soothe my woes. Curiously, she was correct. "I should have listened to Dushka. Poor Jens. Once I learned of his death, I threw my doors open wide. We need a place to grieve. People have been coming and going all day."

Each arrival and departure noted by federal agents, I thought.

I introduced Edith. She and Salka exchanged words of mutual admiration, then Salka returned to the subject at hand. "The papers are intimating he was murdered. Is this true?" When I nodded, Salka gripped my arm. "I cannot believe it. Surely no one hated that boy enough to kill him."

Evidence indicated otherwise. "Do you know where Felix and Marthe Auerbach are?" I asked.

"No, but Felix has the capacity to work anywhere. He's taken to driving around Southern California, seeking inspiration for new compositions. The desert, the mountains. He could be anywhere." She took my arm again. "I imagine the police would like to talk to him."

"And Marthe." As gracefully as I could, I inquired about Jens's music book. Was it possible he'd left it here, perhaps on a book-shelf?

"Unlikely, my dear. It was the size of a Bible, scarcely the kind of thing one could conceal. Had I seen it, I would have recognized it instantly. I'll search for it, though."

Within thirty seconds Edith and Salka had identified half a dozen common acquaintances. "You must meet Ludwig," Salka pronounced. "A new arrival signed to direct at your wonderful studio Paramount. Luddy, come here!"

I detached myself from the conversation and made my way to the garden. The atmosphere was markedly different from that of the salon days earlier. That assembly and its Babel of tongues had been like a Black Forest cake—dark, but with an undercurrent of sweetness for those with palates educated enough to appreciate it. Now only the gloom remained, the gorgeous weather isolating the participants in their grief.

Gretchen hadn't sat down so much as collapsed in the scraggly shadow cast by the dormant lilac bush. The other guests avoided her like a spill they hoped someone else would clean up. I lowered myself onto the grass next to her. Gretchen glanced at me through red-rimmed eyes, utterly bereft, then turned away.

It really was a cruelly beautiful day.

"For the last few weeks as I fell asleep," she said softly, "I'd tell myself Jens was fine and I'd see him the next day. Now that ritual's gone, too. I thought knowing the truth, having some certainty about him, would make me feel better. But it only makes me feel a thousand times worse."

There was nothing I could say to console her, lamenting a love that had never blossomed. There were only questions to ask.

"Gretchen, I need to find Jens's music book."

"Why do you want it?"

"Because other people are looking for it."

The thought stanched the flow of her emotions. She sat up straighter and concentrated on me. "The people who killed him?"

"Possibly. When's the last time you saw it?"

"The last time I saw him. He played at a party, a fund-raiser for the Anti-Nazi League at some writer's house. I wasn't invited, but I knew Jens was playing so I snuck in."

"Where would Jens stash that book? How about the places he'd stay when he needed somewhere to sleep?"

"There's a whole circuit of us he'd cycle through every few weeks."

"Can you ask them to look for the book? Check your own place thoroughly. Jens might have hidden it."

Gretchen climbed onto her knees and nodded her head, ready to snap into action at once.

"Any other possibilities you can think of?" I pressed. "Places Jens would go all the time. A place where, where . . . when you have to go there, they have to take you in."

"I know that. That's from a poem."

"Yes. Robert Frost. 'The Death of the Hired Man.'"

"About home, isn't it? The place where they have to take you in. Jens didn't have a home anymore. None of these people do." She raised an arm to take in the others around Salka's yard. The gesture rang false, some instinct telling me Gretchen had an answer she wasn't immediately keen to share.

"But they have Salka's," I said. "This is as close to home as many of them will get. Did Jens have another place like this? Where, sooner or later, he'd always turn up?"

Gretchen chewed her lower lip. Her resolve gave way first. "I don't know if this is what you mean. But he played a few times a week at a nightclub."

"Which one?"

"Club Fathom, on the Sunset Strip. Do you know it?"

By reputation only, I thought. No wonder he kept it a secret.

"Jens swore no one would take him seriously if they knew he worked there," Gretchen continued. "I said it was like one of those clubs he'd played in Berlin, but he told me Americans thought differently about such things."

I nodded in the general direction of the sea. "I understand he also used to play on the *Lumen*."

"Not for long. He hated boats. Said he'd been on the water enough coming over here."

"Did he ever mention Malcolm Drewe, who owns the *Lumen*?"

Gretchen thought a moment. "Yes. He said Drewe really had this country figured out, and he should act more like him."

Emulating a gangster didn't sound promising. "I also wanted to ask about Felix and Marthe Auerbach."

"I don't really know them," Gretchen volunteered too quickly.

"You said that. Still, they'd come here on Sundays. And Felix works at Lodestar, like you."

"In the music department. He might as well still be in Berlin."

"You really had no idea Jens was studying with him?"

"No." She pouted. "He probably didn't want me to know he was on the lot. Keeping me at arm's length. He didn't like when I'd go to Club Fathom to hear him."

"This is an indel—"

The widening of Gretchen's eyes alerted me a second before Gustav Ruehl roared in my ear. "You again! Why have you returned to this place?"

"To pay my respects to Jens Lohse."

"You lie! You did not know the man! You ask about the Auerbachs, more people you do not know. You inquire about Jens and he is killed! Is Felix next?"

Once again we were the center of attention, and Ruehl was merely getting warmed up. Edith stepped toward us, prepared to intervene. I surreptitiously shook her off. "Mr. Ruehl, please lower your voice. I'm a guest like you."

"Guests are welcome! Are you welcome? No! You are here under the false pretenses. You are here to spy, *ja?*" He spat on the ground at my feet. At least I hoped he hit the ground. "This is how it began and how it will begin again. With people asking questions and making reports in secret. With people who should trust one another—"

Gretchen slapped Ruehl's face, the sound carrying. Across Salka's garden, Edith flinched. Even the few people who'd tried to ignore our argument were fixated on us now.

"Shut your mouth, you wicked old troll," Gretchen said. "Why are *you* here? Not to honor Jens's memory. You hated him. You've always hated him. If you want to dance on his grave, you're too early. You'll have to wait until he's laid to rest in a potter's field."

Gretchen stormed past Ruehl, his head hanging to one side as if her blow had knocked it askew. She marched toward the house and the music room where we'd spoken before. I caught up to her at the door.

She'd regained control of her emotions. More than that, she'd sublimated them, her voice without affect. "I know why Jens didn't tell me he was studying with Felix. What clearer way was there to say he wanted nothing to do with me? Had I known he was coming to the lot, I would have treated him to lunch. I always treated him. I had money and he didn't. He'd rather deny himself a free meal than spend time with me. God, I've been such a fool." She faced me, her expression calm. "You were going to ask about Marthe Auerbach. If she and Jens were lovers."

I nodded, admiring the ease with which she said the word.

"I found them in this house once. This very room, in fact. I was desperate for a moment alone with him, and saw him having a moment alone with her. I didn't even know they knew each other. It's why Ruehl hated Jens, I think. The Auerbachs are the only people who like him, aside from Salka, and he thought Jens was going to tear their marriage apart. I assumed those were Marthe's hairs on Jens's coat the last time he stayed with me, and I teased him about it without saying her name. I shouldn't have." Gretchen smiled tightly. "Do you know what I'd like to do? I'd like to make sure Jens's music book isn't hidden in my home somewhere."

"You don't see it here, do you?"

She gave the room a cursory inspection. "Salka's would be a terrible place to hide anything. She has too many visitors."

I longed to ask Gretchen if she knew her fellow Lodestar employee Simon Fischer and could shed any light on his character, but I'd intruded enough on her fragile state.

After Gretchen left, I searched for Edith. Spotting her in conversation, I signaled I'd be outside. I bid a hasty good-bye to Salka, needing to clear my head.

Down the street, a man in a brown sedan scratched on a newspaper as if deeply immersed in a crossword puzzle. I didn't buy his act for a second.

Emboldened by Edith's example I stared the man down, letting him know I knew he was there. It didn't seem to have the desired effect, so I stared harder. So much so I didn't notice the woman who sauntered up next to me.

"Many cars today," she said in an accented voice. "Salka is having a party?"

"A wake." My eyes remained on the sedan. "Her friend died."

"Yes. The piano boy. A shame. I wanted to use the pool." I sized her up quickly. Her hair was tucked into a broad-brimmed sunhat shading a face bare of makeup. Her brown overalls could have been swiped from a public works truck, the legs rolled up over cheap canvas sneakers. She looked like she'd gotten lost on her way to the beach to pick over whatever jetsam had washed ashore. The woman yawned, stretching both arms over her head. From the flashes of flesh visible in the resulting gaps in the overalls, I deduced she was naked underneath. Just another day in Hollywood. Santa Monica, anyway.

The man in the brown sedan shifted position, drawing my eyes back to him. The daft woman clapped her hands. "A walk shall be my exercise then." She weaved around me, stepping onto some damp grass at the edge of Salka's lawn. As she passed I happened to glance down at her footprint, already fading in the heat. It was about the same size as my own, which was admittedly on the large side for a lady of my gender. The woman's broad strides had carried her out of earshot by the time Edith trotted up to me.

"What did she say to you?" she demanded.

"She grumbled about death queering her plans."

"You know who that was?"

"Yeah, an odd duck."

"Quite. Named Greta Garbo."

Dumbstruck, I squinted down the block. I couldn't see the woman. Or the brown sedan, for that matter, which had taken off after her.

"I'd have put her in something more flattering," Edith said.

19

⬚

"WHY ON EARTH are we putting this dresser back together?" my friend Violet Webb asked. "This is your chance to toss it for good."

"But whoever broke in unstuck the bottom drawer! If I knew who was responsible I'd send a thank-you note."

"Yeah, delivered by Gene and his pals in blue."

I'd telephoned Vi for the skinny on Club Fathom. She suggested coming over to chat, and I explained why that was a bad idea. She then insisted on helping me restore order to my apartment. With the tiny blond dynamo's help, the place was neater than I usually kept it.

Vi might have been small, but she had a powerful set of pipes. Lately she'd caught on with a dance band. I'd booked them at several of Addison's parties. What good was pull if you couldn't use it to give your friends a leg up?

Having rebuilt my bureau, Vi roosted on the windowsill. "I'll say it again. I wouldn't go to Club Fathom without a bodyguard. Who had his own bodyguard."

Club Fathom promised a rollicking good time on the Sunset Strip, a stretch of unincorporated land that, if not exactly lawless, was where local ordinances were less stringently enforced by the sheriff's department. Consequently, it was home to a concentration of nightspots. Club Fathom, on the lower end of the iniquity scale, wasn't dangerous so much as seamy, an establishment to which the word "demimonde" was frequently appended.

In short, an unsuitable venue for a solo appearance yet a possible resting place for Jens's music book.

"Where am I going to scare up an escort?" I asked Vi. "I can't exactly call Gene for this."

"How are things with him, by the by?"

"Fine. In that they're exactly the same."

"Abigail still playing third wheel?"

"Some nights she's a whole sidecar. Let's avoid that boulevard of broken dreams. I need an unattached man. But who?"

"I know." A devilish grin split Vi's angel face. "So do you, cowgirl."

"I'M NOT SURE, ladies." Hank "Ready" Blaylock addressed his comment to the Stetson in his hands. "Kay wouldn't cotton to this."

"Kay doesn't cotton to anything these days," I said. "Where does that leave an independent fella like yourself?"

Long, lean Ready so epitomized the image of the cowboy he might have ambled out of a daguerreotype. All that jeopardized his status as an in-demand stuntman in westerns was a preference for male companionship. Fortunately, he'd met the ideal match for lavender liaisons in my onetime friend turned gossip maven Kay Dambach. Not that Kay was a Sapphic sister; her sole predilection was to reach the pinnacle of her chosen profession. Each provided the other an escort of expedience.

Ready knew Kay's column had created distance between her and me. He also possessed an innate chivalry, which I exploited now.

"All I want is a big fellow by my side to dissuade those of ill intent," I told him. "You won't have to say a word."

"All right. But let's leave now before I think better of it."

I'd purchased the gown for a formal dinner at Addison's, the

rare event that, at Mrs. Rice's insistence, wasn't saddled with one
of her husband's madcap themes. Late regrets from a guest designated me the affair's seat-filler. Rogers ran me to Tremayne's
Department Store, my former place of employment, where I selected a black sleeveless chiffon dress with a pleated skirt and
shirred Lastex waist of flame red. A touch bold for Mrs. Rice's
crowd, judging from her expression that night, but Vi reassured
me it would fit right in at the club. For once, I'd take her testimony over Edith's.

Vi was providing last-minute advice when a taxi pulled up
behind Ready's car. Kay spilled out, spitting mad.

"What's she doing here?" I asked Ready.

He searched the street for a horse he could crawl under. "I
may have told her I was coming to see you ladies."

"Oh, Ready. The eyes of Texas are upon you."

"Good thing I'm from Oklahoma."

Kay made her way gingerly toward us; since achieving a mod-
icum of fame she'd begun applying girdles to her zaftig frame.
"Lucky I got here in time. What goes on behind my back?"

"Hello, Kay," Vi singsonged. "Fine, thanks."

"Nothing's going on," I said. "I needed a ride, and Ready was
gallant enough to provide one."

"Baloney. Addison Rice's limousine is at your beck and call.
What gives?"

Kay's tenacity knew no bounds. I had no alternative but to
tell all and hope she'd get in the spirit of the occasion.

She didn't. Once I'd turned over my cards she wheeled toward
Ready. "No. Absolutely not. I forbid you to go near that scandal
magnet."

"It's not that bad," Vi said.

"You only think that because money changes hands to hush
up the worst of it. I hear that hole in the wall's name more than
I care to admit. Every time a half-witted celebrity wanders in to

see what all the fuss is about there are consequences, sometimes public but more often private. I, for one, can't *fathom* why anyone would sink to that joint's level."

She was already composing copy. We didn't stand a chance.

"You should go with them, Kay," Vi suggested. "They usually have good music."

"It's Katherine. Everyone else calls me Katherine."

"But we're not everyone else. We're the people who knew you when."

"I expected better from you, Vi. After I gave your show a plug in my column."

"And a big help it was. Every subscriber to the *Tustin Herald* turned out in force."

I tried to intercede, but Kay had saved her strongest venom for me. "The very idea I'd help you," she railed, "when you find a body in the hills and don't give me an exclusive. I'd have at least gotten your job right. You know, that job that earns you enough for those fancy duds and keeps you too busy to call me."

Kay's sense of entitlement never ceased to amaze. "Part of my job is keeping the names of Addison and his guests out of the columns." *Even the ones no one reads,* I thought.

"Ready is off limits." Kay scolded him again. "We've talked about this. You have to be squeaky clean for our wedding."

As Ready nodded obediently, I said, "Congratulations. When's the happy day?"

"As soon as I'm big enough to have the ceremony covered by other columnists." She plopped into the passenger seat of Ready's car. "Let's go. You're taking me home."

Hat in hand and head held low, Ready kissed Vi good-bye. After doing likewise to me, he whispered in my ear. "At Fathom, ask for Rory. Tell him I sent you." He got behind the wheel, Kay waving to us like she was Eleanor Roosevelt en route to her next charity event.

"This is a kick in the head," Vi said. "And here you are all dressed up. Now what?"

"Now I try one more idea. A bad one, and a long shot to boot."

"WHY IN HELL would you want to go to a pit like Club Fathom?" Simon asked on the other end of the line.

I still harbored doubts about Simon, owing to the happenstance of his being with me when my apartment was searched. But the way to allay doubts was to test them. Besides, should those suspicions prove unfounded, he'd already demonstrated a willingness to come to my aid.

"Jens used to play there," I told him.

His response—"I'd prefer to take you somewhere classier, but I'll be right over"—made me wish I'd called him in the first place.

20

❖

A BEGUILING SEA nymph swam over to lead us through an underwater paradise, our cares drifting away on the tide.

That, presumably, was Club Fathom's desired effect. The execution played a good bit tackier.

The interior was painted a murky blue, its walls studded with bogus portholes. Fishing nets drooped from the ceiling. Tanks near the entrance contained actual denizens of the deep, mostly elegant angelfish and dapper neon tetras. A fish floated upside down at the surface of one aquarium. I hoped it was waiting to clock in for its shift.

The waitress who met us at the door had been sewn into an iridescent azure dress meant to look like scales. Our nimble nereid guided us to a table by the stage on which Kidd Captain and His Merry Mermen were billed as featured attraction.

Simon, the scent of pomade still fresh in his hair, asked my poison. "I doubt we'll be here long enough to enjoy a drink."

"You have to have something," he said. "If you want people to talk, spend money. And I'd trust alcohol over water here."

"What do you recommend?"

"Doesn't matter. They all have rum."

When the waitress returned, Simon placed our order and I asked for Rory, adding that Ready had sent me. I received the fisheye in multiple senses before she paddled away again.

The cocktails arrived at the same time as the night's first act. A brunette singer approached the microphone, her mouth a

streak of overripe red. "This one's for a friend of the establishment. We'll see you there, Jens." Piano and guitar backed her thin
but not unpleasant voice.

I'll see you there wherever I may be
An easy chair or on a stormy sea
If I am where I never dreamed I'd be
I'll see you there

The song would have been mournful under any circumstances. Simon reached across the table and touched my hand.
"Are you all right?"
"It's nothing. Rum always makes me cry."
Distraction came in the form of a man striding into the club
garbed in ostentatious camouflage: a brown slouch hat and a
camel hair coat as long as a duster. His body language seemed
familiar, prowling with a feline grace verging on feral. He doffed
the coat like a matador working his cape, and my suspicions were
confirmed.
"That's Errol Flynn," I whispered to Simon.
Simon turned his head slightly, nonplussed.
"Robin Hood!"
"Right. I've heard of that one."
"You really don't gawk at anybody, do you?"
"As far as I can tell, the only person worth gawking at here is
you."
His matter-of-fact manner with the words, tossed down like
greenbacks onto the tablecloth, threw me. We weren't on a date.
At least I wasn't. I had an agenda.
I watched a compact figure fly to greet Flynn. His slicked-
back hair and trim wardrobe of vest with no jacket gave him the
profile of some aquatic mammal, like an otter. He leaned close to
the actor and said a few words accompanied by a salacious hand

gesture. Flynn howled with laughter. The man led Flynn up a
few stairs toward a secluded row of banquettes.

On stage, the brunette's eyes shone as she reached her big
finish.

I'll see you there no matter who's in view
I'll let them stare as I envision you
With beauty rare, filling my heart anew
I see you there

She blew a kiss to the heavens and walked off to scattered
applause. A Mae West impersonator, the seams in her face powder visible from the cheap seats, strutted out next, delivering one-
liners with one-tenth the original's verve.

"Mae West has two versions of her costumes made," I told
Simon. "One's looser, so she can sit down in it. That way, no
wrinkles."

Simon deftly feigned interest. He was trying, I had to give
him that.

The waistcoated man bounded down the stairs and summoned a school of waitresses. White shirtsleeves flashing, gold
tie shining in the inky gloom, he was the fish most likely to be
noticed darting hither and yon in this spurious seascape. I wasn't
surprised when he made his way to our table.

"Good evening to you. Rory Dillon." His accent I recognized
from my New York childhood: Irish, with the blunt nasal notes
of the North. "I hope you're better behaved than that last lot of
Ready's friends. Holy terrors they were. Had to clean one of the
tanks after they left."

Simon handled the introductions. Rory held his gaze an extra moment. "A repeat visitor if I'm not mistaken, Simon."

"I may have come in out of the rain once or twice."

"And sure it rains a powerful lot in California. Have you been tended to? Can I bring you anything?"

"Actually," I said, "we stopped in because I understand Jens Lohse used to play here."

"You knew Jens, too? Tragic, that. Did you hear Carol do 'I'll See You There'? Jens's songs are on the bill all week."

"How often did he perform?"

"He was part of the Monday and Wednesday bands." Rory leaned close to the table. "Our dark secret. We call every band the Merry Mermen because we paid to put the name up there. Kidd Captain's the only constant and he's always well lubricated before the curtain goes up. Jens truly dazzled when we took requests. You couldn't stump him at all."

"Thanks to his magic music book."

"That bloody thing. Used to tell him I should have hired it instead of him."

"Is there any chance it could be here?"

Rory considered the idea. "Somebody would have tripped over it by now. You're looking for it?"

"It hasn't turned up anywhere else."

"I'll have a quick look 'round and let you know. Enjoy yourselves in the meantime." With a wink he was gone. The Mae West impersonator still made with the tired wisecracks.

"So you're a Club Fathom regular?" I asked Simon.

"I've been here once or twice, like I told the man."

"And what brought you in out of the rain?"

Simon swigged his cocktail. "The reputation. You hear a place is bad news, you stay away. Until a night comes when you feel like bad news yourself." His eyes dared me to press for details.

Time for a small sip of my own drink.

Fake Mae turned the stage over to a soft-shoe duo, their patter better than their steps. A flutter of motion by the entrance

caught my eye. A woman came in draped in a midnight-blue
cloak. She blinked nervously, terrified her eyes would never ad-
just to the dark. A waitress led her to the stairs. Errol Flynn
greeted the woman warmly and guided her into his banquette
as if she were a Buick with balky steering. When she shed the
cloak, I saw she wasn't Flynn's wife, the French actress Lili Damita.
She was younger than Damita. Younger, even, than me. California, where a girl of twenty-five gets put out to old-maid pasture.

Rory emerged from a service door adjacent to Flynn's booth.
He welcomed his marquee guest's companion, then beat a path
back to our table. "No sign of Jens's book," he said, "unless it's
propping up the foundation of the building. Lord knows it's big
enough for the job. Wish I could tell you more. We'll be doing
a few more of his songs, so stick around. First round's on the
house. Tell Ready all is forgiven, provided he brings that one fella
back. He'll know the one I mean. I'll check on you later." Another wink and he was away again, a barracuda among sharks.

I reached for my purse. "You don't want to stay?" Simon asked.

"He told me what I came to learn. And the entertainment's
unlikely to improve." I dropped a few dollars on the table. "Shall
we go?"

"Provided you don't mind a roundabout route." Simon rose
and held my chair. Then he lumbered drunkenly forward, swerving toward Flynn's banquette. I couldn't see the actor, only his
date, her face flush with compliments and liquor. Simon made a
startled noise and slapped the wall above Flynn's head. "Sorry,
old man. Wrong turn." He reeled backward down the stairs to
where I waited, by the service door Rory had popped out of.

Simon pushed it open. It gave onto a grimy corridor. He
leaned in, checked behind the door, and smiled. Then he pulled
me into the hallway after him.

"What are we doing?" I whispered.

"Building inspection. I work for the county on the side."

A shadow fell on the floor and we heard Rory's clipped brogue addressing Flynn. Simon stepped out and joined them. I followed suit.

Errol Flynn gazed placidly up at us, a man accustomed to having his evening interrupted by strangers. The woman at his side held a napkin over her chest like a shield.

"Sorry for the intrusion, folks," Simon said. "Mr. Flynn, I wanted to tell you how much I enjoyed you in *Robin Hood*."

"Thank you, sir." Flynn's voice was every bit as breezy as I'd hoped. "If you wouldn't mind—"

"Now I'd like to return the favor." Simon rapped the wall behind Flynn, one of the decorative portholes in the center of it. "I thought you should know this wall has been modified."

"Has it?" Flynn said.

"There's a compartment not visible from this room. My guess is the porthole is two-way glass and a camera is behind it."

Flynn studied the porthole over the tip of his cigarette. "Two-way glass, you say." He then grinned impishly at Rory, who hadn't cracked a sweat. "You cheeky bastard."

"I thought if it worked for you . . . ," Rory said.

The woman threw down her napkin. "I don't understand what's happening."

"I'll explain later, pet," Flynn told her.

"But that camera might not provide the best angle. Would you excuse me?" Simon pushed down the stairs past me, seizing a busboy by the collar of his white jacket. He manhandled him to the banquette and shoved him into a seat next to Flynn's now-bewildered consort. "This young man brought your water. Has an odd way of walking, I noticed." Simon hoisted the busboy's foot into the air. The woman yelped as the busboy clawed at the table, sending cutlery clattering.

"There's no call for this," Rory cautioned.

"Yes, there is." Simon hiked up the cuff of the busboy's trousers. Strapped to his ankle was a small camera, two cords extending up the pant leg. "What the porthole doesn't see, the help does."

"Like James Cagney in *Picture Snatcher!*" I yelled.

Simon glanced at me. "You know that was based on Ruth Snyder's actual execution."

"Well, yes, but—"

The most divine sound cut me off. The rich laughter of Errol Flynn, practiced at appreciating absurdity. "Rory, you're a devil and no mistake." He turned to Simon and me. "Sir, madam, I thank you for taking pity on my ignorance. And miss, may I say what a lovely dress you're wearing. Now, Millicent," and with this he faced the woman, "I daresay the prudent course of action is for us to call it an early evening. We can't leave together, so I'll see you to the door and into your ride home. Pardon us, won't you?" With a bow, he swept fair Millicent away, leaving us with Rory and one perplexed and contorted busboy.

"So," Rory said. "I expect you two have more questions."

"GRAND MAN ALTOGETHER, Flynn. Very sporting attitude. It'll be the death of him yet. Fancies himself an Irishman even though he's from Tasmania. Worst of a bad lot, them. But I play along."

Rory's Ulster accent echoed off the ceiling. His office consisted of the bare essentials, as if the room had been stripped for parts. Clearly, his home was the nightclub's floor.

"At least we know how Club Fathom got its sterling reputation." I aimed for a sneer but didn't pull it off.

"People come because they hear it's shady. We can't disappoint them, can we?" A buccaneer's smile from Rory. "Full credit for the idea goes to your man."

"Who?" My heart sank. "Not Jens."

"A Lohse production, start to finish. I maintain it in tribute to his genius. That, and it pays off like a fruit machine. He's the one pointed out people request those booths for a bit of privacy and it wouldn't take much to refit them. The masterstroke was him saying the picture studios have people whose job it is to hush up scandals like the kind that unfold in those booths. The money's already set aside. Be a waste if nobody claimed it."

"How did it work?" Simon asked.

"Exactly as Jens said it would. We send along the photographs. The studio sends over a big fella who yells and breaks a few ashtrays. Whole show's for nothing, because he's there to pay me off. I tack on the cost of the ashtrays."

"But then that star never comes back," I said.

"True, love. He even tells his friends, 'Whatever you do, don't go to the Fathom.' But he won't say why. The friends get consumed with curiosity, and the horses are on the track again. Jens predicted that, too. Nary a name sullied, and the money goes to its earmarked purpose." Rory shook his head, marveling. "A thing of beauty, no? Streamlined. Like something Henry Ford dreamed up."

"It's contemptible," I said. And I meant it.

"Blame your friend Jens. A pure businessman, he was, which is my respectful way of calling him a bastard. He saw all manner of sins at those parties he worked, other clubs. Only he forgot none of it. The mussed hair. The lipstick on the collar. And he turned what he knew into money. I've no idea how many rackets he had going. He'd rope me into things I had no clue about. He'd target legitimate types, society people and the like. Do it indirectly, keep himself out of it. For instance, he had me bump into this actress, Charlotte Hume. Did you see *The Defense Rests?* Brilliant. I tell her I know her husband, say something like, 'He was quite impressive in court last Friday at four seventeen.' A highly specific time sticks in the brain, Jens always said."

He'd stolen the idea from Hiram Beecher. *A crooked number*

plants a hook in the memory, Beecher wrote in *How to Be at Home in the World.* I felt sick to my stomach.

Rory kept talking. "Charlotte goes home and tells the husband, who thinks, 'Jesus, I was nowhere near court last Friday at four seventeen. I was somewhere I shouldn't have been, frolicking with someone not my lovely wife.' After he shites himself, another party bumps into him and requests financial assistance. Jens would throw some of the proceeds my way. Him manipulating it all without showing his face."

I fumed at Rory across his barren desktop. "Why did you tell that story? Why did you mention Charlotte Hume?"

"Because her husband, Donald Hume, is solicitor for and close friend of your boss, Addison Rice." His chair creaked as he sat back. "You think I'd talk to you without first finding out who you are? Not a whisper about your man Simon there, but Addison's name came up soon as I mentioned yours. You made me feel uncomfortable in my own establishment, Miss Frost. I'm only responding in kind."

He'd succeeded brilliantly. How could I make nice with Donald and Charlotte now that I was privy to Donald's infidelity and Charlotte wasn't?

"As ruthless as they come, Jens," Rory said. "Practical, too. Almost knew when to get out."

"What do you mean?"

"Last time I saw him, he said he was packing it in. Selling his operation outright. Names, pictures, detailed record of misdeeds, all on the block. No idea who'd be buying it, though."

I had an inkling. "Malcolm Drewe?"

"Christ, Jens wasn't tangling with him, was he?" Rory shivered. "Jens said he was after a pot of money and had plenty of irons in the fire. Haven't a clue what those other irons might have been. I trust he settled up with his partner first."

"Partner?" Simon asked. "What partner?"

"Here, I'll show him to you." He unlocked a desk drawer and handed Simon a photograph. It had been taken in the corridor outside Rory's office. In it, an angry Jens, hair falling into his eyes, brandished a finger at a smirking blond man.

Whom I'd met before.

Hello again, Mr. Ames.

"Took it myself, with one of the wee cameras," Rory said with pride. "Jens never knew I was there."

"This man was Jens's partner?" I asked quietly.

"Aye. He'd come in when Jens was here and they'd slip away for serious conversation. I asked Jens who he was, and Jens called him a 'music lover.'"

"Why'd you take their picture?"

A sly smile. "It's what Jens would have done."

"Has the man been here since Jens stopped coming in?"

Rory thought a moment. "I believe so."

I turned to Simon. "That's the man from my building."

Simon studied the photograph, his fingers unconsciously massaging the spot on his skull where Peter Ames had brained him. "You're sure?"

I nodded.

"Keep it, with my compliments," Rory said. "I've other ways of remembering Jens. He won't soon be forgotten at Club Fathom."

21

THE BUZZ OF discovery staved off the night's chill better than my coat. As we crunched across the gravel-covered parking lot, I praised Simon for how ably he'd plumbed the depths at Club Fathom, not only sussing out Rory's racket but confronting him about it.

"I'd noticed some odd details on my earlier visits. I didn't put them together until tonight. What I want to know is how you pulled Malcolm Drewe's name out of the ether."

"I'll explain when we're on the road."

Simon's coupe represented several steep steps down from the showy sedan he piloted for Lodestar. As he took out his keys, I glanced again at the photograph of Jens and Peter Ames. Seeing Jens's hostile expression reminded me I had an entirely new sense of the composer now, and my glow of excitement began to fade.

"It's early yet," Simon said. "Where would you like to go?"

I was wondering whether a studio driver could afford the Cocoanut Grove when the doors of the Chrysler next to Simon's car opened. Two men emerged, moving quickly to block us in. One in a brown topcoat, the other in threadbare navy. Simon instinctively swept me behind him. "Help you fellas?"

I felt the photograph get plucked from my hand. Behind me, Peter Ames titled it toward the light. Surprise flitted across his face, only to be replaced by the same smirk he displayed in the image.

"Ah, Jens," Peter said. "Chaos forever in his wake. You got this from that mick pansy, I presume."

"Rory's a pansy?" Simon asked. "You sure? He didn't make a pass at me." He stared levelly at Peter. If they'd ever met before— if, as Gene suspected, they were working in tandem—then I was witnessing two performances worthy of statuettes at the next Academy Awards.

"Thank you for leading me to this." Removing a cigarette lighter from his pocket, Peter set the photograph aflame and dropped it to the gravel. "I didn't know it existed."

"Then what were you searching for at my apartment? Jens's book?"

"Was someone in your apartment? You notified the police, I hope."

Peter wouldn't even do me the courtesy of lying convincingly, his line readings devoid of life. He ground out the smoldering remains of the photo.

"I was there, too. Got a blow to the head for my trouble." Simon stepped closer to Peter. So did the two topcoated underlings. More importantly, Peter retreated. Simon's bravado had intimidated him—and he knew I'd noticed.

Thrusting his chin toward me, Peter asked, "Did Mr. Dillon relay anything else about me?"

"Only that you're a lover of music. I had you pegged more as a film fan. Your name's not Peter Ames. Did you swipe that from *The Mad Miss Manton*?"

"A trifle, that picture. Still, one can't miss a Stanwyck. I understand you know her. Consider me jealous. She's well matched with Henry Fonda in *Manton*. They should do another picture together."

"Do you like Marlene Dietrich?"

Peter's eye twitched. I took that as a no. "I should inquire about anything else pertinent Mr. Dillon might have. Won't be a moment." He spoke a few words in German to his stooges, then walked toward the club. The two men faced us with an uneasy swagger. We were in a dark corner of the parking lot, but enough people were present to cause problems.

Simon smiled at the man in brown. "How goes it, Fritz? You speak English? What about you, Heinrich? *Sprechen sie?*" No reply was forthcoming. "So you didn't hear there are pansies in there? You can go in if you want. The Kaiser's waiting."

Neither minion moved. "What are you doing?" I whispered.

"I speak some German. Peter's orders were vague. I'm not sure these two will actually stop us from leaving. We should find out now while the odds are in our favor."

"How are they in our favor?"

"They're not going to get any better." Simon raised his hands and stepped forward.

Brown Topcoat drove his fist into Simon's stomach. The air came out of Simon in a rush as he slammed into his car. The air came out of me when I screamed.

"We speak English," Navy Topcoat said. "Our orders were plenty clear." He grabbed Simon's hair and jerked his head up.

"What's knittin', kittens?" I recognized the wheedling voice borne on the breeze. I wasn't exactly happy to hear the honeyed tones of Malcolm Drewe's associate Mr. Knoll, but I wasn't put out, either. Knoll scuffed across the parking lot, kicking gravel into the legs of the bilingual flunkies holding us captive. Garrett and the two men behind him picked up their feet, not wanting to jostle the guns they were holding.

Knoll inhaled deeply. "A man can breathe free in L.A. County, almost as free as he can at sea. You sure you want to stand out here, Miss Frost? Might catch your death of cold."

Garrett's brogan nudged what was left of the torched photo. "It's warmer over here. But not much."

"You found something in there and the bad men took it away," Knoll said. "That about the size of it?"

I nodded. "How long have you been following us?"

"Longer than these yahoos, not as long as some square johns could be G-men. Like the circus rolling into town with you at the head of it. All kinds of people interested in you."

I thought of what Malcolm Drewe had said, that you only noticed people following you if they wanted to be noticed. I suspected he was right.

"The blond guy went inside?" Knoll asked.

"We'd like to as well."

"Good idea. Get out of this cold. We'll keep your pals company."

"Don't order any food in there," Garrett said as Simon and I passed him. I assured him we wouldn't. I didn't look back, not even when I heard what I took to be a scuffle, several groans, and a man in a topcoat settling face-first on gravel.

Inside Club Fathom, Simon led the way to Rory's office, telling a nosy busboy I'd forgotten my handbag even though it dangled from my arm. We found Rory propped against the wall, a towel full of ice to his head. A waitress hunched alongside him, her pose popping several stitches in her skintight gown. The drawers of Rory's desk had been hurled across the room, scattering papers everywhere.

"Return customers! The key to success." Rory tried valiantly to stand, then slumped against the wall and slid down again. "The music lover came back as well. Struck me on the head with a gun."

"That's his favored technique," Simon said.

Jens died from a blow to the head. I looked at Simon and understood he'd had the same thought.

"What did he want?" I asked.

"The negative of the photograph I gave you, along with any

others I had. He also inquired after Jens's bloody book. I told him I didn't have it. Apparently my word was insufficient." Rory gestured at the office's disarray. With the waitress's assistance, he got to his feet. "Forgive me, my head's swimming. Only appropriate, given the decor. He was about to put the gun to wholehearted use when Lorraine here interrupted him. Now I'd like to ask her to marry me."

One glance at Lorraine's face made it evident the poor girl took him seriously.

"I'm going to look for him. Stay here," Simon instructed, and darted from the office.

"You really want to marry me?" the waitress asked.

"Permit me to explain a few fundamentals, darling."

I pointed at the telephone on Rory's desk. He nodded. I dug the number Malcolm Drewe had given me out of my handbag. Someone other than Drewe answered. I was told to wait. Neither development surprised me.

Drewe's dry martini voice finally crackled down the line. "Can I be of service, Miss Frost?"

"That escort you provided already came in handy."

"Did you find anything?"

"No. I'm calling with a question. Am I looking for a book?"

"I have no idea. Are you?"

"Very well, I have another question. Did you buy information from Jens Lohse?"

"Now we're talking. Yes. Lohse approached me with a proposition. He had information for sale. I was intrigued, so I requested a sample. What he revealed required a trip to my barber, because it turned my hair white. The things these show people get up to, Christ. It's enough to make me want to bar my daughters from going to pictures altogether, but then I'd have to say why."

"Why pay Jens for the material in advance?"

"I got a bargain. Or thought I did. Jens was willing to slash his price if I paid him at once. Given the quality of what he had on offer, I took a flier. I can afford to be generous. Jens said he needed time to pull the information together, then he'd deliver it. Right when I was starting to think he'd gypped me, you found his body."

"And now you want me to locate this information so you can blackmail people? Because I won't do that." Oh, the valor I could summon courtesy of the Southern California Telephone Company.

"I have no intention of using this material for so crude a purpose, Miss Frost. I simply want to build up my files in advance of my next business venture, whatever it may be. I seek leverage. *That* is what I paid Jens for. What I want you to do is help me recover what is rightfully mine. If it's in a book, bring me the book. I came to your aid tonight, didn't I? Now you come to mine. I'll always be close by."

The click when he hung up sounded nothing like a key bolting a door, I told myself.

SIMON PULLED UP to the club's entrance. He hadn't found Peter Ames. I asked what the scene around his car had looked like. "I'm sure everyone's fine," he said. He drove slowly, eyeing the rearview mirror at regular intervals. I gazed out at the city rolling past the coupe's windows, tarted up with Christmas lights. The trip to Club Fathom had waterlogged my seasonal spirit.

"He was a bad person, Jens," I said.

"Told you I didn't like him." Simon shrugged. "Have to admire him, though."

"How can you say that?"

"His plan with Rory was clever. He didn't hurt anyone, just soaked the studios for money they were prepared to spend.

He was right about that. I've driven Lodestar fixers to those meetings."

"He hurt my friend Charlotte, only she doesn't know it yet."

"You're right, you're right." Another metronomic check behind us. "So what exactly is going on?"

"I think Jens and Peter Ames, whatever his right name is, were partners in a blackmail racket. Jens, for his own reasons, sold it out from under Peter to Malcolm Drewe. Drewe wants the information he paid for. Peter's bent on finding it first."

Simon nodded. "And the information is in Jens's music book?"

"Considering Peter's also after it, it's the likeliest place."

"Then where's the book?"

I sank into my seat. "I have no idea."

We drove a while in silence. "Another question," Simon said. "Where am I taking you? We still haven't eaten."

I thought for several blocks. Starvation and exhaustion duked it out. Only one could claim victory.

"It's best if you take me home. I have to help Santa Claus in the morning."

Simon didn't bat an eye. "So be it," he said.

22

EDITH DIDN'T HAVE to tell me you never upstaged Santa. Addison would be in red, so I chose a forest green silk dress with antique brass buttons decorating the bodice and cuffs. With brown suede pumps I resembled an ambulatory Christmas tree, but so long as no urchins hung tinsel on me I'd be fine.

The bus bearing the boys and their chaperones would arrive at nine sharp. I planned on beating it to Addison's by a good two hours to ensure all was in readiness, leaving time to call Gene. I'd set the kids to gorging on flapjacks and bacon, then greet the stars who would trickle in soon after to nibble pastries and sip champagne. By ten o'clock our young houseguests would be ready to sit on Santa's lap and receive perfectly wrapped presents from the likes of Clark Gable. Come noon, we'd have brought joy to the world. Or at least Brentwood.

I tiptoed past Mrs. Quigley's already open door. Miss Sarah barely glanced up, uninspired by my dedication.

Outside, I spotted a fellow early-bird tenant, Mr. Pendergast, in earnest conversation with a woman across the street. I lowered my head and powered down the pavement, not wanting to be waylaid.

On the streetcar, my thoughts circled back to the previous evening. Simon had taken a punch and stood ready to endure additional punishment on my behalf. I hated that I'd gotten him into this morass, I respected his mettle, and I wondered how I would have responded to his question about possible dinner plans had the Santa breakfast not loomed. I was still contemplating the matter when she spoke.

"Lillianfrost?"

Snapping out of my reverie I looked into the face of a woman holding a folded newspaper toward me. She had a bedraggled appearance, clutching a rumpled coat around herself, the collar pulled tight against a beret concealing her hair. Shoes black with dust had rubbed the backs of her heels raw.

I'd seen her before, talking to Mr. Pendergast. She tapped the paper. It was from days ago, the *Register* article about me discovering Jens Lohse's body. The woman tapped my name in newsprint insistently. "Lillianfrost?"

"Yes, I'm Lillian Frost."

Hearing this, the woman let loose a cry of relief. She swept the beret from her head, setting her blond hair free. At that moment, I realized where else I'd seen her.

"Jens dead," Marthe Auerbach said in a voice thick with hysteria. "Jens dead and I am guilty."

I gaped at her, frozen with surprise. Marthe presented the insides of her wrists to me, ready for handcuffs. "Jens dead because of me."

"Mrs. Auerbach? Marthe? Please, sit down."

She keened again, waking up everyone else on the streetcar. "Lillianfrost, help me!"

I lunged for the pull cord. "Yes, of course, yes. We'll go to the police. Okay? Police."

Marthe sobbed a little. "Yes. Police. Thank you, Lillianfrost." She tapped the newspaper again, in case I'd forgotten who I was.

"SHE ISN'T SAYING much," Gene announced, "in German or English. But it's exactly what she told you."

"She confessed to killing Jens?"

"I scared up a guy to translate. Mrs. Auerbach stated more than once she and Jens Lohse were in love, and she killed him."

"Why?"

Gene sat next to me on the hard bench in the police station's hallway. He'd nicked himself shaving under his right jaw, the spot an angry red. "That's still unclear."

"She hit him with the fireplace poker and heaved his body off the balcony. She admitted all that."

"In those words? No. She hasn't offered any specifics, aside from Jens being killed at the cabin."

"Then she hasn't confessed at all."

"Easy, Frost. What she's said is sufficient for us to hold her. The issue now is her husband. Where's Felix? I asked, and she said he was gone. No, hang on." He flipped through pages in his notebook. "'Now he is free.' Which could be interpreted any number of ways, including she killed him."

I twisted around to look at Marthe Auerbach, an oasis of calm amid a scrum of detectives. She'd removed her coat to reveal a dowdy housedress, and loosely organized her hair. She sat serene and luminous, Joan of Arc awaiting the pyre.

"No," I said, still staring at her. "She didn't kill Jens. She's selling a story. Where's she been all this time?"

"Hiding, she says. In churches and elsewhere. Again, not much detail yet."

"Or ever. I'm telling you, this is fishy. Jens's death is tied into Ames and Drewe and what I learned last night."

"Now that we have a moment." Gene's voice plunged to its sternest register. "I'd like to hear about that. With all the detail you can spare."

I'd revised my script while I'd waited, expecting to dazzle Gene with word of Jens's extortion empire and its pending sale to Malcolm Drewe. But Gene failed to mouth any of the dialogue I had in mind for him.

"Let me get this straight. You went to a nightclub—*that* nightclub—with this Fischer character? I thought we agreed we didn't like him."

"But he doesn't know Peter Ames! Last night proves it!"

"It proves nothing. You weren't supposed to see Ames leaving your place. They could have staged last night's clash for your benefit, to allay any suspicion. A punch in the gut's even easier to take than a blow to the head."

"Why go to such lengths to fool me?"

"Why? I don't know. Any more than I know why you called Fischer in the first place." Gene concentrated on a spot on the scarred green linoleum between his shoes.

"I knew you wouldn't want me to go to Club Fathom alone."

"Damned right. Or at all."

We lapsed into a fraught silence. I glanced back at Marthe. A burly detective handed her a mug. She sipped from it gratefully.

"Can you ask her about Jens's music book?"

"Already did." He still spoke to the floor. "She said she didn't remember any book."

"She's lying. She has to be. You know that, don't you?"

"I'll tell you what I know. I know the captain came down to shake my hand and thank me for wrapping this up."

"Why didn't he shake my hand? I walked Marthe in here. It's my collar."

Gene couldn't conceal his cockeyed smile, but it didn't stay long. "You're right. There's more to this than what Marthe's admitting. Maybe it's that she killed Felix. We'll get her to talk. But you have to understand two things. Jens's blackmail scheme could be unrelated to his death. And when the captain comes a-glad-handing it means we're turning the page. A prime suspect voluntarily confessed, and Lodestar's pressing for a swift solution. Ergo, the case is closed. My doubts aren't enough to keep it open."

Gene had doubts. For now, that would have to be enough.

"If the case is closed," I said, "then Detective Wingert isn't in Dutch for giving Marlene the brush anymore. So he should be willing to talk to me, right?"

"You want I should ask him again? Anything else while I'm at it?"

"I have to get to Addison's Santa breakfast. I'm already late."

Gene stood up. "Let the captain's new golden boy deliver you in style."

23

GENE DEPOSITED ME at Addison's front door shortly before noon. No buses were in sight, and only a handful of automobiles remained around the fountain.

"Everybody's gone." I did a sterling job of suppressing the panic in my voice; only complete strangers, close friends, and those in between could hear it. "That means the breakfast went without a hitch, right?"

"It's fine, Frost. Stop worrying." Gene squeezed my hand, kissed my cheek, and waited with a reassuring smile until I entered Addison's house.

Never again would I know such kindness.

I was accustomed to Rogers giving me the cold shoulder. But when the entire staff shunned me, I knew disaster had struck. I tore through the house, ignoring multiple smashed holiday ornaments and several disturbing brown stains that I hoped were hot chocolate. I sent up a prayer to Saint Zita, patroness of domestics, as I ran.

Addison stood outside his study with William Demarest. The gruff-voiced actor said, "Anyway, I seen plenty worse in the army," then chucked Addison's shoulder and took his leave.

My boss still wore his Santa suit, a pair of child-sized maple syrup handprints on one sleeve. His white beard drooped around his throat like a flag of surrender. His spirits hung even lower. I nearly burst into tears at the sight of him.

"Lillian. Of all mornings to be late."

"I'm so sorry. I called and left a message but . . ." *Oh, what was the use?* "What happened?"

"The breakfast came off relatively well, although we could have used you to greet the children. The presenting of the presents is where things veered off course. You see, we didn't know where they were."

"But I left that information when I telephoned!"

"It didn't make it to me, I'm afraid. I sent the staff to find them, and when they reported back with bulging bags I assumed all was well. I made my entrance as St. Nick, and soon Robert Taylor was handing out presents. One little boy—charming tyke, never saw so many freckles—tore his open rather exuberantly and it shattered."

"Shattered? But we didn't get anything breakable for—"
No. Oh dear God, no.

"Naturally, the poor child got upset. We were tending to him when another boy unwrapped his present, and I saw the problem."

"You were handing out the wrong presents. You were giving away tantalus sets."

"Yes. Crystal decanters filled with alcohol. Bob managed to get the set away from the boy before he swallowed a mouthful of rye. I waded in to recover the others we'd given out." Addison removed his flaccid Father Christmas hat and held it over his heart. "The sight of Santa Claus taking presents away proved traumatic. The lads became unruly. Ran riot all over the house. Some went back for seconds on breakfast and a food fight broke out. Good thing Bill Demarest was here to impose order. I had to plead with the photographers to stop taking pictures. Eventually we located the toys, so the boys didn't leave empty-handed. But by then the mood of the morning had been lost."

"I can't apologize enough, sir. I hated leaving you in the lurch but it was an emergency." I explained my unplanned trip to the police station.

But Addison wasn't listening. "At least Maude wasn't here to witness this. She'd be mortified." He noticed the sticky stain on his crimson coat. "I should clean up. After that I'll be in the lab. Miss Lamarr will be joining me. I won't be available for the rest of the day."

"Yes, sir."

I wandered the house in a haze, spotting signs of battle everywhere. The dining room looked like feeding time at the Griffith Park Zoo had just ended, a battalion of maids already on bucket detail. In the reception room, Donald and Charlotte were tucking wrapped tantalus sets under the Christmas tree.

"There you are!" Charlotte wore a peeved expression but otherwise looked adorable in a black suit with a white blouse covered in festive red dots, jaunty red beret decorated with a Christmas wreath pin tilted toward one ear. "A fine way to treat your hostess. Leaving me forsaken amidst utter madness without so much as a prompter."

Donald wedged another few boxes under the tree. "Must keep these clear of trafficked areas. Otherwise it's a liability." He smiled, and the voice of Rory Dillon saying "four seventeen" sounded in my head. I ignored it.

"How bad was it?" I asked them. "Be honest."

"Well, once the boys finally untied Deanna Durbin . . ." Charlotte trailed off.

I gripped a chair to steady myself.

"Oh, Lord, Lillian, I was joking!"

"This is why you aren't cast in comedies," Donald scolded.

"Mack Sennett thought I was plenty funny, once upon a time." Charlotte patted my arm. "Addison must have painted a dire picture. The boys got rambunctious is all. I got Deanna to lead a round of carols until the baseball gloves and fire engines were distributed, then it was all smiles. Aside from the single miscue, it was a lovely event. Wasn't it, Donald?"

"Absolutely. Nobody's going to sue and now that we know what Addy and Maude got us, we can top them." He wrapped his arm around Charlotte. I heard Rory telling me the time again, a daft Irish cuckoo clock.

Charlotte took my hand. "Now what happened to you?"

I couldn't talk to them. I couldn't face anyone until I'd repaired the damage I hadn't meant to cause. "I delivered an early gift to the LAPD. It'll be in the papers tomorrow. Would you excuse me? I've got a lot to take care of."

Charlotte embraced me so tightly her pin almost embedded itself in my temple. "You did nothing wrong, kiddo," she said. "Remember that."

When the front door shut behind the Humes, I might as well have had Addison's immense home to myself. A voice in my head suggested that, after the morning's events, I might want to take one last look around.

ADDISON REMAINED IN seclusion for the afternoon. I stayed busy, pitching in on cleaning duty, telephoning the Brentwood Boys Brigade to offer my apologies, drafting thank-you letters to our special guests. The activity didn't prevent me from whip-sawing between despair and indignation. On one hand, I couldn't keep a children's party on the rails, so what business did I have organizing bashes for world-renowned adults? On the other, there was nothing I would have done differently. I deserved some of the blame but none of the hostility. So a charity function became a modest fiasco. Big deal. Nobody had died.

The silent treatment finally did in my nerves. I decided to re-fill Addison's stationery order in person. The store wasn't far from Paramount, and I needed cheering up. Rogers devised ways to say nothing louder than before on the drive over. A harried Edith had the gate guards admit me.

On my way through the wardrobe building's tumult, I ran into Adele Balkan, the lively sketch artist who'd shared an office with Edith before her promotion. We paused to catch up.

"Christmas better hurry and get here," she said.

Mere mention of the holiday made me flinch. It would be a long December. "Do you have plans?"

"I need the break. It's tough sledding with Edith in charge." She hesitated. "I know you two are friends."

"What's wrong?"

"She's back to her schoolmarm ways. No singing, no chewing gum. She also changed how we do sketches. If an actress is cast, we draw her as well as the costume. 'A more complete depiction,' she says, but directors *hate* the idea. Roles are recast all the time, and they only want to see the clothes. Edith's making changes just to make changes, and I don't care if you tell her that. I'd better run."

The day's frenzied feeling penetrated Edith's normally tranquil office. She greeted me with the most fleeting of smiles. "Sorry, dear, but today's an absolute misery. The studio's delaying production of Jack Benny's next picture because he insists on going to trial, so down goes my department's schedule like so many dominos. I'll be here all weekend making adjustments. But enough of my woes."

I gave Edith a condensed account of my night at Club Fathom and my morning at the police station. To my dismay, she didn't provide the ready ear I'd hoped for.

"Detective Morrow's point is well taken," she declared. "The investigation of Mrs. Auerbach must run its course."

"But she had nothing to do with Jens's blackmail operation."

"You don't know that for certain. In any case, an organization like the police department must be permitted to follow its processes. Trust in Detective Morrow. He's a good man." She adjusted her glasses. "If you'll permit a personal aside, I'm distressed you spent time with Simon again given the questions about him."

"My other plan fell through. I had no choice." I sounded petulant even to me.

Edith's ringing telephone interrupted. She uttered one "yes," three increasingly emphatic "no"s, and a resigned "very well" before hanging up. "Horses appear to be escaping from every barn today. We'll have to cut this short. Perhaps lunch over the weekend?"

As Edith walked me out, an assistant showed Dorothy Lamour in. The brunette actress was a vision in an ivory suit and spectator pumps, her features more exotic in proximity.

"That hairstyle is you," she told Edith as they embraced.

"I keep hearing that." Edith introduced me then said, "Thank you so much for rescheduling your fitting for the reshoot."

"More sarongs. At least we're poking fun at them in this picture."

"One last wink to your fans before we put you in some contemporary fashions to dazzle them."

"I saw the gown," I chimed in. "It's a knockout." I'd stolen a glimpse of the dress Edith had designed for *St. Louis Blues*, a white number with a pattern of stars cascading down organza ruffles. Dorothy Lamour would look better in that dress than half naked in one of her trademark sarongs. To the women in the audience, anyway.

"Worth four whistles at the least," Edith said. "Maybe five."

"I'm on to your secrets." Dorothy laughed. "You bribe the electricians to whistle when you think I don't like a dress."

"You don't like my dresses?" Edith clutched her agate necklace. "Let's get you in and out as quickly as possible."

"Could you? I'm so far behind on my Christmas shopping and I've got a friend coming from back east to prepare for." As Edith led Dorothy into the salon, the actress said, "And now they're delaying my picture with Jack! Something about smuggling. You always have your ear to the ground, Edie. What have you heard?"

I dallied in the outer office. It had been a trying day. I had nowhere to be. What I wanted was to talk to someone who thought as I did, who saw the world my way. Someone who believed I was right. Edith hadn't come through on that score, and it was because of her I'd unintentionally imperiled a job I loved.

But I had other options. I telephoned Simon at Lodestar. Doing so from Edith's office made it seem positively sinful.

24

❖

SIMON, I LEARNED, had run out to Union Station to fetch a passenger arriving on the *Super Chief*. No one important, I figured; the big names knew to disembark in Pasadena to avoid the hurly-burly. Gretchen, my other errand on the Lodestar lot, was all too eager to arrange a pass at the gate.

She sat at her desk outside Sol Huritz's office leafing through *Variety*. She wore a dress the color of gingerbread I normally would have coveted, but after Addison's botched holiday bash anything reminiscent of Christmas roused my inner Scrooge.

"Where's Mr. Huritz?" I asked.

"His standing Friday meeting at Musso & Frank. What's doing?"

"I wanted to bring you the news myself. Marthe Auerbach turned herself in. First to me, then the police."

"Turned herself in?" Gretchen went pale. "She killed Jens?"

"That's what she says."

Gretchen's collapse was abrupt, from hushed stillness to furious tears in a heartbeat. She wrenched open a desk drawer for a tissue. Behind her purse rattled a photograph of Jens, in an elegant silver frame meant for display. I wondered if she'd hidden it away after he'd died, or if it had always supplied secret solace.

"I knew it was her. I knew it. I never liked that . . . bitch." She feasted on the word as if it were a five-dollar steak. "Keeping her distance at Salka's. Clinging to her so-called genius husband while toying with Jens. She deserves whatever she gets."

Hardly the time to explicate my theory that Marthe was being deceptive and Jens's criminal endeavors had sown the seeds of his demise. Not with that photo stashed in her desk.

Gretchen rose and hugged me. "I can't thank you enough. For finding out the truth, for coming here to tell me."

"I also wanted to see Simon Fischer, who drove me the other day. He's been a tremendous help."

"The man of mystery. Some of the girls on the lot would set their caps for him if he was a few years younger."

"It was a lucky break we met. If anyone else had taken me to Felix's apartment, this would have gone so differently."

"That was no accident."

The sudden chill made me grip my shoulders. "What do you mean?"

"You were almost guaranteed to get Simon. Pretty much any time Felix goes somewhere or someone goes to see him, Simon gets the call. He's Felix's unofficial driver. They have a relationship."

Did they? That came as news to me.

SITTING UNINVITED ON the stoop of a man's building, waiting for him to come home. What would the sisters at Saint Mary's back in Flushing think? *Lillian. We had such hopes for you.*

I'd found Simon's address in the telephone directory. He lived close enough to Lodestar to walk to work. Time to surprise him the way he'd surprised me. All I needed was a flask.

He turned the corner, the sight of me not producing a hitch in his stride. Unflappable, our Simon. He planted one foot on the stairs, towering over me. "Hello, little girl. You lost?"

"I had a big day."

"Care to come in and tell me about it?"

I said yes, certain an entire convent of nuns had wailed in agony.

We entered his sprawling, undistinguished apartment building. The hallways, reeking of cabbage, seemed to double back on themselves as we climbed to the third floor. I lamented not bringing a ball of thread, one end of which I could have tied to the front door like Theseus when he braved the Minotaur in the labyrinth.

Making Simon the monster within the maze, I thought, a notion I swept under the broadloom carpet of my mind.

I told Simon about my surprise encounter with Marthe Auerbach. "You're right," he said. "I don't buy Marthe's story, either. Last night's incident with your pal Peter and Malcolm Drewe's boys has to be tied in."

"That's why you don't believe Marthe? Not because of anything she said to you?"

He peered at me from the corner of his eye. "As I said, I don't really know her."

"Right. You know Felix."

He openly stared at me now. "No. I drive him occasionally."

That didn't square with Gretchen's Lodestar gossip. Then again, perhaps Simon didn't volunteer information to *anyone,* not just the authorities. I'd have to phrase my question more directly.

As Simon slipped his key into a lock, the door opposite his swung open. A wizened gnome of a man emerged, his few remaining wisps of hair erect on his scalp, suspenders straddling the hump on his back. "Thought that was you, Simon," the man said in a rasp tinged with desperation, as if he were afraid of not being heard. He saw me and stopped short, the magazine in his hands only partly extended toward his neighbor. "Didn't realize you had company. Wanted to give this back to you."

"Thanks, Clifford." Simon took the proffered periodical and folded it under his arm.

"Thanks for loaning it to me. That fellow sure knows his onions. Has the whole world situation figured out. I should start taking that magazine again. Didja read it when he ran those *Protocols*? Explains how the Jews have always—"

"Excuse us, Clifford. Can't leave my guest standing in the hall." Clifford, well versed in being interrupted, offered Simon a wave and me a leer before retreating into his cave. With a tight smile of apology, Simon opened his door.

The room beyond was not clogged with appointments. Some thirdhand furniture, a lopsided Murphy bed bulging out of one wall. Piano music drifted in through a window.

"I'd give you the tour, but you just had it," Simon said. "I've a couple of beers on ice, but not much in the larder other than a tin of sardines."

"I've dined many times on sardines. My uncle Danny loves them."

"The painter from Paramount. Why don't I lay things on?" He stepped toward the kitchen door, pausing to toss the magazine Clifford had returned to him in the drawer of a salvaged end table.

I didn't know why I eased that drawer open the instant Simon vanished into the kitchen. Scratch that. I knew exactly why. He'd hidden the magazine from me, casually but noticeably. And maybe I wanted an excuse to second-guess myself, to follow that phantom thread to the front door and freedom.

The drawer contained a few bills, a pair of reading glasses, and some sheet music in addition to the folded magazine. *Social Justice* was banned across the top. *Founded 1936 by Father Coughlin.* That would be Father Charles Coughlin, the fulminating priest of the airwaves. The man my uncle Danny sometimes listened to and took comfort from. *He's not always right, pet,* he'd say, *but he's one of our own, with our interests at heart.*

I appraised some of those interests now. AMERICA'S INSIDIOUS
FOES, the cover teased. "ANTI-SEMITISM" IS A SHIELD. I flipped to
Father Coughlin's column, headlined BACKGROUND OF PERSECU-
TION. Happening upon the phrase "Without attempting to de-
fend Herr Hitler or Naziism," I closed my eyes.

A soft clatter informed me it was too late to cover my tracks.
Simon carried a tray with two beers, and I was happy neither
had been opened; at least the second wouldn't go flat while he
drank the first. He'd borne presentation in mind, fanning cres-
cents of crackers around the open tin of sardines. But it was the
single violet in a tiny vase at the edge of the tray that broke my
heart.

His genial expression didn't change when he spotted the magazine in my hands. "Ah. Found some reading material."

"Do you believe this?"

"I don't know what I believe. The world's a complicated place.
I try to learn things."

"You won't learn anything from Father Coughlin. He's spread-
ing poison and lies."

Simon deposited the tray on the end table, taking pains to
point the violet toward me. "It's a free country. There are a lot
of people out there with interesting ideas. I'm the first to admit
I don't know everything."

The apartment's walls seemed close, the tinkling piano downstairs preying on my nerves. "I'm sorry," I said. "I feel a terrific
headache coming on."

"We don't have to talk to about this now." Simon took the
magazine from me and replaced it in the drawer. "I'd prefer not
to talk about it at all."

"So would I. I think it's best if I go home."

"Very well. Let me drive you."

"I can walk to the streetcar. The air will clear my head."

"Don't be ridiculous, Lillian. I'm a driver. It's what I do."

"You've already done enough." I intended it as an acknowl-edgment of his willingness to accompany me to Club Fathom, but it came out more like a dismissal.

That was how Simon apparently took it, dropping into a chair and cracking a beer open. "Suit yourself. Good night."

I stumbled through a thank you as I stumbled out. I only got turned around once on my way to the building's front door, all the while pondering a new question about simple Simon, help-ful Simon, always ready with a hand Simon. Why would a Father Coughlin acolyte buddy up to a Jewish composer?

KATHERINE DAMBACH'S
SLIVERS OF THE SILVER SCREEN

John Barrymore and wife, Elaine, are winging to the Big Apple to star in a new play. But some say the lure of the Great White Way isn't the reason for the trip. They blame Hollywood's lack of faith in the beauteous Mrs. B's acting abilities.

Life in Los Angeles's loftier climes isn't always a bed of roses. Take yesterday, when neighbors of retired radio tycoon Addison Rice had to endure the whooping and hollering of a busload of boys on loan from less fortunate homes, wreaking havoc at the millionaire's mansion. One eyewitness reports the lads had reason to rampage. Instead of promised gifts from Santa Claus the tots were handed bottles of the stuff Carrie Nation would never ax for.

The tykes understandably stampeded, hurling candy and pie in a frenzy that would have made Mack Sennett proud while filmland's famous faces watched in horror. Perhaps that rotund rascal Rice should stick to grown-up gatherings?

25

MY FRIEND VI exhibited an unseemly amount of pep for any human at the crack of a Saturday morn, much less one who'd sung two shows the night before. I clung pajama-clad to my door frame as I made this observation.

"Had some of Mrs. Q's coffee downstairs. Her joe's the best." She handed me a newspaper. "You should see this."

Kay's column dispersed my early A.M. fog. "Nuts. Addison swore he'd put the kibosh on this story. Kay only ran the item to needle me."

"Don't worry. No one reads her stuff."

"She could at least be accurate. We didn't serve candy and pie at a *breakfast*."

"And that Carrie Nation gag! Wheeler & Woolsey wouldn't have touched it. Everything okay? You look down in the mouth."

"Right now I'm down everywhere." I told her about my trip to Simon's and my fear he'd been using me.

"You went up to his apartment?" Vi gasped.

"I think you're missing the bigger picture."

"And I think you only dallied with Simon because you don't want to talk to Gene about Abigail."

Leave it to a friend to see right through you. "When did you get to be so wise?"

"I've always been wise. But when you're cute and blond, nobody notices."

• • •

I WAS BRIGHT of eye and bushy of tail when Addison found me at my post. His spirits had improved considerably.

"Hedy and I are experimenting with an idea of hers," he announced, dropping several scientific catalogs on my desk. "I'll need you to order the capacitors I've circled and a voltage-controlled quartz crystal oscillator. Don't forget the crystal part. That's important. And schedule a visit from the fellow who installed the air-conditioning in the lab. Hedy noticed some spurious frequencies during yesterday's round of testing."

"I thought things felt off in there."

"Very funny, Lillian. It's all quite temperature dependent, you know." He tapped the catalogs with satisfaction. "Perhaps this break from frivolity has put me back on my true path. More research. Hedy's right. The world's in a bad way, and I can use my training to help."

A laudable impulse, but if the future at Chez Rice held fewer parties and more equipment I couldn't pronounce, it might be time to get my references in order.

I had secured my second capacitor when Gene called. "How'd it go yesterday?" he asked.

He didn't need to hear about the breakfast's descent into shambles, and I couldn't share my suspicions about Simon without admitting I'd visited his apartment. That conversation required being face-to-face.

"Never a dull moment. What's the latest with Marthe?"

"She's sticking to her story, such as it is, so we're charging her with Jens's murder. It's about Felix now. The thinking is he's dead, too."

Not knowing how to respond, I said nothing at all.

My uncharacteristic silence threw Gene. After a moment, he said, "I heard from Carl Wingert. He's still pretty sore, but he'll give you five minutes if you insist on talking."

"I do. Anyplace, anytime. Tell him to name it."

"He did. Today, the Deutsches Haus downtown."

"The—wait, isn't that the headquarters of the German-American Bund? The ones who support the Nazis?"

"Or harmless social club for American citizens of German descent, depending on who you ask. Wingert's a member in good standing. They're having some kind of Oktoberfest Christmas celebration to show they're jolly and not fascists. All are welcome, although if my name ended in '-stein' or '-berg' I wouldn't be in a hurry to belly up to that particular *wunderbar*. Show up any time after three. Wingert will find you. Lots of people will be there. You won't require an escort."

Or at the very least, I noted, Gene wasn't offering to serve as one.

I KNEW I'D loitered long enough in Addison's Cadillac when Rogers violated protocol and addressed me from the front seat. "What is this, a stakeout?"

The three-story house outside the car should have had bicycles and toys on the patchy front lawn. Instead a steady stream of people moved toward the portico and the broad double doors beneath a sign proclaiming DEUTSCHES HAUS in the friendliest Teutonic typeface.

"Hold your horses," I told Rogers. "I'm going. I'll find my own way home."

Rogers, that master of subtlety, replied by gunning the Caddy's engine. The car rounded the corner before I reached the sidewalk.

I joined the flow of people heading into the *haus*. The substantially remodeled building served as home to a host of enterprises. The Aryan Bookstore occupied much of the first floor, copies of Father Coughlin's *Social Justice* visible through the window. I

slipped into the rear of a meeting hall given over to a band relying heavily on a heavyset percussionist whose ham-fisted technique wasn't keeping Gene Krupa up nights. Handbills by the
entrance threatened folk dancing, and floor space had been
cleared. The crowd included several families with extremely ruly
children. A sizable contingent nodded in time with the music as
if fervently agreeing with it. These true believers strutted instinctively, even to the coffee urn for a refill. They were on the as-
cendant, confident in their hygiene and their ideals.

I explored on, entering a room that had been turned into a
reasonable facsimile of a Bavarian pub. A portly man behind the
bar filled an impressive collection of steins with German beers.
Alpine scenes decorated the walls, along with a portrait of Adolf
Hitler. A surprising number of the men wore Bund uniforms of
black pants and puttees with gray shirts, Sam Browne belts a
sought-after accessory.

I received a few cursory smiles, superficial friendliness and
bratwurst being the order of the day. A man rose from one of the
tables, saying a few words to the old-timer next to him before
heading my way. His head was shaped like a lightbulb, the stubble staining his narrow jaw giving him a haggard appearance.

"You're Lillian Frost." He didn't expect me to disagree.

"How did you know?"

"Morrow described you pretty well. And you're the only
woman here doesn't look like she eats pork twice a day. Carl
Wingert." He cast a look back at his companion at the table. "I'm
here with my father. Name was Weingarten once, 'til some clerk
at Ellis Island got bored. He misses the music and food in the
old country. Although this pickled stuff doesn't agree with him
anymore. Suppose we'd better sit down." He sounded like he
dreaded the prospect. "Enjoying the festivities? It's the same
bands and dancers every time. I'm hoping Leni Riefenstahl
crashes the place to liven things up."

"Could that happen?" I'd been following the filmmaker and alleged Hitler confidante's trip to America in the papers, an ongoing misadventure intended to promote her mammoth sports documentary *Olympia* that only led to her being embroiled in controversy at every stop.

"She's holed up at the Beverly Hills Hotel. Couldn't check into her first choice, the Garden of Allah, with all the protests. Rumor is the *bürgermeisters* here invited her, but I'll eat a pig's ass if she shows. Pardon my French."

I sat opposite Wingert's father, who looked enough like his son he was practically a vision of things to come. Little wonder Wingert *fils* was careworn, confronted so starkly with his destiny. Wingert *père* bowed gravely to me as if I were Otto von Bismarck, then spouted a few words in German. Wingert dabbed his father's chin with a napkin. "*Nein, Papa, nein.*" To me, he said, "Don't mind the old man. He's losing his marbles. Never had too big a collection to start with."

"Thank you for agreeing to see me," I said. "I can't help feeling responsible for any hardship you're experiencing."

Wingert waved a hand. "Forget it. I'd catch hell whenever the body was found. You knew him? Lohse?"

"No. I was doing a favor of sorts for Marlene Die—"

"Hey!" Wingert's single syllable stopped me short. "Nix on her name in here. She's not exactly popular with this crowd."

Again I marveled at Marlene. Known the world over, non grata everywhere she went.

"So you pitched in by calling Gene Morrow. Guy's supposed to be a straight arrow, but you hear stories. Any truth to the one about him and his partner, the twenty-grand haul from California Republic a while back?"

"None," I said.

"Sez you. And him." Wingert smirked and sipped from his

stein. His father rambled in German again; Wingert deciding the words didn't merit a reply.

"Can you tell me about your investigation?"

He sparked a cigarette. "That's too strong a word. I got a call from a captain who got a call from some big noise at Columbia. I talked to your friend, thought what she said was sketchy. Still, I went to the rattrap where Lohse lived and spoke to the landlady, what's-her-name."

"Mrs. Fuchs."

"Yeah. It was clear in a big damn hurry there wasn't much for me to do. Lohse got the bum's rush because he'd stopped coming across with the rent. The old lady took messages for him. She and her son had cleaned out his place. I walked through it. Nothing there. I left my number, and that was that."

"What about Jens's car?"

Wingert's eyes narrowed through the smoke. He was losing patience. His father drummed the table, keeping time with music only he could hear. "Yeah, searched that, too. Another goose egg."

"Did you check the trunk? It was locked."

"When a captain tells me to do something, I leave no trunk unopened. I picked the lock, saw nothing but some papers, closed it up tight again. Looked exactly the same when I went back this morning."

He reached over and stilled his father's hand, then deposited two pieces of paper on the checkered tablecloth. Each had a ragged edge where it had been torn away from its binding. Both were weathered from exposure to the elements.

"That's all there was. Go ahead, touch 'em. Rain got into the trunk, along with mice from the looks of it. Morrow said you'd be interested."

Gingerly I picked up each brittle sheet in turn. One bore a

dozen or more penciled measures of music, the odd word in German scribbled alongside. The second featured what I took to be an entire song, notations spilling the length of the page.

"Too bad I can't read music," I told Wingert.

"Neither can I. They'll go in the file in case somebody makes head or tail of them."

Wingert Senior eyed the second piece of paper and said a few words in German to his son. Wingert perked up and asked a question. His father scanned the notes and then, to my amazement, began humming a familiar melody.

"I recognize that!" I exclaimed. "'It Looks Like Rain in Cherry Blossom Lane,' Guy Lombardo."

"Papa used to be in a band." Wingert couldn't completely damp down the pride in his voice.

I was looking at one of Jens's famous musical cribs, a sketch of a song enabling him to bluff his way through it.

Wingert's father nudged his son and pointed at me. Another inquiry followed. This time I knew one of the words. *Juden.* Wingert replied in perfunctory fashion.

"What did he say?" I asked.

"Nothing. He wanted to know if you're married."

"No, I don't think he did."

Wingert looked pained. "Ignore him. He's an old man."

I turned to take in the rest of the tavern. Two men by the door, their starched uniforms more like costumes, gave each other the stiff-armed Hitler salute.

"That's your father's excuse," I said. "What about everybody else here?"

"So there are a few buffoons. That's true of every outfit. Don't lump us all in together. The Bund celebrates German heritage. Honors our contributions to the world."

"Including the work of my friend whose name I can't say?"

"She asked for help, I gave it to her. Plenty of people here wouldn't lift a finger for her."

"Exactly my point. What do you think of Hitler?"

Wingert's father sat at attention at the name. "I think he runs the country, like Roosevelt runs this one. I don't care for either of them. But somebody's got to be strongman of Europe or else the Reds will take over. Adolf's the only one after the job. I say let him have it." Wingert squinted at me. "What kind of name is Frost, anyway?"

"My people are Irish."

"Listen to your own. Father Coughlin, Joe Kennedy. They know what's what over there."

"And what's what is letting Hitler do whatever he wants. That's what you're celebrating here."

"I'm here to get my old man out of the house. Most of these folks just want community, a chance to remember the homeland they'll never see again."

I started as Wingert's father pounded the table. He roared at me in German, making a series of elaborate motions with his hands, vacant eyes suddenly alive with decades of discontent. Wingert spoke over him in commanding tones to no avail.

"Is something wrong?" I asked.

"He thinks you're my sister." He took his father's hand, but the old man shook him loose and fixed me with a murderous glare. We were drawing scrutiny. I stood awkwardly, thanked Wingert for his time, and rushed for the door. Behind me I heard the detective negotiating with his father, the note of pleading evident even in another tongue.

In the hall, I caught my breath and my wits. Wingert's argument that the Bund's activities were akin to Salka's salons agitated me. This swaggering soiree in no way resembled those gatherings of émigrés, aside from the participants being far from home.

But then Los Angeles was a city of exiles, everyone escaping something. Even me. Granted, I hadn't fled fascism but fate. My mother had died when I was young, my father took a run-out powder, and at times it seemed everyone in Flushing knew. I wanted to live someplace where that history wasn't an unspoken part of every conversation. I'd been dealt a bad hand, and as Donald Hume regularly advised, I'd checked my cards, my dealer, and my emotions. Then I dealt myself into a new game in a land where the sun was always on my face, putting the shadows behind me.

A door at the end of the hall stood open to an alley. Two men toted bundles of paper on their shoulders to a closet. Something about their movement—swift, with a sense of mission—cut through my sulk. I waited for the street door to bang shut, consumed by curiosity.

In the closet, stacks of pamphlets had been arranged with efficiency. The cover bore a grotesque caricature of a vulture, with a human face and a hooked nose, blood streaming from its mouth. A star of David loomed ominously above the skullcap on the bird's head. WHAT PRICE THE FEDERAL RESERVE? bellowed a headline over the smoking ruins of a church. READ THE PROTOCOLS OF THE ELDERS OF ZION AND UNDERSTAND THE NEW DEAL.

I slipped a pamphlet free as I heard the back door open again. I emerged from the closet hurriedly, flustered excuse already on my lips—

And looked into Simon Fischer's eyes. Another bundle of loathsome literature on his shoulder.

He stared at me for a moment before saying my name.

I fled past him and down the hall, flying out the front door. Oompah music followed me onto the street. Nothing around but used car lots and funeral parlors, the neighborhood a destination to seek bargains or eternal rest. But two blocks up I glimpsed a façade I knew well: the colonnaded entrance of Claassen's Department Store. I ran toward it, not slowing when Simon called after me.

Passing through the revolving door I dashed to the Millinery department and camouflaged myself with an enormous straw beach hat. Simon entered and slowed to a standstill, flummoxed by the feminine fixtures on display. He shook his head at an approaching salesgirl and revolved his way back outside.

A clerk complimented the chapeau I'd tried on, only to grimace when she saw the pamphlet still in my hand. To remedy the situation I put the offending circular in my purse and said I'd take the hat. It did look rather good on me.

26

GENE PRESSED HIS thumb and index finger to his temples and squeezed. Hardly the reaction I sought. "What are you asking me to do, Lillian?"

"Arrest Simon. At the very least grill him about this."

"This isn't the song you were singing after he took you to Club Fathom."

It was the latest awkward moment in an awkward conversation. The most uncomfortable element: our tête-à-tête transpired on the back porch of Abigail Lomax's house.

From a pay telephone in Claassen's, I'd called Gene. Nobody home. I swallowed my pride, fed in more change, and tried Abigail.

Gene answered. Abigail was fixing a light supper in the kitchen, he'd said.

I taxied to her house, my response to her greeting curt enough to warrant a scowl from Gene. And that was before I laid out why he needed to take Simon into custody.

"I don't understand your resistance," I said. "You were suspicious of him all along. Do you need to hear me say you were right?"

"It's music to my ears, but nothing's illegal about being a member of the Bund. Hell, Wingert's one. That's why you were there. Maybe when the war starts it'll be a different story."

Not *if* the war starts, I noted, but *when*. The prospect of the country drawing up sides, the people in the tavern with Wingert and his aged father aligning with the enemy, made my stomach roil.

"Fine. But explain why a member of that organization, who believes what they're saying enough to circulate this garbage"—I waved the odious pamphlet at him—"would arrange to become the driver for a Jewish composer?"

"It's a corrupt city. Everyone spies on everyone else. I guarantee the LAPD has informants inside the Bund, and for all I know Wingert told the Krauts about them. The mayor, at least the old mayor, had people inside the department. Maybe Fischer's doing his bit for the organization, getting close to Felix to find out if he's a communist. Doesn't Father Coughlin say all Jews are Reds?"

I sat on the porch's single low step. After a moment, Gene joined me. "What do you think Simon did?"

"I think he killed Jens."

"Why? What's his motive?"

"I don't know. But nothing he's said or done makes sense."

"Neither does what you're suggesting. If he killed Lohse at the Auerbachs' cabin, why drive you there?"

"Because it's his job. And maybe he *wanted* the body to be discovered. To implicate Felix, or Marthe, or both of them."

Gene looked dubious, but at least he was listening. "Then why throw the body off the balcony to make it look like suicide? He'd be better off leaving Jens in the house."

"Maybe he did. Suppose Simon killed Jens at the cabin. The Auerbachs show up, find Jens, and *they* throw his body into the canyon for the reason you suggested. They're strangers here, and it's not like things are cozy between America and Germany at present. They panicked."

Gene said nothing, so I did some panicking of my own. "Can you ask Marthe if that's what happened?"

"Typically the captain frowns on us talking suspects out of their confessions."

"Then you've got to hold Simon. At best, he's an anti-Semitic lunkhead who's taken an unhealthy and inappropriate interest in Felix Auerbach."

"How is that grounds for arrest? If I took in every anti-Semite the jails would be packed. And if snooping under false pretenses is a crime you'd be apprehended for your ongoing Mata Hari routine. I'll do what I can, but I already know it won't be much."

We sat next to each other, listening to the *clink* of dishes from the kitchen. Abigail kept a lovely home. It was more than two conjoined apartments crammed with clothes. Any man would be content there.

"Why were you in Fischer's apartment?" Gene asked. "Was it to investigate him? Or because you wanted to be?"

A question he was entitled to ask. Instead of replying, I volleyed with one of my own. "Why are you at Abigail's again?"

"Because you were at goddamned Bund headquarters!" Gene vaulted off the porch and stalked around Abigail's tiny yard. I couldn't tell if he was upset or wanted to continue the conversation away from open windows. "I checked on her, she was alone, I said I'd stop by. We've talked about this."

"I know. Yet I don't know anything. About us, I mean. You'd think I'd be an expert on the subject." I hadn't planned on broaching this thorny topic. Now we rushed headlong toward it. In for a penny, in for a pound. "What are we doing? Are we together? Are we a couple?"

"You know how I feel about you."

"If I did, would I ask? How do you feel about Abigail?"

"Like she needs me."

"Do you know that? Have you talked to her about it? Maybe she doesn't want to say no when you ask her to come out with us. Maybe she can't."

"I've known Abigail my whole life. I'm trying to help her."

"It's possible your help is keeping her from getting on with her life."

Gene seized my hand, pulling me to my feet—and away from Abigail's house. He spoke in controlled tones that papered over his anger. "Suppose she's fine with how things stand. Suppose I am, too. Where does that leave you?"

Facing my biggest fear, I thought. Why shouldn't they be pleased with the status quo? Gene got to feel noble and Abigail protected, leaving only me dissatisfied. "The squeaky wheel, I guess."

"Are you making this a choice?" Gene asked. "You or her?"

YES! I screamed in my heart. *I want you to choose. And I want you to pick me.*

"Of course not," I said. "I want to know where we stand. I want to know we're together."

Grabbing me by the shoulders, Gene pulled me into the shadows at the side of the house. He pressed his hand to the small of my back, his lips to mine. The kiss was at once deeply welcome and wholly unsatisfying, meant to prove something to me, not reveal a truth about him.

Or perhaps, again, I was the problem. Thinking too much, feeling too little. I allowed myself to fall into the moment.

We separated, Gene a mere outline in the deepening dark. "You're my girl. Abigail is my friend. Maybe I don't balance everything as well as I could. But you can't blame a guy for being confused. Not when his girl goes to another man's place."

He had me there.

MY FACE STILL burned when I entered the house alone. Abigail sat in her parlor, sipping coffee. Her open smile made me feel like a louse.

I sat down for some civil discourse. "Has"—*What was that silly memory trick? Leaping rabbit!*—"Warren called you? He asked for your telephone number." More like I forced it on him after our disastrous bridge foursome, but he had it.

"Not yet. Maybe he's taking his time. He certainly had patience with your bidding."

What prompted that wholly deserved dig at my poor bridge play? Was she annoyed I'd horned in on her evening with Gene? Or was she gently ribbing a woman she regarded as her friend? Was I once again my worst enemy, forever in my own way?

I stood up, startling Abigail. "Long day. I should go."

"What? No! Let's all take in a picture. You've seen most of them, so you should choose."

"Pick one you'd like. Have fun." I retrieved my purse and headed for the door the way Marlene would. Back straight, head high, exalted in my suffering.

Abigail was right. I had seen a lot of pictures. Maybe too many.

I WALKED TO a streetcar stop to regain my composure. I boarded too preoccupied to notice the queer condition of the sky—low-hanging clouds tinted a bright orange from below—until the frowzy woman sitting nearby pointed it out. "Heavens! Something *huge* is on fire!"

"Right. They're burning Atlanta tonight."

The woman peered at me. "I beg your pardon?"

"Not Atlanta, obviously. It's the gate from *King Kong*, some other sets. I still don't see why when there's no Scarlett."

After a moment the woman moved farther down the car. Who could blame her?

I paused in the lobby to holler a hello to Mrs. Quigley. My landlady bustled out in a peach kimono, her hair and humor high. "I've had the loveliest evening with your friend!"

Simon appeared in her doorway. Head tilted down toward Miss Sarah, eyes locked on mine.

Mrs. Quigley babbled like a particularly oblivious brook. "Such pleasant company! And after taking a nasty blow to the head in my building."

"Couldn't let that delicious stew of yours go to waste," Simon said.

"You didn't eat downtown?" I asked.

"No. Don't care for the food there." He said good night to Mrs. Quigley and for once she took the hint, leaving us in the lobby. "Can we go to your apartment?"

"Right here is fine."

"We have to talk about tonight."

"No, we don't. You're allowed to believe what you want. It's a free country, unlike Germany. We'll be fighting them soon enough, apparently. But you and I don't have to fight. I'd rather you just leave me alone."

Simon closed the distance between us in an instant, his eyes now blank, his demeanor icy. "You don't understand. We have to talk about you. We know why I was at the Deutsches Haus. But why were you there? Are you following me?"

"No. I had other reasons."

He edged closer. "Name them."

I couldn't have concocted a lie if I'd wanted to. "I was meeting someone. A detective investigating Jens's murder. It's a coincidence you were there at the same time. Like you and Peter Ames turning up together."

Simon's smile had me backing toward the stairs. He lowered his head again, brandishing the nasty scar he'd acquired from Peter, goading me with it. "So I arranged this myself, did I? Good. Keep thinking that. Think whatever will keep you away from me." He retreated a step, clicked his heels together and offered a *heil* Hitler salute before turning to the door.

I scampered to my apartment, defying the instinct to flick on the lights so I could peek out the window. I drew the curtain aside to see Simon climbing into his car. A match flared as he lit a cigarette. He sat smoking under the vivid orange clouds for a moment before his car pulled away. I pressed my head against the glass.

It was still there when a blue Ford rumbled to life and followed him.

LORNA WHITCOMB'S
EYES ON HOLLYWOOD

Early birds at Mines Field report George Burns is
Gotham-bound once more. Expect Gracie's husband
to commute to New York's halls of justice as often as
a Long Island lawyer. We hear Monday will bring
big news out of the Big Apple. Something about the
Chaperau smuggling case, George? . . . All of Culver
City joined in Saturday night's chorus of *Smoke Gets
in Your Eyes* as David O. Selznick incinerated his car-
bon copy of Atlanta. Some residents caught unawares
jumped in their automobiles to flee the flames . . .
Foreign film director Leni Riefenstahl is in town to
preview her latest picture, not parley politics, but the
fetching fräulein's visit has been marred by anti-Hitler
protests. She's even been heckled in the street, she
says. So much for Hollywood hospitality.

27

::::

MY EXPEDITION TO the Deutsches Haus had annexed my sub-
conscious. After a restless night dreaming of storm troopers cho-
reographed by Busby Berkeley, I awoke craving linzer torte. I
sought out Miss Sarah, who benignly tolerated my presence.

The regal feline accompanied me to the ringing telephone.
Edith sounded like she'd been downing coffee since sunup. "Am
I rousing you from slumber?"

"No, the Germans took care of that."

"You can explain that comment over lunch. We discussed the
possibility the other day. Do you have plans?"

"Nothing but mass. Father Nugent works Pat O'Brien into his
homily every Sunday. I'm always curious how he'll do it. When
and where should I meet you?"

"The studio at your convenience. No rest for me, alas."

"Even God rested on Sunday."

"Yes," Edith said, "but I have it on reasonable authority his
tailor still toiled away."

A ROYAL-BLUE DRESS with a shirtwaist top cinched by a belt of
dark pink suede—and a matching pink hat, of course—seemed
appropriate for communing with powers celestial and terrestrial.
After Father Nugent's reading from the Gospel According to
James Cagney, I headed to the studio.

The whole lot seemed mid-doze, my footfalls echoing as I ascended to Edith's office. Still, I heard the susurration of sewing machines, the wardrobe building's ceaseless heartbeat.

Edith greeted me at her door. "I heard you coming. It's impossible to sneak up on anyone around here on Sunday. Are you ready to eat?"

"Always. Is the commissary open?"

"Lunch has been arranged," Edith said.

Together we lugged a picnic basket outside. "My housekeeper Cora packed a lunch," Edith said. "More economical than going to a restaurant. Saves time, too."

"Meaning you can slave away at your desk while you eat."

"If I'm going to come in on a Sunday, I'm going to be efficient about it."

She unpacked our repast while I jockeyed two chairs into the shade. Fried chicken wrapped in waxed paper, creamy potato salad, dark brown homemade bread, and enough oranges for a chamber of commerce advertisement. I thumped the basket on the bottom, but nothing else tumbled out. "No partridge in a pear tree?"

"In the second basket. Cora worries I don't eat enough."

I wondered if the bounty truly was due to Cora's concern, or if I was understudying for a guest who had canceled. Then I saw Edith tackle a piece of fried chicken with gusto. Fearing I'd be left with scraps, I dug in, too.

Around mouthfuls of food, I recapitulated my jaunt to Little Germany and Simon's surprise appearance on my doorstep. "You were right about him," I admitted. "Gene was right. Everybody was right about Simon except me."

"And what exactly did you think, dear? Did you think he was innocent, or interested in you?"

Only Edith could be incisive while inhaling a picnic lunch. "Both, I suppose. Now I know it's neither. Simon has to be involved. He knew Jens and the Auerbachs, he lied about his relationship with Felix, and he's hiding his affiliation with the Bund. I can't understand why Gene won't arrest him."

"There's no evidence, for one thing, and Mrs. Auerbach's confession complicates matters enormously. I imagine Detective Morrow doesn't want to move until he knows why she turned herself in. When he can act, he will, and decisively."

Edith's levelheaded empathy, her innate ability to view situations from every perspective, undoubtedly helped her navigate the treacherous shoals of her job. It could also make talking with her maddening. Because as usual, she was right.

A man with his trilby cocked at a jaunty angle spotted us. "Look at all this food," Billy Wilder marveled. "Are there refugees coming?"

"Tuck in, Billy," Edith said. "You remember Lillian Frost. What brings you to the lot on a Sunday?"

"An aborted script conference was the excuse. The true reason is the couch in my office. I sleep better there than anywhere else, except the theater during DeMille's pictures." He appraised the serving plate and rubbed his stomach through a shabby sweater vest nearing the lint stage of its career.

"Help yourself," Edith encouraged again.

"We can play that word game you were all fired up about in the commissary," I said.

"What fun!" Edith said. "I wouldn't mind a crack at it."

"That game can't be played in the out-of-doors. Entirely too much fresh air. Perhaps after my nap, I could be persuaded otherwise. And a spot of lunch, if you're being so kind." He grabbed a plate and selected a piece of chicken. Then a second. He heaped potato salad between them, which he shielded from scavengers with a slice of bread. "I shall seek you good ladies out later."

"He took the biggest pieces," I said as he strolled off.

"A sure sign he'll become a director. And we ate the big pieces before he got here. We've dealt with the matter of Simon. How are you otherwise? How's work?"

"Addison's talking about scaling back on parties and devoting himself to research. Plus the Santa breakfast debacle reminded me I don't really know how to do my job. It's like I'm constantly auditioning for it."

"That feeling never goes away."

"Charlotte said the same thing. That can't possibly be true for everyone in Hollywood. Even you?"

"It's not just Hollywood." Edith set down her plate, eyes shifting to the surrounding buildings before continuing. "Do you know why they gave me this job?"

"Because you deserved it."

"Because I was the cheapest alternative. By far. The studio pays me a fraction of Travis's salary. And every few weeks they bring in prospective replacements. I'm doing all I can to solidify my position, like dragooning you into helping Marlene. I need everyone I can get on my side."

"You didn't dragoon me—"

"Sometimes I'm tempted to chuck it in," Edith said flatly. "Stop fighting for this job. Call Walter Plunkett, who's designing all those glorious costumes for *Gone with the Wind*, and throw myself on his mercy. 'Let me sketch for you, Walter, anything, just to be part of what you're doing.' Because I'll never get such an opportunity here."

I had no idea what to say, so I did what I usually do in such situations. I tried changing the subject. "Speaking of Selznick, did you see the fire last night?"

Edith's gaze moved to the wardrobe building. "They hate me, you know. The girls. And not just because I'm making them work on Sunday."

"Nobody hates you, Edith."

"Resent me, then."

"It's not that, either. They . . ." I trailed off, marshaling my thoughts. "Did you really forbid the girls from singing and chewing gum?"

"Someone told you that, did they?"

"You won't get a name out of me, copper."

"I had to impose discipline. Travis had let things become entirely too lax. He could get away with that, being a genius."

"That's not how the girls see it. They don't understand how someone who came from their ranks could concoct a rule so—"

"Draconian?" Edith smiled.

"I was going to say silly."

"Point taken. But you've identified my problem. I did come from the ranks. Meaning everyone, from the girls to the executives, views me as a sketch artist who's risen above my station, nothing more. Somehow, I have to make this job my own. And I don't know how to do it."

Had I any advice, I wouldn't have the chance to offer it. Barney Groff dispelled the notion he might have favored more casual attire on the weekend, shrouded in a black suit that likely came gratis with a coffin of his native earth. "At least somebody's working," he said to Edith, once again paying me no mind. "I need to talk to you."

In private went unsaid. I helped Edith pack the picnic basket while Groff batted a newspaper against his hand.

"Might this pertain to the Chaperau matter?" Edith asked.

"Only damn thing I've dealt with for days. To think this all started with some loose-lipped Kraut. All while the goddamn Nazis are blitzing through Europe. Bad enough they already interfere in our operations. That bastard Gyssling insists on weighing in on movies *before* we make them. Can't upset the Germans or they won't approve our pictures. They're not approving them anyway, so who the hell cares what he thinks?"

Groff tossed his newspaper onto the grass, more trash for me to collect. I reached for it. GYSSLING MUM ON RIEFENSTAHL TRIP. The photograph below the headline showed a balding, pudding-faced man in an ill-fitting suit—identified as German consul in Los Angeles Dr. Georg Gyssling—being hustled out of a building by numerous grimly determined men. Not surprisingly given their nationality, every member of this flock of flunkies was blond.

But only one of them I'd seen before.

Peter Ames stood at the edge of the frame, his face angled away from the camera as if aware of its presence—and, by proxy, mine. Peter, whatever his right name, was a Nazi. A servant of the Reich.

I wanted to alert Edith but Groff had already started walking. I handed her the basket, keeping the newspaper. "We'll talk later," she said, and strode after Groff. Leaving me alone in the Sabbath tranquility of the lot with my discovery.

28

❖

THE WELCOME MAT outside Gustav Ruehl's house surprised me. The ill-tempered writer didn't seem the type to put a premium on hospitality. Another surprise was Ruehl's house itself, a charming imitation saltbox more befitting a New England parson.

But the biggest shock was my presence at his home in the first place. I paced outside it, venturing from the door to Addison's car, where Rogers studied me in bafflement. I was uneasy about bearding Ruehl in his den. But I needed to know more about Peter Ames, and Ruehl, with his rabid insistence the German artists of Los Angeles were under observation, was the only person I could think of, despite and perhaps because of his decision to despise me.

I could glimpse Santa Monica Bay from the street, the sight of the *Lumen* steeling my resolve. Malcolm Drewe's gambling ship was the devil on my shoulder I strove to ignore. The corresponding angel apparently had Sundays off.

I hammered on Ruehl's door praying he wasn't at Salka's salon. The esteemed author answered. He'd rolled up the sleeves of yet another black turtleneck, giving the impression I'd intruded on some intense mental labors.

"You!" He stepped onto the welcome mat, obscuring its message, and slammed the door behind him, the resulting gust of air fragrant with pipe tobacco. "Leave here at once."

"I want to ask a simple question, and I won't go until I do. May we talk inside?"

"No." Ruehl folded his pasty white arms. "I do not admit anyone to my home, especially agents of the American government. This is my right, in this land of the free and the home of the brave. I am free to bravely refuse entry to all, including spies and assassins."

"I'm neither, Mr. Ruehl. A young man died and I think someone should be held accountable. One question, two at the most. Can we please talk inside?"

Ruehl seemed more amazed than I was when he flung his door open. I trailed him into a small room stuffed with heavy oak furnishings selected in stubborn opposition to the house's airiness. The aroma of pipe tobacco, with its hints of vanilla, reminded me of my uncle Danny, and for a moment I felt charitable toward Ruehl.

He seized my elbow, bringing those salad seconds to a close. "Do not make yourself comfortable. Ask your question away from prying eyes and go."

"About those prying eyes." I presented the newspaper to him, Peter Ames's face circled in red. "Do you know this man? Behind the German consul Dr. Gyssling?"

Ruehl's eyes went wide, mouth puckering. He looked like a beached fish, stunned to be on dry land with no notion of how to get back. He was frightened. Which meant I was, too.

"He—his name is Kaspar Biel. If you were to ask at the consulate, which I do not recommend, they would tell you he is a, a . . ." Ruehl fumbled for a word in his nonnative tongue. "A secretary, *ja*? But this is a falsehood. Biel is a foot soldier for the Reich without parallel, loyal and cunning."

"He's a Nazi."

Ruehl snorted. "Yes, a Nazi! Born in America but raised in Germany. He returned to attend school. Princeton, I believe, in New Jersey. Then he worked at UFA, the Berlin film studio, for a time. They call him . . . what is your American phrase? 'The bright penny.' He understands both nations, so who better to

watch over Germans who have fled the Reich? He is not someone you want to cross." He peered at me from beneath his massive
eyebrows as if hiding under them. "Have you crossed him?"

"It looks that way."

He smiled cruelly. "I would tell you I'm glad I'm not in your
position, but I am. Biel and his masters have not cared for me for
some time. It's one of the reasons why I am so dedicated to my
work, work which you have interrupted. Now that you have likely
brought me to Biel's attention again, I ask you to go now. *Please.*"
The last word was charged with anguish.

Ruehl banished me to his doorstep, enshrouding me in tobacco one last time. As I walked to Addison's car I spotted a man
in a Buick up the block, ideally positioned to keep vigil on Ruehl's
house and note my departure. Ruehl's fervid fears had been on
the mark. Surveillance seemed a given these days. I had grown
all too accustomed to being watched, and wondered if this was to
be the way of the world from now on.

EDITH, NATURALLY, WAS still at Paramount when I telephoned
with my news and my theory. I needed her to confirm the worst.

"Jens was a Nazi spy, wasn't he?" I asked.

After a long pause, Edith said, "It certainly appears so. It stands
to reason the Nazis would want to monitor the émigré community. The best way to accomplish that would be to have a man
inside that world."

"A regular at Salka's. That photo Rory Dillon took in the
Fathom Club doesn't show Jens meeting his partner in crime.
He's getting his marching orders from Kaspar Biel."

No more would I think of him as "Peter Ames." I'd refer to
him by his right name, one that didn't conjure the trustworthy
visage of Henry Fonda.

"What better location for a clandestine meeting than a club

where Mr. Lohse set up the cameras?" Edith said. "He was gathering information for the Nazis and decided to profit from it himself via blackmail."

"All this time I thought Ruehl's surliness toward me was a persecution complex. Maybe it's something else. What if Ruehl discovered Jens was spying for the Nazis? He already had it in for Jens because of his affair with Marthe Auerbach. Ruehl kills him only to have me turn up looking for him."

And you were alone with him in his cute saltbox house. I shuddered.

"Here's another possibility," Edith said. "Marlene stressed Mr. Lohse's odd behavior. Suppose the strain of his double life, informing on his fellow exiles, made him come apart. The Nazis, say this Kaspar Biel, might then kill him. They'd not only remove a liability, but implicate a prominent Jewish composer in his death."

"That could be why Jens was selling his information to Malcolm Drewe." I was determined to paint a silver lining on this darkest of clouds, to salvage some shred of hope for Jens. "He wanted out from under Kaspar Biel."

"Then the question is why would he, as Mr. Drewe indicated, accept far less for the information than he could have received? Mr. Lohse clearly needed money on short notice for some purpose. But what?"

"And we *still* don't know where Jens's book is."

"Your productive afternoon raises another concern. Didn't Mr. Lohse volunteer for the Hollywood Anti-Nazi League?"

"Yes, Gretchen said he . . . Oh dear Lord. You don't think Jens was spying on them, too?"

"It did occur to me." Edith paused. "I understand they're having a strategy session tonight at the Garden of Allah."

"I may stop by."

"Would you object to company? It's my night off. I'll pass along some advice acquired at the writers' table. Eat beforehand, and a lot. Cocktails will be involved."

29

❖

STRICTLY SPEAKING, WE didn't require a chaperone to gain entry to a Hollywood Anti-Nazi League meeting. I'd learned if you gate-crashed an affair grousing about the service and demanding champagne you'd blend into the wallpaper, while any modestly behaved nonluminary would be viewed askance. Still, given the political nature of the evening, having a friend in place seemed a wise precaution.

"Tonight's session is the kind where they read minutes and things," Charlotte Hume said when I called. "But I could stand to put in an appearance. Shall I meet you there?"

The Garden of Allah being a compound, I wanted to scout the property. I had my taxicab drop me at the corner of Sunset and Crescent Heights, unaware of what a deathtrap that intersection was, particularly once night fell. Vehicles barreled out of the dark, chasing me back to the sidewalk. By my fourth aborted foray I was fighting back tears and searching for a burial plot. *Either I cross Sunset or they lay me to rest on Crescent Heights Boulevard.* At the next lull in traffic, I charged forward. The cacophony of car horns summoned a final burst of speed that propelled me onto the hotel grounds. Heart thundering in my ears, I let the Garden of Allah envelop me.

The hotel began life as a mansion for silent movie queen Alla Nazimova, who christened it after herself in jest. Once she encountered career woes and transformed her estate into a hostelry, the name—now with a gratuitous H she couldn't abide—stuck.

Within a year she went bankrupt, selling out to others who made the hotel a success. The actress still lived on the grounds, suffering a quintessentially Hollywood fate: reduced to paying tenant on her former domain, her name living on after she'd been forgotten.

The hacienda that had been Nazimova's residence fronted on Sunset Boulevard, its windows largely lightless. The action took place in the two dozen bungalows encircling a swimming pool. I moved along a cobblestone path bordered by stucco walls and shrubbery. Ice tinkled in glasses somewhere ahead, music spilled out of a cottage to my right, and from the pool emanated splashing and low laughter of both the male and female variety. The night air was fragrant with sumac, and positively fecund with disreputable possibilities.

A bicycle bore down on me. I braced for impact, but the rider swerved at the last second, an impressive feat given he was steering with one hand. The other held a paper bag that clanked as he came to a halt. He wore a once-white jacket, and his massive blond head resembled the chewed end of one of George Burns's cigars. "Almost made me lose my deliveries," he drawled. "You look a mite turned around."

"I don't know at which bungalow I'm meeting my friend."

"They're villas. Which one did he tell you to go to?"

"He?"

"Come on now, missy." The man extracted a bottle of scotch from the bag. As he twisted the cap off and helped himself to a slug, I realized his grin had been rendered permanently sidelong from sizing up angles. "The friend who told you to meet him. You ain't blond, so that rules out villas four, seven, twelve—"

Footsteps clattered up the path, punctuated by soft feminine cursing. Charlotte, concentrating on her footing, almost collided with a stucco wall. "She's with me, Ben."

"Miz Hume. If you'll excuse me, I'll finish my rounds." Ben sealed the scotch and pedaled off into the gloom.

"His rounds," Charlotte scoffed. "Should be fixing these blasted paths. Murder on a girl in heels. Give me a minute before we face these people, sugar."

The frolicking in the pool had finished for the nonce. I sidestepped a telephone extension cord snaking across the grass toward parts unknown. In her dress of silk crepe with burgundy and white checks topped by a tight-fighting burgundy jacket, Charlotte looked equally ready to demonstrate concern over global affairs or bat eyelashes over highballs. "I hadn't planned on coming tonight," she said. "Donald says it's silly, being in the League. But my career has reached a stage where it's vital for me to have an identity separate from acting—and from Donald, if we're being honest. I want to be my own person, do you know what I mean?"

My stomach clenched with that blue-plate special feeling. Here I was using Charlotte when I knew her husband had strayed—and she didn't.

Charlotte perched on a chaise longue and proceeded to make a meal of a cigarette. "So what's your reason for being here? Anything to do with your recent escapade?"

"Partly," I hedged. "Hearing about what's happening in Germany makes me want to do my bit for the fight. I've been burying my head in the sand long enough."

"Good for you. This outfit could use people with your organizational bent."

More footsteps, then Edith appeared poolside. "Lillian! You darted in front of my car like a deer a moment ago. I honked at you. Didn't you hear me?"

"I misinterpreted it. Edith Head, Charlotte Hume."

Charlotte was on her feet at once. "Lillian speaks of you so often I feel I know you intimately. My hope was we'd meet in your salon, you about to fit me into something divine."

"I look forward to that day. You're blessed with a flair that makes every outfit elegant. Including your prison uniform in *Sisters Up the River.*"

"Bless your heart. Terrible picture. Why do we never see you at Addison's parties?"

"Don't blame me," I said. "I hand deliver the invitations."

"And I'm always flattered. But I can seldom get away from the studio. Tonight's a treat."

"I don't know about a treat," Charlotte said. "You'll come to our holiday cotillion. No excuses accepted. The season is fast upon us, not that you'd know it from the way they skimp on decorations around here."

"You and Donald are throwing a Christmas party?" I asked.

"With Addison laying low, someone must take up the slack. Any interest in planning it with me? I'll sweet talk Addy into letting me borrow you."

"You're not serious."

Charlotte nodded deliberately. Edith spoke up. "It's always a good idea to work with new faces, expand one's horizons. Loan-outs are a common studio practice."

"What's good enough for Paramount is good enough for me. If Addison okay's it, I'd love to."

"Wonderful!" Charlotte said. "I'm useless when it comes to entertaining. If our first coproduction is a success, perhaps we can poach you away and make the arrangement permanent."

"Excuse me?"

"Donald and I have talked about hiring someone to do what you do for Addison. We need you more than he does. We may not host as many parties, but ours are more important because Donald's not retired. He's still looking to land clients at the firm.

And my career is finally taking flight. I have to start making an impression as a gracious hostess. I only know how to fix grits and that ain't exactly gonna wow ol' Louis B. Mayer. I'm just a country girl."

"And I'm shanty Irish."

"So together, we're perfect! We'd make Marion Davies look like a dray mare!"

I was flattered by the offer, and if Addison was serious about shrinking his social calendar I might have to consider it. Plus after the Santa breakfast debacle it was gratifying to learn I could land on my feet. Which only made the burden of knowing all was not well at Casa Hume weigh more heavily.

Charlotte interpreted my unease as hesitation. "Think it over. Now must we see these people? The Trocadero is within walking distance."

"We're here," Edith said. "We might as well go in."

Charlotte snuffed out her cigarette. "I should have eaten first. Always helps to line your stomach in advance."

THE GARDEN OF Allah's management had their cheek. If what Charlotte led us into was a villa, then I was Marie of Roumania. The bungalow was congested with dark furniture and light banter, the latter courtesy of two dozen or so visitors with more tumbling into view whenever a door opened. Charlotte, unperturbed by the scene, waved at a petite woman whose smudge of a face housed impossibly dark, vibrant eyes. The woman weaved her way through the throng to us.

"I doubted we'd see you tonight, Char," she said in a sleepy croak, like a frog awakened from a beautiful dream. "Purely an administrative session."

"Yes, it all looks highly administrative, Dotty. I bring fresh meat. Lillian Frost, Addison Rice's girl Friday. Edith Head, Paramount's queen of costume. Meet Dorothy Parker. The League's chief troublemaker."

"I'm familiar with Miss Head." Dorothy half smiled at me. "If you can find a spare inch amongst the rabble you're more than welcome to it."

When encountering someone new in Hollywood, praise always made the strongest opening gambit—but never of the expected. Declaring I'd read Dorothy's scabrously funny poetry until my copy of *Enough Rope* had fallen apart or gushing over the script she'd cowritten for *A Star Is Born* smacked of the obvious. The trick was to single out some secondary attribute. Clothing was my standard choice but Dorothy, casually clad in tennis shoes and gray knit skirt, didn't provide much to work with. So I improvised. "Chief troublemaker? Was it you who kept Leni Riefenstahl off the premises?"

"Can you imagine her staying here? As a resident I couldn't allow it. Former resident, I should say. Now I visit on a day pass most nights." She spoke louder, addressing the room. "Fraulein Riefenstahl is on this evening's agenda, children! I've heard murmurings about her movie! Tittle-tattle as well!" The room rumbled in response.

Edith removed a bottle from her capacious handbag. "My contribution to the refreshments, Mrs. Parker. Have you ever had Fernet-Branca?"

Across the villa, Gretchen prepared drinks behind a bar. I allowed the crowd to jostle me in her direction. Most of those in attendance fit readily in the three categories of Hollywood scriptwriter: brooder, drunkard, and wisecracker hell-bent on topping his friends' jokes. I overheard a few references to the war in Spain but for the most part the chatter didn't stray from the standard subjects of preview cards and paychecks.

Gretchen had accessorized her blue and white striped shirt-waist with the forbearance of a grieving widow. She smiled wanly

at me. "I had to get out, and Jens and I normally would have volunteered tonight." She hoisted a cocktail shaker. "This is about
all I can do."

I watched her fix a martini and thought, *Dear God, that's too
much vermouth.*

"What did Jens do to help out?" I asked.

"Whatever put him at a typewriter. One keyboard's just like
another, he'd say. He was faster than any secretary including me.
He'd run up volunteer lists, donation records, anything."

All valuable information he could then funnel to Kaspar Biel.
Jens likely wreaked untold damage. A man snagged two marti-
nis from Gretchen with a "Thanks, doll," grimacing as he sipped
one. Edith and a woman I didn't recognize drifted by behind him,
Edith showing me the high sign.

"How's by you? Anything new with Simon?" Gretchen drew
out the first syllable of his name girlishly.

The clamor and constant elbows in my side were getting
to me, because I answered honestly. "There's something fishy
about him."

"You bet. The extra years he has on you."

"No, about him and Jens."

Gretchen slammed the cocktail shaker down, gin geysering
into the air. "What do you mean?"

"He knows more than he's letting on. About Jens, the Auerbachs, everything. I'd look into it, but we didn't part on good
terms." I gazed soberly at her. "Could you ask around Lodestar
about him?"

Gretchen was already nodding. "Absolutely. I'd rather do that
than fix drinks for a bunch of phony crusaders." She snagged her
coat, intent on tackling the task immediately.

I wasn't about to stop her. "Whatever you do, don't try crossing Sunset Boulevard," I called after her.

"Good heavens, you didn't venture across that thoroughfare,

did you?" The male voice bore traces of intoxication and famil-
iarity. Robert Benchley, the humorist recognizable from the hi-
larious special features he made for the pictures, sat in a leather
wing chair seemingly jettisoned in a corner by movers. "That
road's a menace. Come sit by me and recuperate." He hooked a
foot adorned with a pearl-gray spat on an ottoman and drew it
closer to him.

I deserved a rest. I accepted his offer and introduced myself.
Benchley, with cocktail already in hand, picked another off the
floor. "Fortify yourself with this. I keep one in the hopper for that
express purpose. You couldn't be more right about the perils of
Sunset. I've resorted to taking a taxi from one side of that street
to the other, on days when I can face the driver's derision. Still,
it's from such challenges that character is birthed. What brings
you here this evening?"

"A friend."

"Mrs. Parker?"

What the hell. I nodded happily. "And you?"

Benchley held his glass aloft. "Rumor says it's where the liquor is."

"Are you a member of this august organization?"

"I suppose my name's on a piece of paper somewhere. The
Hollywood Anti-Nazi League. Well, I'm most definitely anti-Nazi,
as all right-thinking people are. And I am in Hollywood, though
frequently I'm at a loss to explain why. All of which renders me
eligible for League membership, bearing in mind it's preferable to
be in a league of one's own." He chuckled merrily, and rewarded
himself with a sip of his drink. "The whole outfit's a bit too Red
for my blood, but that's one man's opinion. Not a very bright
man at that."

Dorothy Parker ambled by, and Benchley waved to her. "Your
friend's washed ashore, Mrs. Parker!" Dorothy speared me with
a smile reserved for a woman who'd shown up wearing the same

outfit. I feared Benchley had noted her reaction, but he was gazing contentedly at the window.

"Then there are sunsets that bring no perils at all. I prefer
nighttime because birds rest then. Tell me, Miss Frost, what do
you know of birds?"

Stumped, I said, "They're quite good fried."

Benchley's laughter was entirely disproportionate to my comment. "That they are, quite good fried. I dislike birds intensely
myself."

"Why?"

"Because they have it in for me." He stared at the window even
though all he could see was his reflection. I caught a glimpse of
Edith in the glass. "Our most learned scientific minds say rep-
tiles are descended from dinosaurs, but it's my considered opinion, not that anyone's asked, their true progeny are birds. You
can see it in their eyes, that utter lack of mercy. The term 'bird-
brain' is used to describe someone of low intelligence, yet what
do we know about the workings of the avian mind?" He looked
at me. "Do you think it's possible when we hear, for instance, the
song of a lark, it could be a cry of pain? As if from a migraine?"

"Possibly. Another of your theories?"

"Yes, one that brings me great joy. Speaking of headaches . . ."
He gestured at Ben the bellboy, tramping past carrying several
empty bottles of gin. "Benjamin! I require several of your finest
aspirins from Schwab's."

"Naturally. Main Street all the time around here. You want
'em by the pill or by the bottle?"

"Let's splurge on a bottle. I'm planning a corker of a hangover.
And keep something for yourself. I know you would anyway, but
this time I want in on it."

An apparition manifested across the room: Edith frantically
signaling me, her hands like hummingbirds. I made my excuses
to Benchley and pinballed over to her.

"You must help me find a conversation. I overheard a snippet of it and I—"

A voice rose above the hubbub, the words it uttered finding me like darts.

". . . Nazi spy . . . Dietrich . . ."

The man's voice faded in the din. "Let me guess," I said. "That's the one."

We set off, eavesdropping on people then slipping past them, bulldozing across the bungalow until we heard a promising exchange.

"So Eddie's the spy?"

The nasal tones from earlier held forth again. "No, the spy-buster. He's campaigning for the part."

"Probably a good idea. Get that Red stink off him."

"It'll take more than one role to do that."

A knowing, two-man laugh, then the crowd parted like the Red Sea in Cecil B. DeMille's *The Ten Commandments* to unveil the speakers, brothers in tweed and spectacles, each clinging to a glass and his allotted resentments.

"And the Breen people are letting this happen?" the mustachioed one asked.

"They'll raise holy hell, talk up the 'national feelings' clause. But they can't kick too much. The story's true. It's been in all the papers."

"And they're Nazis, so who gives a damn about 'national feelings'?" Mustache shook his head in wonderment. "Somebody's finally showing some guts, and it's the Warners."

His friend turned to catch us listening. I brazened on as if crossing Sunset again. "You talking about a picture?"

"That's right." Mustache beelined over to me. *Confessions of a Nazi Spy*. About that espionage ring the FBI broke in New York. Warners is whisking it into production with Eddie Robinson."

"And did you say Dietrich?" Edith asked.

"They want her in it," the nasal one said. "Only because she's German. I wouldn't put her in anything at this point."

"Forget her. Box office poison." Mustache edged closer. "I'm Elliot, by the way."

"Hi, Elliot." We'd birddogged the dialogue for nothing.

"I hear Anatole Litvak's directing." Elliot turned to his friend. "Say, he's a member. Is he here tonight?"

I never heard the response. Litvak was a Russian whose principal credit was *Mayerling*, which may or may not have been produced by . . . noted smuggler Albert Chaperau. Known to his friends as Nate. My worlds had collided.

I started to laugh. Edith joined me. In seconds, we were doubled over in hysterics. Elliot dutifully inquired if we were all right.

"Dandy," I said, wiping my eyes. "Have a lovely night."

After another lap of the villa, Edith and I had discovered that no League member had any recollection of Jens Lohse. "It's like he made no impression at all," I said.

"A useful attribute for a spy, I'd imagine. Shall we go?"

Edith stopped to say good-bye to some Paramount colleagues. As I scanned the bungalow for Charlotte, Dorothy Parker placed a hand on my elbow, a slightly soused seraph with an unreadable face.

"Did I hear tell you're leaving? That's a shame. I'd hoped we could find a quiet moment to talk. Would you do me the honor of calling me? Tell me you'll call me, Lillian."

I vowed to do so. Her dark eyes locked on mine. "I will hold you to that."

Fancy that, I thought with glee as she slipped away, Dorothy Parker seeking my company. I stepped aside to permit a few latecomers entry.

"She won't take your call."

I spun around. Charlotte's face was cruel in its blankness.

"What, Dorothy's lying?"

"Oh, no. Right now she wants you to call, desperately. Right now she'd rather be on the phone with you than in this room full of people. Trouble is, when you call she'd rather be at this party. That's the tragedy of our Dotty. Good night, sweetheart."

"*MAYERLING'S* DIRECTOR TAKING on a Nazi spy ring," Edith marveled. "It truly is a small world."

The night air was crisp, carrying the faint undercurrent of decay that passed for winter in Southern California. We hiked through the Garden's unpaved parking lot to Edith's car. I girded my loins. A night drive with Edith packed more thrills than a Republic serial.

"We have much to discuss," she said.

"Really? I thought this trip came a cropper."

"No, this information I learned elsewhere. I only came here tonight to tell you. I didn't feel comfortable repeating it over the telephone or in front of others."

I piled into the car, closing my eyes as Edith reversed out of her parking space. "You'll remember Mr. Groff—Now what's this?"

She stopped short. I cracked an eyelid. A blue Ford had come to a halt behind us, the driver sitting motionless.

The gears of Edith's car squealed as she pulled forward, almost clipping the sedan parked next to us. A brown Ford roared out of the dark and boxed us in. The driver of this vehicle clambered out and glanced down at the dust coating the cuffs of his pants, then walked over to Edith's window.

"I'm going to scream," I screamed.

"Easy, Miss Frost. Miss Head. Let me show you my identification." Agent Elisha Carpenter of the Federal Bureau of Investigation presented his credentials. "Why don't you ladies hitch a ride with us?"

30

✦

AT LUNCHTIME, PERSHING Square would be crowded with sec-
retaries and switchboard operators sunning themselves under the
stubby palm trees. But at night the downtown Los Angeles park's
fountain stood forlorn, the slender men moving in the shadows
more interested in private, not public, spaces.

The Federal Bureau of Investigation's office was a block away
in an uncommonly narrow building, its fire escape tucked discreetly on the side. A trio of bas-relief panels over the entrance
depicted history's march, the eras each figure represented dis-
tinguishable solely by costume. Edith gazed up at it approvingly.
Below, a quote etched in stone: OPPORTUNITY IS MORE POWERFUL
EVEN THAN CONQUERORS AND PROPHETS. BENJAMIN DISRAELI. I'd
have to bear that in mind.

Opportunity had been scarce on the drive from the Garden
of Allah. Once we'd set off Agent Carpenter proceeded to ignore us. Edith and I barely spoke. I used the time to rehearse my
most persuasive case regarding Jens Lohse, the mysterious Simon
Fischer, and the impending Nazi threat in Southern California.

Carpenter hustled us past a shuttered bank sharing the building's lobby. The Bureau's offices upstairs were unusually busy given
the hour, staffed by staunch young men in starched shirts. No
weariness in their voices. Nary a hint of stubble at ten P.M., the
agents undoubtedly shaving in shifts beneath a framed photograph
of John Edgar Hoover. Gene's face occasionally betrayed the
toll of long, frustrating days. These men were a different species

altogether, emissaries from a world where law officers shined their shoes each morning and hung up their jackets at night.

The man whose office Carpenter led us into exemplified the operation's no-nonsense air. Jet-black hair precisely parted, skeptical eyes positioned in his broad face as if with the aid of calipers. Which only made the gap between his front teeth more incongruous, giving him the appearance of an exasperated jack-o'-lantern.

"Miss Frost," he said. "Special Agent Virgil Deems."

His name, I noted, was a sentence. *Virgil deems.* As in, *"the agent judges."* Not that I read anything into that.

"And you would be Mrs. Head of Paramount Pictures' Costume department."

"Miss," Edith corrected.

Deems consulted paperwork on his desk. "Yes. You received a divorce but kept your married name. Interesting." He scribbled an addendum to the file, then concentrated on me. "You've been running us ragged all over greater Los Angeles. We decided after your recent activity the time had come to have a chat."

I nodded, prepared to tell all. Carpenter asked if I wanted a glass of water. I said yes. I had a lot of talking to do.

Deems shuffled papers, a transparently theatrical gesture. Knowing that didn't make it any easier to wait him out. I gulped some water. Edith stirred beside me, poised to come to my aid.

"We picked you up as you were leaving a meeting of the Hollywood Anti-Nazi League for the Defense of Democracy, correct?"

I almost choked in my haste to reply. "Yes."

"Are you aware of the extensive Communist presence in that organization?"

"I know no such thing. It was my first meeting. We were only there to—"

"I'll direct the conversation, Miss Frost." More fussing with papers, Deems making like a spinster piano teacher. When he finally looked up, my eyes were instantly drawn to the gap between his teeth. He pressed his tongue into the space. "You are familiar with one Albert Chaperau?"

I turned to Carpenter, expecting him to be armed with the feather to knock me over. Edith shook her head, every bit as mystified as I was.

Again Deems's tongue tapped the space between his teeth, like a convict testing the bars of his cell. He was going to do it every time he spoke, and I would be powerless to look away. "I asked a question, Miss Frost: Do you know Albert Chaperau? Born Nathan Shapiro, currently under arrest in New York City? We have it on the authority of your employer Addison Rice you were in attendance at a dinner party with him in Manhattan on the night of October twenty-first."

"Yes. I was there. I— Forgive me, but . . . you brought us here to talk about Albert Chaperau?"

"Nathan Shapiro," Carpenter said helpfully.

"Yes, Miss Frost, and so far you haven't told us anything. You do, in fact, know Mr."—a glance at Carpenter, a touch of the tongue—"Shapiro?"

"Yes. But he's not important."

"Is that so? Then why were you at Paramount Pictures in the company of Mrs. Head—sorry, Miss—discussing him with Jack Benny, born Benjamin Kubelsky, and George Burns, aka Nathan Birnbaum?"

"Excuse me," Edith said, "but how did you know that?"

Carpenter answered from behind me. "Their right names were in *Modern Movie*."

"No, how did you know Lillian and I talked to Mr. Benny and Mr. Burns? Did someone at Paramount provide that information? Someone in my department?"

It's a corrupt city, Gene had said. *Everyone spies on everyone else.*

"We're the FBI, Miss Head. And we'll deal with you in due course. Now, Miss Frost. You then followed these conversations with a visit to an organization with known Communist ties."

"I'm sorry, Agent Deems. I'm confused. I thought I was here regarding Jens Lohse."

Deems raised one eyebrow the Bureau-sanctioned height to indicate mild puzzlement. Carpenter stepped in. "Musician found dead up in the hills. Austrian, I think."

Swinging his pumpkin puss back to me, Deems said, "Why would we be concerned with him?"

"Because he's involved with the Nazis! They probably killed him!"

"Did they?" Another look at Carpenter, another note in the file. "Returning to October twenty-first at the home of Justice Lauer—"

"Wait. You're only interested in Albert Chaperau? Then why was the FBI watching Salka Viertel's house and the homes of her guests like Gustav Ruehl?"

"Ah, I understand your confusion. We are indeed aware of the activities at the Viertel residence and monitor them accordingly. But we aren't watching them at present."

"I saw you there! Not you yourself, but other FBI agents."

"That's correct, Miss Frost. But we weren't watching Mrs. Viertel or any of her guests. We were following you. We've been following you for weeks."

"Me? Why?"

Deems sighed. "Because as I've repeatedly stated, you know one Nathan Shapiro, also known as Albert Chaperau. A smuggler whose efforts don't stop with Messrs. Kubelsky and Birnbaum."

"Benny and Burns," I said petulantly.

Deems's voice assumed a tone tailored for a courtroom's acoustics. "We have reason to believe other individuals in the motion picture industry profited from Mr. Shapiro's activities. We further

believe, given your history with Mr. Shapiro, the advantages be-
stowed by your position with Mr. Rice, and your friendship with
Miss Head, you know who these individuals are, and may have
delivered contraband to them."

"Absurd," Edith erupted. "Lillian would never engage in such
behavior. She's the finest young woman—"

"To be conducted personally to an audience with Malcolm
Drewe, a former smuggler who now owns a gambling vessel subject to multiple injunctions? To be involved in an altercation at
a nightclub in unincorporated Los Angeles County?"

"It's all right, Edith." Up went my white flag. The Frosts always know when they're beaten. I told the agents everything I
knew about Albert Chaperau, which was nothing they hadn't already heard. Throughout, Edith held my hand. Deems and
Carpenter tackled my story, which never changed. One of the
benefits of telling the truth, Uncle Danny regularly counseled,
was having less to remember.

Having worn down their resistance, I said, "*Now* can I tell you
what Edith and I have been doing? The reason I've been leading
you on this merry chase?" I laid it all out: Marlene Dietrich's role
as catalyst, my voyage to the *Lumen*, my suspicions of Simon,
Jens's link to Kaspar Biel and the Nazis. Edith corroborated when
necessary.

Agent Deems, I noticed, never wrote one word down.

His tongue grazed his ivories again. "Are you finished?" I nodded. "Good. None of that concerns us."

When I finally found my voice it was at a higher pitch than
usual. "But Jens Lohse was murdered! It's an official homicide investigation."

"Then I suggest you relay this information to your friend Detective Morrow."

"But you're the FBI! Jens was a Nazi spy!"

"So you allege."

I wanted to tear my hair out, but I'd spent too much time on it that morning. "Don't you read the papers? Every day we're closer to war."

"Miss Frost, we know what will be in those papers before they're printed. The United States is some ways off from war. Meanwhile, there are people in this community—your community, Miss Head's community—who think the law doesn't apply to them. People who perform under aliases and fraternize in politically questionable organizations. Those people concern us."

"So you don't care about Jens's death and what it might mean. You're only interested in snaring movie stars for dodging import taxes on jewelry and fancy clothes."

"Lillian, please," Edith said sharply. "Show these gentlemen the proper respect. We may not be privy to all the facts." Her deference shocked me—until I spotted a glint in her eye even her glasses couldn't conceal.

Deems puffed himself up. "Listen to your friend, Miss Frost."

"There are issues here of which we are unaware," Edith said. "You recall Mr. Groff found it unusual the authorities were pursuing a case of noncommercial smuggling. He did some checking at my request."

"Hold the phone," Deems said. "Mr. Groff?"

"Paramount's chief of security. He's likely in your records."

I spelled his name, as Hiram Beecher had taught me.

Edith continued. "I telephoned friends in New York who work for various ateliers and, as such, have their ears to the ground. It was reported Mr. Chaperau returned from Europe in October with twelve pieces of luggage. Nine—fully three-quarters of them—went through Customs without inspection thanks to his so-called diplomatic clearance. The complete contents of that luggage were not in his hotel room."

"Meaning they'd already been distributed in New York." Whatever thread Edith was pulling, I wanted to help.

Carpenter and Deems both made uneasy sounds. Edith blithely spoke over them. "Nine pieces of luggage of undetermined size—trunks, for all we know—containing undisclosed amounts of undeclared couture gowns and jewelry. My friends say all of New York society is on the qui vive, waiting for the other hand-stitched shoe to drop. More than a few significant people are living in abject terror of being exposed as a result of Mrs. Lauer's indiscretion."

Deems rapped his desk. "They broke the law."

"Undeniably true. But to whom are New York society people likely to be connected?"

"Oh my God," I yelped. "President Roosevelt."

"Formerly Governor Roosevelt of New York. It wouldn't do for some of the president's wealthiest supporters to be seen flouting the law in order to save a few dollars, particularly with the European situation so grave. But Mr. Groff confirmed that's what will happen if the focus of the Chaperau investigation remains in New York."

"Now see here," Deems blustered.

Edith remained unruffled. "My thought is . . . suppose the FBI's Mr. Hoover took it upon himself to spare the president a scandal."

"Why would he do that?" Carpenter tugged his shirt collar.

"The world runs on favors," I replied. I understood now what Edith was doing. She wasn't speculating. She was recounting facts, direct from backlot Borgia Barney Groff. Facts she'd planned to impart on our drive home. Facts she was now using to shame the FBI.

"He could accomplish this," she went on, "by shifting the investigation's focus to Hollywood."

"Sure," I said. "Paint Chaperau as an unscrupulous film producer. Demonstrate his accomplices aren't greedy New York society types but uppity Los Angeles show people. All of whom also happen to be Jewish."

"Hey," Carpenter growled, leaning menacingly into my eyeline. Deems's tongue pounded like a piston against his teeth. I didn't care. It was as if the men had vanished and Edith and I were chatting in her kitchen, bottle of Fernet between us.

"How does this hand play out?" I asked. "In theory."

"In theory, the federal government offers Mr. Chaperau a deal. He pleads guilty. In return, the FBI stops blackening his name. Mr. Chaperau then serves a minimal sentence, and the president avoids embarrassment. Similar deals are tendered to Mr. Burns and Mr. Benny, the terms strongly endorsed by their attorney Mr. Donovan. Who, as it happens, is known to President Roosevelt. If they admit wrongdoing and pay their fines, they won't face prison and their cases will be handled with a minimum of fuss. Everyone saves face."

The ensuing silence was like a fifth presence in the office. Deems shifted some papers so he could neaten them.

"Paramount wouldn't film a scenario so full of holes," he said. "Although it sounds like justice would be done."

I had met scores of influential people while working for Addison, but this was my first intimate glimpse at power being wielded behind the scenes, and it made me feel unwell.

"So in order to keep from exposing a few Park Avenue swells as tightwads and making our commander in chief look guilty by association," I said slowly, "the FBI is willing to let Jens Lohse's killer roam free. Even if he's a Nazi."

"Miss Frost," Deems began, his voice wintry.

Again Edith rushed to my aid. "It's a matter of priorities, Lillian. But priorities change. These men are responsible for the Albert

Chaperau investigation, no matter what motivated it. Once that's settled, I'm sure they'll turn their attention to matters of true import."

Deems didn't quite shrug, didn't quite nod. It was the best we could hope for.

Edith had deftly called out the FBI men as errand boys while sending me a message. *Hold your tongue. Let's just get out of here.*

So I swallowed my anger at their apathy, at the manpower squandered on following me. And I smiled. And I asked if there was anything else.

"Not at present," Carpenter said. "We'll be in touch."

"Could someone give us a ride back to my car?" Edith asked.

Deems shook his head. "Given the circumstances, Mr. Hoover would frown on that."

I couldn't help myself. "This is why I prefer getting hauled in by the Los Angeles Police Department. They always see a lady home."

31

❖

"LILLIAN!" ADDISON'S VOICE boomed across the lobby as I closed his front door. "What do you think of the Perisphere?"

"I think it's the salt of the earth. Why it spends so much time with that snooty Trylon is beyond me. Once the World's Fair opens next year watch the Trylon drop poor old Perisphere for Robert Montgomery."

"I mean as a costume for Marion Davies's New Year's Eve party." Addison placed his hands over his considerable stomach as if to prevent it from overhearing. "I wouldn't need much padding. And Maude could go as the Trylon. That'd be mostly headdress, and she loves an excuse to stand in one place at these things. They haven't been officially unveiled yet, but they're already iconic."

"I think it's a swell idea. I doubt anyone's gone to a party as a Flushing landmark before."

"Are there other Flushing landmarks?"

"The park bench at Kissena Lake where Jimmy O'Shaugnessy kissed me. Although some historians call the event apocryphal, among them Jimmy O'Shaugnessy. Will we be joined by Mr. Hume?"

"He's on his way. I telephoned him right after you called this morning, per your suggestion."

Addison accompanied me to my desk, holding forth on the myriad wonders slated for exhibition in my birthplace at the World's Fair in April. As I hung up my coat, a deliveryman presented himself. He held a gold box large enough to require the use of both arms, tied with gilt-edged crimson ribbon.

"Miss Frost? The butler said to bring this to you."

"That's for *me*?"

"If you're Lillian Frost." He accepted a gratuity and left in the vain hope of retracing his steps to the front door.

"Don't see a card." Addison chuckled. "Any guesses who it might be from?"

"If it's not you, then I'm fresh out of ideas." Gene, I knew, wasn't given to surprises or extravagance. The notion of Simon fluttered into mind, and I shooed it away.

One tug loosened the bow. Off came the lid. A profusion of multicolored tissue paper burst from the box. Like Howard Carter at Tutankhamun's tomb, I started to dig. And dig. And dig. Shreds of every shade tumbled to the floor. Even Addison pitched in, unable to resist the fun.

I struck plain brown cardboard and suspected an elaborate prank. Addison sifted through tissue paper as I overturned the box. I heard an object hit the floor. A small one.

A matchbook. With the image of a ship on it.

The S.S. *Lumen*. For a voyage of fun!

A friendly reminder from Malcolm Drewe that he continued to have me on his mind, awaiting word on the whereabouts of the information he'd purchased from Jens. I cast a glance over my shoulder at Addison's sun-dappled yard, unsettled by the sense my life had become a movie watched by a constantly expanding audience—Drewe and his cronies, Deems and the FBI, Kaspar Biel and who knew how many other Nazis. Worse, I had no idea when or even if I was ever off camera.

"What is it?" Addison asked of the matchbook.

"A joke. Not a very funny one."

Donald Hume cruised into view, his eyes widening at the sight of the box on my desk. "Christmas came early! And I didn't bring you two anything."

I picked up the telephone. "We should get started, gentlemen. I'll arrange for coffee. By the time I'm finished, you may want something stronger."

"HOW I DEARLY wish," Addison said, swilling a midday high-ball, "I'd never heard the name Albert Chaperau."

"Amen, brother." Donald paced the floor. "All this time counseling you to check your cards and your dealer, and it turns out the whole house is rigged." He looked at me in wonderment. "Groff really believes this is about protecting Roosevelt?"

"He swears it."

"It does play." Donald pointed at Addison. "You were at the dinner with Chaperau, and everyone in town attends your parties. The FBI likely figured you could have provided even bigger names than Burns and Benny."

Addison nodded. "And given your recent running around on Marlene's behalf, Lillian, I can see how they'd view your behavior as suspect."

"Me, a conduit for contraband? I can only pray this is over."

"If Groff's right, it is," Donald said. "No one benefits the longer this drags out. The government convinces Chaperau, Benny, and Burns to plead guilty, and this goes away in a single flash of bad publicity. Everyone contrite, chalk it up as a misunderstanding."

"And hope the public forgives Benny and Burns for their mistake." Even I heard the doubt in my words.

"On that, we wish them luck. But it doesn't affect us." Donald clapped his hands and rubbed them together. "You're in the clear, Addy, old boy. Uncle Sam has moved along, and so should we.

On to new business. Namely, your crop of freshly minted patent applications."

A line clearly indicating *Exit Miss Frost*. I returned to my desk and a ringing telephone. Another delivery from Malcolm Drewe, maybe? Perhaps this prompt a used coaster from the *Lumen* wrapped in ermine and left in a brand-new Duesenberg. I picked up the receiver.

"Lillian? It's Gretchen Corday. I've been calling all morning." Her voice sounded oddly hollow. "I was thinking about what you said last night at the Garden of Allah."

That conversation from a thousand years ago, before I'd been scooped up by federal agents and discovered I was a pawn in a game being played on behalf of the resident of 1600 Pennsylvania Avenue. "Right. What part of what I said, exactly?"

Gretchen's voice dropped to a whisper. "Simon Fischer being involved in Jens's death."

"I didn't say that. I suggested he knows more than he's letting on."

Steel entered her hushed tones. "I did some digging at Lodestar today. Before he took you to the Auerbachs' cabin and you . . . found Jens, the last time Simon had driven out there was August twenty-sixth."

"I know. That's what he told the police, and the studio confirmed it."

"Only he's lying. I can prove it. Do you have any idea how many records a studio keeps? And how easy it is to get the *right* ones when you say you're trying to clear up a discrepancy that will cost someone their job?"

I squeezed the phone so hard it creaked in my hand. "Gretchen, what did you do?"

Her voice assumed the dangerously serene quality of someone staring at the ocean in the moments before their final walk into it. "The records the front office showed the police say Simon didn't drive to the cabin for months. But the ones buried in the motor pool that I looked at this morning? Those say Simon Fischer drove Jens to Felix's cabin on the morning of December first. That's the day the police think he died, isn't it?"

"Yes, it is. Can you—"

"I saw him, you know. Simon. He returned a car while they pulled the records. He smiled and looked right through me." She paused. "I'm going to talk to him."

"No. Gretchen, please—"

"I'll find him and tell him I know what he did."

"Don't do that. You'll tip him off. Let me call my friend with the police and he can arrest Simon."

"He'll only lie again. He'll lie about killing Jens."

"Not now. We have proof, thanks to you. Don't go near him, Gretchen. Let me call the police, okay? Gretchen? *Gretchen?*"

She didn't answer.

"KEEP CALM, LILLIAN." If Gene's voice at the other end of the line were any indication, he could stand to heed his own advice. "Take a breath and talk me through this. What you're suggesting is that not only Fischer lied. So did Lodestar."

"Yes, but at least their lie makes sense. They acted out of instinct to protect their interests. They didn't lie to help Simon. They did it to minimize their involvement and Felix Auerbach's."

"They wanted it to look like Auerbach, their employee, didn't know Jens was going to be at his cabin."

"And to do that, they had to conceal that Simon drove him there."

"He could just be sticking to a story the studio gave him," Gene said. "Trying to hang on to his job."

That's not why he lied to me, I thought.

"Then ask him. You can prove he's lying, ask him why he did

it. But please, do it now before Gretchen spills the beans. You've got to. I told you, the FBI won't. They don't care."

"Don't worry, Lillian. I'm putting my coat on now. I'll pull the motor pool records and bring Fischer in for questioning. And I don't need the FBI's permission to do it."

32

MY UNCLE DANNY had a soft spot for what he called "weepers," soapy ballads that jerked tears the way a frontier dentist pulled teeth: with minimal regard for artistry. At any gathering Danny would belt out one sad song after another, a dry spark of mirth in his eye as every other orb in earshot misted over. His repertoire covered fallen women, ghostly children, lovers parted by death. The title of one of his perennials, "A Bird in a Gilded Cage," echoed in my head as I walked the floors of Addison's magnificent house. I may not have been sporting fancy plumage but I felt trapped in a luxurious prison, and only word from Gene would set me free.

Addison, detecting my unease, invited me to join him for lunch. I declined, which set off his alarm bells; I never passed up food. Upon hearing my dilemma, he had a telephone extension run to the table. "Just like the Brown Derby," he said with a smile. The phone didn't ring, meaning I scarcely tasted the poached salmon with creamy dill sauce or my two helpings of apple brown betty. After lunch Addison repaired to his workshop, leaving me to my lonely vigil.

I checked the radio for news, dreading reports of gunplay at Lodestar, Simon reacting like a mad dog when confronted by Gene. I pounced whenever the phone rang, dealing with the merchants on the other end brusquely, vowing I'd add a bonus to their holiday gift to make up for it. As the afternoon wore on it grew more difficult for me to hoist my hopes with each call. By three o'clock, when I recited "Rice residence, Miss Frost speaking" for the umpteenth time, I had gone numb.

"Lillian, it's Gene."

I nearly wept. "Where are you?"

"Edith's office at Paramount. Can you come here? Right now?" He didn't sound like himself. He sounded empty. Beaten.

"Of course. Is everything all right?"

He laughed, forgetting to include any amusement in it. "Ducky. I don't understand anything anymore."

ROGERS DROVE ME to Paramount in his customary silence. But I thought I spotted something like concern in the look he threw at the rearview mirror as I bolted from the car.

Edith sketched at her desk, her gay crimson scarf at odds with the funereal mood of her office. Gene sat across from her, hat in hand, feet splayed as if bearing up under a great weight. His toothache smile grieved me.

Barney Groff commanded the room, accusatory finger already stabbing in my direction. "About damned time you got here. First you're no help on the Chaperau business. Now you're screwing up something even more important."

"Go easy on her, will ya?" Gene said in a voice from the bottom of the sea.

"She has a great deal to learn," Edith said. "We all do."

Edith's telephone rang. Groff answered it. "Now? Have him wait." He slammed the receiver down so hard the bell echoed. Edith winced.

Groff loomed over me. "You know how the Nazis gained power in Germany?"

Experience had taught me even if I knew the answer to a Barney Groff question, he didn't want me to say it. The point of the exchange was for me to admit my hopeless ignorance. I got on with it.

"No."

"Disaffected veterans. Soldiers from the Great War who chafed at the way the country was treated after Versailles. That was this bastard Hitler's first audience, the muscle that allowed him to take over. He tried the same routine over here, but it hasn't succeeded. You know why?"

"Because we won the Great War?" I said meekly.

Groff glowered a moment before continuing. "Because the right man heard about it. I'm not telling you his name. You don't need to know his name. It's enough to know he's a lawyer, a veteran himself, a true American patriot. And a Jew. Worked for the Anti-Defamation League. He found out veterans were being recruited into the Friends of the New Germany, the group that came before the goddamned Bund, and you know what he did?"

Groff didn't want input from me anymore. He was on a roll.

"He told them to join. To remember everything they heard and report back to him. Even paid their expenses, out of his own pocket." A shake of the head in amazement, Groff relishing the story. "Who else would do that, would have the foresight and the commitment necessary? The things he learned about what the Nazis were doing, were planning to do, terrified him. This tough, clear-eyed man, this *American* knew this was big, knew he needed money and support. First he turned to the B'nai B'rith, but they couldn't get their act together. Then he tried the establishment Jews, the downtown crowd. Businessmen, lawyers, real estate people. Respectable types." He charged both words with withering contempt. "They wrung their hands, said how terrible it was, how they had to do something. And between them they couldn't scrape up a lousy thousand dollars."

Gene pushed out a breath and sat back, having heard the song before.

"So what did our man do? He made the stop of last resort. A move of pure desperation." Groff stabbed his finger into his own chest hard enough to bruise. "He came to us. The show business Jews. The pants pressers from back east. Making too much noise and too much money in a low-rent business. But we knew what was going on in Germany from our dealings there. We were *awake*."

He framed the scene between his hands, directing now. "In 1934, he arranged a meeting at the Hillcrest Country Club. The club Jews built, because none of the existing places in town cared for our kind. Everyone was there. Mayer, Thalberg, Selznick. Our own Manny Cohen. Even Lubitsch. And me. We heard what this man learned from veterans brave enough to cozy up to the Krauts. We understood the threat. And we alone stepped up to foot the bill. The men who run the studios spent tens of thousands of dollars on—"

"A spy ring," Gene said.

"A fact-finding operation." Groff wielded the phrase with the precision of a scalpel. "One that unearthed the truth about the Nazi connection to the Bund years ago. I've never been prouder of anything this town has done. Even the downtown Jews are kicking in their fair share now, because of what we've learned." He turned the full force of his righteous fury on me. "And you almost brought it all crashing down."

"Mr. Groff, please," Edith said. "Lillian still doesn't know what you mean."

But I did know. Only one explanation was possible, even if I couldn't force my mind to accept it.

Groff stood his ground. "Because of Dietrich and this goddamned Lohse business—some two-bit composer nobody wanted to hire, for Christ's sake—our efforts are at risk. Because you had to sic your pet cop on our top man."

He walked over to the door. Wrenched it open. Gestured into the outer office with exasperation. *C'mon, you missed your cue.*

Simon Fischer strolled in. A look of apology on his face.

HE NODDED AT Gene and Groff. Bowed to Edith. Turned to me with an expression saying *I can explain.*

"So you're him." Groff eyeballed Simon with vague disappointment, the star attraction not living up to his billing. Likely he'd expected a raffish sort with William Powell's panache, not a slim fellow with a scarred face and a detached disposition. Groff had heard of Simon's exploits but had never clapped eyes on him before, while Gene and I had been dealing with him for days without understanding who he was. To Edith, he'd merely been a name. Simon was a mystery man to us all, but in different ways.

"Then you're a . . ." I couldn't say "spy," knowing the word would provoke Groff's wrath. "You're not really in the Bund?"

"No. As I said, I don't care for the food." A smile played beneath Simon's features without quite surfacing.

"He's *our* man, Miss Frost," Groff said. "The first line of defense against Nazi agitators. And you damn near had him arrested."

"How was I supposed to know?"

"Quit sweating her. She did nothing wrong. We're letting the cat out of the bag to a few more people, that's all." Simon directed his words at me. Groff might as well have been at the other end of a telephone line. In, say, Scranton.

"I for one would like to hear more about your efforts," Edith said to Simon.

"The group I presume Barney told you about came to me. Said I fit the bill for what the Nazis are looking for, a veteran at a loose end in life. Which is a nice way of saying I didn't have a job. They put me on at Lodestar. Sure enough, a few weeks later a couple of grips mentioned the Bund meetings. Told me I'd hear some things I agreed with. What I heard I passed along."

"To whom?" Gene asked.

Simon pointed at Groff. "Ask the poo-bah."

"Your department," Groff snapped. "The district attorney. People in Washington. Fat lot of good it did us."

"Why?"

"Because it came from Jews." None of the disdain in Groff's eyes sounded in his voice. "Nobody in a position of authority cared. They said, 'Consider the source.' Plenty of solid citizens think Hitler's got it figured right. Remember when the Dies Committee people were here back in August? Investigating 'Un-American activities'? We played ball with them. Opened our books, offered to have our people testify. But Congressman Dies wanted no part of it. To him, 'Un-American activities' means communism, and communist means Jewish. You think he wanted a bunch of Jews, in show business at that, telling him to stop waiting for the Reds to holler 'Boo!' and concentrate on the Nazis instead? He doesn't want to hear the Bund is working hand in black leather glove with the Reich, delivering money to Nazi agents and bringing in propaganda."

"I hate to sink your U-boat," Simon said, "but the Bund isn't the danger you're making it out to be. Most Germans in the U.S. won't give those clowns the time of day. And the ones who are in the Bund mainly like sitting around talking about how much better it is in the Fatherland. Those meetings are like listening to ex–New Yorkers say how much they miss the Dodgers and Giants."

"They plan kidnappings." Groff's finger jabbed the top of Edith's desk. "They talk about murdering studio executives."

"So do writers on every lot in town. They're a bunch of second-generation burghers marching in circles and shooting off guns in the hills. When the Bund does kill somebody, it'll be with food poisoning at one of those goddamn Oktoberfest dinners."

Groff shook his head as Simon spoke, bridling at being contradicted. On his own lot, yet. "You don't assess information, Fischer. You collect it."

"I was also told to collect it from an actual Nazi spy."

"You mean Jens Lohse," I said.

Simon's eyes met mine. "Yes."

Gene cleared his throat. "How'd you know he was a spy?"

"Unlike the blowhards at the Bund, he acted like one. I was taking him to Felix Auerbach's apartment, and I knew from the questions he asked about Felix what he was after. I arranged to become Felix's semiofficial driver. I also started watching Jens and building a dossier."

"All on his own," Groff interjected. "No supervision from us."

"Once I confirmed my suspicions, I sent word along. You may recall, Barn, I received a commendation for my initiative."

"Yeah," Groff said. "That medal come in the mail yet?"

Gene positioned himself between the two, prepared to hose them off if need be. To Simon, he said, "Then in your estimation, Jens Lohse was a Nazi spy."

"Yes, but small potatoes. He wasn't in a position to acquire military intelligence or tell you what was rolling off assembly lines at Lockheed. He was a piano player."

"But he was spying on the émigré community," I said. "He had access to the records of the Hollywood Anti-Nazi League."

"True." Simon took pains to sand the harsh edge off his voice when he addressed me. "And Hitler and his cronies are vain enough to want to know what the émigrés are saying about them. But a sewing circle of composers and intellectual novelists isn't causing the Führer to lose sleep. And you hardly need an inside man in the Anti-Nazi League when their every move is reported in *Daily Variety*. Jens's true value was as a go-between. He was always in people's homes, entertaining at various clubs. That afforded him plenty of opportunities to meet with high-level Nazi assets who can't risk being seen with the likes of Kaspar Biel. That was my interest in Jens—who did he meet *after* his regular rendezvous with Biel at Club Fathom?"

"You knew all along who 'Peter Ames' was," I said. "That's why Rory Dillon recognized you. You'd been following Jens."

"For months. What I didn't know was who you were, why you were interested in Jens, and why Biel was interested in you."

A silence followed. Edith filled it. "You'd tied Mr. Lohse conclusively to the Nazis. Surely you passed that information along to your organization."

"And we told the FBI." Groff's smile made me wonder if vultures grinned when they spotted a vulnerable animal below. "They were unmoved."

"You're telling it to the LAPD now." Gene ignored Groff's snicker. "You drove Lohse to the cabin the day he was killed."

"Yes. He said Felix had moved their lesson there."

"Did you see Felix?"

"No. Not him, not his wife, not a car."

I couldn't contain myself. "Did Jens have his music book?"

Simon nodded. "I never saw him without it."

"You lied when I asked about this," Gene said.

"My hands were tied."

"Blame us if you must," Groff said. "We didn't want Fischer compromised, and Lodestar was already in hot water because the kid was found at Auerbach's house."

"This fact-finding outfit of yours. Is it investigating Nazis or covering your asses?"

Groff spread his arms, taking in all of creation. "What can I tell ya? Sometimes the twain meets. Point is, we knew Fischer was a dead end, so we saved you some time."

Gene clenched his jaw before turning again to Simon. "You're familiar with all the players. Who killed Lohse?"

"Best guess? You have her in custody."

"It's *Marthe*?" I gasped.

"I'd love to pin it on Biel. Marlene Dietrich had it right, Miss Head. Jens was falling apart. The pressure of spying on his friends had gotten to him. If I could see it, so could Biel. Jens was at the end of his usefulness to the Nazis. They could have killed Jens at the cabin knowing the Auerbachs would take the blame. But Felix's absence is impossible to ignore. Whatever happened up there comes down to the three of them and intense jealousy. And only Marthe can tell the tale."

Gene pinched the bridge of his nose. "Which she has so far refused to do, aside from admitting her guilt."

"A-1 job you boys in blue are doing." Groff chortled. "To date all this *mishegas* has done is jeopardize the one serious effort to combat the Nazi influence in Los Angeles. On the word of an actress who couldn't buy a hit. I swear to you, Dietrich will never work in this town again."

33

BARNEY GROFF APPROPRIATED Edith's office for some final words with Gene and Simon. She and I adjourned to her salon. The waiting racks of Dorothy Lamour gowns visibly calmed her. They did wonders for my constitution as well.

"We gave Mr. Groff an early gift. He hated having to bottle up that story. I daresay recounting it made his holidays." Edith peered as if she could see around me into her office. With those glasses, anything was possible. "So that's Simon."

You didn't need my years in Catholic school to hear the judgment freighting her voice. "You don't care for him."

"On the contrary, I find him impressive. Likely the ideal man for the vital task he's undertaken. But we heard about the toll such a life had on Mr. Lohse. I can't conceive how difficult it must be for him."

Neither could I.

Groff summoned Edith back to her office, dismissing the rest of us. Simon approached me, Gene sticking so close I thought they were handcuffed together.

"You'll want your usual ride home," Gene said.

Simon cleared his throat. "I'm happy to drive Lillian. We haven't had a chance to speak since she learned the sordid truth about me."

I questioned why Simon made his case to Gene, seeking his permission and not mine. Gene stepped back, leaving the decision to me.

"I should hear him out," I told Gene.

"As you wish." He turned toward Simon. "I don't envy you your work, Fischer."

They shook hands, and with a nod to me Gene headed out. Simon extended his elbow. I thought I saw a glimmer of disapproval in Edith's eyes as I took his arm.

Or maybe it was light reflecting off her glasses.

WE SAT ON a secluded bench on the Paramount lot. I gazed up at the pepper trees, thinking they might be the same ones that loomed over George Burns when Customs agents braced him.

"I'm sorry for deceiving you," Simon said.

"You had no choice. It's your job. It must be lonely."

"Actually, it's the opposite. Always somebody to see, another stein to hoist. These Bund members are eager to talk. It's why I find it hard to take them seriously." He cracked a half smile. "Anyway, I don't have to lie anymore. I can be honest with you, which for me is a great luxury. I like you, Lillian."

I resumed my survey of the pepper trees, unable to look at him. "You do?"

"I told you before. You're not under any illusions, unlike every other woman in Los Angeles. You see through these people. You're grounded while everyone else's head is in the clouds."

If he intended his forthrightness to be flattering, he was in for a rude shock. "I see through these people? That sounds like you don't care for anyone who works in pictures."

"I don't, generally. They're unserious. They dabble in politics, they judge everything by appearances, they prize their careers above all else."

"And I like show people, so I guess I'm unserious, too." I shook my head as if that would restore order. Simon's romantic interest had been playacting, a fabrication necessary for his mission. Quandary avoided. I should have been relieved.

So why, now that I knew Simon played for our side, did I feel put out?

"Can we talk about Jens?"

That warranted a full smile from him. "This is what I'm talking about. Always on the job."

"You genuinely think Marthe killed him?"

"Unless Felix miraculously returns to tell me otherwise. I'd give anything to find him."

"Too bad Felix's best friend won't talk to us."

"Who, Gustav Ruehl?"

"He's taken an intense dislike to me."

"I don't see how that's possible." Simon paused. "He may not deal with you, but I might have a chance with him."

"I doubt it. Ruehl's suspicious of everyone. Right now he's locked in his house puffing on his pipe, waiting for the Nazis or the FBI to beat his door down."

"His pipe?"

"I smelled the tobacco when I was there yesterday. It was a lot like my uncle Danny's brand, has a vanilla scent."

Simon nodded, his eyes on his hands as if watching to see what they'd do. "I did some research on Ruehl when I learned he and Felix were close. You'd never think it to look at him, but he's one of those German health fanatics. Eats nothing but vegetables, embraces physical culture. He doesn't smoke a pipe."

A chill ran through me. "And Felix?"

"He'd light up in the car whenever I drove him home. Lovely tobacco. Hint of vanilla."

"You don't think . . . we have to tell Gene."

"Not yet. If Felix is hiding with Ruehl, it's because he's afraid of the police. But he knows me. I can convince him to turn himself in." He took my hand. "Come with me."

I waited for the rational side of my brain to weigh in, to counsel patience, to mention Gene again. But that voice didn't speak up. Instead, the impulsive one took the floor.

"Where's your car?" I asked.

I POUNDED ON Gustav Ruehl's door with a confidence borne of having a man who'd killed while wearing the uniform of his country behind me. No telltale waft of tobacco greeted me when the saturnine scribe jerked his door open. He proceeded to upbraid me in German, his eyebrows ready to shoot their quills. When he halted mid-rant, I knew Simon had emerged from the shadows.

"Afternoon, Mr. Ruehl. Name's Simon Fischer. I'm a friend of Felix Auerbach's. If you'd tell him I'd like to say hello?"

Ruehl's eyes scanned the street in panic. No one was paying us any mind. "What do you—I don't understand."

Simon stepped around me, his frame filling the doorway. He spoke as if he were on stage, projecting his voice to an unseen audience. "He'll know me. We listened to the second Louis–Schmeling fight together. Not that it was much of a bout. Felix felt terrible for Schmeling. Not because he lost in one round, but because Schmeling was no Nazi puppet and had to go back to Germany in defeat. Tell Felix. We'll wait."

"Why do you say this? There is no one here. I am alone." Ruehl threw up his hands and looked at me incredulously, expecting my support.

At first I thought I imagined the muted whiff of vanilla. Then Ruehl stopped agitating and lowered his arms in surrender. Muttering in German, he beckoned us inside. On my previous visit, I'd attributed the house's gloom to a decorating sense that reflected the novelist's outlook on life. Now I understood every curtain was closed to prevent anyone from seeing his guest.

I heard a door at the end of a corridor creak, followed by foot-steps. I recognized Felix Auerbach from the photograph of him and Marthe at their cabin. His skin looked sallow, his bald head more fragile and egglike. As he shook Simon's hand, he sucked on his briar pipe like he drew his very breath from it. "Another friendly face at last," he said in a pronounced but navigable Ger-man accent. "Someone had to find me. I'm glad it was you."

Simon introduced me. Felix executed a sharp bow from the waist. "The woman who discovered poor Jens, and to whom my wife surrendered herself. An overdue honor."

GUSTAV RUEHL'S BACK garden made an unlikely confessional. Gardenia shrubs surrounded us, scenting the air. When the flow-ers were buds they resembled seashells, containing secrets. In bloom, they revealed themselves in a fleshy display that would raise hackles at the Breen Office.

Scratch that. The garden served as an ideal confessional.

"Funny, I never cared for this weather." Felix smiled at the sun as he spoke. "But when you're trapped inside all day, hiding when the police come to ask questions, you crave warmth and light. Marthe took to it at once. Now she is denied it, too. You have seen her? She is well?"

"My friend with the police is taking care of her," I said.

Felix nodded sadly. "I knew she was having an affair with Jens, but I said nothing. I couldn't blame her. She is younger than me, living in a foreign land. And my own ego was a factor. I valued being seen as a teacher again. Some days I was certain Jens con-tinued our lessons only to be near Marthe, but other times his work would improve and I would think . . . I would think I was truly educating him."

He stared at the wrought-iron legs of Ruehl's patio table. "Then came the day I made an impulsive trip to our cabin to work. I arrived to find my prized pupil lying dead on the floor. In my shock I made what seemed a logical assumption, that Marthe had killed Jens and fled."

"You saw no one else near the cabin?" Simon asked.

"No. After the fires the area had been largely quiet." Felix took a sip of water. "My only instinct was to protect her. I dragged Jens to the balcony and heaved him over the side, hoping his death would be seen as a suicide, and then I cleaned the cabin." Without thinking he crudely pantomimed disposing of Jens's body, his gestures making me flinch. "That's when Marthe came in, expecting Jens. She was, to say the least, surprised to see me. I, in turn, was surprised she said nothing about my discovery. So after brooding for a time, I took her away."

I spoke up. "How did you get her to go with you? What did you say?"

Felix swept a hand over his scalp, smoothing the memory of his hair. "I told her, 'I know what you've done. Come. We must leave.' She thought I meant the affair, because she had no idea Jens was dead. But she is a good wife, my Marthe, and did as she was told. We drove through the night to a place in the desert I like. Secluded, good for work. And there we sat, in silent recrimination. Marthe believing I was in a rage over her infidelity, me convinced she had murdered her lover."

"How long did this . . . confusion last?" I asked.

"It shames me to say almost thirty-six hours. I started fumbling toward a reconciliation. I said Jens was dead and Marthe made a logical assumption of her own, that I had killed him in jealousy. So more time passed with us both in the dark. Finally, we came to understand the truth. Someone else had murdered Jens in our home. And in trying to shield my wife from harm, I had unwittingly helped conceal the crime."

After a moment, Simon prompted, "What did you next?"

"We drove back and consulted our dear friend." He waved at

Ruehl, who impassively accepted the tribute like a stone bust of himself. "Gustav said Jens had not been mentioned in the newspapers, meaning it was possible no one yet knew he was dead. At that point, we hatched a scheme. We would return to the desert, only this time we would not stay in secret. We would take pains to be seen, we would talk about the weather for the past week, we would . . ." He turned to Ruehl. "How did you put it?"

"Make a big noise. I read it in *Black Mask* magazine. One of the only publications to tell the truth of the proletariat in this country."

"Yes, yes. We would then go to the cabin and find Jens ourselves, telling the authorities we had been on holiday."

Ruehl rapped a knobby knuckle on the table in front of me. "But our plan was ruined when first you arrived at Salka's house searching for Jens, then went to the cabin and found his body. We didn't have time to establish the, the . . ." He snapped his fingers, seeking help.

"Alibi," Simon said. "I read *Black Mask*, too."

"At that point, we were at a loss," Felix said. "Gustav was good enough to put us up while we decided what to do."

"Why not go to the police?" I asked.

"Because Felix is too valuable an artist to submit himself to the brainless and corrupt thugs of the state!" Ruehl erupted. "It would be a further blow to the civilized world to subject him to a jury of American nincompoops who think strumming a ukulele while signing about the moon in June is the summit of musical achievement!" Spittle flew from his lips. I almost admired his ability to whip himself into a frenzy. Charting his blood pressure could win a specialist the Nobel Prize.

Before I could launch a foolhardy defense of Rudy Vallee, Felix spoke. "We were in shock. Then Marthe took matters into her own hands. One morning I awoke to find a note from her. She believed her actions had brought death to Jens and disgrace to me. She wanted to atone. So she stole away and turned herself over to the authorities through you, Miss Frost. She thinks by accepting blame for Jens's death, I can resume my career. As if I would want to without her by my side."

Now he is free, Marthe had said of her husband when she'd surrendered to Gene. Yet here he was, still confined.

Simon touched Felix's shoulder. "We'll make this right. Lillian and I will help you and Marthe with the police. Right now the important question is, who *did* kill Jens?"

"Marthe believes it was the Nazis. Soon they will kill everyone, she says. They simply started with him."

Ruehl began pleading with him in German, but I wasn't ready to stop talking. "Was Jens's music book at the cabin?"

"Of course. It was his constant companion. I took it when we left. I meant to destroy it, but I couldn't. It's all that's left of the boy."

"Could we see it?"

He went into the house, returning with an object clutched to his chest. After so much talk about the book, I didn't know what I expected. A jewel-encrusted cover, perhaps, securing vellum parchment. Certainly not the plain brown cardboard monstrosity before me, binding held together with tape, pages jutting out at wild angles. Maybe it was a case of appearances deceiving on purpose. Secrets valuable enough to get Jens killed were within this unassuming collection of potential paper cuts.

"You've looked inside?" I asked.

"Yes. It was the only music I had to keep me company." Felix opened the book. I noticed a few crude renderings of crude subjects sketched inside the front cover and flushed with embarrassment.

"There's a piece Jens was working on for Marlene Dietrich. He mentioned it a few times. It starts as one of Jens's silly little songs. Scandalous jokes of the sort he was somewhat known for.

But partway through, he stops writing *for* Dietrich and instead writes *to* her. The lyrics become a confession. Jens admits he was working for the Nazis as a spy. Likely he told them many things about me. He certainly yielded information on Dietrich to them. He wanted her to know why. It's actually quite a sad tale."

Felix placed some folded sheet music before me. Lyrics—in German, naturally—ran beneath the notes. Felix tapped one page. "Here is where the truth comes out. Rather ingenious. A casual reader would never notice."

I picked up Jens's musical mea culpa, the notes meaningless to me, its words in a language I didn't comprehend. A smaller sheet of unlined paper fluttered loose. *Dezember* written across the top, the two columns below a rudimentary calendar. Jens had a busy Christmas season planned. I recognized several names. *B. Rathbone, E. Flynn. Fathom* appeared several times, and a return engagement on the *Lumen* had been scheduled. There was something ineffably sad about Jens keeping track of engagements he wouldn't live to see.

I flipped through pages dense with music, sometimes in an orderly fashion, more often a dozen or so jumbled measures scrawled in haste. Occasionally I'd find a progression of notes independent of a staff, floating free in space. Words in German marked some of them. Others were preceded by letters or numbers. I couldn't make head or tail of what I was reading.

Felix pored over the book with me. "A few grossly simplified arrangements of popular songs. As if Jens heard them on the radio and wanted to remember them. Mostly melodies, a few chords, enough for him to trick the untrained ear. The rest?" He puffed out a dismissive breath. *"Kauderwelsch."*

"Come again?"

"Gibberish," Simon said.

"Musical nonsense. Well, some of it is music. A few measures that might be the beginnings of a song. But it's mostly scribblings. Notes jotted at random."

"And the other writing? The words, letters, numbers?"

Felix shrugged. "Only Jens could explain it."

A dreadful sinking feeling overwhelmed me. Either I'd been mistaken about the book's significance or, if I'd indeed found the trove of information Malcolm Drewe had paid good money for, neither he nor I could interpret it.

"Now if you will excuse me," Felix said, "I must make myself presentable for the police." Ruehl protested, but Felix waved him into submission. "What choice do I have? I regret leaving Germany. I wish Marthe and I had never come here."

"You can't mean that," Simon said.

"But I do, my friend." Felix's smile scarcely concealed his pain. "Germany is full of devils, but they are devils I know. America is a land of demons I have never met."

LORNA WHITCOMB'S
EYES ON HOLLYWOOD

FLASH! Selznick has finally settled on his Scarlett. Word is Paulette Goddard, long-rumored front-runner, will be posing in petticoats when cameras roll. And if Mr. S. should need to burn Atlanta again, he has a thousand screen tests he can use for kindling . . . Marlene Dietrich is no longer carrying a torch for Columbia. The tempestuous Teuton terminated her contract with the studio now that Frank Capra won't direct her in *Chopin*. Europe, we're told, beckons to the actress . . . Pity the poor toyless tots whose fathers (and even mothers!) are gambling away their Christmas Club savings on those chancy games of chance found floating on the *Lumen* and its like . . .

34

DETECTIVE HANSEN, GENE'S oh-so-lovable partner, had worn a knothole in the sole of his shoe. I knew this because said footwear was propped on his desk and pointed at me.

"Tell me why these two always rate special consideration." He swung his toe from me to Edith, trim in slate gray.

Gene fashioned an erudite retort. "Pipe down, Roy."

Edith opted for a more diplomatic tack. "I'm dressing Dorothy Lamour at the moment, Detective."

Hansen, who never missed a picture, tried to mask his enthusiasm. "Lotta sarongs in this one, I hope."

Gretchen arrived, all doe eyes and matching tentative footsteps. Visiting a police station was clearly a novel experience for her. I waved her over and made introductions.

"There's *three* of 'em now?" Hansen barked, forcing Gretchen a startled step back. "Why don't we wait for the tour bus to come through? Anybody else coming?"

The sight of a naturally prompt Marlene Dietrich shut him up. She looked majestic in a wool suit in black and white stripes, the feather crowning her otherwise modest black hat long enough to pick up radio stations in San Diego. "Hello, boys!" she called in response to the hoots and shouts of her name, snapping off waves like a victorious general in a passing motorcade.

Box office poison, my aunt Fanny.

Hansen could only gawp as Dietrich embraced me. In the air around her hung the scent of My Sin, a floral perfume with spice and strength I'd sampled when I worked at Tremayne's Department Store. I needed a few more sins under my belt to carry it off, so of course it suited Dietrich perfectly.

I presented Gretchen to Dietrich as "Jens's dear friend." Gretchen practically curtsied. "Jens adored playing for you," she said.

"I could not have asked for a finer accompanist."

"Ladies, if you'd come this way?" Gene opened the door to one of the station's less scrofulous interview rooms. "The accommodations aren't much, I'm afraid."

Edith drew me aside. "It's a true kindness on your part, including Gretchen."

"It may not be, considering what she's about to learn. But it seems right she's here."

Dietrich strode around the room, intrigued by her mean surroundings. Gretchen sat meekly at the table. Gene reappeared, carrying Jens's music book. A panting Hansen stood behind him. He'd dashed down the hall and splashed water on his hair. The improvement was minimal.

Gene placed the book before an antsy Gretchen. "We'll leave you to it."

"Thank you, detectives." Dietrich walked up to Hansen, looking him square in the eye. "I appreciate all you do."

Gene had to drag his partner bodily from the room.

"There it is," Gretchen said softly of the book. Dietrich made a tiny sound of agreement.

I extracted Jens's final composition. "I thought it only right you saw this, Marlene, because Jens was writing it for you. And it will answer many of Gretchen's questions." I already knew what the pages said, thanks to Simon's translation. How Dietrich would react to Jens's confession was the question.

The actress sat down, hooking her long legs beneath the chair.

She chuckled as she read the lyrics. I knew she'd reached the more revelatory passage when she pressed a handkerchief to her face. Even her tears maintained a Prussian sense of order.

"It's tragic," she said. "He stops writing this most amusing song and admits he is coming undone. He has been spying for the Nazi regime against his will for months."

Gretchen gasped. "Does he say why?" Edith asked.

"He left family behind in Austria. A mother too old to travel, a sister ill with consumption. After the Anschluss a Nazi named Biel approached him in Los Angeles and said his family could be made more comfortable if Jens assisted them. Spy on the émigrés, deliver messages to and from those who could not openly meet with their Nazi masters. Jens had no choice but to agree. He invented fictions when he could, told the truth when necessary. He spoke of me to them, and begs my forgiveness. The silly boy."

Edith patted Dietrich's arm, knowing her principal responsibility was to console the star before her. I mirrored the action with Gretchen.

"But he has decided to end this charade," Dietrich continued. "He has a plan to raise enough money to move his family to the United States. Then, he will leave Los Angeles forever. The next time he plays for me, he writes, it will be in a free Berlin." Again she brushed her cheeks with the handkerchief. "I told you I could sense his troubles. These blasted Nazis will never give us any peace. Their shadow falls even here. This is who is responsible for Jens's death, yes?"

I spoke up. "The police think it's a possibility. It's why they can't release the papers to you."

"I don't want them. I doubt I could ever perform this song. It's too personal, too raw. It needs work." She read the lyrics again, thin eyebrows arcing ever higher as she translated them

on the fly. She hummed a melody softly then, to my astonish-
ment, began to sing.

> What have I done to deserve this? You wouldn't say I
>   had earned this.
> How did this life become mine?

> My lovers sport their darkly tinted glasses when visiting
>   my mansion in the hills.
> Tess is an actress, Bess a designer, Rose is a poet (I pay
>   the bills)

> I cultivate a fashionable skin tone—lightly bronzed is
>   right for '39
> I've built a bungalow down by the seaside, my friends
>   come by to eat (we never dine)

> I live at the beach, lemonade within reach
> I eat only salads and never sing ballads

> What have I done to deserve this? You couldn't say I had
>   earned this.
> How did this life become mine?

> How did I make my way, without a penny—Berlin to
>   Paris, then across the sea?
> I often think of those I left behind, and hope they have
>   no need to think of me.

> Honest men whose character outshines mine, gentle
>   girls as kind as I am cruel.
> Should they be here enjoying what I savor? Should I be
>   there? Or am I just a fool?

How can I frolic in the sun
When friends are falling one by one?

Why does Fortune treat me kindly
Yet punish those I left behind me?

I would offer to switch places—
But could I leave such pretty faces?

What have I done to deserve this? God knows I haven't
    earned this.
Why did this life become mine?

Edith handed Gretchen a handkerchief while I reached discreetly for one of my own. I knew I'd heard the one and only performance of Jens Lohse's last song, sung by the very woman for whom it had been composed.

"It tries too hard," Dietrich said clinically. "We would have improved it. But his talent was at work. He was writing about his guilt, and mine. He was transforming his pain into art. Until he could write no more."

"There will be a venue for that song someday," Edith said.

"Much must change first. Jens is an early casualty of what is about to happen. It's partly why I'm going back."

"To Germany?" I couldn't keep the alarm from my voice.

"No, not while that man is in charge. I go to France. Close enough to smell my native land, taste its food. Perhaps I will make films there. Word of my catastrophic box office performance has yet to reach those shores." She smiled. "But I shan't leave until after Christmas. Earl Carroll's Vanities Club opens that night. It will be the event of the year. And before then, you must allow me to cook for you. I will prepare a true German Christmas feast. Roast goose, some dumplings."

Gretchen smiled for the first time that morning, her reddened eyes alight. "Potato or bread?"

"Potato. My *kartoffelklösse* have made many a traveler weep from homesickness. Do you cook, my dear?"

"All of my mother's recipes. It wouldn't be *Weihnachten* without her *gänsebraten* and *semmelklösse*."

Dietrich smiled dreamily. "*Rotkohl* simmering on the stove for hours."

My stomach growled despite my not understanding a word after "dumplings," showing who the true brains of the outfit was.

"Come, we will compare notes on cooking in a more genial atmosphere." Dietrich stood, all business, and kissed Edith. "Again, my eternal gratitude to you and Lillian. You surpassed my every expectation." Her gloved hand touched my face, the leather cool against my skin. She leaned in to buss my cheek only to turn her head and press her lips against mine. Her eyes were open, which meant, I supposed, that mine were, too. She breezed out of the office with Gretchen on her arm, and I smelled of My Sin at last.

While I regained my equilibrium, Edith fussed with Jens's book. "It seems underwhelming now that you've recovered it. Any indication of where Mr. Lohse's bounty of secrets is?"

"It's my opinion you're looking at it."

"What do you mean?"

"Felix said most of this material was gibberish. My theory— well, Simon and I developed it together—is that the gibberish is actually a notation system. Jens had to keep track of every scandalous tidbit he came across while working, but didn't want anyone to know he was doing it. So he developed a code in the language he understood best."

"Music."

"Exactly. It's an idea out of Hiram Beecher's book *How to Be at Home in the World*, which Jens and I both read. 'Only you know how the river of your memory flows,' Hiram wrote. Jens scratches down a few notes that remind him of a name or location. Letters and numbers clarify the meaning. To anyone else, they're a composer's scribblings. To him, it's a way to recall information to pass along to Kaspar Biel or use for blackmail purposes. My guess is Jens planned on transcribing it for Malcolm Drewe while hiding at the Auerbachs' cabin, but never had the chance." I tapped the page before Edith, containing a good two dozen unconnected measures of music. "This could be dirt so filthy it would keep Louella Parsons and Lorna Whitcomb going for years. And the only person who can read it is dead. Jens took all his secrets with him."

"Except the one he left for Marlene. Remarkable." Edith closed the book, flashing a grin at the ribald drawings inside the cover. "What does Detective Morrow make of your suggestion?"

"He deemed it interesting."

"Does he believe Mr. Biel is responsible for Mr. Lohse's death?"

"That notion he dubbed intriguing. The police still think one of the Auerbachs killed him. We only have Felix and Marthe's word for what happened."

"While scant evidence implicates the Nazis."

"Gene contacted the consulate anyway. They stonewalled him." I slapped the table in frustration. "But Biel did it. Simon insists Felix and Marthe are innocent. There's no one else it could be."

"There is another possible culprit," Edith said slowly. "I thought of it earlier, and Jens's confession only fanned the flame. He stated he was collecting money to deliver his family from Austria. He did so by turning the spying he was compelled to do for the Nazis to his own ends. Blackmailing society people, extorting the studios."

"And selling all his information to Malcolm Drewe."

"For which he was willing to accept less money, in order to receive it up front. Why would he ask for such terms? Suppose

Mr. Lohse needed to move his family at once, with Mr. Drewe's immediate payment providing the last of the necessary revenue. What would he—and they—live on after that? Particularly if he planned on leaving Los Angeles for good?"

"Rory Dillon said Jens had other irons in the fire."

"Simon said Mr. Lohse's primary role as a spy was serving as go-between, ferrying information to and from higher-placed assets."

The hair on the nape of my neck stood at attention. "You think Jens was blackmailing other Nazi spies?"

"Surely the names of those agents are the most valuable intelligence Mr. Lohse possessed. What better way to raise a great deal of money? He could act indirectly, again using Mr. Dillon and others. His targets would not want to admit to their Nazi handlers they had been compromised. One of those individuals could have acted on their own to kill Mr. Lohse—the only person who could conclusively identify him as a spy—without knowing it was Mr. Lohse himself blackmailing him."

I sat back in my chair. "So some illustrious Los Angeles resident who met Jens at a party or a club and is secretly a Nazi agent could have killed him."

"Conceivably. All that remains is to determine that person's identity."

"Piece of *gugelhupf*. We don't even need Jens's magic book to figure it out. I'll just invite Kaspar Biel around and ask him. He already knows where my place is."

"Don't joke, Lillian, you— What's wrong?"

"Nothing. I just thought of someone other than Kaspar who might know where to start."

"SO WHAT YOU'RE telling me," Malcolm Drewe said with understandable exactitude, "is I'm never going to get what I paid for."

I nodded from my position opposite him in a booth at Marie's Pantry. I had arranged to meet him at the café near the Santa Monica water taxi landing. I hadn't gone to the assignation alone, either. I'd instructed Rogers to park Addison's car two blocks from the restaurant. When he'd done so, I dropped a dollar onto the front seat next to him.

"Marie's has the best peach melba in town. Have some, my treat. You don't have to sit with me or acknowledge my existence. Just go in ahead of me and leave after I do."

Rogers held the bill up to the light; had it been a coin, he'd have bitten it. When I arrived at Marie's ten minutes later, he was comfortably ensconced at the counter. He'd ordered strawberry shortcake and seemed to have gotten the better of the deal. Drewe was already waiting.

"Jens didn't lie," I told him. "He had what he sold you. But it's in a form only he could read."

Drewe shoveled shortcake into his mouth, the peach melba apparently wildly overrated. "You're telling me there wasn't one name in it you recognized?"

"Johannes Brahms, but he hasn't had a hit in years. Jens used a musical code to remember everything, and did so because it would only make sense to him."

"He said he had incriminating photographs. Where are those?"

"Locked in a bank somewhere, or squirreled away at a friend's place under the floorboards."

"All noted in his magic book using his secret code, now lost to us mortal men. So they'll molder away and not turn a buck for anyone." He laughed uproariously and continued attacking his shortcake, the flashes of vivid red on his teeth disquieting. "I'll say this for you, Miss Frost, I like your nerve. Not many people would deliver this news in person."

Before I could explain why I'd done so, Drewe's man Knoll slid into the booth. He cocked his ginger head toward Rogers.

"That goon at the counter is with her. And the pair of them are being followed by guys look like federal agents."

Drewe lowered his fork and stared at me. At least he'd closed his mouth. "They probably are federal agents," I said. "But they don't care about you. They're only interested in Jack Benny."

I sipped my disappointing coffee and waited. Drewe continued staring, so I pressed on.

"I had a reason for bringing you this information directly. I wanted to ask a question."

"Go ahead."

"What do you know about Nazis in Los Angeles?"

"Nothing. I get enough grief from local politicians. What do I care what foreigners do across the sea?"

"We could all be concerned before long. You want your customers looking up from the roulette wheels to see U-boats out the windows?"

"Portholes."

"You know everybody worth knowing. I was wondering whether you'd heard if anybody worth knowing was overly sympathetic to the Nazi cause."

Knoll shifted. He wanted to hear the answer, too.

"If I tell you," Drewe said, "you owe me."

I swallowed hard, tasting burnt java. I didn't want to consider what owing Malcolm Drewe might entail. But I couldn't think of anyone else to ask. "Fair enough."

"Plenty of people think like me, that what happens in Europe is none of our business. Lindbergh, for one. He'd know, since he was in such a damn hurry to get there. There *are* people who want the Nazis to come out on top. Some of them are quite well known." Drewe grinned, his teeth now licked alarmingly clean. "One of them got famous robbing from the rich to give to the poor. Doesn't sound like a Nazi, does he?"

35

IF THERE WERE ever a time I could wear slacks without fear of reproving glances, it would be a golden December morning with a nip in the air, spent at the north end of Griffith Park watching cricket. Then I pictured the veddy British expatriates clotting like cream at Addison's parties, considered what Edith would recommend, and decided more traditional attire was the safer bet.

The Hollywood Cricket Club had been founded in 1932 by C. Aubrey Smith. The venerable character actor's stiff-upper-lipped visage had come to exemplify Englishness after decades of playing earls and majors in films like *Little Lord Fauntleroy* and *The Lives of a Bengal Lancer.* Smith had carved out a slice of his native land in the hills for the playing of his favorite sport. Any male British subject who arrived to test his fortunes in Hollywood soon received a note from Smith summoning him to the nets. I'd learned of a Wednesday morning practice staged largely to put Nigel Dansby-Hall, scribe of the Broadway smash *Ten for Elevenses* and newly signed to a contract at Warner Brothers, through his paces on the pitch. Rogers drove me to Griffith Park, his silence more respectful since witnessing my showdown with Malcolm Drewe. Or so I liked to think.

I drifted through the club's pavilion, a rustic structure with a fieldstone fireplace, a wood plank ceiling, and that essential comfort of any colonial outpost, a well-stocked bar. Outside a handful of people sat scattered on low bleachers around a field of an uncommonly rich emerald hue. Beyond lay a lushly wooded stretch of Griffith Park, oak, California sycamore, and pine all rustling in the breeze.

C. Aubrey Smith stood by three wooden stakes driven into the ground at one end of the field, shaking his leonine head at a fair-haired man I presumed to be Dansby-Hall. A ball cowered between them. "I say," Smith bellowed, "not to put too fine a point on it, but you are familiar with the accepted rules of the sport, what? Where the ball is to be bowled and so forth?" Dansby-Hall nodded in dignified embarrassment and cast blame down at his ill-fitting equipment, likely borrowed from a club member.

One of whom I was there to see. I climbed the bleachers for an unobstructed view of Errol Flynn, every bit as impressive a specimen as he'd been at Club Fathom. A man whose name was on Jens Lohse's calendar, and Malcolm Drewe's lips.

"I'M NOT SAYING he's a Nazi, you understand." Drewe pushed the remains of his strawberry shortcake aside. "He came to mind in response to your question, that's all."

"Why, exactly?"

"I can tell you three things about Mr. Flynn. I could tell you more, but I don't want to be accused of corrupting an innocent. That's Errol's job." He snorted. "One, he's Australian—Tasmanian, you want to be precise—but thinks of himself as Irish. You Irish, Miss Frost?"

"My people are."

"Then you know bog-cutters love whiskey and the church, and hate the English. The English hate the Nazis. And the enemy of my enemy is my friend. That's as much thought as Errol's given the situation. Although with the state the world's in, I sometimes believe the people in charge think the same way. If Errol's disposed toward the Nazis it's because, like him, they loathe the limeys." Drewe shrugged. "Yet he still plays cricket. Go figure."

• • •

CRICKET EARNED POINTS for fashion. Many of the players at the edge of the field wore blazers boasting magenta and black stripes. Flynn had shucked his, standing among his teammates in a crisp white shirt, as much at ease in the bulky pads protecting his lower legs as his own skin.

What purpose the pads served, I had no inkling. I knew nothing about cricket, the sports section of my brain jammed with what I'd learned from watching the Hollywood Stars with Gene—and that only because Barbara Stanwyck owned a share of the baseball team. I didn't want to ask those around me for pointers, not because I feared they wouldn't reply but because I sensed they yearned to; I wasn't prepared to face normally reserved Englishmen bubbling with enthusiasm.

"Real English grass, you know," one of them said to a compatriot. "Smith had the seeds brought over."

"Surprised the water took to it," his friend replied, and both chortled merrily.

No, I would definitely be parsing this game on my own. As Dansby-Hall retrieved the ball and made another sortie, it occurred to me C. Aubrey Smith had created an oasis for expats much as Salka Viertel had. Two tribes of émigrés, one reveling in the opportunities afforded by the glorious sun overhead, the other peering up at the golden orb suspiciously.

Speaking of orbs, the ball pitched by Dansby-Hall rolled to a halt three feet from Smith's two feet. Flynn turned to his teammates and offered a critique that provoked gales of laughter. I wondered anew if I looked at a Nazi spy.

DREWE RAISED A second finger. "Two. Errol went to Spain earlier this year. Craved a firsthand look at the war."

"I remember that. He wrote about the trip for *Photoplay*."

"Then you remember he was supposedly wounded."

"Some of the papers reported he'd been killed." I blinked at Drewe. "Wait. 'Supposedly'?"

"There are all kinds of questions about Errol's trip. For instance, he told the Loyalists he'd raised a million dollars from his Hollywood pals and brought the money with him, earmarked for ambulances and hospitals. Repeated the story everywhere he went. Only he never raised a penny."

"Hold on. If he's supposed to be a Nazi, why would he pledge aid to the Loyalists?"

"And another thing. Errol went to Spain in the company of Hermann Erben. Austrian, some kind of doctor, by all accounts a true-blue Nazi. Stories I've heard say Erben used Errol to get to the front lines for some purpose of his own. Are these stories true? Beats me. But could a guy like Errol be a dupe?"

Drewe sat back and brandished his teeth in a way that made me glad Rogers was sitting nearby.

EITHER AUBREY SMITH harrumphed or someone had fired up a Rolls-Royce. "You don't have to listen to me," he roared to the hapless writer. "I've only won one bloody Test cap, and that was fifty years ago. Perhaps the game has passed me by. New techniques and all that. This soft tossing of yours could be the way of the future." Dansby-Hall kicked at the green, green grass. "We'll try you with a bat in your hand, what? You want to grasp the narrow end."

Simon vaulted up the bleachers. He dropped down next to me, staring at the pitch in contempt. "I never know who to feel worse for, people playing cricket or watching it."

"Amen. Give me the Stars at Wrigley Field any day."

"Baseball's just as boring."

I decided not to contest the point. "Thanks for coming."

"Thanks for calling me. I figured after we brought Felix to your friend, our conversations were over. I missed them."

And so, I had to confess, did I. Simon saw me differently than Gene did, in his eyes, I was more mature, more mysterious. A woman of hidden depths, including some I'd concealed from myself. Gene likely had a truer sense of my nature. But there was no denying I liked the person Simon thought I was—and, by extension, the person who viewed me that way. Not that I could admit that to Simon. I could hardly accept the thought in my own mind. So I stuck to the matter at hand.

"Did you learn anything?"

"About Flynn? Not much. He's popular down at the Bund. Heard him referred to as 'one of us' a few times, but that could mean anything. All those burghers think of themselves as lean panthers of men who are catnip to women."

"Do you think he could be a spy?"

"No one would suspect him, I'll say that. He meets a lot of people, travels extensively. His reputation as a man given to excess could work in his favor. But he'd be more valuable as a public spokesman, a friendly face saying, 'Hey, folks, Hitler's not all bad.' He's not doing that, I notice." He squinted at the actor, still contemplating. "The Bund's in a lather over something else today. You've heard about Leni Riefenstahl's disastrous trip."

"Credit Dorothy Parker and the Anti-Nazi League for that. I doubt she'll sell her documentary about the Olympics to one of the studios."

"They're too terrified to look at it. Walt Disney told her he wanted to screen the film but those Reds in the projectionists' union would blab about it." Simon laughed. "She's finally showing *Olympia* tonight."

"She is? Where?"

"The California Club downtown. No advance publicity, but word's out at the Bund. A very private screening for club members, sportswriters, athletes who are in the picture. They say Johnny Weissmuller will be in attendance. It's supposed to be a celebration of human competition, very apolitical."

"Good luck with that."

"She's showing the apolitical version."

"There's more than one?"

"What I hear, Leni has three different *Olympia*s in her bungalow at the Beverly Hills Hotel. Tonight's doesn't include a single shot of Hitler. Pure sport, appropriate for all audiences. Then there's the version that premiered on *der Führer's* birthday. As you might expect, he has a starring role in that one. One of the Bund bigwigs let slip Leni secretly screened that print at her bungalow. Gyssling, the consul, wanted to see it and invited some other Nazi personnel. Quite the top ticket, possibly the only time Leni's uncut version plays in the States."

A crack of the bat rang out, so loud I expected to see the Hollywood Stars' own Frenchy Uhalt trotting around the bases. Instead there was only Nigel Dansby-Hall, looking chuffed as the English say, watching the ball he'd struck bounce across the turf.

"You could bloody *run*, man!" Smith trumpeted. "Just for appearance's sake!"

Dansby-Hall took off at a sprint while fielders chased after the ball. I stopped following the action, my focus now on Flynn, who in turn devoted his energies to a woman at the base of the bleachers. Not his bride Lili Damita, or Millicent from Club Fathom, but a redhead. I wondered if Flynn needed a social secretary to keep his conquests straight, and if I should apply for the job.

"When was this secret screening?" I asked.

"Right after Riefenstahl arrived."

"Would Nazi agents in Los Angeles have gone?"

Simon chewed on the idea. "They'd be taking a hell of a chance."

"Not so much at the Beverly Hills Hotel. There are meetings

and parties there every night. Visiting one of the bungalows without being seen is even easier. Nobody there but other Nazis. You wouldn't need a go-between."

Simon considered Flynn again. "It's feasible. But would a notable person risk being found out for that?"

"An exclusive, once-in-a-lifetime screening of a movie featuring a star turn like no other?" I turned to Simon. "I know your opinion of show people. What do you think?"

DREWE, I REALIZED as he lifted finger three, had a better manicure than I did. If I handled that much money, I'd splurge on nail care, too.

"And finally, lest we forget, Errol's an actor. Actors always want to prove themselves. You give Errol a chance to do what he does in pictures for real? I don't think he could resist it, any more than women can resist him. He's helpless in that way. You know why?" Drewe leaned forward, all three polished digits tapping the tabletop. "The poor bastard has to be Errol Flynn. All day, every day. Even to himself."

PRACTICE APPEARED TO be over now that the ball had been recovered. Before Simon could stop me, before I could stop myself, I marched down the bleachers toward the field. Smith waved Dansby-Hall closer and studied him up and down. Then, with a hearty bark, the actor thrust out his hand. "Good show. Matches every Sunday. Grand to have you aboard."

Unless I was mistaken, Dansby-Hall brushed away a tear.

Flynn, bidding farewell to his teammates, had draped his blazer over his shoulder and consequently looked even more delectably roguish. I wouldn't have to fake a swoon, because the genuine article barreled toward me. I braced for impact.

The crash came when Flynn spotted me, his eyes narrowing in recognition. "Hello," he said as if he'd just wandered out of the bathroom wrapped in a towel, the whole world his hotel room. "Haven't we met before?"

"We have. Here and a few other places." I waved at the field. "I enjoyed watching you."

"Cracking good sport, isn't it? Come again Sunday and you can watch me work up a sweat."

Okay, this was getting difficult. I'd have to work fast. Time to pilot the palaver toward the subject of Riefenstahl's film and see if the actor gave himself away. "Is cricket in the Olympics?"

"A very good question. I happen to know it isn't, not since an exhibition match in 1900. High time that changed, don't you think?"

"Quite. Do you like the Olympics?"

"I like all kinds of physical activity. Especially when it's judged and prizes are awarded."

Oh, come on. I was beginning to think if Flynn was a spy he ranked with Allan Pinkerton. Thanks to his one-track mind, he couldn't be fazed. He glanced past me at the redhead, pouting in wholly nonsuggestive fashion. "Would you excuse me? We'll continue this conversation on Sunday. Perhaps over a pink gin."

Flynn dashed over to his titian-haired temptress. Simon caught up to me as I walked away from the pitch.

"You're crazy," he said, and I detected a hint of admiration. "The verdict?"

"I have no idea. Flynn could be too smart for me, too dumb for the Germans, or both."

"Still, it was a valiant effort. Now what?"

"Now we go to Fräulein Director and ask her."

36

❖

"I HATE TO sound like one of the scripts I'm too often forced to read," Edith said, "but I have grave reservations about your plan. And there's a stain on your shoe." Nothing related to wardrobe escaped Edith's vision. I curled up on her office sofa so I could scrub the smudge of grass I'd carried from the cricket field.

"I'm going to a preview, hoping to wangle a chat with the director. I've done it before."

"Not in a room full of Nazis."

"And Olympians. Stalwart examples of clean living. *Johnny Weissmuller* will be there. It's practically a public event."

"A screening with minimal publicity is hardly a public event. It is, quite literally, a meeting in a darkened room. You don't even know you'll gain entry."

I grinned with both pride and exertion; the grass stain on my white leather spectator oxford proved stubborn. "Addison's a member of the California Club. When his social secretary inquired about the venue, the management was happy to extend an invitation to tonight's special event."

"Very efficient. One might even say ruthless. Please stop rubbing that shoe, Lillian! A little white vinegar and water will remove the stain. Be sure to daub it on." She exhaled and placed her palms flat on her desk. "I don't understand why you're prepared to take this considerable risk."

"Because I can't go on reading papers and watching newsreels hoping everything will work out. I have to *do* something. I have to act. I mean, the Nazis already invaded my apartment." Having given voice to the thought, I recoiled from it. "Anyway, it's not risky. It's only a movie."

Edith nodded, but not in agreement. "What does Detective Morrow think of this proposed derring-do of yours?"

"I haven't told him. I already know what he'd say."

"Then the sole supporter of this scheme is Simon."

"Better than just me." Only then did I realize Edith regularly referred to Simon by his Christian name. She still called Gene "Detective Morrow" and spoke of me as "my friend, Miss Frost." That she didn't extend this formality-as-respect to Mr. Fischer troubled me. "You don't support it, then."

"No, I don't. It's potentially dangerous. And Errol Flynn is no Nazi agent. An adventurer and a libertine, but not a spy. It's my understanding Warners would put him in any movie but wouldn't trust him with an address book."

"If it's not Flynn, I can persuade Leni to tell me who it is. I know I can."

Edith canted her head at a slight angle, which I knew meant *Not bloody likely.* "If you insist on going ahead, I insist you inform me the instant you're free. Tell me what if anything you learn from Miss Riefenstahl and I'll convey it to Mr. Groff. He can deliver the information to more receptive ears in Washington. Don't telephone. Come directly to the lot."

"It's a long movie, Edith."

"I'll be here. Some of the girls will be working late, and I'm going to demonstrate my solidarity. I may even permit them to chew gum." A half smile as she shuffled the sketches on her desk. "We have to finish the costumes for Bob Hope's next picture. Our friend Preston Sturges worked on the script, although he's disowning the entire enterprise and making noise about directing again. I take it Simon will accompany you tonight?"

Now that I'd noticed her constant use of his first name, I cringed when she said it. "No. He can't risk running into anyone from the Bund."

"Then who'll act as translator for you and Miss Riefenstahl?"

The room went white. "Translator? Doesn't Leni speak English? She did in *S.O.S. Iceberg.*"

"The film with Rod La Rocque? Heavens, you do see everything, don't you? What little dialogue she had was dubbed. Her command of English, I'm led to believe, isn't strong. And I imagine nuance will be of the utmost importance."

"Then I need an interpreter, fast. What about Marlene?"

Edith burst out in laughter. "You'd entertain that idea after hearing her plan to assassinate Adolf Hitler? Besides, Miss Riefenstahl would never tell Marlene what you want to know. You must approach Miss Riefenstahl purely as an American admirer of her artistry and craftsmanship."

"There's Gretchen."

"Can you trust her, given her feelings toward Mr. Lohse?"

"I don't have much choice, given the time constraints."

The only problem: Gretchen was nowhere to be found. I couldn't raise her at Lodestar or at home. I hung up the phone, feeling utterly foolish for not thinking this caper through. "Not to rush you, dear," Edith said, "but in five minutes I have to meet some cowboys at Western Costume. I regret to say you may not be able to talk to Miss Riefenstahl this evening."

"Cowboys."

"Yes, we often rent their costumes when there's no need to have them custom-made." Edith scrutinized me. "What is it? You've thought of something."

"I know a cowboy whose fiancée happens to speak German. But do I want her help?"

• • •

"*MAN SOLL DAS Fell des Bären nicht verteilen, bevor er erlegt ist,*" Kay said, unfolding her napkin.

"That's why I called you. What's it mean?"

"Basically, don't count your chickens before they hatch. But it's German, so there's a bear in it."

My one-time chum and I convened at Lucey's, a restaurant on Melrose directly opposite Paramount. The old world charm and convenient location made it an informal studio clubhouse. I spotted a few faces from the commissary writers' table surrounded by empty glasses and hoped they'd turned in their pages for the day.

Kay signaled for coffee. "Before I agree to sit through Leni's monstrosity—it's *four hours* long—I need to know what's in it for me."

Any appeal to our former friendship would fall on deaf ears. Kay put her career first. Our hatchling Hopper wouldn't be cajoled into cooperating easily.

"The *Olympia* screening's still fairly hush-hush," I said offhandedly. "Could be an exclusive."

"I don't care for sports."

"Any of them? It's the Olympics. There's got to be one you like. What about an interview with Leni Riefenstahl?"

"That I'm in favor of. The press is being unfair to her. She only wants to sell her picture. The town's high-hatting her because she's a woman."

Who may or may not be der Führer's girlfriend, I thought, *and is certainly his cinematic hagiographer.* "It's an interesting argument."

"I made it in print. You do read my column, don't you?"

"Never miss it." I tried to restrain myself and failed dismally. "I saw Addison earned some ink."

"Hm? Oh, the Santa Breakfast." Acting like she didn't remember. Kay knew she had me in a bind, so out came the saltshaker for my wounds. "That was choice stuff. I could use more of that."

She pointed her coffee spoon at me. "My question is, why are you so hot to talk to Riefenstahl?"

"I can't say."

"Like fun you can't. This is tied into another juicy murder, isn't it? That's why we're meeting across from Paramount. You were in there huddling with Edith Head."

"I *was* visiting Edith, but about another matter." No way would I mix Edith's name up in this muddle now that Kay was involved. But the viper had to be sated somehow. "And yes, there is a murder involved. And yes, there might be implications for a movie studio."

"And yes, you'll give me an exclusive if Leni comes across."

I fumed. I debated. I relented.

"Of course."

Kay smiled, growing accustomed to getting her way. "*Wunderbar! Lassen sie uns ins Kino gehen!*"

37

NO ANGRY MOB seethed outside the California Club on South Flower Street, so close to the FBI offices I craned my neck to check Agent Deems's window. The gracefully imposing Italian Renaissance building looked like where a middling Medici might have stashed ill-gotten gain. Once inside, though, I felt transported to old Heidelberg. A constant low buzz of German coursed through the reception area, barrel-chested men clustered together anxiously.

"If you see the director, sing out," I told Kay. "I'm not staying for the picture if I don't have to."

"How about a yodel if I spot Johnny Weissmuller?"

"Will another Tarzan do?" I indicated a tall man with a shock of dark hair and the air of an animal in a zoo, all coiled swagger and haunted eyes. "Glenn Morris, the decathlon champion. He starred in *Tarzan's Revenge* with Hedda Hopper, which was bad even for a Tarzan movie. He's also in *Hold That Co-Ed*."

"Good Lord, you really do see everything."

"Not the first time I've heard that today."

A commotion erupted as several figures swept into the room. I recognized Georg Gyssling, the Reich's consul in Los Angeles, from the newspaper. He beamed at a woman with sharp features and an uneasy smile. Judging from her regal manner, she could only be Leni Riefenstahl. Although the close-fitting jacket of her chic black velvet suit was buttoned up to the pointed satin collar, the peplum showcasing her hips made it plain the entire ensemble was designed to seduce.

Glenn Morris loped toward her but faltered in the face of the crowd. Kay buttonholed him at once. The star of a lousy jungle picture still counted as a star.

Nearby, a bespectacled man observed the scene with amusement. He wore a tired gray suit, hairline retreating up his forehead like a vanquished army.

"Always a circus," I said, affecting a world-weariness.

"No matter the venue." A German accent seasoned his English. "Ernst Jäger, Miss Riefenstahl's publicity chief."

"Lillian Frost. I've come from Paramount Pictures." Technically, the Paramount-adjacent Lucey's if one sought to split hairs. But countless confessional sessions had taught me to phrase falsehoods that would stand up in court.

Jäger tried to douse his enthusiasm. "Really?" He looked at Riefenstahl, surrounded by admirers. "This is why we came to America. She's in her element tonight."

"And a stunning suit."

"Leni is acutely aware of the effect well-chosen garments can have." He smiled. "You haven't seen *Triumph of the Will*. Her film of the party congress in Nuremburg. Leni wore a white great coat so her camera crew could always find her. Even amidst hundreds of thousands, she managed to cut a figure."

The guests headed toward a set of double doors. With a promise to introduce me to Riefenstahl, Jäger took his leave. Kay reappeared at my shoulder. "That Morris fellow won't win any medals for copy, I can tell you that."

A ballroom with gold flocked wallpaper had been converted into a theater. "Don't worry, kid," Kay said as we settled into chairs in a back row. "I heard tell of a dinner break."

A silver-haired gent who never dropped his name rose to say

a few words, chief among them a request not to publicize the California Club's role in the screening. Then the lights went down.

THE OPENING OF *Olympia*, "Part One: Festival of Nations," picked up when the director appeared au naturel.

The sequence had been slow and a touch pretentious, the dramatic music and shots of Greek antiquity not exactly a grabber. Then several women appeared, stretching and posing in the altogether in the out-of-doors. The nudity didn't seem prurient but strangely mystical, the women engaged in some primitive ritual. For the first time I understood the term "sun worshipper."

Then I leaned forward in recognition. One of the women bore familiar features, keen and focused. It was Riefenstahl herself. I risked a look toward the front of the room and saw her gazing at her own body, enraptured.

Talking to her now, I thought, *will certainly be different.*

People continued entering the auditorium, hoping to slip into the screening unseen. I stopped noticing them as Riefenstahl's film began to exert a peculiar hold. I'd grown used to hearing snippets of a boxing match or a horserace on the radio, an announcer's booming voice over a single shot from a ballgame in a newsreel. Riefenstahl deployed a wholly different technique, more fluid and intimate. Her cameras got close to the athletes, capturing their nervousness and determination. Slow motion made sprinters appear to be flying, the hop-step-jump competitors ready to take leave of the earth. I rooted for Jesse Owens, naturally, my heart thrilling each time he breasted the tape. But soon I saw him the way Riefenstahl did, not as an American or a Negro but a magnificent, perfectly tuned machine. The victories didn't belong only to him but the human form, his every action a triumph of physicality. Several times during the film I sensed where shots of Hitler had been excised, his presence weighty even in its absence. But watching athletes excel at the very thing they had been put on God's earth to do gave me a child-like feeling of hope, a confidence everything would work out.

As part one ended, I joined in the applause without thinking. *Olympia*, I had to admit, was a singular achievement, even if the Reich had bankrolled its production. At least I'd be able to offer words of genuine praise to Riefenstahl, standing at the front of the room accepting the ovation with an entitled expression in her eyes.

Provided, of course, I didn't picture her naked.

"THANK GOD HITLER was cut from the picture," Kay whispered. "We'll be out of here earlier."

The audience milled in the California Club's forecourt, where a light supper—translucent slices of meat on bread the size of postage stamps—was being served. Not that anyone wanted to eat after studying sculpted bodies for two hours. Better we should run sprints around the buffet tables.

Grabbing a few moments with Riefenstahl seemed unlikely, given the adulation she was receiving. She positively glowed, especially when speaking with the Olympians in attendance. A preening Georg Gyssling kept bringing dignitaries and club members into her orbit, and the filmmaker would accept their praise then turn back to the closest athlete.

"Let's split up," I told Kay. "Come at Leni from different sides."

"The classic pincer movement. See you at the front."

I picked my way through the audience and three miniscule sandwiches. Riefenstahl stood several people away, the back of her suit to me. Just past her, Kay had gotten bottled up with some Nazi functionaries. I steeled myself for the final push.

"A splendid turnout this evening," a voice said in my ear. I willed myself not to quake and turned toward Kaspar Biel.

A whiff of chlorine hung in the air around him, as if he'd emerged from a swimming pool before slipping on his charcoal-gray suit. Or perhaps he bleached himself thoroughly before dealing with the public. His eyes contained a glimmer of dark merriment over a professional smile.

Time to wipe it off his face.

"Good evening, Peter. Or are you Kaspar Biel at official functions?"

"Yes, an inquiry from the police indicated you'd learned my true name. A real-life Rumpelstiltskin. A German tale, you know. Shall I spin straw into gold for you now?" He chuckled, and my fingers almost flew at his face of their own volition. My frustration at that moment was total. I wanted to hurt Biel, to make him fear I had dirt on him.

"I also learned what you forced Jens Lohse to do. What made you look for him?" My voice was small but hard, alien even to me. Stranger still, I liked the sound of it. "Something had you out there beating the bushes for him. Let me guess. His family in Austria went missing. Jens had raised the money he needed to get them out of the country. You heard they were gone and realized you'd lost your hold over him."

The gleam in Biel's eyes faded, his jaw tightening. I'd struck somewhere near the truth. It wasn't much of a victory, a faint flickering hope that before his death Jens had been able to deliver those who mattered most to him from a dire fate. But it would have to suffice.

Biel changed the subject. "You're the rare American to see *Olympia*. What did you think of the first installment?"

I couldn't praise it, not to Biel's face. "I don't follow sports, I'm afraid."

"A pity. Then let us speak of matters of greater import." He edged closer, the chlorine scent intensifying. "Who should play Scarlett O'Hara?"

His query, screaming in from left field, struck me dumb. Biel happily continued. "Paulette Goddard seems a disastrous choice, don't you agree? Scarlett is so contentious a character, at once monstrous and likable. Who among your actresses possesses both these qualities? Surely not Miss Goddard."

He'd snared me in his web, the bastard. "Her relationship with Chaplin won't help her chances, either."

"For me, there is only one choice. Tallulah Bankhead."

"Are you crazy? She's too old."

"But authentically southern. From a noble lineage, no less, her father speaker of the House of Representatives. Can you imagine? The product of one of your most prominent families taking the lead role in a great story of American history. The symmetry is overwhelming. Rest assured that's how we would mount the film in Germany."

Reason enough for Selznick not to do it. "You wouldn't cast Miss Riefenstahl?" I gestured at the actress and filmmaker—

And to my amazement saw her in conversation with Kay, Ernst Jäger chatting amiably alongside them. Kay spotted me and her eyes widened, commanding *Get over here.*

I sidestepped Biel and moved toward her. But Biel repositioned himself, blocking Kay and Riefenstahl from view. "The other choice for Scarlett would be a neophyte. A complete unknown. I gather Mr. Selznick has considered this option as well."

I smiled tightly and tried to maneuver around Biel but he kept pace, unwilling to let me go.

"The approach brings reward, but greater risk. A novice can find herself in over her head so quickly, make mistakes that cost money and time. She can ultimately prove far more trouble than she is worth." He placed a hand on my elbow, and I told myself I didn't feel it go cold. "But then, eliminating an unknown isn't much of a burden. Who would notice?"

The lights flickered. It took me a moment to realize Biel wasn't responsible. Behind him the crowd started drifting back to the auditorium. Kay, now on her own, threw a curious glance at me. My opportunity, lost.

That smile, disconnected from any human emotion, returned to Biel's face. "Showtime. Part two begins. Enjoy it along with the remainder of your evening, Miss Frost."

Upon regaining the ability to move I scampered back to my seat, where Kay was waiting. "How about next time you listen to Leni while I chat up handsome flyboy types?"

"What did she say?"

"What do you mean what did she say? I don't know what you want to ask, so when I found myself next to her and that Jäger fellow I complimented the movie. Glenn Morris skulked past and I asked if we'd see him in part two. Jäger laughs. Leni says she and Morris were an item during the filming. She tells me when Morris won his medal, he tore open her blouse and kissed her breasts in front of half of Berlin. Says it like it happens every day. I look at Jäger and he shrugs. *Shrugs.*" Kay shook her head. "If she's Hitler's girlfriend, you'd think she'd have a better press agent."

MY HEART STILL hammered in my chest as *Olympia*, "Part Two: Festival of Beauty," began. Fortunately more disturbingly casual onscreen nudity distracted me, this time of the male variety, sweaty men swatting themselves with leaves. I didn't bother gauging the audience's reaction, knowing that to do so would mark me as scandalized. Instead I stared doggedly ahead until I ceased viewing the men as men but instead as groups of muscles operating in harmony—once again, as Riefenstahl did. To her, a finely trained body was the apex of beauty, hence part two's title. She lovingly photographed Glenn Morris like a force of nature, the closing image of him superimposed over the American flag prompting spontaneous applause.

The aquatic sections showcased Riefenstahl's technical acumen. Cameras skimmed the surface of the water during the yacht races, huddled next to men straining against the oars in the rowing events. The bodies of divers were as at home in the sky as they were in the water, a figure in midair occasionally landing on a platform as the film played in reverse, the camera sometimes plunging into the pool alongside the athlete.

The final shot, of smoke from the extinguished Olympic flame floating into a heaven pierced by spotlights, reduced me to tears, both of joy and fear that two years hence events would prevent the world's athletes from meeting again under the banner of competition. This second film felt truer to Riefenstahl's spirit, celebrating sensation and grace, reaching for the beautiful without a thought for what might be crushed underneath.

The lights came up. The crowd roared. Biel was nowhere in sight.

"Come on," I told Kay. "We're talking to her."

AN ALCOVE PROVIDED sanctuary while Riefenstahl's welter of well-wishers waned. Two sportswriters passed us. "Her film's a hell of a piece of work," one of them said, "and I wish I didn't think so." Glenn Morris wandered at the periphery of the crowd, abashed. But then how were you supposed to react when you'd been depicted as a Greek god? He spotted an opportunity and charged toward his onetime paramour. There was no rending of garments or kissing of breasts, simply a clasping of hands and the exchange of a few words. Then Morris stole away, hopelessly at sea. I felt sorry for him.

Still no sign of Kaspar Biel. I grabbed Kay and barreled through the stragglers toward Riefenstahl and Ernst Jäger.

He clucked and fussed at Kay, Riefenstahl's alarmingly direct gaze betraying only a dim recognition. Her eyes next assessed me, and I thought *In* S.O.S. *Iceberg she should have played the title role.*

My name surfaced like two rocks in a stream of German, Kay, making introductions. Jäger took over, the only word I understood "Paramount." Mention of the studio prompted the raising of two eyebrows, one Riefenstahl's, one Kay's. I'd propagated a lie in two languages. The sisters at Saint Mary's would be proud.

Riefenstahl spoke, Kay translating. "So nice of you to come. Did you enjoy the screening?"

I told the truth. "It's a powerful film."

Her response was followed by a self-effacing laugh a touch too transparent; as an actress, she made a fine director. "Perhaps you will tell your employers."

"I will. I'd love to line up some big names to excite Americans about your film, let them know what it is. An ode to the human form in all its glory."

Riefenstahl nodded vigorously as soon as Kay started translating, her next words a torrent. "Yes. This is what I've told Ernst and anyone who will listen. But how do we do this with the world situation being what it is?"

Now or never. "You've had other screenings in Los Angeles."

Kay conveyed my words in German. Riefenstahl nodded. Jäger frowned. I pressed on. "Surely you met people you could enlist in your efforts."

I refrained from biting my lip as I awaited her reply. "Yes, a few. But they might be reluctant."

"Perhaps *we*"—I leaned on the plural, putting the full weight of Paramount Pictures behind it—"could help enroll them in your campaign."

After listening to Kay, Riefenstahl consulted briefly with Jäger. She then turned to me, her smile at last genuine. "We'd appreciate the help."

"Tell me who to call." I prayed she wouldn't say Errol Flynn's name.

A door behind Riefenstahl opened. Georg Gyssling bustled in, shoulders hunched and forehead gleaming. Kaspar Biel stood behind him, his eyes never deviating from mine.

Gyssling flashed a spotlight smile, then spoke in German to Riefenstahl. Biel's comment, in English, was directed at me. "Miss Riefenstahl must depart."

He held the door open. Gyssling gestured for Riefenstahl to proceed. The filmmaker hesitated, looking at me. Biel spoke, his words sounding harsh even without benefit of translation, and I felt myself disappear from Riefenstahl's view, a feature no longer visible on the landscape. She strode off down a corridor, Gyssling and Biel in her wake, Jäger scrambling to keep up.

I hooked my arm in Kay's and ran after them, calling Riefenstahl's name. She and Biel spoke in raised voices, as if I were a squalling infant they'd chosen to ignore. Riefenstahl adjusted her hat so I wouldn't even appear in the corner of her eye. She reached the exit, where two brown-shirted men waited. Gyssling threw the door open to the night and ushered Riefenstahl out. Biel followed without a backward glance. Jäger turned to us—"Lovely meeting you!"—and darted through the door before it slammed shut. The sentries remained, faces blank, barring us from pursuing them.

AN OLD MAN in a tattered coat and a new homburg stood opposite the California Club's entrance. "For shame!" he hollered at Kay and me. "That film glorifies Hitler! For shame!"

"Can it, pops! It's a free country!" Kay bellowed back. "Word's out about the screening. I'm still in the dark about why we're here, but I'm guessing tonight's expedition was a bust."

"In so many words." I didn't want to talk about it. I wanted to go back and let the man in the homburg heap more abuse on me. I'd been so close, and I failed.

Naturally, Kay was in chirpy high spirits. "Still, I don't regret coming. That picture was a marvel. Never saw anything like it. They should show it in schools. The Hitler-free version, I mean. I'm sure Leni would be fine with it." Sensing my despair, she surprisingly took pity on me. "You gave it the old college try, Lillian. Fancy that, telling them you were with Paramount. It was working until golden boy queered the deal. Who is he, anyway?"

"He's with the consulate. He thinks Tallulah Bankhead should play Scarlett."

"Stick to politics, Horst. Leni was explaining you could help get the picture seen and he told her to forget it."

"What exactly did he say?"

"You don't want to know."

"Now I definitely do. What did he say about me?"

Kay exhaled. *Very well, if you're going to force me to repeat gossip . . .* "He said you didn't work at Paramount, and that you were—how did he put it? A nonentity."

A nonentity. *Very apt,* I thought. "What did Leni say in response?"

"Only that she should have known."

"That's it? She came on like quite the chatterbox."

"It was some kind of German folk wisdom, I suppose, a new one on me. She said what you offered was too good to be true, and like the man said, when the hand is dealt it's not enough to check your cards. You also have to check your dealer."

I stopped dead on the sidewalk. Behind us, the man in the

homburg continued to harangue the late exodus. Electricity sparked from my every nerve. *I knew.*

"Those were her exact words?"

"Give or take. Why?"

"I know I don't work there, but how soon can you get me to Paramount?"

38

I PILED OUT of Kay's car at the Bronson Gate, fending off demands for an explanation. "All will soon be revealed," I said.

"Quit talking like Orson Welles on *The Shadow*. I'd better hear every last detail. Remember, I'm in line for an exclusive." Tires scraping the curb, her roadster roared off into the night.

The lethargic gate guard perked up at my name. "Miss Head left a message. She's taking a walk around the lot, but her office is open. You can wait for her there."

A pair of seamstresses speaking Spanish shuffled out of the Wardrobe building, offering weary smiles as I passed. Inside I heard the rhythmic clack of a sewing machine. Cameras would be rolling in a matter of hours, and costumes would be ready and waiting.

Light from a lamp Edith had left burning spilled across the sketches on her desk. I sneaked a peek at her creations, to be worn by Bob Hope's costar in his latest comedy. A flowing skirt with gay stripes accompanied by a Dutch girl hat altered to look more like a doily, and a rather severe black dress suitable for a funeral. Edith had scribbled "dueling scene" on the second illustration; if Bob Hope was participating in an *affaire d'honneur*, he wouldn't be the one destined for the casket. Not with his billing.

Even Edith's artistry couldn't provide distraction from what I'd discovered. Donald Hume was a Nazi agent. Jens hadn't blackmailed him over his infidelity but his political leanings; the "other woman" he'd been with at 4:17 had been Leni Riefenstahl. In fawning over her after the clandestine screening of the full Führer version of *Olympia*, he'd relied on his canned wisdom, which she'd repeated to Kaspar Biel. On the ride to Paramount I'd grilled Kay, asking her to parse Riefenstahl's words. Yes, she admitted, upon reflection the director did seem to be quoting someone as opposed to citing a maxim. The intensity of my questioning only fueled her interest. Kay made bulldogs look lazy when she thought she'd sniffed out a story. I'd soon have to figure out how to handle her.

At the moment, though, what I wanted to do most was review the night's events with Edith. I paced her office suite, the implications looming larger in my mind with each trip.

From the outer office, I heard a noise in the hallway. I swung the door open, tempted to holler a greeting into the quiet, knowing Edith wouldn't find it amusing.

Never was I so grateful for my Catholic school reticence. Kaspar Biel quickstepped along the corridor, reading signs with ferocious concentration.

I didn't wonder how he'd gained entry to the lot. I didn't go back to the office for my handbag. Instead I slipped toward the stairs and started down with all deliberate speed.

I intended to loop around the building along Marathon Street and have the gate guard call the police. But upon reaching the door I abruptly retreated and pressed my back to the wall. One of the brown-shirted men from the California Club stalked past the window. I scurried to another exit.

It was eerie being on the lot at night, the normal vibrancy stilled at that hour. Ghosts already held sway on the studio grounds, vestiges of forgotten films and neglected actors hiding in plain sight, surfacing at unexpected times in surprising places. Under cover of darkness, they had free rein.

My plan was to cut over to the closest gate fronting Van Ness

Avenue and seek help there. But as I reached the path, I spotted the second of the brown shirts jawing with the gate guard. A compatriot who'd allowed Biel and his bullyboys onto the lot, I thought, and fled in the other direction.

Soundstages loomed on either side of me like beached ships, dormant at present yet still emitting energy. I angled toward Melrose Avenue and another source of salvation.

Ahead of me, a few guttural words of German. Unless it was one of their single multisyllabic words. My feet scuffled on the pavement as I scrambled away. I didn't hear the voices go silent so much as feel it, like a chilled liquid engulfing my skin.

I moved faster. Passing John Engstead's photography studio, I spied a space even darker than the night surrounding it. One of the doors had been left open, a forest of lighting stands around it. I weaved between them and ducked inside.

My eyes slowly adjusted, the contours of the room revealing themselves. The studio as always was jammed with furniture. I felt my way to the wall, intent on using it as a guide until I located a telephone.

I screamed before I reached one. It was my natural reaction to finding a woman sitting alone in a pitch-black room. I nearly screamed again when she didn't budge in response.

I'd proceeded far enough to risk a light. I fumbled for a lamp, found one on a table, flicked it on.

A cigarette extended toward me, seeking a match. Behind it, dead eyes. Only in Hollywood could I encounter, in a moment of extreme distress, a celebrity.

The "woman" was Cynthia, Jack Benny's mannequin costar in *Artists and Models Abroad*. She hadn't been packed up after her latest photo shoot, the fair-haired facsimile leaning forward as if hanging on my every unsaid word, cigarette poised.

From outside Engstead's studio, whispers. I doused the light. And did the only thing I could think of.

I took a seat opposite Cynthia. She was shorter than me, so I perched at the edge of the chair with one leg hooked underneath me and the other outstretched, somewhat provocatively, for balance. I draped a blanket over my shoulders to mask my clothes. With the hasty removal of a few pins, my hair fell free and concealed most of my face. Lastly, I raised my arm as if I, too, held a cigarette. I told myself Cynthia and I looked like a pair of catty friends comparing notes in a cocktail bar, about to launch into lines from Clare Boothe Luce's play *The Women*.

Men, I thought across the dark to my scene partner. *Always the wrong ones chasing you, am I right?*

Two flashlight beams punctured the gloom. They picked out furniture covered in dusty sheets, struck mirrors that reflected the light back, prompting hushed profanities. Someone bumped into something.

A last inhalation through my nose, then I temporarily gave up breathing.

Through a scrim of hair I glimpsed Biel, wielding his torch like a sword, surveying the room. The chunkier of the brown shirts followed him. Biel's beam played over Cynthia, then drifted to me. It moved up, down, and up again, halting at eye level like a cruel taunt.

The beam returned to my mute cohort, moving almost caressingly over her features. Biel spoke softly in German. The only word I understood: "Cynthia."

Leave it to me to be pursued by a Nazi who read Louella Parsons.

The beams and their bearers continued through the room. Satisfied, Biel and his sidekick plunged back onto the lot.

I remained motionless for several more seconds, until the blanket over my shoulders slid off as if nudged by an unseen presence. I took that as my cue to leave.

"Nice working with you," I whispered to Cynthia.

The lot had grown even more quiet. I darted toward the Bronson Gate. Before I reached it I heard a steady drum of heels against pavement. I ducked out of sight and waited.

The figure that appeared was too short to be Biel or either of his lackeys. There was only one person it could be. I hissed at Edith from the shadows.

She understood the situation quickly. "We'll avoid my office. My keys will let us into the admin building."

AFTER LOCKING THE door behind us, Edith led the way to a windowless interior office so we could turn on all the lights we wanted. Her first telephone call was to studio security, resulting in guards being dispatched across the lot. Her next was to Barney Groff, who was tracked down at the Brown Derby.

"They're bringing a phone to his table," Edith relayed. Of course they were.

She spoke to him briefly and then, to my stomach's dismay, held out the receiver. "He wants to talk to you."

The giddy hubbub of the Derby greeted my ears, and I badly wished I were there. Groff's brusque demeanor froze my earlobe. "I want this direct from you. There are Nazis, actual Nazis, on my lot?"

"Yes, sir."

"Put Miss Head back on." I returned the phone to her. The rest of the call lasted six seconds.

"We're to wait here," Edith said. "So. What's new?"

My digest of the night's proceedings came out in a gush, sans governor, Edith bracing herself against the onslaught.

"It all fits," I said, forcing myself to wind down. "Donald Hume is an attorney. He represents countless influential people in Los Angeles. He'd be the ideal spy. Addison's new inventions alone would be of value to Germany. And Donald and Charlotte are always at parties, so it would be easy for him to meet Jens and exchange information."

Some of those meetings, I thought, may have taken place in Addison's home. While I was nearby. I shivered and kept talking.

"Plus Jens was blackmailing Donald. Rory Dillon told me, and like him I assumed, as with most of Jens's blackmail victims, it was about being unfaithful."

"It is, in a sense," Edith said. "Mr. Hume is being unfaithful to his country."

"Jens had Rory reach out to Charlotte because he couldn't very well go to Donald himself and say, 'Pay up or I'll reveal you've been talking to me.' Then Donald eliminated the threat by killing Jens."

"It's quite sound," Edith said, nodding slowly. "And, may I say, astonishing. You're the only person who could have made these connections."

"I know. It's practically a miracle. I've been trying to figure out which saint I should offer up a prayer to."

"That's the problem, my dear. Who else will believe it?"

Like that, I was adrift.

"You've convinced me Mr. Hume is a Nazi operative with a concrete motive to kill Mr. Lohse. But what evidence do we have? A rough translation of what Mr. Hume may have said to Miss Riefenstahl is damning to you—and yes, to me—but imagine bringing this to the FBI. They would do nothing, in part because they've made clear what their priorities are but mainly because it's far from conclusive."

I felt queasy. I knew I had no argument to rebut her but struggled to mount one out of sheer pigheadedness. "I'll tell Gene. He'll believe me."

"He certainly will. And he'll do what he can. But if anything, he'll be more limited in his responses than Mr. Hoover's men.

They are choosing to ignore this situation, at least for the time being, while Detective Morrow has already contacted the German consulate and been rebuffed. Anything he attempts now would be without the sanction of the police department."

More arrows in Gene's back, which bristled with a quiver of them thanks to me. *You'll still ask him to do something*, I thought. *And he'll still try.*

Tears of frustration welled in my eyes. I was determined to stop them from falling, because apparently I couldn't accomplish anything else.

"What am I supposed to do," I asked, "if I know the truth but can't get anyone to act on it?"

Edith tilted her head, a deliberate gesture, I realized later, to keep me from reading her eyes.

"One can always dress up the truth," she said. "Put it in a new wardrobe so it resembles the truth others are seeking. The FBI, for instance."

A sharp rap on the door prevented her from elaborating. Barney Groff entered, attired in a single-breasted tuxedo doubtlessly described by his tailor as "Stygian." His hair, normally lacquered in place, stood up in stalks. He caught me staring and tamped it down with his fingers, then smiled. "Problem solved," he announced with a thorough lack of modesty. "It's once again safe to traverse the lot."

"What happened, Mr. Groff?" Edith asked.

"Turns out one of our guards was a Bund bum. He let the Nazis on, so now he's out on his *tuchus*."

"And the Nazis?" I inquired.

"They were also shown the gate, after the time-tested concept of private property was explained to them. Point by point. In meticulous detail." He flexed his hands as he spoke. "The blond one required extra tutoring. But the lesson finally sank in."

He held the office door wide and gestured that we should

leave. As he did, I noticed a fine spray of blood on his dress shirt, some of the bright red drops vanishing into the pleats as he moved.

Again, Groff noticed my attention. Again, he smiled. It was the first time I'd seen the man truly happy.

39

I'D CHOSEN MY vantage point carefully. Upper deck near the stern of the *Lumen*, with a view of the floating casino's landing stage. I watched one of the water taxis doggedly approach, swells be damned. Another benefit of my perch: an overhang that kept most of the night's light rain off me. The weather didn't dampen the spirits of those who'd made the trip. Over a dozen people clambered out of the launch. With firm determination on unsteady legs, they made their way inside.

Once again, I didn't recognize a soul among them.

Malcolm Drewe appeared out of the dark next to me, raindrops glittering like rhinestones on his mohair coat. He gazed down at the passengers. "More seagulls, here for the free dinner. I can tell by their clothes."

"Seagulls?"

"They eat, shit, and leave. You spot your party?"

"Not yet."

After a dubious grunt, Drewe brushed moisture from his coat and ambled back inside. I couldn't blame him. There'd be a wait until the next launch arrived, which might or might not be carrying Donald Hume.

I TRIED TO do things the right way at first. But Edith, as usual, had correctly foretold the future.

Agent Deems made it abundantly clear the FBI had no inter-

est in any additional information I had acquired about the identity of a well-connected Nazi operative and his possible role in
the murder of Jens Lohse. He did, however, remind me his door
remained ajar should I care to discuss Albert Chaperau. I didn't
bother mentioning Donald's name.

As for Gene, I held nothing back. When I'd laid out every
specious supposition and harebrained hypothesis, he appraised
me over my coffee table, then shook his head.

"I'm sorry, Lillian. I can't do anything."

"I was afraid of that."

"I'd talk to the consulate again, but it's been expressed from
on high I'm not to pester them anymore."

"I didn't realize I'd gotten you in trouble."

Gene waved my concern away. "Part of my job is annoying
the right people. Including my superiors. The bigger problem
is the Auerbachs. When Felix resurfaced, Marthe recanted her
confession. But the DA's still going to prosecute her for Jens's
murder."

"I understand. I have to ask, though. Do you believe me?"

Gene glanced out my window. Miss Sarah, slinking across the
sill, forced him to look back at me. "Honestly, Frost? It's not much
to go on."

"OF COURSE I believe you," Simon said, his gaze steady over
my coffee table. "What do you need from me?"

Executing Edith's plan without Gene's help would require a
lot of cooperation. Simon was merely the first stop.

"The exact date of the secret *Olympia* screening."

"Why?"

"I'm going to follow through on Jens's plan. I'm going to blackmail Donald Hume."

• • •

NOW THAT I knew to avoid booths with portholes, I would have ventured into Club Fathom alone. Still, I preferred showing up in Simon's company.

Rory Dillon's sleek appearance wasn't dented by his nonplussed expression. "You want me to do what?"

"Exactly what Jens had you do before. Tell Charlotte Hume it was a pleasure to see her husband, Donald." I turned to Simon.

"On the evening of November twenty-fifth," he said.

"He's still catting around, with the missus up there on the silver screen." Rory winked lasciviously. I doubted he could wink any other way. "But why do you care?"

"Charlotte's my friend."

"Strange show of affection. I expect a cut of the proceeds."

If he wanted a share of the prison sentence coming Donald's way, he was welcome to it. "You'll have to earn it. A few days after you see Charlotte you'll telephone Donald to arrange the meeting. I'll tell you what to say."

IT DIDN'T TAKE that long. The day after Rory's second casual encounter with Charlotte, he telephoned in a lather. "Your man called me! Hume. Or his office did. How the hell did he know it was me talked to his wife?"

He's a spy, I thought. "How many dashing Irishmen with shady reputations can there be? What did he—or she—say?"

"'Mr. Hume doesn't understand your instructions.' Didn't have a clue what she was asking, the poor wee girl."

A cagey move on Donald's part, using his secretary Marjorie to keep himself at a remove. No wonder the Nazis prized him. "And your response to the poor wee girl?"

"The time and place you gave me. I said I'd settle accounts with Mr. Hume then."

"How'd she take it?"

"She said she didn't know if he'd be available but she'd relay the message. A lovely voice she had, quite posh. Should hire someone like that myself. My part in this drama is through, right?"

"Yes."

"Remember now, I'm in for a share of the winnings. I may even turn up at that boat to make sure I get it. Always wanted one of those free turkey dinners."

I HADN'T SPOTTED Rory on the *Lumen*, but I had no doubt his representatives were present, along with Malcolm Drewe's men. Drewe had been unstintingly generous with his support since I'd persuaded him to play along with Edith's scheme.

We had met at Marie's Pantry again, Simon at my side, short-cake on the table. No more peach melba for me.

"We found the person responsible for Jens Lohse's death," I said. "The person who kept you from getting what you paid for."

"And you want to give me his name so I'll mete out some frontier justice? That's not how I operate, Miss Frost, no matter what you've heard." He looked pointedly at Simon, intimating I was the one who'd brought muscle along, forgetting about Knoll and the other men lounging in and around the diner.

"That's not what I want. My friend and I would like to confront this man and ideally bring him to the authorities. At the very least, he could give you the money you paid Jens. But there's a chance this could go wrong."

"And it never hurts to have something that could go wrong take place in international waters. Is that it?" Drewe gazed wistfully out at Santa Monica Bay, resenting every moment he spent on shore. "Tell me your event's requirements. Perhaps the *Lumen* can accommodate you. We do aim to please."

• • •

ON THE SHIP'S deck, I shrugged deeper into my coat against the chill. I'd stuck a few extra pins in my hair to keep my hat on against the insistent breeze, but I'd foolishly forgotten my gloves. Time to warm up inside while awaiting the next taxi of tinhorns.

To maintain Christmas spirits Drewe had sprung for punch stations serving gratis wassail to the bettors, each manned by a Santa. The Saint Nick nearest me had clearly been sampling from his own ladle. The wavering gaits of the *Lumen*'s passengers were only peripherally related to the rolling waters beneath.

I moved among the crowd and rubbed feeling back into my hands. Knoll sat a table, an untouched glass of punch before him and a vacant smile on his face. "Silent night," he said as I passed. His left shoe tapped the grip tucked under the table. "Your suitcase is ready when you need it. *If* you need it."

If indeed.

THE UNLIKELIEST COCONSPIRATOR in Edith's plan proved the easiest to convince.

At our meeting with Barney Groff, he greeted me with his customary indifference. Edith explained that the German assault on Paramount Pictures spearheaded by Kaspar Biel was, in fact, caused by Donald Hume.

"Lillian tried to alert the FBI," she said, "but they're preoccupied with this Chaperau matter."

"Of course they are." Groff fumed, so hot he almost didn't need a match to spark his cigarette. "How the hell is it we see the threat the Nazis pose and Hoover's boys can't? Or won't?"

"It's a shame, Mr. Groff."

His eyes narrowed. "So what do you propose to do?"

"It occurred to me," Edith said, "that as long as the FBI *believes* they're investigating Mr. Chaperau, they'll do so diligently. Par-

ticularly if you inform them of a recent development that has you
concerned."

The security chief looked skeptical, so I spoke up.

"You tell them I'm in cahoots with Chaperau after all. After
his arrest, I hid couture dresses he smuggled into the country in
the wardrobe department here at the studio. I exploited my
friendship with Edith. Paramount is utterly blameless and just
wants to help. You tell the FBI I'm a nuisance who causes you
nothing but aggravation."

Groff looked from Edith to me and back again as he weighed
the idea. Then a smile broke on his face as pure as the dawn. For
the second time in a week, he was truly happy.

THE FBI'S SHADOWING of me escalated immediately. It felt
creepy, but I got used to it. On the day Donald Hume was to
meet his blackmailer aboard the *Lumen*, I arrived at Paramount
with a suitcase. Purely for show, of course, along with my visit
to Edith's office. A rack of stunning gowns waited there: wild,
adventurous creations unlike Edith's usual designs. I said as much.

"These aren't mine, dear. They're the dresses from Paris used
in *Artists and Models Abroad*."

"Starring my good friend Cynthia." I knew I was keyed up
about what we were attempting when I couldn't properly sali-
vate over the sartorial smorgasbord before me.

"No sense waiting," Edith said. "Open your suitcase."

"But I don't need actual dresses. I only want the FBI to think
I have them."

"Props and costumes, which in this instance are one and the
same, lend shape and definition to a performance. And that's what
you're giving tonight." She stepped back. "Is that what you'll be
wearing?"

• • •

THE FBI AGENTS dogging me scrambled to board the same water taxi. On the *Lumen*, they watched me entrust my suitcase to Knoll with palpable excitement.

Edith's plan was simple. Donald Hume arrives to confront his mystery extortionist. I present myself and hand him the suitcase. The FBI sweeps in and snares us both. Groff blows the gaff, with Edith offering bona fides for the dresses in my grip. The studio moguls then pressure the FBI to investigate Donald on charges of espionage and murder. Even if the gambit failed, Donald would be of no use to the Nazis as a spy after the incident.

And if Kaspar Biel showed in Donald's stead? I'd holler bloody murder until the FBI or Drewe's minions came to my aid. An international incident in theoretically international waters would force the government's hand. I merely had to bring the concerned parties to one location and stay calm.

But the designated hour had come and gone, multiple launches ferrying no familiar faces. I had to consider the possibility Donald had stood me up. There'd been no word from him since his secretary called Rory Dillon; there wasn't supposed to be. Earlier I'd taken the dicey step of telephoning his office to ask if he'd be available for a meeting with Addison that night. His perky secretary Marjorie—Rory was wrong; her voice wasn't that posh— replied *No, Mr. Hume has an engagement this evening, let's see, what other times would be convenient for Mr. Rice?* I hung up certain Donald and I had a date with destiny.

I hated invoking Addison's name. I hated keeping him in the dark about Donald even more. But I needed confirmation before impugning his longtime counselor.

Dealing with Charlotte was another matter. In the midst of my machinations she telephoned, the sound of her voice startling me. "What are you doing?" she asked.

Wishing your husband was only cheating on you.

I stuck to neutral answers and didn't rise to any of her gossipy conversational bait, willing the call to be over. At last, she got to the point. "Addison will spare you to help plan our Christmas bash! Isn't that fabulous? Still interested?"

"Let's see what the next few days bring," I said.

THE LAUNCH WAS but a distant speck on the pitch-black sea, slowly growing larger. I had time to stretch my legs.

Simon fed change into a slot machine, pulling the handle as if testing his reflexes. He subtly indicated the adjacent one-armed bandit. I took a seat and rooted in my purse for coins. We'd argued about the wisdom of his being on the *Lumen;* I was concerned his presence could scupper his cover story at the Bund. Simon had again gazed at me levelly, paying me the compliment of his full attention. "You need someone on that boat whose sole concern is protecting you. That someone will be me."

Now he murmured at the tumbling wheels of the slot machine, which made him seem like an authentically degenerate gambler. "How much longer do we wait?"

"We may have waited too long already. Drewe's starting to doubt me."

"Are you all right?"

"I'm fine. Actually, I don't know what I'm doing. And I have no change."

After surveying the room in the slot machine's polished exterior, Simon surreptitiously palmed me a nickel. Into the slot machine it went.

Three cherries. Naturally. I fed a nickel from my winnings in and kept playing.

"If we decide to bail on this barge," Simon muttered, "any thoughts on how we do it?"

"The FBI should leave me alone. The trouble is recovering my suitcase from Drewe. He might kick."

"I'll deal with him if necessary. I'll row you back to shore myself if it comes to that."

I couldn't help turning toward him, ready to offer my deepest gratitude. One of the FBI agents furtively spun away to assess a sheet of horseracing odds. We were being watched.

Wordlessly I shoveled nickels into my purse and walked off, careful to leave a coin behind. I always paid my debts.

THE FEWEST PEOPLE yet tumbled out of the water taxi, having commenced their imbibing on terra firma. None of them was Donald Hume. It was more than two hours past our meeting time. I had to face facts. He wasn't coming.

I stood outside, freezing, watching the launch's skeletal crew ready the boat for the return voyage. The plan had made sense— to Edith, to Simon, to Barney Groff, to me. Yet nothing had come to pass, aside from J. Edgar Hoover's choirboys eyeing me anew.

Where was Donald? I shivered in my too-thin coat as the rain fell harder, pocking the surface of the bay below, and reviewed every step in our scheme. How could it have failed? Could Marjorie have mangled Rory's message to Donald?

My next thought chilled me more than the night air. *What if Donald had never received it?*

Gene. I had to talk to Gene. I needed a telephone, desperately. There were none on the *Lumen* I could access. I couldn't ask to use the ship's radio, not with Drewe already harboring suspicions about me.

A blast of the water taxi's horn made up mind. I drew my coat around me and raced toward the landing stage before the launch—the *Caroline*—pushed off. I couldn't signal Simon, not

without siccing the FBI on him. And I couldn't risk Drewe knowing I'd slipped ashore. I'd hightail it to Santa Monica, telephone
Gene with my latest fear, and be back aboard the *Lumen* in two
shakes. No one would even notice I had left.

Or so I told myself.

40

⬚

THERE WEREN'T MANY passengers on the *Caroline*, most people possessing the sense to ride out the rough weather on the larger vessel. Plus the Lumenarias went on again at ten. A half-dozen swells braved the swells in the launch's bow, protected from the elements. A baby-faced sailor in a peacoat and watch cap sprawled in his seat in despair, mourning the loss of his pay. A white-haired drunk, stuffed with free turkey, dozed off with his face aimed at the heavens. I feared he'd drown sitting up.

The *Caroline* charged toward shore, the lights of Santa Monica a promise destined to be broken. I steadied myself against the railing, realized with regret I'd have to make two more such crossings this evening, and started for shelter.

The sailor's legs blocked my path. I could have tried slipping past, but the deck was slick with rain. And I frankly wasn't in the mood. "Excuse me," I said over the wind.

"I don't believe I will," the sailor replied, and I no longer had to call Gene and warn him about Charlotte Hume because Charlotte was right in front of me, brandishing a pistol that perfectly complemented her peacoat. Then again, black went with everything.

Props and costumes, Edith had said, *lend shape and definition to a performance.*

She'd tucked her hair under the watch cap, the coat concealing her curves. With her hands in her pockets and her head angled down in the classic pose of a sailor fleeced at the start of shore leave, no one would give her a second glance. I was cer-

tain I hadn't: I had the sinking feeling I'd passed Charlotte on
the *Lumen* repeatedly.

"Donald won't be joining us. Donald doesn't even know about
this. Men can only get into trouble, not out of it." She sat in masculine fashion, legs splayed, shoulders hunched. The gun lev-
eled at my stomach was invisible to those at the front of the
Caroline. "Were you behind this all along?"

I didn't see the point in feigning confusion or surprise. Not
with my friend. "No," I said.

"Then it *was* Jens. So I can end this once and for all." Her eyes
ticked past me to the dark waters of the bay, dappled with rain
now falling with some force. They then shifted to the drunk, still
out like a light. "Almost at the busiest part of the channel."

"People know I'm here."

"Dozens of them, from what I saw on that boat. But nobody
knows I'm here."

"How long have you known you were married to a Nazi?"

"I didn't have a clue until the first time that slick mick am-
bushed me and I mentioned what he said to Donald. Donald
cracked immediately. Told me every detail of his silly intrigues.
The Germans sure can pick 'em. Donald's terrified of them. So I
stroked his forehead, told him it was nothing. Then set out to
make it nothing."

A wave struck the launch. I stumbled against the railing. Charlotte shifted as if she'd sensed the swell coming, the gun still
aimed at me. She moved like an old salt, completely at home in
that peacoat. The power of wardrobe could not be denied. I'd
have to tell Edith, if I lived through the night.

"Donald couldn't think, so I thought for him," Charlotte said
"The only threat facing him was Jens. Without him, no one could
prove anything about Donald. It didn't take long to realize Jens
was also the blackmailer—and sleeping with his music teacher's
wife."

"You tracked him to the Auerbach cabin."

"I'd been looking for a challenging ride for my horse." Charlotte smiled at the memory. For an instant I could glimpse the woman I knew—and I was petrified. "A lovely canter through the hills and back. Never saw a soul. Donald has no idea what I did. All he knows is no one followed up with any demands, so he believes his worries are behind him. So did I, until the Irishman came back."

"You didn't pass along his second message," I said. "You called the Irishman pretending to be Donald's secretary."

"I assumed he was a go-between, but it couldn't hurt to put a little fear into him. I got to the *Lumen* hours ago. I saw you arrive, and all those men watching you. I decided to wait you out. If you left on your own, I'd follow you. Arrange an accident at sea."

"Why? Why are you protecting Donald? Why are you doing this?"

"Because I'm going to work with *Capra!*" She bellowed the name into the wind, invoking the director like some ancient god who would smite her enemies. "After years of struggle, of rejection, I'm finally being seen. Not by casting directors or sleazy agents, but the names on the screen. Other actors. Directors who matter. They are *seeing* me. Do you understand what it means when those people see you, acknowledge you exist? They are making me real. If Donald is exposed as a Nazi agent, that goes away. They'll stop seeing me. I won't be real." She stared through me to the water, the storm raging in her head far more tumultuous than the one behind me. "I won't be my own person. I'll be the floozy married to Hitler's stooge. I won't be *me*. I won't be able to share my gift. I won't permit that to happen."

Her recitation took on a religious fervor, the won'ts becoming her cant. I knew she had every intention of pulling the trigger. Yet I had to ask the one question that had formed solidly in my mind.

"That job you offered me. It wasn't real, was it?"

The words needed a moment to penetrate her haze. "No."

She glanced at the shoreline, then the channel marker, and flicked the gun at me. The time had come.

"Put the weapon down, Mrs. Hume."

The *Caroline*'s skipper approached us, billed cap pulled low over his eyes. He had a gun of his own in his hand.

And, incredibly, Gene's voice.

Charlotte vaulted toward me. At that moment the drunk from the rear of the launch pounced, moving with the reflexes of a much younger man. He seized Charlotte's arm, her gun clattering to the rain-slick deck. Charlotte writhed in his grasp and unleashed a fierce animal wail. Already she could tell the right people had stopped seeing her. She could feel herself disappearing, each missing molecule causing untold pain.

I blinked through the rain at Gene. His eyes practically shined with calm. "LAPD officers have been on these launches all night. I ever tell you I hate the water?"

Questions elbowed each other aside in my brain, desperate to be asked. Instead I collapsed against Gene, burying my face in his borrowed coat that smelled of fresh rain and another man's cigarettes. And I sobbed.

THE ANSWER TO my most pressing query came when I spotted the figure standing beneath a streetlamp at the water taxi landing. Her stylish tartan umbrella would have given her away even if her petite frame hadn't.

Gene had to help me off the boat, my legs suddenly petulant about obeying orders. He and the erstwhile drunk then led Charlotte toward a waiting police car. She drifted between them in shock; one tap of a finger on her shoulder and she'd change direction.

Slowly I walked over to Edith. She extended her umbrella but I remained beyond its reach, feeling unworthy.

"How did you know?" I asked.

"I didn't. But I know actresses. I saw it as a possibility."

"Why didn't you tell me?"

"You and Charlotte were friends. I didn't want to plant a seed of doubt until I was sure. So I told Detective Morrow."

I'd applied the same logic in keeping mum about Donald to Addison. It only seemed fair Edith use it on me.

"You're soaked. Come in out of the rain," Edith said.

"In a minute. You should go to Marie's Pantry. I recommend the strawberry shortcake."

Edith nodded and walked away. I watched Gene guide Charlotte into the police car with an almost respectful gentleness. A little more than three miles away, the *Lumen* bobbed aimlessly. That's where Simon was, out at sea, where he couldn't help. While I was on largely dry land with Gene. There was no doubt in my mind Edith had planned that, too.

KATHERINE DAMBACH'S
SLIVERS OF THE SILVER SCREEN
EXCLUSIVE

Happy Hollywood marriages are as rare as hen's teeth, but those who know Donald and Charlotte Hume called them the exception that proved the rule. The bond between the powerful lawyer and the up-and-coming cinematic star was a true love match.

Did I say "was"? Apparently it still is, for although Charlotte is cooling her high heels in the Lincoln Heights Jail, accused of murdering Austrian song-smith Jens Lohse, husband, Donald, is standing by her side.

The police allege Charlotte and Jens were lovers and she took his life in a jealous rage. Despite that, the influential attorney will drop all current clients and devote himself to defending his wife on the capital charge.

So what if debonair Donald hasn't tried a case since he was a wet-behind-the-ears pup right out of USC Law? Connubial commitment trumps legal experience. Or does it? Only time, and a jury of Charlotte's peers, will tell.

41

❖

"SOMEONE DONNED THEIR gay apparel," I told Edith as I entered her office. She'd foregone her muted tones in favor of a bright red shirtwaist with a white placket and matching pockets. "I should dip you in hot chocolate like a candy cane."

"Perhaps later. I thought I'd dress for the occasion. I'm throwing a holiday party for the girls in Wardrobe."

"That's a swell idea. Will you be playing Santa?"

"At my height? I'll forever be typecast as an elf."

"That seems appropriate. Elves do the hard work, while Saint Nick hogs all the press."

Edith concealed a smile. "Quite right. This afternoon I'm only making the punch."

"You're not putting Fernet in it?"

"No. It's not really for mass consumption, is it? What have you been up to?"

"Mainly helping Addison find a new lawyer. Although I did see *Artists and Models Abroad*. Extremely silly and just what the doctor ordered. I'm going again for the assembly line of beauty alone. To think I ran around the *Lumen* with those gowns in my suitcase. That scene with Cynthia—Jack Benny and Joan Bennett ran the same dodge I did!"

"Of course. Nothing's original in Hollywood."

Edith's secretary leaned into the office in a dither. "Miss Head, I— Um, Dorothy Lamour is here."

The actress breezed in, gorgeous in a green dress with a red tropical print that acknowledged both the season and her famous jungle girl roles. Still, her appearance hardly warranted the secretary's pixilated reaction. After effusive hellos, Dorothy said, "I'm showing a friend from back east around and he asked to meet you, Edie." She went to the doorway. "Jack?"

The man stepped into Edith's office as if afraid he'd misheard the summons. He was shorter than me, the grimace on his face indicating he'd logged that fact. His massive head and blocky frame seemed to have been carved out of a single slab of stone. The dark circles under his eyes clashed with the surprisingly flashy blue-and-gold tie around his throat.

Speaking of throats, mine closed up. I recognized the man.

"J. Edgar Hoover, Miss Head. May I say I'm a great fan of your work." His cadence was clipped, patrician. He turned to me. "Miss Frost."

How I mustered a nod, I would never know.

Edith recovered her bearings at once. "You and Dorothy are friends?"

"We've known each other for years," Dorothy said. "When I sang at the Stork Club, Rudy Vallee introduced me to the regulars like Walter Winchell. But Jack was the one I really wanted to meet. Can he tell a story!"

Hoover flashed a perfunctory smile. "Dorothy, might I have a moment with Miss Head and Miss Frost before we continue the tour?"

Dorothy happily blew air kisses all around. Apparently, knowing Hoover meant regularly being dispatched in that fashion.

He waited until the door closed behind her. "I wanted to meet you both after hearing about your efforts. Your tenacity is to be commended. We'll need more of it in the days to come. I'd like to reassure you that the Federal Bureau of Investigation is acutely aware of all German attempts to gain undue influence within our borders and would have acted at the appropriate time."

Sure you would have, I scoffed. Hoover's head snapped toward mine, and I was certain he could read my thoughts.

"You were wasting your time suspecting Errol Flynn, Miss Frost," he said. "We're familiar with his political convictions, such as they are. The man is a danger only to himself."

Some automatic reflex deep in my brain again managed to move my head up and down in response.

"I also wanted to allay any concerns on your part, Miss Head, about how the Bureau kept apprised of your involvement in the matter of Albert Chaperau."

"I believe I know," Edith said. "Dorothy?"

Another blink-and-you-missed-it smile from Hoover. "Old friends often discuss their respective workplaces. Dorothy passed along studio gossip about your meeting with Mr. Benny and Mr. Burns. And gossip, I'm sure you'll agree, is a valuable form of intelligence."

"I'm not about to put an end to gossip."

"I daresay I couldn't do that, either." The expression on Hoover's face hinted he'd like to try.

"Sir?" I sounded faint, and couldn't tell if my voice or my ears were failing me. "If I could ask, what happens to Mr. Chaperau and the others now?"

"The matter is resolved," Hoover declared. "Mr. Burns sensibly decided to plead guilty. At present Mr. Benny insists on maintaining his innocence, but he will assuredly be convinced to do otherwise and initiate the process of putting his mistake behind him. The American people are a forgiving people."

I fought the urge to hunt for the radio microphone into which Hoover seemed to be issuing his official remarks.

"As for Mr. Chaperau," he continued, "he will hold his tongue and serve his time. Time that may not be as long as he thinks."

"I'm afraid I don't understand," Edith said.

"Mr. Chaperau understood the risk he posed and acted to minimize it. He will be rewarded for that discretion. Now more than ever, we must protect the rule of law. That begins with protecting our duly elected leaders."

He paused as if waiting for the echoes of his oratory to fade then rubbed his hands together, a friendly gesture he'd no doubt poached from an underling. "Now. Dorothy said we might peek into your salon, where you do the fittings."

"By all means. It's right next door."

"Excellent. I hope you won't mind if I call on you both again should my business take me to this fair city?"

Edith nodded. I followed her lead.

"I wish you ladies happy holidays. 1939 should be a splendid year for the picture business."

"We have *Persons in Hiding* from your book to look forward to," Edith said.

"And *Gone with the Wind* might even come out," I added.

"Yes." Hoover hesitated. "Vivien Leigh will play Scarlett O'Hara."

"What?" I yelped. "But she's English!"

"Mr. Selznick's made his decision. I think it's an inspired choice. Good day to you both." With an oddly formal bow, he left to find Dorothy Lamour.

Edith and I stared at each other. "I don't suppose he planted some kind of listening device in here," she said softly.

"I wouldn't put it past him."

"And he's in the salon now. That's where the secrets really come out. I should have Mr. Groff inspect both rooms once Mr. Hoover departs." She chuckled. "Shall we have lunch?"

Halfway to the door she returned to her desk to jot down a note. Barney Groff would be receiving a call.

$\bullet \quad \bullet \quad \bullet$

THE PATH TO the commissary was festooned with wreaths and decorations. Only the mild weather prevented it from being a winter wonderland. "What are your holiday plans?" Edith asked.

"Up in the air at the moment. Addison's wife, Maude, is back from her trip. She had a difficult crossing, and the mood in Europe left her feeling tense. Plus the unpleasantness with Donald has been weighing on Addison. So they'll spend Christmas in seclusion, at their place in Arizona."

"Desert Christmases can be lovely. You won't be joining them?"

"They have staff there. Besides, I have to get to work on Addison's January social calendar. He's decreed 1939 will be a year of bashes and ballyhoo, starting with a New Year's Day brunch. The studio will be closed, so your attendance is expected."

"I do have to eat. You'll be at liberty on the twenty-fifth, then. What will you do with yourself?"

"Gene's arranged a dinner."

"Just the two of you?"

"No. Abigail will be there." I paused. "But Gene invited another detective to keep her company. Nice fellow, he says."

"That should be grand."

I certainly hoped it would be. I had similar expectations for my dinner with Simon the following evening. He'd been disappointed at being left on the *Lumen* during my showdown with Charlotte. "Now that this is over, we should spend some time together," he'd said. "You know who I am. I'd like to get to know who you are. It would have to be away from those fancy Hollywood places, though. No big names, no bright lights. That doesn't work for me. We'd have to go someplace off the beaten path. A little dark and disreputable."

If that's what it takes, I'd told him.

Edith wouldn't be pleased with my decision. But then Edith didn't need know to everything about me. Although when she fired a sudden suspicious glance my way as we reached the commissary doors, I realized she came as close as anyone ever would.

INSIDE THE USUAL ritual played out. Edith greeted everyone she passed by name, occasionally pausing for a few words. I affected a look of worldly patience. Let the assembled bigwigs wonder who the woman in Miss Head's company was. A well-regarded Park Avenue couturier, perhaps, trying California on for size. Or possibly the enigmatic star of a new film that was all the rage in Paris. Certainly not a too-tall girl from Flushing who'd lucked into the world she'd always dreamed about.

A roar erupted from the writers' table. Edith led the way to the ruckus. Billy Wilder jabbed at the piece of paper in another man's hand.

"These are the words you come up with? Does the studio know they're paying you as a writer? There's no wit to them, no élan, two words which, incidentally, I had in this round." He took note of Edith's approach. "Our esteemed Head of costume! Tell me, when will the commissary feature something inedible named in your honor? That's when you'll know your position is secure. It's cheaper to keep people on salary than reprint the menus."

"Say," another wag called out, "what's this I hear about J. Edgar himself being in your office?"

Wilder shushed his confederates. "Can we please discuss more significant matters? Your friend Preston Sturges is threatening to direct again. You know everything. What's he saying?"

"One thing I don't know," Edith said, "is why this word game you play fascinates you so."

"It's a keen test of intellect. We go around the table calling out letters until we reach twenty-five. You write them in a grid and make words of three, four, five letters. Whoever has the most wins."

Wilt, I spotted on Wilder's card. *Tilt. Spun.*

"That doesn't sound too difficult," Edith said.

Ovoid. Slid.

Following a long, awkward pause, all eyes at the table shifted to Wilder. Who shrugged.

"Anyone with a brain can play."

Spavin. No, that was six letters. I wondered if it counted.

"I've got a brain," Edith said.

Wilder pushed out a tortured sigh of impressive duration. "Miss Head has a brain, she says. Very well. Prove it." He gestured at the writers closest to him. "Shove over, boys. New shooter."

Vapid. That would work.

Edith sat demurely.

"I've got a brain, too," I said.

"What is this world coming to?" Wilder rubbed his face. "All right, gentlemen, make room. Time to see what the ladies are made of."

✳ Author's Note ✳

We wove a lot of fact into our fiction in this book, although on occasion liberties were taken. Herewith, a few words about sources and what's true. Any errors are our own.

A happenstance discovery of a news item regarding the Albert Chaperau affair inspired *Dangerous to Know*. It amazed us we'd never before heard about an international scandal involving two of the biggest stars of the era. Our description of the dinner party at the Lauer residence on October 21, 1938, is drawn from period accounts. Elma Lauer pled guilty to smuggling charges and served three months in prison, while Justice Edgar Lauer resigned from the bench and public life. In exchange for his guilty plea, George Burns received a suspended sentence and paid a substantial fine. Jack Benny initially protested his innocence in court, but was ultimately persuaded to take the same course of action as his longtime friend. He would pay more in legal fees than he would in penalties, an outcome that would flummox the skinflint character he famously portrayed. While our story depicts him at a personal and professional low point, our research confirmed that Jack Benny was unquestionably one of the funniest individuals of the twentieth century, his work on radio, television, and film deserving of new audiences.

What of the man behind the scandal? Once convicted for his role in the Lauer case, Albert Chaperau cooperated with the government in their efforts against Benny and Burns. His sentence of five years was "reluctantly reduced" to two by the presiding judge in recognition of this assistance. On April 12, 1940, Chaperau was personally pardoned by President Franklin Delano Roosevelt. The cited reason was his help in obtaining guilty pleas in the smuggling cases as well as his corroborative testimony in an unrelated judicial corruption trial. And we're certain that's all it was, not the names of the dozen or so businessmen and "socially prominent" people found in Chaperau's papers upon his arrest and never publicly revealed.

As for the peripheral players in the scandal, Rosa Weber, the maid who informed on the Lauers, was paid a reward of $6,714, or twenty-five percent of the total fines and penalties collected as a result of her information, and was never heard from again. The attorney who represented Jack Benny and George Burns, William J. "Wild Bill" Donovan—wonderful fellow, used to be in the Coolidge administration—was chosen by President Roosevelt to head the O.S.S., the World War II intelligence organization that served as a forerunner to the C.I.A. Lillian's boorish tablemate at the Lauers' dinner, the mysterious international financier Serge Rubinstein, was murdered in his Manhattan townhouse in 1955. The case remains unsolved. Lillian's whereabouts at the time have not been accounted for.

The saga of the spy ring founded by attorney Leon Lewis and initially funded by studio moguls to combat the Nazi influence in Southern California is a fascinating true story, its details only now beginning to emerge. We are indebted to Laura Rosenzweig, Ph.D., who wrote her doctoral dissertation on the subject based in part on Lewis's personal papers, for answering our questions. Her forthcoming book *Hollywood's Spies: Jewish Surveillance and Resistance of Nazi Groups, 1934-1941* (New York University Press) will shed some light on this too-long-overlooked aspect of Los Angeles history.

Many books have been written about the exodus of artists

from Europe to California in the years before World War II, often spotlighting Salka Viertel's role as the doyenne of this exile community. The most illuminating of these is Salka's own memoir, the sadly out-of-print *The Kindness of Strangers* (1969).

For a matchless look behind the scenes at Paramount Pictures in the 1930s and 1940s, read 2015's *It's the Pictures That Got Small: Charles Brackett on Billy Wilder and Hollywood's Golden Age.* Anthony Slide deftly edits Brackett's diaries to provide a glimpse at one of the most successful, if contentious, partnerships in movie history. Ernest Marquez's *Noir Afloat* (2011) is the definitive work about Southern California's gambling ships. Future generations may well know Hedy Lamarr more as an inventor than an actress; the patented frequency hopping technology she developed with composer George Antheil (who scored several Paramount films in the 1930s) for use with Allied torpedoes prefigured many contemporary communication networks like GPS and Wi-Fi. In *Hedy's Folly* (2011), Richard Rhodes pays tribute to Lamarr as an intellectual adventurer.

Other truthful tidbits: Every actor dubbed "Box Office Poison" by the Independent Theatre Owners in May 1938 bounced back nicely, thank you. Marlene Dietrich would have one of her greatest triumphs the following year in *Destry Rides Again,* featuring songs written expressly for her by Friedrich Hollaender. Dietrich's plan to deal with Adolf Hitler? One of her own devising. There really was a Cynthia, an eerily lifelike mannequin who became the 1930s equivalent of a Kardashian sister. Leni Riefenstahl's *Olympia* did screen for a select audience at the California Club on December 14, 1938, as part of Riefenstahl's trip to the United States. The Chopin script that Frank Capra longed to make was finally filmed in 1945 as *A Song to Remember.* Charles Vidor directed Cornel Wilde as the composer, with Wilde netting an Academy Award nomination for Best Actor. Merle Oberon played George Sand. Travis Banton designed her costumes. The movie's not very good, but the wardrobe is to die for. And yes, FBI director J. Edgar Hoover and Paramount actress Dorothy Lamour were indeed friends. All of which demonstrates that it truly is a small world, and Hollywood perhaps the strangest place in it.